Talking to My Hand

TALKING TO MY HAND

Stories

Arthur G. Typermass

iUniverse, Inc.
New York Bloomington Shanghai

Talking to My Hand
Stories

All rights reserved. No part of this book may be used or reproduced by any means, graphic, electronic, or mechanical, including photocopying, recording, taping or by any information storage retrieval system without the written permission of the publisher except in the case of brief quotations embodied in critical articles and reviews.

Copyright © 2008 by Arthur G. Typermass

iUniverse books may be ordered through booksellers or by contacting:

iUniverse
1663 Liberty Drive
Bloomington, IN 47403
www.iuniverse.com
1-800-Authors (1-800-288-4677)

Because of the dynamic nature of the Internet, any Web addresses or links contained in this book may have changed since publication and may no longer be valid.

ISBN: 978-0-595-47841-5 (pbk)
ISBN: 978-0-595-60615-3 (ebk)
ISBN: 978-0-595-51831-9 (cloth)

Printed in the United States of America

This is a work of fiction. All of the characters, names, incidents, organizations, and dialogue in these short stories are either the products of the author's imagination or are used fictitiously.

Quotations from "Everglades" by Harlan Howard
"Unchained Melody" by Alex North and Hy Zaret
"Good Ole Boys" by Bob McDill
"By the Rivers of Babylon" by Brent Dowe and Trevor McNaughton
"I Can't Get Started" by Ira Gershwin and Vernon Duke

Now and then we had a hope that if we lived and were good, God would permit us to be pirates.

—Mark Twain

Contents

Trapezoo'd

The signs were unmistakable to anyone who didn't need a Seeing Eye dog. Flyers in varying pastel colors were put up haphazardly around the parking lot and entrance gate, looking from a distance like so much strewn confetti. The message was heartfelt, direct, and not a little frantic:

> You can help save your Tropical Paradise Zoo!
>
> Escalating costs have caused your community zoo to operate at increasing losses, and it is in danger of having to close its gates forever.
> The zoo is trying to obtain a state grant as a landmark environmental preserve, so
> that it can continue to be one of south Florida's greatest attractions.
> We implore you to write or phone legislators to help see our request reach fruition.
> There is also a petition you can sign as you exit the zoo today. Survival depends
> upon your support. Please help!

It was high season in south Florida, and families were clicking through the turnstiles at the zoo as fast as the desk could process them. More messages advertising the zoo's plight were tacked up in prominent locations.

"Hey Marge, do you see this?" one already harried father of three toddlers called out to his wife as they strolled along the gravel pathway.

"Whassat, Jim?" the woman responded, more occupied with a tightly bound bag of popcorn that had split it seams and with charting her children's whereabouts than whatever was on her husband's mind.

"The zoo's going to close, it looks like. Says they can't make ends meet, and they're looking for some kind of grant to bail them out. I don't get it. They sure charge enough. Do you know it cost us $48 just to enter the place?"

Margery Conway appeared noncommittal about the zoo and told Jim to stop crabbing; they were on vacation, and you had to expect to spend money. Besides, if this zoo shut down, it being a must-go attraction in town for the kids, they'd have no alternative but to steam up north to The Mouse and pay *those* prices, and that would be a fine how-do-you-do.

Jim muttered to himself as the family entourage plowed ahead. A small crowd was gathered at the zebra pen; as Jim moved up to it, he could see that the attraction was two entwined black-and-whites cavorting away in a compromising position and looking like a lumpy ball of bicolored twine in the process. Occasional cheers emanated from some of the onlookers. He was transfixed until he heard his wife bellowing, "Jim, pull yourself away! We got ground to cover."

He said, "A minute more, Marge. This is educational."

His middle boy, Jimmy, asked to be lifted up above the crowd to see. "Maybe later, Jimmy. Mom wants us to move on."

They turned a corner to the alligator pond, where four of those creatures were stretched out on a grassy bank, as silent and immobile as the still Florida air. Jim Conway said, "They don't do squat. At least the zebras have a life. Maybe we need another batch of condos and malls, and it'd be better if the place did shut down."

The Conway boys, ages three to eight, took all of this in. The older guy, Matt, looked up at his father and asked him, "Dad, did anyone tell the animals?"

So there it was. After all those years, the zoo was on the edge of being a goner.

A helicopter fussed and sputtered at low altitude over the Tropical Paradise complex, much as it had done frequently in recent weeks. Today its passengers were Crandall Coastman, one of the region's prominent real estate developers, and two bankers from Everglades Trust, Lucas P. Boniface, executive vice president for commercial loans, and his assistant, Carly Joe Tee. If Coastman had been a licensed pilot, he would have taken the chopper up himself, so well did he know the flight pattern as a result of escorting groups of potential lenders up to survey the site over those weeks.

"Lucas, look down at it," he said, "more than nine hundred acres of prime land just salivating for quality development." The banker was hesitant to do so; he glimpsed the scene gingerly, being spooked by the clear vinyl sheet that was fluttering in the air currents and that was all that stood between him and oblivion down below. Coastman would have looked too, were it not for the fact that he'd done so countless times already; better still, there was the distraction of a preferable option alongside of him, that being a view of Carly Joe's unblemished thighs stopped midway by the hem of a black silk miniskirt.

"Ah see it, Cranny, ah see it. Hey, lookee, Carly Joe, there's some kinda big cat runnin' round under them trees," Boniface said, then in an instant picking his head back up. Carly Joe, a recent Vanderbilt graduate and a Phi Beta Kappa to boot, and who was on the cusp of a promotion to junior loan officer at Everglades, was motivated to display enthusiasm, and half lifted off her seat in compliance with his command, revealing still more leg and driving Coastman into a palpitating frenzy. He wasn't ready to commit, but the developer favored this banking team over the others he'd hosted, so today's meeting held more potential for him than previous ones. "So what all you got in mind?" the banker continued.

The developer rapidly fixed his thoughts back to the task at hand. "Well, here's the thing," he began, "that down there is known in these parts as the Tropical Paradise Zoo, or the TPZ for short. That's not to be confused with the TPC, which, as you may know, is a golf course."

"Oh, that's a funny one, Cranny," Boniface laughed. "Hell, man, we can do a golf course anyway—maybe want to get rid of them tigers, though." Trying to overcome his in-air jitters, he went on with the conversation, turned to his comely assistant and said, "Hey, Carly Joe, get happy, this ride sure beats a day in the office, dontcha know."

Carly Joe, now seated as demurely as possible, flashed a set of bright-smiles at both men, at the same time tossing a full mane of honey-blonde hair for final effect.

Gawd, thought Crandall, *if she comes along with the deal, I'd even pay an extra eighth on the interest rate.* He continued, "The golf course, we'll have at least one, Luke. See off to the west a bit, there's the mall, to the north some office and bordering the zoo to the east we have Starfish Point Golf and Country Club. What we're gonna do with this land is create south Florida's largest and finest community. They'll be a clubhouse at the center with every amenity.

"Golf-orientated, just like I said. And the residential, why we'll have a range from villas to Single-family homes up to 20,000 square feet. We'll use the lakes already there and create some new ones, some of which'll have man-made beaches. I mean to tell you, this is the last prime parcel of this size available within a hunnert miles, maybe anywhere in the South."

Boniface was tiring of the sales pitch, having heard the line about "last prime parcel" from every developer he'd ever talked to. He figured the phrase must originate in Real Estate 101 or some other training manual for them. Anxious to end the tour, he went direct: "What ya lookin' for from Everglades, Cranny?" A small banty-rooster sort, with thick glasses and reddish-sand hair that went off in numerous directions from a square face, Boniface could pass for a Teddy Roosevelt mutation. Appearances to the contrary, he enjoyed a reputation for being one of Florida's savviest lenders and one who gave no quarter should a loan head southward. Word on the street was never to screw Lucas P. Boniface.

After a deep breath, Coastman said, "We need $900 million for phase one as I see it.

That gets us all the infrastructure, the golf, and about a third of the residential. You know, Luke, that once we start sellin' the sites and the homes, that this'll be self-financing. Cash will flow like the mighty Mississippi during spring rains."

The ride was ending; they were touching down on a helipad at the regional airport.

The banker listened to the end of the pitch with a poker face; although no stranger to big numbers these days, what he had heard about this project moved the bar a notch higher.

"Whoa, now, Cranny, that's just for developin' and buildin'. What ya gonna do to pay for the property in the first place? Can the bank assume it'll all be Coastman Construction equity?"

"Aw, Luke, now don't you fret a bit; sure we got equity. Of course, we still gotta negotiate the purchase price."

They landed and were exiting the helicopter, Coastman thanking his pilot and the bankers nodding in agreement; the developer was savoring one last view of the way in which the tarmac breezes caused Carly Joe's skirt to dance merrily around her.

"How much, Cranny?"

"What? The equity or the price?" Coastman asked.

"Each. In whatever order you wish." Boniface awaited an answer, his jaw jutting upward at the other's throat.

"I got maybe a hunnert mil to put up, but I'll need to get that back, or most of it, when we start the sales program. As for the property, it's a family that owns the TPZ, and I know they want to—have to—sell, and we're on track to sit down and do a deal with them."

The comment was not what the banker wanted to hear. He had hoped Coastman was further along. Hell, Everglades' business was loans, big loans, and well secured ones at that, and he liked the ideas that Crandall advanced, at least in principle. But the guy should have been at a more advanced stage in his process before grabbing him and his disarming assistant on the joyride. *Developers! This one didn't even own the property yet.*

Nobody had to tell the animals about the growing threat to their home. The posters having been on display for some weeks now, most of the visitors would talk about the message on their initial walk-through. Species of macaws overheard the ongoing conversations, and the colorful birds, well known for clarity of voice but little known for perceptive hearing comprehension, commenced to chat up the developing situation among all the other permanent residents of the TPZ. The multitasking macaws, clever besides, would telegraph their messages after sundown, when all parties had left the park other than a handful of keepers and maintenance personnel. Once the humans were out of earshot, the chattering would commence:

Now hear this, now hear this
Zoo closing, zoo closing
Bad for us, bad for us
Need to meet, on the street

And so, the word was getting out and around.

The zoo had a proud history. Originating with the Nightingale family and pieced together when land was cheap and with the town's support, the founder's son, Louis B. (Shooter) Nightingale, Jr., assisted by his own son, Louis III, affectionately known as Three Sticks, currently ran it. The old man had really gotten into the swing of it all by going native, prowling around the property in outback gear, purchased at a going-out-of-business sale by J. Peterman, and pointy-toe boots (not alligator, though; he knew that would be offensive), topped off by a bush hat that shaded a burnished copper face whose signature feature was a pomaded handlebar mustache. He'd never missed a workday at the TPZ.

On this particular Friday, Shooter was reviewing the zoo's most recent financial results, which showed a pool of red ink despite a record number of visitors streaming into the park. He was convinced by now that the fundamental economic position of the zoo was untenable; the revenue needed to offset embedded and rising fixed costs required increases in admission charges that would be prohibitive. He believed that a campaign to fund-raise through some sort of grant was the best direction to take to rescue the enterprise, although it would likely be a lengthy process even if they got encouragement from appropriate organizations.

Failing that, a sale on some basis would have to be entertained, although he clearly did not want a sale and the experience of a "The End" on what had represented his life's work.

Shooter III breezed into his father's office, curtailing for the time being the old man's concentration on the dismal statistics in front of him. Reading weariness on his father's face, the son surmised correctly that the latest figures showed no respite from the zoo's losses.

"Hardly surprising then, Dad, is it?" he said after hearing a grudging confirmation from his father.

The two could not have appeared more dissimilar. In contrast to the crusty demeanor of Shooter Jr., the son was of less than average height and almost frail looking with a narrow face, faintly sunken features, and pale flesh. His hair was jet black, and he had lately adopted a combed-straight-back, slicked-down do. He might easily have been taken for an extra in *American Psycho*.

"Look, I hate to come on like a broken record, but we oughta sell this place."

"Hell no, son." The old man was resolute, the chin firm, the fingers clenched.

Three Sticks let fly with a titter, "You know, Pop, it's been said that a 'no' is in reality a request for additional information."

"Is that what they taught you in graduate school? And, need I remind you, it was on my dollar," Shooter responded. "It's too damn bad your mama isn't here to rein you in."

It had been a father-and-son relationship for many years. Shooter's wife, Zelda, had died when her only child was four years old, and the old man had never remarried. The son hardly ever knew his mother.

Shooter III was well-educated, with an undergraduate degree in poly sci from Duke followed by an MBA from Florida, the latter with a concentration in real estate. What he was doing at the TPZ in ninety-degree weather wearing a charcoal grey Armani three-button cut, all buttons fastened, was anybody's guess, but something approaching the truth was that he could not get a job elsewhere. He interviewed poorly, looking ashen to start with, and he stammered repeatedly in face-to-face recruiting situations or, to compensate, more often he would come on in a super aggressive manner with an especially high pitch to the voice. Either gambit was certain to raise the hackles of the most jaded corporate recruiter and, as a result, he was usually out the door before the seat could be warmed. Thus he found himself locked in the family business, a home being defined as where you were taken in.

"Hey, I'm not seeking an argument," he told his father. "I came to tell you that Coastman keeps calling. I'm sure he's hot to buy us out, taking all those bankers on fancy chopper rides all over the place lately."

"Yeah, and probably scaring the piss outta my animals," the old man chimed in.

"Well, I'm going to talk to him."

"Go ahead son, but I got to tell you it ain't worth a camel's breath if you do."

Three Sticks was undeterred. "Let's face it, our time is past. We can't charge enough to keep the place going and deliver the value people want. Hell, most of 'em go up to The Mouse or The Gardens, anyway. That's the big leagues up there, Pop, and here we are bleeding in the boonies.

We oughta consider ourselves lucky as all get out, sitting on the most desirable piece of real estate in the region. The kind of prices we're seeing here, why we'll take our money, man, and sit on the beach in Rio for the rest of our lives."

"Are you done now?" Shooter asked plaintively. "All right, you've spit your wad. Maybe there'll be a time when we have to talk about it, but not just now. Let me be."

Again alone, he unlocked each side top drawer in his faux African desk, a massive hunk of furniture modeled on one that he had deeply admired on a tour through TR's Sagamore Hill home some years ago. On the one side, the drawer contained a World War II SS Luger pistol.

The other held a new bottle of Knob Creek bourbon. He then rapidly bolted each drawer.

Just want to make sure it's all still there, he thought.

Two

There was a culture within the zoo population that had nothing to do with human beings. It was a command hierarchy, a social structure, and a workable system of communication among the animals. It was nothing new, having been in place for years. Animals being brought into the park were initiated in the ways of the order. Some newcomers put on an attitude of resistance, often symbolic of pride in their particular species, and a few were displeased to be zoo denizens in the first place, but a rotating welcoming committee of long-term residents was quick to outline the prevailing ground rules, at the same time warning against dissent therefrom. While hardly without differences of opinion, the zoo animals exhibited a high level of harmonious living.

Crime was rare, murder nonexistent for as long as anyone could recall, and there was little competition among them, animals possessing no money whatsoever. There was, on the other hand, an established pecking order in the park.

Leadership roles had traditionally been undertaken by the big cats, who had power, poise, image, and beauty—traits that represented qualifications for political success. Lion King, by original acclamation and current default, was the titular chief executive of the TPZ, but power was shifting towards the younger leopards, panthers, and tigers.

The tropical birds' roles of information dissemination presaged the animals' town meeting that the big cats had set up for the following midnight. In front of the zoo's stage, which served up daily presentations of animal tricks and stunts, stood concrete bleachers for daytime human spectators; these stands were now filled to capacity by animals facing the big cats' leadership committee arrayed on the platform. "Come to order," Snow Leopard intoned, banging a paw on the cold platform for attention.

"Curious that the meeting isn't being run by Lion King," Zebra said to Antelope, next to her in the third row of the stands.

"I heard that, you Africans," Snow Leopard countered, addressing the two by native habitat rather than genus, a form of put-down and an opening for Snow Leopard to establish position.

"All of you—observe Lion King. Does he look like the meeting chair?"

Alongside of Snow Leopard, Lion King was fast asleep, wheezing and snoring; from time to time his mane would shake involuntarily, spewing its contents of embedded gnats and lice directly in front of him. Snow Leopard went on in a conciliatory way, "This is not to say that we do not revere him for his wisdom and guidance. He will always be our dear leader. But I say that it is time for a torch to be passed to a new generation, particularly at this moment of crisis.

"Hear, hear," rumbled Tiger and Panther, who flanked the other two cats like defensive ends.

"Allow me to proceed then, animals," Snow Leopard continued. "As you have already learned, there is a plan afoot to close the zoo. It isn't the first time we've been so alerted, but this time, it is serious. Our task is to formulate a plan of action, the first step being to name a committee to evaluate options." Leopard looked toward the back as Giraffe entered the theater. "Good of you to join us, Giraffe," he said. "Unfortunately, we've run out of seating, except in the front row, where you'd block out everyone else behind you."

"Okay, I'll stand," Giraffe responded in a jaunty tone.

Snow Leopard said, "We'll want you on the committee because you're—how shall I put it—an obvious presence."

"Oh, thank you, thank you." Giraffe seemed flattered, an accommodating lady.

"She's too damn nice," Tiger muttered.

"Yeah, but she occupies space," Leopard said, "and she'll tower over all those humans at any negotiating table we may have to be at. She can look down on all the cards they may be holding, if you catch my drift."

Tiger turned huffy. "What makes you think she'll fit in any room?"

"A minor problem. Who knows whether we'll be indoors anyway … but you've given me a good idea, Tiger. We get those humans in close quarters with the likes of us, hot, smelly, wet—hell, it'll be over in no time at all. Now, where is Porcupine? I don't see him in the group."

The animals looked around. Rhesus Monkey raised a hand, in the process revealing a pungent armpit. "He's been delayed," Monkey began, "acting in a porcographic movie."

A threshold of tittering coursed down from the audience. "Spines on fire!" two myna birds were chanting.

Snow Leopard banged a paw once again for order, lest the meeting lose control.

"All right, then, I'll deal with him when he shows up. He's a weapon, animals. I expect we'll have to meet with the humans, and when we do, why, we'll just throw Porky right on the bargaining table, where he'll terrorize them with the threat of getting pricked—get it?"

"You really believe that will intimidate humans?" asked Swan.

"Maybe you can get by on your clean looks," said Leopard, "but we need some strong-tail tactics here. See, I know what you are all probably thinking. You know *Animal Farm* by heart.

"Well, what good was Orwell? He thought the future ended in 1984—not much of a forward thinker. And you have all laughed at Larson's *Far Side*. But that was all bullshit, and I'm not offending anyone 'cause there's no bulls here, them being low-life farm animals in the first place."

Tiger growled at him, "Hey, cat, you're gettin' carried away."

Porcupine showed up, out of breath, and shuffled to an open seat in the front row.

"So—how was it?" Leopard said, managing the faintest of smiles.

"Spine-tingling" answered Porky. "The reason I'm late is our prickers got completely intertwined, and we had to, ah, disengage with great care. The taping ran overtime, but the director said the extra footage was worth it. He's going to add a special feature to the DVD and expects it to be a big seller in the adult section."

Bear raised a paw and was recognized. "I'm tired of havin' my name taken by all the teams and getting nothing fur it" he barked, "and that goes for my friend Buck here, as well."

Snow Leopard fixed a steely gaze into his eyes. "Look, Bear, you're getting off point here, but I'll comment anyway. Tiger and Lion have put up with that for years, and they're not complaining. What would you get anyway? We got bigger fish to fry, Bear, no pun intended."

"Well, maybe I could get a tryout at linebacker," Bear said and sat down.

Lion King shifted his massive frame and let out a bellow; the crowd stilled. He rose up on his haunches. "I have heard quite enough. My ears sting me. Snow Leopard, you have asserted yourself, now do something besides talk—form your committee. This meeting will then end."

Evidently spent by his outburst, Lion fell asleep on the cool floor. Snow Leopard promptly selected Tiger to be second-in-command, Bear and Giraffe to be responsible for security, Porcupine to be chief negotiator, and Macaws for communications.

He had no idea what to do next.

Crandall Coastman and the Everglades bankers were in the throes of a sumptuous dinner at the top floor of the Coral Sands hotel, at a table with an unobstructed view of the Gulf.

The bankers wanted to know where Crandall was headed with his project in order to decide whether to spend the time now or move it to the back burner. There'd be questions, but they could hang until dessert and cordials had been served. No need to interrupt the enjoyment of these fine vittles, as Coastman referred to the food in his best down-home manner. Carly Joe Tee, who was a Midwest transplant to Florida, was amused by the competition in southern patois between her boss and the developer. Of course, the part of Florida they were in was about as southern as, say, Indiana. Carly Joe recognized after a few months at her job that nearly everyone there was from somewhere to the far north or west. *These two guys really were throwbacks,* she thought.

Out of a corner of an eye, the developer picked up on the entry and seating of Shooter Nightingale III, arm-in-arm with an auburn-haired size four in a size two dress that was being tested for tensile strength. "Excuse me a minute, will ya," Coastman whispered to his dining companions as he rose to approach the couple across the room.

"Wha-ya, Mr. Nightingale junior, as I live and breathe. I'm Crandall Coastman, who has been callin' you, and seein' as you are here, I hope you will not mind my friendly intrusion—"

Nightingale looked up, cutting off his preamble curtly by saying, "I recognize who you are, and the name is Nightingale the third, for clarification. That said, I'm happy for your acquaintance."

He smiled; actually it was more of a smirk.

"And who might your lovely partner be?" Crandall was displaying a froth of saliva around the right side of his mouth.

Three Sticks smiled broadly. "Are you sure it's me that you're interested in, Crandall? Allow me to introduce Delia Castle."

"My pleasure," purred Coastman, who remained standing, not having been invited to sit, and would not be, but he hardly minded as it afforded him a peek at the top third of the young lady's torso straining against that dress.

"Delia is into commercial real estate, as are you. I'm making some introductions around town for her."

"Well, I wish you luck, young lady," came the reply as Coastman turned to leave, "nice sayin' hello to you both. I'm havin' to get back to my guests." Addressing Three Sticks on the way, he said "Let's talk soon, son." Back at his table, he thought, *real estate, my butt. I know everyone in town who's in it. He's trying to kid a kidder.*

It was noteworthy that Delia Castle did not open her mouth during the meeting. Had she done so, it would have revealed an endearing New York accent in the best of *The Nanny* tradition.

"So what'd you find out from Shooter III?" Boniface asked Coastman.

"Aw, it was just a friendly intro, no big deal," the developer said as he dug back into his grouper almondine.

Both Luke Boniface and Carly Joe Tee couldn't help being fixated on Delia Castle, for undoubtedly differing reasons, and it was Boniface who eventually inquired, "Who's the looker with him?"

"Name was Delia something or other. More competition." Coastman was eschewing additional elaboration, leaving the bankers uncertain of the import of that last remark.

He wasted little time in calling Three Sticks. For his part, young Shooter anxiously awaited the next conversation; in fact, it would have been a push bet as to which man's fingers reached for the telephone initially, such was the level of anticipation. The two met off-campus, so to speak, at a tiki bar on Marco Island.

"Ah'll come right to it," Coastman said. "I'm offerin' up a hunnert mil for the zoo property, take it or leave it."

"You need it bad, dontcha," Three Sticks replied with the trace of a leer. "Well, maybe that's not too shabby for an opening bid, but it won't get it done. The way I figure it, the zoo sits at the epicenter of what you have to have for your development, maybe a golf course around which all the high-end residential would revolve. I happen to know that you have already assembled adjacent land to the east and the south." (That comment was a bit of a stretch; Three Sticks had picked up on local gossip, but he'd been too lazy to research recent land transactions which would have confirmed that indeed the developer had bought up considerable surrounding acreage.)

Coastman leaned back and grinned after taking a long pull on a gin and tonic. "If you so smart, how come you're not in the real estate bidness like me, huh? Look, an offer is on the table and it's your place to accept or reject. Nothin' more or less."

After the sun had descended in the calm Gulf sky and the completion of half a dozen more drinks, the two shook hands on a purchase price of $107 million. The developer neglected to ask—and Three Sticks hardly volunteered—whether the latter had the authority to make a deal. And the younger Shooter, in his haste, failed to learn if the offer was all cash, funny money, or some combination of the two. Nonetheless, both left the bar and went their separate ways, each assured that good work had been done and a night of untroubled sleep awaited.

Had Coastman addressed the issue of payment, he'd have expressed no intention whatever of using cash or, if forced to do so, would pony up as little as would fly. No matter; now it was time to take the deal to his bankers and begin documentation on the loans and the purchase of the TPZ. What really counted was the deal had been made, and at a favorable price to be sure.

There was a modest amount of public support for the salvation of the zoo. Local politicians met with the Nightingales to express their concerns for the impact on the community and its cultural tradition. They made certain that photo ops preceded any sit-downs and that they would be seen and heard expounding sincerity on the evening news. The TPZ arranged for a benefit concert by Neil Young for a fund-raiser, along with special guest Pete Seeger right in the zoo's center, which was lightly attended and generated $200,000 which, after paying the performers' out-of-pocket expenses and advertising, yielded about half again as much for the zoo. Shooter thought that would help keep it all afloat for a few more months. Young was upset because he believed he was brought there to sing on behalf of Canadian geese; finding none there, he stormed off halfway through his gig. Seeger sang a protest anthem lauding the red tide, but someone whispered to him that the red tide had nothing to do with the Russian revolution and, in fact, was a very bad thing for the ecology of the Gulf Coast. He seemed confused, but not nearly as much as the audience, who had expected Bob Seger.

Shooter appeared detached during all of the activity. Three Sticks listened politely and offered little talk, other than the platitude that *at the end of the day* the TPZ was private property, and, therefore, the owners had a right to do with it as they saw fit. All the heads at the meeting nodded in understanding of such eternal truths; all stood up, shook hands, and promised to see what could be done.

All were merely dancing a minuet. The animals would have no such luxuries.

It was shortly after the foregoing that the meeting on Marco took place; proud of his negotiating prowess, young Shooter could hardly wait to inform his father about the sweet deal he'd made, and how it would solve all of their problems. He had to approach the old man with humility, though, recognizing his sentimental attachment to the property.

Sucking it up, he entered his father's office calmly and in a matter-of-fact manner disclosed the fact that he, and he alone, had reached an agreement to sell the zoo, that it would be in the best interests of all involved, and that, by the way, it was at a "fantastic" price.

Shooter cast a laser-like glint at his son. "Now have ya?" he asked.

"The price, Pop, it's … $107 million. Can you believe it?"

"Well, no, I can't, actually. No." Shooter answered laconically, leaning back in his office chair made out of wildebeest hide.

"Pop, aren't you pleased? Proud of me?" Three Sticks was showing an emerging tremble.

Shooter remained placid, although he had opened his desk draw and had begun to caress the cold steel of the Luger involuntarily. He looked his son straight on and said, "Well, I guess the time has come to call in the dogs to piss out the campfire."

Three

The first set of draft papers for the property transaction were prepared by Coastman's legal staff and sent on to the Nightingales. Shooter waved at the package of contracts and shipped it all off to the family attorney, Buford Swope, with a full measure of reluctance because he knew that not merely would a hefty fee be in the offing, but that Swope would be reminding him of certain embedded facts surrounding the property. Sure enough, the call came through from Swope while Shooter was behind his antique desk sipping Knob Creek straight up and massaging the pistol.

"Y'all can't do it, Shooter," the attorney began without even so much as a hello. "Who in hell made this deal? Wasn't you, was it?" Buford Swope was a casting agent's image of a backcountry lawyer, with a drawl that dripped syrup and, in the flesh, jowls that extended to the shoulder and tousled grey hair that hadn't seen shampoo in months, all encased in a rumpled white linen suit.

"Hell, no, Buford," Shooter responded, his blood up now. "It was my son. I didn't tell him to, but there it is."

"Doesn't he know? Buford inquired. There was a heavy pause in the conversation.

"Aw, shit, he doesn't know. Ain't that the case? Well, I guess there shouldn't be any surprise. Y'all had little need for it, up until now."

Shooter said, "Hell's bells, he's been so hot to trot lately, the damn subject hadn't come up. Lord knows, I didn't expect it to come around this way."

Buford Swope told him that there needed to be some explaining between father and son before he'd start to run the clock grappling with the papers; he'd keep them nearby and await instructions from the client.

The land, and the zoo that occupied it, was the creation of Shooter's mother, Cora Nightingale, nee Cora Lee Madison (she was related, albeit distantly, to those famous names in American history).

She married a stockbroker named Louis Nightingale, who turned out to be as poor a gambler as he was a broker. With all of the money in the marriage hers, she'd had the foresight to have a prenup, forward thinking inasmuch as such agreements were unusual and suspect in the days of supposed trust and devotion. Thus, when Louis wound up in a bed in the Sands Hotel in Las Vegas with his throat slit ear-to-ear, she hardly missed a beat. Freed of him once and for all, she was able to indulge in a passion for animals and nature. The Tropical Paradise Zoo was created. Louis had left her with nothing other than their only child, Louis "Shooter" Nightingale, Jr.

Shooter grew up around and, much of the time, inside the zoo. It became instilled in his life, a form of calling like his mother's, and when Cora Nightingale died in 1990 he took over the management, as natural a transition as could be imagined. Under his stewardship, TPZ grew in its collection of species, the expansion and development of new grounds for animals, and additional exhibits within the ample piece of land wherein the zoo was situated. It resulted in a burgeoning of visitor traffic every succeeding year.

Shortly before her death, Cora revisited and revised her will and estate papers. While she owned a respectable amount of financial assets, the TPZ was by far the most valuable asset that she possessed. Her last will and testament expressed her wishes for the Tropical Paradise Zoo:

> Upon my death, my ownership of the property known as Tropical Paradise Zoo (TPZ) and all my landholdings surrounding same shall pass in perpetuity to a trust to be entitled Friends of Humanity Trust, which trust shall exist for all the sole benefits of the inhabitants of said property …

The document went on to define the term "inhabitants" as being limited to any and all members of animal species and genus as may reside in the TPZ. It was signed by Cora Nightingale as grantor, and by L. King as grantee for the trust. Underneath King's line was the undeniable paw print of a rather large creature.

The papers were filed in accordance with the State of Florida some two months preceding Cora's death. Shooter Nightingale first learned about the will only as it was read to him by Buford Swope shortly after his mother was laid to rest—which resting place happened to be in the center of the zoo's Monkey Island. The brief interment ceremony was punctuated by the incessant chattering of a coterie of Cora's favorite simians coming from the trees above. The minister was heard to remark that the lady would have adored the serenade, this even after his black suit was repeatedly bombed by offerings from on high.

Shooter was the only person in the office when the reading occurred. He was visibly puzzled by the whole turn of events and said something to the effect that although he was certainly no attorney, it seemed as though the will left a lot of unanswered questions.

"Well, old buddy, dontcha think I tried to tell your mom about that?" Swope commented. "But she was resolute; that's all she wanted it to say. The intent was that the zoo would go on indefinitely."

"And Florida accepted the document without question?"

Swope grinned. "You know this ole state, Shooter. The guy there jes' took his fee and went on to the next nutcase."

Shooter slumped in his chair and then went on to ask what this meant for his place in the whole situation. Swope told him that since all the papers were silent on the status of his TPZ role, the law would support a continuation of his position as manager of the asset in keeping with the will's intent. Should the son walk away from such duties, which of course was his right, Swope, in his role as executor of Cora's estate, would be empowered to find and install new management, so as to carry out the mother's wishes. Shooter proceeded to plunge into the management of the zoo in the subsequent years with insight and enthusiasm, the true architect of its growth. Following the settlement of the estate, he had nothing further to do with the matter—until now.

Three Sticks was counting inventory of laminated alligator heads in the zoo's gift shop when Shooter came through in his signature six-pocket bush jacket and pith helmet (he thought the crowds loved it, believed him to be an explorer, or maybe had lost his way from The Mouse's Animal Kingdom up north) and whispered in his ear, "My office, when you are finished here, son. Soon."

As the two faced one another across the old man's desk, Three Sticks appeared to have forgotten about the father's cold reception to his news about the deal as he asked Shooter about whether the flow of draft papers had commenced.

"Now hold on, son," Shooter held a palm up to him. "Before we get to that—if we do—we need to talk about a related issue. That's what we're doin' here." He then laid out the terms of Cora's will and estate arrangement, something he'd never disclosed to anyone. The son, neatly attired as always, this day in a midnight blue Zegna four-button silk suit, crisp white shirt, and a thin solid-black tie, listened intently as the story unfolded.

"So you're telling me that the family doesn't own the zoo?" Three Sticks was dumfounded.

Shooter was building up to a victorious grin. "Now you are catchin' on, son, lookin' as though all that education is kickin' in. It's true. It ain't ours."

"Which means that they—" Three Sticks was making a fey gesture in the direction of the animal areas.

"Bingo!" The old man rose up. "And you didn't even need a lifeline to reach the correct conclusion."

"So what about the sale? There was a handshake, a deal, pop," the son continued.

"Well, I suppose you are just gonna have to unshaken them sweaty fingers, then. You had no authority anyway, the way I see it. Of course, there may be another way." He waxed pensive for a moment.

When the son asked plaintively what that might be, Shooter offered that if a sale had to take place, why then the prospective buyer could deal with the owner.

"But they're animals!" Three Sticks exclaimed.

"Aw now, real estate developers deal with animals every day of the week, if you catch my drift. Hell, our animals are better 'n some of the humans anyhow."

Buford Swope was leaving his office on an oppressively steamy Friday afternoon. He was decked out in a linen suit and wrinkled white shirt accented by a red bow tie, all resting under a straw hat modeled after a 1937 style with turned-down brims, a narrow black band, and a nipple on the crown. The hat nearly left his head from the force of a whoosh from the car coming to a screeching half in front of him as he stepped off the curb.

Three Sticks pulled alongside in a yellow Jaguar convertible with Delia Castle in the passenger seat. "Why, Mr. Louis, the younger," Swope was saying in a syrupy manner. "And who might this comely maiden be?" Regaining control of his head, he managed a slight doff of the Panama.

"Hop in, counselor, we need a conversation," said Three Sticks, "Delia, in the back." Swope took notice of the fluidity of motion that Delia demonstrated as she climbed from the front and executed an effortless glide into the squishy rear seat. As they sped away, the lawyer introduced himself to her, no such courtesy having been extended by his host.

"I know all about it from Pop," Three Sticks told him, looking straight ahead at the road, his hands clutching the wheel like a vise, "and I got questions for you."

"Well and good, but the clock is runnin', and," Swope looked at his watch, "it starts now. First off, father and son, are you two on the same page?"

"Maybe. Look, what I want to know is, if there's no animals around in the zoo, do we own it then?"

The lawyer squinted at him. "You thinking about something, Louis? Mebbe I don't want to hear this conversation."

Three Sticks was sounding somewhat cooler. "I know this is hypothetical, but we all realize the whole arrangement is—uh, eccentric—and doesn't cover a lot of 'what ifs.'"

"I'll grant you that," Swope responded, "but I don't have any easy answers for you. Your Grandma wanted it to remain a zoo. But if it wasn't a zoo any longer—"

"Then what?"

Swope chuckled, "Thas' why there are lawyers, son. I think under that—unlikely—circumstance, the land could well wind up with the state under eminent domain."

"Couldn't the family claim, though, that it's rightfully theirs?"

The lawyer went on, now energized by the discussion. "Ah'l say you could make a case that the family maintained the property for its intended purpose, but that economic conditions now dictate that it's no longer viable. Further, the state could be petitioned to fork over compensation for what it takes."

Three Sticks asked, "And we'd get that, me and Pop, right?"

Swope laughed again, this time louder and longer. "Guess that's what we got the Supreme Court for. Shee-it, I'd like to argue that case. Trouble is, a case like that wouldn't be decided in my lifetime and"—his face bore a stern look as he turned in Three Sticks's direction—"not maybe yours, either. And now, Louis, I've said my piece and would like to get out of this little joyride. Drop me off."

"But we're in a swamp here." They had come to a stop.

"It's okay, Louis. Ah'd be leavin' one swamp for another, an even trade. Nice to have met you, young lady." Swope opened the door, exited, and showed one final hat move to Delia.

"Chawmed, likewise," she said as the car sped off in a cloud of Florida dust.

Four

On a Sunday afternoon towards the end of high season, Carly Joe Tee took her twin five-year-old nephews to the Tropical Paradise Zoo. The preceding Friday at a staff meeting with her boss, Luke Boniface, she was told that the "zoo deal," as he was wont to refer thereto, was moving forward with paperwork flow at an early stage, and that she should begin reading the draft purchase/sale and loan agreements. Anticipating then that the zoo's days may well be of the numbered variety, she wanted to have a look before it became history. Having done Monkey Island, seen the big cats perform their lunges and high jumps (somewhat perfunctorily, Carly Joe thought, but the boys were enthralled just the same), and then pony rides, they were headed for the exit when stopping by the exotic bird section. She never failed to admire the birds' flamboyant colors and the range of iridescent hues that characterized the animals.

"I used to have a parakeet," she said while gazing at the birds. "A he or a she, I never was certain; it was powder blue and I named him or her 'Thunder' because we bought it in a thunderstorm."

"What's a pa-keet?" asked Will, the more vocal of the two.

"Oh, it's related to these birds, Will," she replied, "but a lot smaller." Carly Joe picked up that all the species represented—parrots, macaws, canures, toucans—perched themselves front and center along the wire mesh cage, as much examining the human traffic as vice versa. "Hi there, Red," she started to converse with one multicolored parrot who could have served as an ornament on Long John Silver's shoulder.

"Hi there yourself!"

"Hey, he can talk back," Phil, the other twin, said.

"Talk back. Talk back."

"So beautiful," Carly Joe said, "and so sad it'll have to end."

"What's have to end?" Will was asking, now tugging on his aunt's sleeve, a sure sign of *let's go home now*.

She knelt down to the twins and said, "Because, boys, the zoo is being sold, and there will be new houses and stores here in its place. That's why I wanted to come here with you guys today, to see the animals before they go away."

"Where are they going, Aunt Carly?"

She held back a developing tear and merely shook her head. The birds had fixated on the conversation and remained gathered at the cage front. Carly Joe could swear she heard them utter the words "zoo sold" and "going away" coming in continuous chatter from inside the cage, as she and the boys made their way out. The last exhibit before the exit was African animals, and she noticed that it was vacant. A small sign pinned to the fencing informed that it would be down temporarily, since the contingent of zebras and antelopes were "on loan." *Cryptic message, isn't it,* she thought, *but perhaps things are beginning to happen.*

How the animals learned that the TPZ was held in trust was through Shooter Nightingale, this after Buford Swope reported to him on his unscheduled meeting with Shooter's son.

"I think you boys are gonna have to come clean and disclose to all interested parties," the attorney told him, "if'n you don't want to open a can of worms—or maybe a den of lions is a more apt phrase."

The following evening at sundown, the zoo having closed its gates for the day, Shooter, in a freshly starched bush jacket and swigging a new bottle of Maker's Mark, stood in front of the bird cage and beckoned all of the exotics to listen.

"I don't own the zoo," he began, coherent enough to employ terse statements so that the messages would be clear. "My mother put it in trust for you animals."

The birds started to chirp and sing nervously among themselves.

"Lion King is the trustee. The zoo is—in effect—yours. That's all I have to say."

With that, Shooter took a lengthy draw from his reservoir of bourbon, about-faced on his faux lizard boots and stalked back to his office.

The birds wasted no time disseminating his message to the committee organized by Snow Leopard and Lion King, although there was uncertainty within their ranks as to what a trust was and why Lion King was a trustee. Toucan did not understand the modifying words "in effect," but Myna bade her not to nitpick. "You always have a bird's-eye view," he said. Ultimately the birds understood that they were communicators, not analysts, just like the news anchors on the evening television programs that the humans watched.

Snow Leopard met with Lion King shortly after the news began going around. Not many of the animal groups had received the messages just yet, and Leopard wanted to hire a squadron of carrier pigeons to spread the word, but Lion King was not ready to accede to his proposal.

The former approached the old big cat with deference, keeping his naturally aggressive tendencies in check. He prided himself on his leaping abilities, both physical and mental, but this day he was seeking information from his old mentor of the "what did he know and when did he know it" nature.

"So, LK, you cannot recall signing off on this trust agreement with the humans, or when that might have taken place?" he inquired.

Lion King expelled a deep sigh that created noisome waves of air around them.

"I've signed many things, footballs mainly, so it's hardly surprising that my print may have been on such a paper."

"You know what this means. The zoo belongs to all of us. We can keep our home here. All you need do is exert your power," Leopard said.

Lion King's gaze was straight, its path interrupted only by the heavy-duty mesh façade fronting his lair and a vending machine in the distance. "I think about Africa often, Snowey," he said. "When I was little more than a cub, I became a good hunter, bringing home food every day, not only for myself but for the family."

"Like what?" Snow Leopard was having to endure a ramble of a dissertation, he was coming to realize.

Lion King forged ahead. "You know what the best was? Open impala with snake oil sauce on the side. To die for, if you follow; not me, of course, the impala. And the skies, Snowey, the skies. Why you've never seen such vivid sunsets like those over the great savannah. Purple, deep rose, and, burnished gold, all the colors of nature and then some you would not believe nature could produce, the hues changing and blending continuously in a living kaleidoscope. However, you've never been to Africa—you're an Asian, is that not true?"

Snow Leopard spoke softly. "Not even so. That's my heritage, to be sure, but I've lived almost all of my life in the confines of this zoo, being brought here as a toddler. I suppose you could say I'm a city boy."

"I understand," Lion King said, "you haven't had the freedom experiences some of us animals have had, but the point I'm making is that … perhaps there is an alternative to all of us remaining here."

Leopard seemed taken back. "But King, we're all safe here; we get fed every day, and if we assume control the menus may improve—so what could be so bad?"

"You mean this monotonous slop they place in front of us? We'd still rely on the humans for food service, and I for one would not care to rely on their good nature. No, the zoo cannot compare with the thrill of the hunt. Moreover, it isn't in our makeup to be so protected and dependent. That robs us of our true destiny. Wouldn't you like to prowl the mountains of Asia, Snowey, attack a yak, have sex with an ibex?" Lion King let out a deep bellow, his form of laughter at his own rhymes.

Snow Leopard conceded that though it all sounded inviting, he didn't know whether it would be for him. Lion King looked him in the eye and said, "I'm getting old for all of this, Snowey. I may only have this one chance to return, but for many of you younger animals a whole new world would open, and that might be a good thing."

Eager to move on with business, Snow Leopard brought up the subject of communicating with the zoo animals about what had been learned about the control of the zoo. "Are we ready to utilize the birds to distribute the message to our brothers and sisters?"

Lion King continued to stare ahead, hearing Leopard's query but not immediately reacting to it. "Snowey, do you know why ducks walk single file when they cross roads?"

This time it was Leopard's turn to laugh, hardly believing his mentor was waxing comedic. "No, I don't.

"Well, neither do I," Lion King deadpanned. "I also think ducks are the only animals that can travel by walking, flying, and swimming. Do you know of any others?"

"If you give me a week, I probably could come up with an answer," Snow Leopard responded.

Lion King faced him. "Maybe so, but we do not have a week. Go and mobilize the birds."

Five

Three more animal pens had been emptied out over the next several days. The pattern of events had by now caught the attention of some of the zoo's staff, and Shooter was subsequently informed of these developments; lately he'd been out of his office more than not, conferring with Swope and following up on the possibility of outside financial aid for the TPZ, the latter to no avail.

As soon as he was told, he sent for Three Sticks, who was nowhere to be found. "When he shows up, tell my son to come see me," was all he could say at the time. Things were dire enough, he knew, without the loss of animal attractions, and he could not help but be deeply suspicious of his son.

His instincts were dead-on and would be proven out shortly. Three Sticks had been busy methodically clearing out the zoo population and hiring a crew of laborers, who loaded the animals into unmarked trucks in the gloom of night to be taken south to the Everglades. There, they were set free, their freedom being short-lived as they melted into the swamps and thickets of that vast wilderness with its mysterious terrors. Most would never be seen again.

Three Sticks actually was engaged in the latest iteration of his so-called project, along with Delia Castle functioning as sidekick. This was to be the most ambitious caper yet in his plan to cleanse the entire zoo of its animals in the hope that once this "final solution" (as he had termed it) had become a *fait accompli*, the Cora Nightingale will and trust arrangement would be moot. So on a bright Florida morning he and Delia were barreling north along I-75 in a king-size pickup truck, its bed occupied by Giraffe, Wildebeest, and Mountain Gorilla. A day previous, he'd made a deal with the operator of a new game preserve theme park nine miles east of Disney for the sale of the animals.

Park management was intent on head-to-head competition with the colossus of Orlando and had evidenced a strong need for animals to fill the place, and rapidly. Three Sticks was convinced that as soon as this initial delivery was consummated, there'd be no stopping him from his eventual triumph.

The prize in this morning's batch was Lady Giraffe; his customer had breeding her in mind. Three Sticks was effusive in praising her attributes. "She's got long legs and a very light tan coat—she'll make a super catch for some lucky stud." He and Delia were exultant in the cab of their truck, belting out the old Kingston Trio hit "Everglades."

> He was born and raised around Jacksonville
> A nice young man, not the kind to kill

They were about to start on the next verse when everything came apart at mile 117. At an overpass with a sixteen-foot clearance, and with the vehicle clocked at eighty-two mph, nineteen foot Giraffe was decapitated. The force of the collision caused the truck to spin and then veer toward the right shoulder of the highway, where Three Sticks was inexplicably able to gain control without rolling over.

They steamed to a halt, now some three hundred yards beyond the overpass. As they turned back toward the grisly scene, they could see indistinctly through the truck's blood-spattered back window a long gathering line of cars and trucks backing up, tires screeching and whining, and an occasional *crump-clang-bong* of metal meeting metal.

"Louie, get out!" Delia, shouting at a transfixed Three Sticks in the driver's seat. She jumped to the ground. "Oh, shit … yuck …" Delia saw the still twitching carcass of Giraffe in the truck's bed, limbs splayed over the sides, blood running from below her neck in rivulets through the bed's indentations. A now-dazed Three Sticks joined her. Neither of them noticed that in the chaos Wildebeest and Gorilla had climbed over the back of the truck and disappeared into the brush.

"Louie, I'm gonna puke …" Delia wretched by the roadside.

They were both sitting alongside of the truck when the patrol car pulled up. The state trooper, dressed in high spit-polished boots, light grey uniform, hard hat, and Prussian-blue sunglasses, ordered them to step out of the vehicle. "We are out of the vehicle, officer," Delia responded, doing her best to flash a toothy smile, a modicum of composure returning.

"So you are, so you are," he murmured. "License and registration, then." Delia could see bloodstains on his gloves; a glance toward Three Sticks was futile, so she climbed back into the cab and retrieved the papers from the glove compartment, handing them to the trooper. "Well, we got ourselves some kinda mess, here," he said, turning to the truck's rear, where, with a final thump and fountain of blood, Giraffe had finally come to inactivity. "You were driving?" the officer asked Delia.

"No, he was."

At that, the trooper knelt down on the ground and leaned into him. "You are aware that there's a head back aways of this … animal … belongs to you, or the rest of what you were transportin' here. Now, you gonna back up this truck on the shoulder; I'll follow, and you pick up this thing, load it back in so's I can begin to clear this up. Then we'll take a little run down to the station. Okay?"

Three Sticks, staring off into the distance, lifted himself up to comply with the order.

It was the lead story on the evening news.

"Good evening southwest Florida. This is Ted Martinez reporting," the handsome young Latino man in the tan suit was saying. "We begin with a horrific traffic accident earlier today on I-75 where a truck, apparently transporting animals including a giraffe, collided with an overpass at mile 117—or, the giraffe did, so collide, that is, let me very clear about that—causing the giraffe to lose its head. Literally, lose it. Not go crazy, have the head … uh removed …"

The camera moved to Ted's news partner, a pert blonde.

"That's right, Ted. The police reports indicate the head was severed cleanly, then the truck lost control up the road. A man, now identified as Louis Nightingale III, and his companion, a Delia Castle, were involved. Fortunately, neither was hurt. Back to you, Ted."

"Thank you, Muffy. It took four hours to clear the highway. Traffic was backed up for seven miles. We understand that it is flowing normally at this time."

Muffy added that it was fortunate that the road was cleared in time for the rush hour and asked Martinez what they were doing there in the first place with a giraffe.

"Nightingale is an executive with the Tropical Paradise Zoo, and he was taking the giraffe up north for sale. In addition there was a gorilla and another animal in the truck at the time."

"And what became of them, Ted?"

"The gorilla was captured at a nearby McDonalds, in the drive-thru line. The other—I'm told it was some kind of beast—well, it's still missing."

She asked him about Nightingale and Castle.

"They were released in the custody of Nightingale's father, 'Shooter' Nightingale. No charges have been filed as of yet—I was told—because the police cannot find an appropriate violation in their rule books. They are still researching it. Now over to you for the rest of the day's news, Muffy …"

House arrest, of a sort. Three Sticks was sent to his old room in the Nightingale family home, where Shooter would glower in his direction from time to time. Delia Castle achieved a measure of local prominence by an appearance the following day on a morning TV show, where she renounced any further relationship with Nightingale III. "I can do a lot better without him. Wait and see."

Snow Leopard and Lion King met again, now in a crisis mode. "We can't abide this, LK," the leopard began. "They're killing us off."

"This … Lady Giraffe thing … it makes us look bad. I agree with you. Get your forces together and retaliate."

Carly Joe Tee had left work and entered her car when she felt a kind of intermittent jabbing at the back of her neck. "What the—" she exclaimed, and turning backward saw Porcupine standing on his hind legs.

"Now do as we say, and you won't get hurt. What you felt was just a gentle tap. There are stronger pricks in my quiver."

At first, she was amused. "You're just a porcupine. And who's 'we'?" As if on cue, Bear reared up from a prone position on the floor and bared a set of teeth that were in dire need of whitening. Carly Joe was nothing if not a quick study. "Okay, I'm starting to get the picture," she said.

She was instructed to drive to the zoo, a route she knew all too well; Porcupine temporarily relaxed his quills while Bear's foul breath wafted toward the driver's seat. She was relieved that it was only a short drive. When there, the two animals escorted her to a small shed that housed wheelchairs for the disabled and strollers for the young, all available for rental for the applicable visitors. The shed had one small window. "We'll see that you get food just like we do, thrown in on the ground," Porcupine said. "You'll see what it is to be a hostage, just like us."

"What the hell do you want?" she screamed at them.

"Help. Your help." With that, the door was shut tight and padlocked.

"Suppose the visitors want the carts tomorrow, Porky?" Bear asked.

"Use that feeble brain of yours, fuzz-face. They'll walk, just like we do."

Crandall Coastman was in conference with his legal staff. As much as he privately applauded Three Sticks's single-handed effort to clean out the zoo to expedite development, he seethed when he was informed of the true nature of the zoo ownership and when he assumed that he had been deceived.

One of his lawyers opined that Three Sticks really did not have adequate information or the talent to use it to deceive anyone successfully, but that did nothing to assuage the developer's feelings.

"Look, I think what that idiot was on to was the right thing," he said. "If we can find a smarter way to get rid of these animals, we'll have everyone we're up against by the balls. So I say, let's proceed with a program of extermination."

His audience sat in silence.

"What? Don't you like my idea?" he asked.

Finally, the general counsel cleared his throat and spoke. "There is a problem. This … incident with the giraffe … well, it appears the animals retaliated by seizing someone as a hostage."

"Who? Don't keep it a secret. You damn lawyers have too many secrets."

"It's the banker from Everglades, Carly Joe Tee, Mr. C."

Coastman exhaled. "Oh, the young one. Well, that shouldn't stop our deal."

The counsel continued. "On the contrary. The bank and the police don't exactly like it, and they don't know where the animals are keeping her."

"All right, then. So now what?" Coastman asked.

His counsel responded. "The animals are out for revenge and will only release her if we agree to a meeting, so we talk to them."

"Through who, Dr. Doolittle?"

The staff chuckled en masse in an attempt to warm the frosty atmosphere.

The company's counsel went on. "They want to meet as soon as possible to address their grievances. They will communicate via the talking birds. Shooter and Buford Swope will be there along with the bankers. They wanted to meet in a closed room, but we think it best that the meeting be held in an outdoor environment and will set up tables at the zoo on Monkey Island. They are agreeable."

The developer asked, "What do they want?"

"We are about to find out, Crandall."

At the start of the meeting, Snow Leopard requested a moment of silence in respect of the memory of Lady Giraffe. "We have lost 'a towering presence,'" he intoned, "but we do not want to hold a grudge. We believe that the past is the past and that our purpose today is to resolve our differences, with all due respect." The humans barely suppressed a groan.

Observing Porcupine stalking the center lane of the conference table, a nervous Luke Boniface asked, "Can't you get him to take a seat?"

"I'm only here to offer my quills, should we come to sign an agreement," the animal said, "and, besides, if I sit, I tend to burrow under, and if you don't remember where I'm at and you sit down, well ... you can figure out the consequences. Trust me, it's in everyone's best interests to keep me in sight."

"That's enough for now, Porky," said Snow Leopard, eager to get on with the agenda.

The meeting did not begin amiably; the Coastman group claimed to have made a bona fide purchase of the TPZ in good faith, and the animals refuted the claim, saying they had a right to void any such agreement, and they demanded to remain in their adopted home. Shooter was asked to review the zoo's financial condition, after which he made a conciliatory statement about his heart telling him that he'd choose for everything to remain as is, but that the reality was that the zoo could not afford to keep going and that some kind of disposition agreeable to all parties was the only practical solution.

"Look, I mean to have this property one way or the other," Coastman said in a crusty manner. "So what do you all want? I had a deal at a hunnert and seven mil, and I stand ready to pay up." He sat back, arms locked across his chest in a defensive manner.

Swope, representing the Cora Nightingale Trust, huddled with Snow Leopard and Porcupine.

Lion King was into a morning snooze. Swope looked to the people at the opposite side of the table and reported that the animals didn't think that the amount was enough.

Coastman reddened. "Goldang it, a deal's a deal. You animals have no morals!"

The remark set them off. The monkeys in the trees started to chatter, the talking birds flew off to communicate the perceived slur to the zoo proper, and Bear began to murmur once more about compensation for his name; all the while, Lion King continued to sleep through.

Up to that point the bankers had not spoken. Thinking the meeting was already tilting out of control, it was Carly Joe Tee—less than an hour after her release from the cart shed—who stood up and exclaimed, "Enough from all of you. Humans, clear the table! Animals, stay behind with me!"

Lucas P. Boniface turned ashen, and his carrot hair frizzed up as though it had been subjected to a thousand volts. He glared at his comely assistant and in a quasi snarl said, "Young lady, you all are lucky the cavalry came to your rescue from these critters, but now you are makin' a career decision. You know what you're about?"

"I've never been so sure in my life," she answered in a determined tone. All conversation ceased and gradually the people rose and vacated the room. Her demands having been satisfied, she commenced to confer with the animals.

After an hour passed, Carly Joe beckoned the negotiators to return to the table; they were rounded up from vending machines, benches, and port-o-lets. "Okay, missy, we are all ears," Boniface said once they were again seated.

"All right, here's the deal," Carly Joe said. "They don't want your money."

Coastman rose to the bait. "Well, that sounds good to me, but I heard earlier that my offer on the table was not enough, so what gives?"

She went on. "I meant that they have no need for money—for themselves. But they'll take it all right, because they do want it for other purposes, such as new game parks in Africa and elsewhere. And there are a few other things."

"Here comes the catch," Coastman's lawyer whispered into his boss's ear.

Crandall held up a palm to him. "Wait. Go on, young lady."

"They are prepared to vacate the zoo," she said. "By the way, I would appreciate you all addressing me as Ms. Tee, befitting my position as in-training to be junior loan officer of the Everglades Trust."

"For now," Boniface muttered under his breath.

"Okay, so they'll leave. What else do they want?"

"They want to go home," she said.

The Coastman team, and then Shooter and Boniface, began to confer amongst themselves.

"Fine with us," their lawyer said at the conclusion of a brief huddle.

"It's not that simple," Carly explained. "See, they would all be going different places, ancestral homes and the like. There are some special requests, too."

"Such as?"

Carly Joe was consulting some notes she had scribbled down during her session with the animals. "Snow Leopard, for example. He wants to go to Las Vegas. It seems that's where he's from.

He was sold to the zoo as a cub and wants to trace his early years and maybe perform there. Then there's Bear; he's had his heart set on a tryout in Chicago as an outside linebacker; in fact, he insists on it."

Shooter interjected, "I love him dearly, but he always was trouble. Still, you'd better accede to his needs."

"So, you begin to get the picture, Mr. Coastman. The property will be yours for the price, but before it happens there's a big logistical task to be completed."

"At my expense, I suppose," Crandall said.

"That's the deal." Carly Joe was all a grin and managed a flip of her hair for emphasis.

Over the next two days, the details of the transaction were worked out. Coastman's staff arranged to charter a fleet of military surplus cargo planes to move the zoo's animals to their ultimate destinations. All were slated to move except for the alligators, who would stay in place and serve as outdoor furniture for the planned championship golf course. That appeared to please everyone concerned. "Couldn't move 'em, anyway," Shooter offered. "They haven't ventured from their places in years; well, maybe a few inches at lunchtime but that's about it."

"We'll build the course around them," the developer said. "I want one or two just off the tee box on the par-three fourth hole, and that will run parallel with the seventeenth, where we'll add a couple more in the second cut of rough. Should be quite a challenge for the players."

They were wrapping up negotiations—Carly Joe Tee was leading the talks, having been the only person to gain the confidence of all the parties—when a snag developed. She approached the Coastman group. "We have a little problem."

"Now what?" their lead attorney asked in a testy way.

"It's the penguins," she answered. "They want to go back to Antarctica, and the planes can't land there on the ice."

Crandall, listening in, said, "Who do they think they are? They'll just have to settle for somewheres else."

Carly Joe retained her cool demeanor. "You see, Mr. Coastman, penguins are hot right now—well, cold, actually, but you get what I mean. They do movies; they're number one in T-shirt impressions and key chains and think they've got leverage."

"All right, I get your point. So what do you suggest?"

She told him that the only means of transport to Antarctica would be by ship and that she had located a Russian fishing vessel that was available. "They are prepared to sail from Spitzbergen as soon as we give the word. The vessel is a touch smelly, but the penguins will love it. They'll have raw fish all the way down."

"And what'll that cost?"

"I can get it for a favorable price, only two million, because it's down time for them. I recommend we grab it." Carly Joe's lilting tone of voice made it seem like the world's greatest bargain.

Coastman was apoplectic. “That’s the last straw. It had better come to the end, missy, or I’m walking.”

She told him that *was* the final point. “If you agree, we are done here.”

The developer slumped in his chair. “Go ahead. Done and done.”

Six

Eight months later, Crandall Coastman was admiring Delia Castle as they lay side by side in his Tuscan-style king-size bed. Beyond the walls of his twenty-room manse, a rainy Florida evening held sway, the only audible sound being the steady beat of the drops on the bedroom windows. The rain provided a threshold to any other sounds that might be extant, but the plain facts were that the home was so large that Coastman could have been being burgled blind in another wing of the place and would never have heard it, rain or not.

"My, you are one pretty thing, Ms. Castle," he warbled.

"Why, Mr. Coastman, you are so flattering," she sang in return.

He kept his eyes on her perfectly proportioned body, a centerfold proxy in alabaster, while he gently ran his fingertips along her dips and swirls. His angular form cozying up against her, his own skin looked like a slice of Neapolitan ice cream, striated tones of white, pink, and brown, the product of outdoor site work under a hard hat, arms tanned and face reddened under the sun while the rest of his body remained fully clothed.

"And you are one ace salesman," he said to her, "so let's us have a little ole celebration." He shifted to an upper position.

"Please, Mr. Coastman …" Delia said in a contrived plea.

"Look at me. Is there a letter in your bag …" He sang in an atrocious voice, clearly in a buoyant mood.

His hiring of Delia to head up condo sales at the development, formerly on the site of the Tropical Paradise Zoo and now known as Flamingo Trace, proved a wise move. She evidenced a special rapport with New York customers, who were turning out to be the largest group of high-end homebuyers for the new project. Her commissions were on pace to earn her more than six hundred thousand for the year. *Not bad for Dorcas Cohen, a little girl from Forest Hills,* she thought. The name was her original, not Delia Castle, which she had fessed up to Coastman, being somewhat apprehensive about it. He not only laughed it off, he thought it a brilliant sales gimmick for the New York crowd, and it seemed to work. Delia would often begin the sales pitch with an introduction, followed by a "You know, they made me into a Delia for professional reasons, but oim acshully Dorcas Cohen—so you can call me that." More often than not, it won them over.

This night, he concluded quickly. She begged for a cuddle, but he was rolling over.

"Gotta get up early tomorrow, doll face," he told her. "I have an early tee-time with Three Sticks."

After the sale of the zoo concluded and Coastman began to work the property, Three Sticks, suddenly disenfranchised, approached the developer about a job. "You owe me, Cranny," he implored in an emotional high-pitched whine. Coastman offered up no resistance to his plea and within the next week Three Sticks found himself in charge of the pro shop, which was housed in a trailer while the course and the clubhouse was under construction. At first the job left him little to do, but after four months the holes were more or less ready for play, and he was soon afterwards able to open his shop to fee-paying customers. Crandall had played the course only once before, so he was looking forward to this day's round, even though it was with Nightingale III. *I'll play my game and tune out his bitching and moaning,* he thought.

Soon after Three Sticks hooked up with Coastman, his father, nowhere to be found for several weeks, resurfaced as a cast member at Pleasure Island in DisneyWorld. He played himself, a famous old hunter in suitable attire, seated in a dimly lit library in the park's Explorer's Club, where he regaled the paying customers with tales made up as he went along. There was talk of a series of gigs with animals on one of the national morning television shows.

The day was bright, the previous night's rain having moved on and leaving Flamingo's greens soft and welcoming. The players were evenly matched; Coastman carried an eleven handicap, and Three Sticks was one or two strokes within, having improved by playing often in his capacity as pro shop head. Their game was close as well, and by the time they came to the seventeenth hole, it was a dead heat. Three Sticks decided to press, and Crandall in response gave off an indifferent shrug of acquiescence. The developer's drive found the fairway two hundred yards out. On the tee, Three Sticks went into a full coil, rushed his downswing, and hit a vicious hook along a creek.

"Well, ah hope ya'll can find that." Coastman was smug as they climbed into their cart. "We'll drive to mine, then you take the wheels to look for yours." Three Sticks left his playing partner at his ball and rambled off in the cart to the left side. Coastman hit a six iron that clipped the right side of the green and then took a hop into the bunker alongside. It was a piece of bad luck, as he was smelling a par and knowing Sticks was in trouble, but he figured if the lie wasn't too bad, he'd be up and down in no more than bogey, which might still be good enough to win the hole. As he walked up toward the green, he glanced backward, seeing no sign of Three Sticks or the golf cart. A course ranger approached. "Hey, Mr. Coastman, how's the round going?" Sensing distraction on Crandall's part, the ranger asked, "Lost your playing partner?"

"Looks like I have, Howard. Too much concentration on my shot, I guess. I'd have figured he'd be up by now."

The ranger, an affable retired Hoosier, said, "It's been known to happen. Let's go back and pick him up."

The cart was parked precariously on a slope that bordered the fairway and led down to a creek, appearing as if the softest of Florida breezes could send it into the murky waters below. There was no sign of Three Sticks. As Coastman and Howard shuffled down the slope and peered into the creek, they saw tinges of what might have been blood, mingling in oily fashion with the brackish green of the water. A pang of apprehension visited each of the two, then grew into a tangible spasm in the gut as they watched an eight-foot alligator emerge from the swamp and take up a position on the opposite side in full sunshine; the animal shut its eyes and seemed to evidence a posture of satisfaction. "Uh oh" was all the ranger could utter.

Walking ahead, they at first had overshot the body that had come to rest abutting a peninsula of thick reeds. It was only when the rivulets of blood had trailed off that they doubled back and discovered Three Sticks's corpse, not quite quartered but crudely chewed up in three sections. One leg, still clothed in half of a Tommy Bahama pair of cream-colored slacks, slapped lazily against the bank.

"Let's go back to the clubhouse, Mr. C," the ranger said. "We'll get some help out here right quick. In fact, I'll call on the cell. Also, let me warn the foursome behind us."

"Yeah. Tell 'em the seventeenth is temporarily closed for ground repair," Coastman said. *Oh well, he insisted on the press.*

High on a cliff, overlooking the expanse of the Serengeti, Lion King was comfortably perched, observing the migration of animals across the moveable panorama in front of him. Evening was coming on, the skies presenting ever-changing hues; his massive head turned toward the approach of Mbala Ojibwe, climbing the dusty trail to the animal. "King, I have brought you news of your friends from the bird messengers!" Mbala was jubilant in his role of this service to Lion King, who had recently evidenced interest in the whereabouts of the now far-flung alumni of the Tropical Paradise Zoo.

"Ah, Mbala, talk to me; let us not waste time," Lion King said.

There was no paper trail; Mbala had committed everything he had heard to memory.

"There is a message from Snow Leopard, King," the small, wiry nut-brown African man began. "When he left the zoo—as you immigrants termed such places of confinement—"

The lion interrupted. "Please, Mbala, there is no place for your editorial comments. Your role is to report the facts to me in an unabridged fashion."

Mbala continued. "He went to a … Las Vegas … whatever that is—"

"I'll explain later. Go on."

"Yes, great King, I will take care not to stray from the message. Leopard was seeking out two human tormentors, for it seemed he'd been abused as a young cub by these trainers. It was to be a mission of revenge, and, following its completion, he had hoped to land a job at one of the major hotels as a headline act. Well, he was too late. One of the mean trainers had already been taken down by a tiger. Having been denied satisfaction that was rightfully his, Snowey had no recourse but to pursue his job search. However, the whole act had closed by this time and he was told that there were no openings for leopards. The tiger had wrecked it for all of the big cats."

"So?" Lion King was waiting.

"He's still looking. May I continue?"

"Please do."

Mbala reported that Porcupine had made his way to California to act in adult films. "His next release, 'The Thrill of the Quill' is generating a great deal of buzz … or is it burr? I'm not sure.

Then, there's news of Bear. He realized a lifelong dream by gaining a tryout with the Chicago team and making it as an outside linebacker. Oh, King, I do not understand this terminology—"

"I do, Mbala. It's native to America. Go on."

"It didn't exactly work out, Bear said," Mbala was relating the story. "He was repeatedly penalized for … uh … unsportsmanlike conduct—Lion King?"

"Yes?"

"How is it that an animal can be punished for conduct attributable to a man?"

Lion King pondered his associate's question for a while and then made a vague statement about imbalances in the universe. Mbala let the answer pass; the lion asked if there were any further details in Bear's message. "Yes. It appears he mauled a quarterback beyond recognition. That led to his suspension for the remainder of the season as a player, but the team has given him a job as a mascot.

I do not understand the word … Quarterback … maybe this man was deformed beforehand, and Bear's tactics were misunderstood."

"Perhaps, Mbala. Is that all?"

"Yes. That is all."

Their conversation was interrupted by a commotion welling up from the plain beneath them. Loud laughter was interspersed with occasional gunfire. Lion King instructed Mbala to see what it was all about.

In a desert-colored Hummer, with its top off and side doors removed, sat Lucas Boniface and Buford Swope. Each was playing with a 12-gauge shotgun, and a half-gone bottle of Jack lay on the floor. "Hey Luke, did you pick any of 'em off with that last blast?" Swope asked.

"Dunno. I was trying for one of them vultures, but the light's fading fast."

Swope said, "You know, I don't think we're allowed to kill these suckers."

"Aw, we came here to skip a bunch of bullshit. Besides, they got enough animals to go around for ever'body."

"Good point, Buford. I'd keep it in mind if you're grabbed by one of them tribesmen."

Swope laughed and took a pull on the bottle. "And here he comes now."

Mbala approached the two and explained that, as an emissary of Lion King, the leader of the Knjatta preserve, hunting was prohibited and would they please refrain from such disrespectful activity. Mbala was nothing if not diplomatic. They readily agreed to comply with his request, and he went on his way.

"Nice guy," Swope said.

"Yeah, for a—" Boniface needn't finish the thought. "Hey, good buddy, it's time for dinner anyhow. Let's head back to camp. I hear there's grilled hippo steak on tonight's menu."

They both howled, their laughter floating around the endless savannah. The safari trip was a perk from the Coastman organization, a "l'il thankee," as Crandall termed it, for seeing the deal through.

"Tell me, Luke," Swope was asking, "were you pissed when that Carly Joe took over the deal?"

"Naw. I was fixin' to retire anyhows, and that just moved up my agenda a little. At the time, sure, I didn't like it, but she took a risk and pulled it off." Boniface paused. "I'll sure miss the eye candy, though."

The night was pristine and loaded with stars. Lion King was finishing a dinner of grilled rhino cheeks that Mbala had prepared. "That was tasty, almost as good as in the raw."

"Do you miss the hunt?"

"Oh, yes. But those days are past. Moreover, I am part of management now, and it would not be seemly if I was seen as a recidivist predator in our very own park, would it."

Mbala laughed. "No, I suppose not. King, do you hear the voices from below?"

He had picked up on the sound of song rising in the cooling air.

I guess we're all gonna be what we're gonna be
So what do you do with good old boys like me

"Are those your friends from earlier, Mbala?"

"I believe so. They do not sing well."

Lion King said, "It disturbs our tranquility. Is this the price we pay for opening up our preserve to these … visitors?"

Mbala answered. "Those who come here are all different—colors, sizes, habits. Sometimes I am amused, sometimes puzzled, by their actions."

The big cat fixed his gaze on a particularly vivid star. "Mbala, do you know why ducks always walk in a single file?"

"I think, King, that the leader has a map and the others merely follow."

"Very good, Mbala. Now I understand."

Means of Disposal

As soon as Callman saw the lion bound across the neighbor's lawn, he sensed that this would not be an ordinary day. The lion was female; he was pretty certain of it, as the animal was not in possession of a mane, and was moving away from him, thanks be to God. Then the neighbor appeared in her terry cloth bathrobe and pink flannel bottoms, seemingly shooing her away as though the appearance of a lion was an everyday street occurrence. His last glimpse was of two legs up and a swaying tail disappearing beneath a gentle rise and then a view of a placid horizon where land yields to the bay in the seaside town in which he lived.

When did lions move in here? he wondered. *Dogs of all manner surely, but lions?* Or were his eyes deceiving him? He continued on his way and turned the corner at a sharp right angle; only one more block to the train platform, a familiar refuge and, hopefully, devoid of any further morning jolts. Climbing the aluminum platform stairs, he looked furtively to the left and the right for reassurance that the lion had indeed moved on. A handful of commuters were distributed along the line—nothing out of normal here. *Good. Menace another place, not in my back yard,* he thought.

On the platform he exchanged greetings with Harry Primbo, late of Sydney, who worked in town for one of the Aussie beer companies (what else?). After a couple of nods and good day, mates, Callman was about to bring up the sighting and perhaps seek validation thereof, but then he thought better of it. Best not to be believed to be a whack-job, he reasoned, especially not in the presence of an Aussie. *Do they have lions, there,* he wondered. Well, probably, they must have every kind of creature imaginable and then some. The train crawled to a stop and everyone boarded in their individual silence, a signal that the day's call had officially begun.

Evan Callman's destination was the headquarters of Integrity Investment Management Corporation, where he was into his fifteenth year of service. Integrity, known in the trade as "double-eye," had a reputation as an upstart in the financial industry; it was new and aggressively managed (competitors think recklessly managed), the creature of a merger between Consolidated Stockbrokers Inc. and Select Traders Corp. in the boom times of the latter years of the twentieth century. There were few, if any, aspects of the investment business that Integrity was not into. Callman was responsible for the administration of services for Integrity's clients. An important component for the company, its top bosses loved the link between selling stocks and bonds and customer service, a natural package for cross-marketing the full range of functions that the firm could offer. Callman was hardly the type of go-getter who would be out pitching the business, but once it was obtained and brought in-house, he would take it on and guide operations on a trouble-free basis, generating ongoing revenue, that is if the client were kept happy, which proved to be the case in the vast majority of accounts. For this he was quite well compensated and thus was able to enjoy his home in the quaint seaside town, the recent presence of lions notwithstanding.

He was able to walk from the train station to the building, some fifteen city blocks, always finding the morning walk invigorating despite the monotony of the same surroundings along the way—there were some minor route variations available—but now that the weather was on the upswing on this late spring, almost into summer, day, it was a particularly pleasant interlude for him.

His office was on the second floor of Integrity's twenty-one-story building, which rankled him to an extent. The higher-ups at the company were situated, not surprisingly, higher up, and he made a mental note to begin a campaign for loftier surroundings; he and his team were cramped anyhow, what with the growth of the business. But all in due time; pick your spot for success, he always believed. Nodding in greetings to staffers, he made his way to his office. First thing, he checked with his admin assistant, Noemi Lorca, about the day's schedule. Integrity had long ago done away with personal executive secretaries other than for its CEO and his immediate coterie, instituting a level of AA's, who each served a group of managers. Noemi was efficient and striking in an olive-skinned, raven-haired way. A salute to her Hispanic heritage, she was Evan's selection and a good conduct mark for the company's diversity score.

"Okay, Noemi, tell me about today, but gently please," he said to her. "I've had a shock on my way to the train station, already."

Giving no reaction to the boss's failure to divulge more, she looked up as he brushed by and said, "The meeting with the North Coast people is set for 10 a.m.; that's the new account with … ah … five thousand participants."

"Have we got everyone from here on tap for it?" he asked.

"As far as I know, but I'll confirm it," she answered. "You have the systems group from IT, payment processing, customer service protocol, legal department …"

"Good, good," Callman said. "Sounds like the usual suspects have been rounded up; let's hope there's room around the table for all of them. Oh, and by the way, while I'm thinking about adequate space, remind me to take up a request for moving …"

At that, Noemi rose erratically from her swivel chair in reaction to a threatening word and said in a tremulous voice, "Moving. You can't mean …'

"No, no," he responded reassuringly, while thinking, *damn, I never should have used that word.* "I don't mean re-lo, just getting added space right here. We need it."

Calmed down, Noemi said, "Yes, I will remind you, Mr. C." She continued, almost as an afterthought, "Mary Ellen Dunn wanted to see you after the meeting."

"Isn't she going to attend?" he asked.

"Yes, but she asked to see you anyway; just some face time, I guess."

Callman seemed to shrug, then said, "Okay, just before lunch, then. Is there anything else?"

Noemi looked down at a scratch notepad, then said to him, "Oh my God, I almost forgot. Mr. Grader called early—he wants you to come up when you get in. *Mi Dio,* I am so sorry, Ev—Mr. C."

Before her sentence was completed, Evan was out the door, tie being straightened, and in front of the elevator bank on his way to the twenty-first floor.

Mr. Grader was Lowell Grader, the company's CEO, a courtly gentleman from Aiken, South Carolina, who could exude a kind of steeliness packaged inside a covering of sweet molasses. The sort of summons that Callman received from him was either the opportunity of a business lifetime or an express elevator ride down to the lobby and out to the street, nothing possible in between. Within minutes, he was ushered into the top floor office, handsomely adorned with several striking examples of abstract art. Callman, however, was edgy, and was in no frame of mind to admire the boss's office ambiance this morning. "Evan, please, let's sit over on the sofa." Grader stretched out his six-feet-three lean frame and motioned for him to sit. He focused in on his guest and began, "I'll get right to it, Evan. You know that a special committee of the board asked for a review of Integrity's products and units, yours among 'em, and the results are comin' back, not all yet, mind you, but we already know that we are going to put yours up for sale, and—ah'm afraid—that would mean we'd have to let you go."

Callman, at first stunned, swallowed hard and regained composure. "You know my business unit has made tremendous profit contributions, beat our bogies every time—"

Grader cut him off. "Evvy, Evvy, sure I know. Why do you think we're able to sell it? It just isn't, well, the right fit for Integrity going forward, that's all. The Wall Street boys want to see us in something more exciting. Your business is steady, makes money, but it doesn't have the pizzazz to move Integrity's stock."

"So what about me? Am I offered up to go along with the potential buyer?"

The CEO paused, effected a kindly face, and said, "Not really. I'll level with you. We've already had an offer. Came out of the blue. Brought to us by Morrison Brothers. The buyer would re-lo the whole shebang, Evvy, and fold it into a giant processing center they already have up in North Dakota. Trust me, y'all know I'm from South Carolina. I wouldn't like to go to North Dakota, and neither would you."

"Then that's it," Callman said.

Grader said, "Of course I expect you to keep this to yourself for now—it's not yet a done deal. The buyer will insist on a full accounting review of results as a part of their due diligence. And if they want you to consult, I'd want for you to be available—at a handsome fee, naturally. So, look, you're not leaving empty-handed. The board is cognizant of the impact you have had on this company, and we'll negotiate a favorable exit package for you. And, I might add, the buyer wouldn't even ask for a noncompete. Why, man, with your skill, you'll be out knockin' em dead in no time at all. I'd bet the ranch on it."

As though he had a ranch to bet, Evan thought.

"You sleep on it, Evan. Git your numbers together. We'll talk again at the end of the week." When Callman left the CEO's office, Grader asked his secretary to call the head of Integrity's audit department.

The scheduled client meeting went on for two hours. Evan more or less sleepwalked through it, putting up a stoic façade, no one else knowing what he knew. He would have been bored anyway, even under normal circumstances, having been through the drill countless times in the past. Everyone went their own way after the meeting concluded; upon returning to his office, he saw Mary Ellen Dunn waiting outside, and he motioned for her to enter and close the door as she did so.

Positioned behind his desk, he looked wearily across at her, and said, "I thought … we agreed … not here, Mary Ellen. But then, here you are, so what is it?"

Mary Ellen Dunn, having logged nearly as much service at Integrity as he had, appeared the picture of the parochial schoolgirl she had been before joining the company. Her dark tartan skirt and white silk blouse, topped with a light blue merino wool cardigan, led up to a rather flat face framed by matte brown hair parted perfectly in the middle. She emitted the impression of a woman striving to attract a minimal amount of notice. She started, "I know, Evan, we did agree, but look, I …"

He was no longer in any degree of a positive mood. In a clipped tone he told her to get on with it; his day was busy, and others might be speculating on what was going on between the two of them. "All right then, it's the money. Or some money. When am I going to see some of it?" She hesitated, then went on. "There. It's been said." She managed a faint smile, a gesture of a burden having been lifted.

"I've told you, when the time is … ah … appropriate. I'll let you know when. Okay?"

She answered, "That's all you can say?"

Callman stood his ground, face downward to desk papers, and said softly, "Yes. It is. Better you leave for now." When he looked up, Mary Ellen Dunn had gone, as silently as a leaf floating from a tree.

Lunch hour was at hand, an important juncture in the typical Integrity workday. Callman by now, having repaired to his black vinyl desk chair, had left his door open, and a trio of staffers looked in on him, asking about lunch plans. "Thought we'd go over to Eduardo's on Ninth," Ed Kelly said. "How about it, Evan?"

"Nah, I need to play catch-up, Ed, but maybe later in the week if you want to," he responded, an effort to remain genial. As the group headed out of the office, he found himself alone momentarily amidst a quiet patch in the surroundings, fleeting in the usual bustle of activity but markedly so this day, he felt, considering what he had already been subjected to. He unlocked the middle drawer of his desk and smiled to himself, recalling an old joke. It seemed that the senior partner of a law firm began each workday with the routine of opening the middle desk drawer, glancing in at its contents, then immediately shutting and locking it. This ritual was well known to his co-workers for all of the years that he had served the firm. When he died unexpectedly, his office had to be cleaned out, and the item of greatest curiosity was the revelation of the contents of that drawer. The staff gathered around the desk, the middle drawer having to be pried open, for the attorney had taken the key with him, figuratively if not literally. Finally opened, they found it to be empty save for a small yellowed paper taped to a lower corner on which was written "hot is on the left, cold on the right."

Callman's drawer had no such legend, but like the old attorney, its contents were known only to him. And, again like the old attorney, his movements were quick and darting, open and shut, and then a sense of reassurance that things remained in their rightful places. He rose, walked to the men's room, performed his release and ablutions, and went to take his suit jacket from a closet before leaving for lunch by himself. *Well, it was that kind of a day, wasn't it, and not half over,* he thought.

The rumbling began just as he crossed his office's threshold.

The company's head office building was one of those nondescript structures put up in the 1980s, an example of dull architecture but engineered for lean and efficient work flow and, moreover, built at leaner cost. West of Seventh Avenue, it was not a location that anyone had much use for—in the city's version of no-man's-land—and it was surrounded by a polyglot of neighbor businesses ranging from garment distributors to photography studios. Yet it served its employees well from the standpoint of ample mass transit options, which was one reason why management had not entertained a move despite the continued growth of the business. That, and the fact that the real estate was fully paid for would make almost any move in Manhattan expensive and, some would say, a wholly unnecessary proposition.

After years of dormancy, the area had begun to perk up. Gentrification, the construction of new office and residential towers, spurred a population influx and brought with it related amenities such as stylish new restaurants and other services. Several construction projects were under way in the company's immediate vicinity. As Callman would approach the building lately, it seemed as though he was sheltered by a continuous and makeshift overhang of wooden boards supported by steel rods and struts, a not very temporary mélange of street infrastructure. Helpful to some degree on rainy days, it was otherwise unpleasant to be around.

He never made it out his office door. He was at first only faintly aware of an onrushing cacophony of thunderous sound accompanied by a flash of blinding light (sunlight intruding on the artificial dim of the office?) and then a disorganized pattern of crunching, grinding, and even a shrill whistling sound as the air around him rapidly grayed, filling itself with dust and smoke, becoming charcoal along with all power shutting down. There emerged a time of silence like a form of respect to a momentous event just having passed, and then came the resumption of noises, new ones, creaking and wrenching, presumably the back end of some form of storm.

Callman felt himself knocked to the ground, such ground as had stayed in place.

Unsure whether he had blacked out, he rose and ran his fingers all around his head and body to determine the extent of any damage. His initial conclusion was that there was none, which was reinforced by his ability to stand and walk, although—to what?—visibility being barred by pervasive dust, moving cloudlike in the closeness of the atmosphere. After an indeterminate amount of time had elapsed, he reasoned that he was more or less an intact person. Despite the haze, he concluded that some sort of force had blown out the exterior wall of the building alongside of his office and, undoubtedly, all adjacent areas. Through the fetid air, he could see the outline of his desk, as solid as ever, but little else remained of the walls that had heretofore closeted his corporate universe.

I must start moving around, he thought. He did. Sifting through rubble, a few feet at a time, making his way along the path of the building's façade, he soon saw light—daylight—ahead. Where the apparent impact had been, there were shafts of light beaming in on a distorted and mangled tableau of structural materials: concrete, steel, wood, wire. It was remarkable what went into the assembly of human shelter. Indeed, the random pattern of the debris had created a ramp way, such that from the original second floor he was certain that if he followed the traces of light he could pick his way safely out to the street below.

As he maneuvered gingerly, step by step, fingers feeling deliberately around and through the piles of rubble, he came upon a body, making its appearance at first as merely two feet protruding from a blanket of steel beams and cinder blocks. Callman poked around this surprising apparent apparition with apprehension. *Was there movement? Would something spring up upon a touch?* He was able to clear away much of what had brought it to ground. He found the substance of what was a clearly dead man, a face … remnants thereof … swathed in blood, beyond disfigurement into some other territory, now unrecognizable to anyone. His clothes, bloody as well, were dust-infused but not particularly torn up, having acted like some nuclear shield covering its own interior explosion.

Sometimes revelations only come after an event has taken place; that attribution for the point of inspiration can be assigned. For Callman, this would turn out to be such a moment. *I can do this,* he thought. *But time is limited. Before long, there will be sirens, EMT trucks, the whole thing. Better move fast.*

He groped his way back to his desk. Some of the gray dust had begun to disperse. He keyed open the middle drawer, removed a slim folder contained therein and returned to the body. Still in its place, Evan bet that this guy was someone homeless, and his odds improved when, after rifling through his pants pockets, nothing, absolutely nothing, was there. So here it was, a nameless person wiped from the rolls of humanity and offered up as a gift to him.

With no time to waste, and acting with a motivation and dexterity he did not know he possessed, he was able to switch clothes with the body. He stuffed his own wallet back into his pants pocket, pants now on the dead guy, placed his watch on a grimy wrist, and, with a flourish, slipped his commuter rail card and house key into the suit jacket's breast pocket. *Voila!* It's dead Evan Callman.

One last task remained. Although the guy was in horrific shape, it wasn't bad enough. The man's size and body contour was not that far off from his own, at least as much as could be estimated, but the face—ah, the face. *That we must rectify*, he thought. For what seemed an eternity but what actually took up less than eight minutes, he used all of the strength he could summon to repeatedly bash in the dead guy's face with concrete forms and, just to break the monotony, steel bars. Although he understood that complete satisfaction could not be achieved in this grim task, he declared victory when the guy's head took on the look of a pepperoni pizza that had somehow fallen to earth from a multistory window. He then lifted as much as the beams and blocks as could be lifted and dropped them on top of the body, shook the dust from his hands, and began to trace the light lines that would lead him out into the springtime afternoon. As he started out, he became aware of sirens wailing in the distance and coming closer. No longer with a watch, he had already lost track of time, but his sense was telling him that the rescue effort was taking much longer than it should have. *So much the better*, he thought as he made his way down.

Almost there, he remembered that in his zeal to produce a bona fide dead Evan, he had left his wallet intact in his (former) pants pocket. On a path to the light, he realized there was no money, no cards, no anything on his person. *Gotta go back*, he said to himself. The sirens were closing in. Climbing back over, he reached the body and quickly fetched the wallet. There was over four hundred dollars—a large amount to be carrying—but he had stopped at the ATM on his way in to the office, and he peeled off most of it, along with one of the four credit cards he carried. *Leave the rest*, he thought. *All right, then, it'll still look authentic. Now, back down, no time to lose.*

He was on the street, having emerged much like an airline passenger sliding down a chute after an emergency landing and after having bludgeoned his fellow passengers to gain position. Crowds were already gathered on the sidewalk, and, this being anyplace other than New York, the roughed-up man in blood-soiled and crumpled clothes would have been an object of concentration. But not here. He crossed the street hurriedly just as the sirens, in the form of the police and firefighters, came to a screeching stop at the curb fronting Integrity's headquarters building.

One of those vest-pocket parks was across the street, and he stopped to plant himself at a back table alongside one of the granite walls that bookended the little park. Thus seated, he was hopeful that his appearance would be less than conspicuous. From his vantage point, he could now see what had happened.

An enormous construction crane with a wrecking ball on its business end was parked at a forty-five-degree angle to the street. The crane operator had climbed down from his cab and was approaching the growing phalanx of uniforms. Callman could only surmise that the crane operator had taken a massive swing at the adjacent construction on Integrity's block and had missed his target by a lot, like a fastball pitcher losing control and heaving one into the dugout. The building, more specifically the floor that until moments previous had housed his office and business unit, now looked like some Middle Eastern structure after a suicide car bomb attack, its front lain open and its interior contents revealed to all.

After pausing to catch his breath, he began to move away from his perch, intent on getting distance from the area. He walked—calm now—to the subway, which he reasoned was the most anonymous refuge available to him.

Descending the top steps, which held the bright rays of the sun up to the emergence of the cool and dank platform, he used cash to buy a MetroCard and got on the first uptown train that pulled in.

Being early afternoon, the subway car was hardly crowded, and, again, as he furtively surveyed his surroundings, he saw that the few passengers took little notice of him. He thought that the first thing he must do is to buy some different clothes and ditch what was presently on his back. However, not anywhere in upscale Manhattan. Maybe one of the boroughs. The train was headed north, so he rode on as far as 138th Street in the Bronx and came out of the subway. This was an old-time shopping area, now largely Hispanic and never, ever, high-end. It was just what was needed. Within two blocks, he found a discount clothing store sandwiched in between a bodega and a laundromat, and, once inside, quickly selected a raincoat (to cover the mess underneath) and a pair of size 11 shoes from a bin (the dead guy's shoes were killing his feet). Finally, he located a pair of khakis in a 36 waist and a designer knockoff sport shirt in an L. The whole thing cost him $90 before tax, and he didn't look half bad—probably a little too swift for this Bronx neighborhood.

"Do you have a bathroom here?" he asked the portly Indian proprietor.

"No, sir. There is McDonald's up the street; please go there." The man virtually bowed in contrition to the question. McDonald's it was, where he made for the men's room—thank God empty—changed and stuffed the bloody garments into the store's bag, and walked out. Allowing himself a faint whistle as he did so, his posture took on an erect form, driven no doubt by his fashionable new threads.

He would exercise some caution disposing of dead guy's clothes, utilizing two, perhaps three, city waste cans, much like OJ did out in LA, whose bag was purportedly never found. Hopefully, he would have equivalent luck. Then it was on to figuring out what to do with the rest of his life. Hunger making its inevitable entry into his body, he put the big picture on hold and went into a coffee shop, ordered up a BLT and a Dasani water which, with tip and tax, ran another ten. At this rate, cash was dissipating rapidly, which was one more thing to think about.

The coffee shop had its wall-mounted TV on, and the owner kept switching channels between *Passions* and *Power Lunch*, depending on the direction of the stock market and the opinion of one of the soup fans at the counter. While on the network broadcast, *Eyewitness News* broke in with a bulletin. Callman's attention turned from his sandwich to the screen. The daytime newsman came on.

"... the Channel Seven chopper is over the Integrity Building and correspondent Tom Astleton is on the street. Tom, what can you tell us about this accident?"

"Well, Steve, here's what we can piece together. About an hour ago, a wrecker's ball swung mistakenly into the Integrity Building at its second floor. As you can see, there is a great deal of construction activity on this block and apparently the work was meant for an adjacent structure."

"Thank you. We can now see that there was significant damage to this building. Can you tell us whether or not there were any injuries?"

"Well, Steve, as we look towards the scene, there is considerable police and fire presence, and they are beginning their investigation, which will involve sifting through that part of the building that has been damaged. So we don't know just yet."

"That's all for now. We'll have an *Eyewitness* update for you at five o'clock, or earlier, should there be breaking news. Now we will return to our scheduled programming. For Channel Seven, this is Steve Epstein."

The screen reverted to the soap opera that had been so rudely interrupted. The customers started to talk amongst themselves. "Bunch of assholes, whatya expect," one said.

"Imagine busting in on a show for that shit?"

"Only in New York, man. They hire these aliens, bums, to run those cranes. Bet he was nonunion. Probably never swung a ball in his life."

"Hey the Mets could use him, huh. Scare the piss out of the on-deck batter! Like Ryne Duren. Remember him?"

Evidently nobody did. There was a pause before one more piped up, "I bet anything he was aiming for someone in there; that's what they'll find out. How could he be so far off? Don't make sense."

Callman swallowed the last of his BLT and walked out. No one saw him leave.

Two

Georgina Callman had just entered the house and heard the phone ring, which she picked up on the third ring, beating the recorded message by one ring.

"Is this the Callman residence?" a flat-toned voice inquired on the line.

"Who's calling?" she asked.

"Is this Mrs. Callman that I am speaking to?" the drone continued.

"Hey, you didn't answer my question," she said, annoyance creeping into her response.

"No—but you've not answered mine either, ma'am. But I'll assume that you are, in fact, Mrs. Callman. I am Detective Bruno Kiel of the NYPD, and I have something to tell you. It concerns your husband, Evan Callman. Now … will you identify yourself for me?"

Attention taken, Georgina cut in with "Yes, then, this is she. What is it? I've got to run in a minute—he's all right, isn't he?"

"Look, Mrs. Callman, there's been an accident involving your husband down at his office and—"

Suddenly in panic, she said, "Tell me, then, now."

Kiel, still in a drone mode, went on, "… please allow me to finish. I am very sorry to tell you that a man was killed earlier today in the collapse of his building … ah, a part of the building, and we believe that man to be your husband."

There was a heavy silence at the other end of the telephone.

"Mrs. Callman?"

"Yes, yes. I'm here. You say you 'believe' it is him. Are you certain? Could there be some mistake?"

Kiel continued, "I have to ask you to come to the city to identify this body. And, sure, there could always be an error, but I must tell you that we are certain that a man trapped underneath the rubble of the accident was … is … in fact, your husband, but any such determination must be made with your positive ID."

She stammered in response, "How … uh … did all this happen, Detective?"

"Look, ma'am, when you get down here we'll go through all that happened, so, no, not on the phone. I also must prepare you for the fact that Mr. Callman … the body … is not in very good condition. I would advise you, if at all possible, to bring someone with you for your own comfort. I can tell you from experience that this will be difficult and you will need support—"

"Not if it's someone else, and you got me down there on a hunch," she chipped in.

He went ahead as though her last remark was nonexistent. "I know your town police department and have arranged for one of the officers to drive you down within the half hour. You should not consider coming in yourself."

Kiel then proceeded to give her the address of the morgue where they would all meet. Conversation over, Georgina cradled the phone receiver, unpacked the grocery bags she had carried in, and placed her purchases in their rightful compartments. *Best to keep busy,* she thought while awaiting her ride into the city.

"Mrs. Callman?" Kiel asked as he stood alongside of his desk and shook hands with the woman facing him. "Let me introduce my partner, Sergeant Emshawn Hamilton."

Kiel was a large man, rangy and swarthy with leaded eyebrows that shielded deep-set hangdog eyes. Hamilton was his equal in stature and seemed to Georgina to present an effective Samuel L. Jackson persona. Standing on either side of the diminutive, black-haired Georgina Callman, they each sensed that her size belied a steely demeanor. She gave a barely perceptible flick to her long straight hair and said, "Now, Detective and Sergeant, can we get on with this? I'll want to finish here so that I can proceed with the arrangements—that is, if it becomes necessary."

Kiel went on to caution her that what she was about to see would be alarming, to say the least. "Since I do not see anyone with you, I take it you didn't bring a companion along?" he asked her.

"Well, there wasn't much time, was there? People are occupied this time of day." The two policemen exchanged glances.

"All right then, we'll just go ahead," Kiel said, "but I must again emphasize, ma'am, that Mr. Callman … He … is extremely disfigured from the accident and that you must be prepared for …"

"On with it, Detective."

Kiel nodded to Hamilton. *Is this lady an ice queen or what,* he was thinking, and both policemen instinctively flanked Georgina as they walked into the morgue. They approached a stainless steel gurney in the room's center; in fact, the only one on display there at the time, and, as if on cue, deftly removed the white sheet from the recumbent body. Georgina did, in fact, shudder and emit a muffled gasp as she first viewed the corpse laid out in front of her. "Look, ma'am, we've done our best to clean him, but, as you can see, what is left of the face is virtually unrecognizable," Kiel intoned. "I've never seen anything quite like this; oh, maybe after nine-eleven, those bodies that were still in one piece, and I'm sorry to have to put you through this, but we need to have a positive ID from you."

The dead guy's face was hardly more than a lopsided coating of what was once flesh over a skull that must have had most of its bone structure shattered. One eye seemed to be completely torn away from its socket. *They could have placed that one back in its holder,* she thought, as she observed that the ears had been mashed to a pulp, and the nose, or what had been a nose, was at a right angle to whatever substance held it in. Hair was matted down and had turned to a noncolor, a pasty grey.

Kiel turned to face Georgina. She remained silent. "Well, ma'am?"

"I … I … yes. As best I can tell, it's Evan," she answered. "You say his effects were on him?"

"Well, I did not say," the detective said as he managed a faint smile, "but you may have those, of course. There was a wallet, commuter train ticket, keys, some money. About what would be expected. Now, you just told us 'as best.' Naturally we'll need stronger affirmation. Do you recognize the clothes—that is, even in this condition?"

Georgina continued to stare at the body. The more she did, the more doubt entered her mind, but she was determined not to let on to these two characters. *And yet, with the gross disfigurement, how could anyone tell who this was merely by looking,* she thought. *The man's size was about Evan's,* she added to herself. She said, "The clothes, well, yes, it looks like what he went out with this morning, but you know, I never pay attention to that sort of thing …"

"Any distinguishing physical characteristics that you can tell us about, Mrs. Callman? It seems that there is some hesitation on your part." Kiel was doing all the talking. Evidently, Samuel L. was there for corroboration. Georgina put forth a small smile; she was tempted to tell them Evan had an especially long cock, but that might only prompt the unveiling of that gallant member now in terminal repose, a sad end to such unfailing service.

"Ah, not really, no. Look, Detective, I'm satisfied, it's him. So let's end it here, okay?" she responded, once more a lady in control.

"It's my decision, gentlemen. Moreover, in the Jewish religion it is required that those who have died are … uh … taken care of immediately. I want the body to be sent to the funeral parlor in our town. I'll leave you the number and address. Now, if it's acceptable to you, I'd like to sign any statement you need and then go home. I'll want to stop in at the mortuary in advance of Evan's arrival there later on."

The officers agreed to her wishes and promised that the body would be on its way as soon as the funeral parlor arranged for transportation. It was hardly in their best interests to keep Evan Callman on his steel bed any longer than necessary. After all, there had been no evidence of a crime being committed, and they would want to move on to the cases that inevitably would be rolling their way as the warmish evening progressed. They were shorthanded anyway, with most of the station being up in Central Park at the annual picnic and softball game. Kiel and Hamilton walked back to the office area of the station. Paperwork was placed in front of Georgina, who scribbled her name on various forms without bothering to ask what any of them meant. The young policeman from town had stayed to drive her home.

"Mrs. Callman," Kiel asked in the doorway, "did your husband favor shoes that were a size or more bigger than his feet?"

"Why, what an odd question, Detective." This time the lady wore a smile and thought that Kiel had studied his interrogatory technique under Columbo.

He said, "Maybe not, ma'am. You see, the shoes are size 11D and the feet, or what's left of them, appear to be a nine or so. Seems strange to us."

She faced the officers squarely. "I don't know about that. Some people just need extra wiggle room. Good afternoon, gentlemen." With that, Georgina took her leave, deliberately not looking behind on a venue she hoped she would never see again.

Once out of her earshot, Kiel said to his partner, "I dunno, E-shawn, that's one cold lady, and I'm not convinced of what just went down. What do you think?"

Hamilton said, "Think? I think we move 'em out, just as she wants. We're gonna have bigger fish to fry than worry about some white-bread guy had the misfortune to get slammed by a wrecking ball."

Tapped out of anything further to add, Kiel shrugged in resignation. They were done there. Hamilton's phone was ringing, as was Kiel's a moment later.

He was sitting in a rear booth of yet another coffee shop in the west end of Chelsea when the 6:00 p.m. news came on.

"… And now for an update on that earlier midtown accident, where a misguided wrecking ball took out a section of the front of the Integrity building. We have learned that there was one fatality inside the building as well as three minor injuries to passerby at the time of this incident. The fatality has been identified as Integrity executive Evan Callman, who was believed to be in his office at the time of this tragic event and, it appears, in the direct path of the ball …"

Evan hunkered down in his seat as he saw a quick flash-bite of him on the screen. *Now where did they get that likeness?* he wondered, and then figured it must have come from some part of his corporate personnel jacket. He scrunched down a bit further. The broadcast continued.

"… Standing with me is Detective Bruno Kiel of the local precinct. What can you tell our viewers, Detective?"

Kiel went on to describe the horrific state in which the man was found, making reference to nine-eleven for comparison, and expressing condolences to next-of-kin and fellow workers, all the while shaking his head in an empathetic manner. Then the interview switched to one of the man's co-workers. *My God,* Evan thought, *it's Trulett Maddox, large as life up there on the TV.*

"Why, I just left Evan in the office. A few of the others and I were on our way to lunch. But Evvy—Mr. Callman—he stayed behind. He sometimes used the lunch hour to get caught up with what was on his desk, when things quieted down for a while. That's the kind of man he is—or was. Ah, if he had only gone along with us. He died at his desk, a real hero for our company. I tell ya'll, it's a sad day for Integrity."

Maddox appeared to brush back a tear with a silk handkerchief. The newsman went on.

"That is the story, then. A devastating miscalculation and an innocent life is lost. You know, Maggie, (he was addressing the studio anchor in a heartfelt way) we use the term TGIF so casually, but on this particular Friday it came home to reality, because as senseless as this is, had this not happened on lunch hour, the injuries, or even additional deaths in that office section might have been more extensive …"

Maggie, the anchor, reacted. "You nailed that one, Vince (the newsman), it's a lesson for all of us never to skip lunch. You never do, do you?" After a noticeable titter on Vince's end, the broadcast meandered to other stories in the naked city, and Callman exhaled, trying to collect his thoughts and regroup.

All right, he thought, *I've got some money left, enough for a couple of days but not much more. I could use the credit card maybe one more time, it's got an ATM function on it, because notice of the death of Evan Callman probably would not hit his banking transactions just yet.*

There would, of course, be electronic trails that would certainly raise eyebrows as to the timing of any future withdrawals; it was a risk he might have to assume. Then, there would be the events surrounding his demise; they would occur over the next forty-eight hours or a bit more and then cease. He needed to get through that block of time. As for his appearance, he would not be able to alter that right now, not in any significant way; a cap, dark glasses, and perhaps some hair coloring might see him over the span of time between the present and his getaway, which had yet to be planned out. Down the road, there was the issue of new identity, but that would have to wait as well, although he had started to give some thought to that in the recent past, in some of his quiet moments.

He got up and repaired to the street, evening closing in. Tonight, and maybe for the next couple of nights, he would ride the subway, catching catnaps as he did and exercising care to stay clear of any late-night stalkers who may be fellow travelers. He stopped to purchase those few items that could change his appearance, but he was not overly concerned about recognition for the time being. After all, no one who would know him would be on the subway after dark, and the TV flash of his countenance was brief and altogether forgettable. He soon found a McDonald's that had a clean bathroom—*it is remarkable the unheralded service this chain provides to America, spiffy bathrooms everywhere,* he thought—and applied some instant dark hair color (Callman had naturally blond and thickly curled hair, lightly flecked with grey), donned an NYC baseball cap and dark glasses bought from a street vendor, and descended once more into the subway.

Daytime was problematic. However, there were all-day movie houses open, and he knew that the Mets had an afternoon game at Shea Stadium against the Brewers. *Now wouldn't that be a rip,* he thought. *Anyone notice the dead guy in the right field stands? Yeah, the one with the raincoat and the shades. Kinda overdresses for the occasion, but, come to think of it, showers are in the forecast, and he could be the only one who's prepared.*

He was tempted to stroll by his building, to see if there was anything to see. He had to fight that idea; it was too great a risk to take, and there would be, no doubt, little activity there, save for the obligatory yellow tape across the scene and the street cleanup. The office, such as it was, would have to be relocated temporarily. Better to stay clear of it.

Two days following his untimely passing, on the obit page of the Times, Evan read his own notice in the Times along with a column about him. Generally, the grey lady of journalism reserved that space for celebrities, intellectuals, moguls, or oddities. But, there he was.

Evan Callman, 47, Executive

Died unexpectedly after a construction accident damaged his office building. Mr. Callman was a Senior Vice President at Integrity Investment Management Corp. He was generally credited with developing Integrity's global administrative services business to its pre-eminent position in today's marketplace.

A 1980 graduate of Wesleyan University and holding an MBA degree from New York University, Mr. Callman was also a retired U.S. Army Captain, having served five years in its Finance Corps. He leaves behind his wife, Georgina, of Quiet Sound, Connecticut, a brother, Mark, and his parents, Max and Minnie.

The formal notice was hardly cut-and-dried and brought a wide smile to Evan's face.

Callman, Evan, suddenly on June 6. Loving husband of Georgina, brother of Mark, devoted son of Max and Minnie. All services private. In lieu of flowers, friends are encouraged to offer contributions to Bide-A-Wee of the tri-state area. "Evvy, beloved master, why did the Lord need you so soon? Your work here was hardly complete. May you rest in my thoughts and those of your family forever."

—Your grief-stricken and loyal bichon frise, Quasimodo.

By day three, his entire body ached from fitful naps on the city's mass-transit system, and his new clothes were starting to reek. By then, he had seen most of the current movies, and he considered himself to be a worthy contender for a reviewer's job, should any of the incumbents ever decide to step down as a movie critic. He thought that the fanfare had probably ended, everyone on to better things, and it was high time to make some moves.

Three

He was on the 9:43 p.m. train out of Grand Central, headed in a northerly direction. Lightly populated, it was a late train even for dedicated workaholics, and it was too early for the theatergoers to be returning to their suburban aeries. He had not seen his home platform since that fateful day that began with the lion sighting, but he was not about to go to that station anyway, for fear that one of his neighbors might be de-training along with him. No. He would go to the station four stops down the line and then grab a taxi to the main street of his hometown, where he'd be dropped off in front of a restaurant he knew. Once the cab turned the corner, he'd walk the eight remaining blocks to his house. It was a trip he had to make. Daytime, when he might have been fortunate enough to find his wife out, he believed too risky because of neighbors and other assorted activity that could immediately blow his cover. Night, with Georgina all but certain to be abed, posed yet another issue—her recognition of him and the unavoidable *tete-a-tete* but it was in his mind the lesser of several evils.

He was counting on one or more of the doors to the house to be unlocked, Georgina being one of those souls who, when it came to home security, was indifferent, an anomaly within the context of her sharp tongue and otherwise suspicious nature. Evan would occasionally prod her to install an alarm system, but her attitude seemed to be that when the day came that she no longer felt safe without one, it would be time to sell. She rarely locked doors, but now, following his departure, it was hard to say what she would do. The last thing he needed was to be apprehended in a faux break-in. If doors and windows were locked, he'd have to leave.

Luck, if anyone could call it that, was with him. The front door was not locked. As softly as he could, Evan turned the knob and entered the house. The little dog yapped, a mechanical reflex that he expected and did not mind because once inside he understood he would not go unnoticed.

"Quasi, shh, shh, what is it?" came a woman's voice from the bedroom upstairs. The little dog approached him, offered a series of reassuring sniffs and then retreated to her doggie bed at the foot of the stairs to the second story. He proceeded up the staircase. "Now go to sleep, Quasi, will you, all right …" the woman's voice trailed off for a moment, but then evidently hearing more unannounced sounds, she said, "What, what is it?" and then he was made aware of a lamp turned on and a rustling of sheets and bedclothes.

Georgina Callman was half out of her bedside when she saw the apparition facing her, not ten feet away. She managed a "what the hell …" before sinking back to her bed for a form of support to brace her for what she was witness to.

"Quiet, calm now, Georgie," he said, palms up toward his wife in a mode of contrition. "Yes, it's me, as you can tell and I …"

Now she was up and striding towards him, bedsheet around her (Georgina always slept nude; he found that endearing) barely covering a breast that seemed momentarily to fly solo (he could not suppress an ongoing admiration of her breasts, her finest physical attribute, he always thought, and never failed to remind her of that when the situation favored him). "It is you, isn't it?" she exclaimed, now facing him, touching—no—pinching, his cheek. Then she took a step backward and said, 'What kind of crap did you put on your hair?"

That was the Georgina Callman he knew, having regained composure and vitriol. "Oh, it's only temporary. Look, I have to talk; I don't have much time, I've got to … uh, pick up some things, and then I'll be out of here. Promise." He grinned.

"Evan, what the shit is this all about? You're dead, goddamit, and now here you are in front of me with a shit-eating smirk. What do you mean, leaving? Not without some kind of explanation."

"You don't want to know."

"Oh, yes I do, Evan. You put me—everyone—through this. You bet I do."

He moved to sit by the bed. Georgina remained fixed in place. He told her that some things were better left unsaid. "It could be detrimental to our future."

"Future? What future? You're a bag of ashes in the mudroom right now."

Callman smiled again. "I'm so glad about your devotion to my memory, Georgie. I'm overwhelmed."

She responded, "And I am underwhelmed. So, if it's not you—obviously—who is that in the Medaglia d'Oro can, anyway?"

"Is that where I am, in a coffee can?" he asked.

"Temporary, Evan, just like your spit-shine black hair. So, I'll ask again, who is—was it?"

He told her about the accident and his discovery of the body nearby. "It was some homeless guy, and then an idea came to me …"

"A homeless guy? I sat shiva for some bum nobody knew? I'm keeping a vagrant's ashes? You gotta be kidding." She started to walk away, to leave the bedroom. "This is too damn much. I'm calling the police—now. Getting you the hell away from me and into custody."

Evan sat on the edge of the bed and said, "No, you are not going to do that, Georgina."

"Like hell. You tell me why."

"I will. Because if you do, the whole thing will be exposed, unraveled. It would not be in the best interest of either one of us. Trust me. Because I bet the company people have already been to see you or talk to you about my life insurance. Huh?" Callman, calm, awaited her response.

It turned out that they had, and Georgina nodded faintly in the affirmative.

He went on, "I would have figured as much. Integrity is noted for service, particularly when it comes to one of their own. And in my case, my group insurance policy called for a face amount of five hundred thousand, and twice that amount in the case of accidental death. And this sure as hell was an accident. So it's a cool mil, wifey. You're not about to throw that away. Have you got the money yet?"

She told him that the check was waiting merely on the processing of the death certificate through the claims department of the insurance carrier and was expected to be in her hands within the next two or three days.

"I would have thought so, Georgie. That is why you are going to hold still. Not a bad payoff, wouldn't you say? It's a little like that old film noir, *Double Indemnity*. You remember that one, don't you? It was the only movie ever made about insurance."

Georgina, a classic movie buff, was not about to be topped; Evan was overstepping his boundary. "Yeah, I remember it, but I'm not sure you do, Evan. Don't you recall what happened to Fred MacMurray in the end?"

"Touche', Georgie," he said. "However, I won't replicate MacMurray's fate." He was becoming tired of the banter and began to depart. "I'm going to grab a few of my things, and then I'm off."

Georgina followed him as he stuffed articles of clothing into a country club duffel bag lying on the floor of their bedroom closet. "You gonna tell me what this is really about, Evan?" she screeched at his back. "It's about leaving me, isn't it?"

He finished stuffing his meager possessions, rose, then left the room and hastened down the staircase. "Who is it, Evan? Is it the mousey brown-haired Irish kid? Or is it the spic with the boobs bigger than mine? You shtubbing her? Or both of them, are you? The mick or the spic?"

He made one final turn to her while she was in full rant at the top of the stairs. "I'll be in touch, Georgina. Everything's going to work out. Have a little faith in me."

With that, he was back into the soft night air once more. He had one more stop to make there, which was the garage, a detached structure several feet from the house.

There, behind a masonite panel in the garage's north wall, he retrieved a decaying Knicks backpack. Two items were inside: a silver key and four envelopes containing twenty thousand dollars, mostly in hundred-dollar bills but including a smattering of twenties. The hundreds might turn out to be problematic, but it was what it was, and he would just have to deal with it. He took the backpack, replaced the panel on the wall, and left the premises.

The walk back to town was peaceful. No one was out. He entered a bar, called a taxi, and drank a Foster's on draft while awaiting his ride. He thought about his Aussie neighbor, Harry Primbo, as he enjoyed the cold one. *Another dime in your kick, Harry,* he thought, feeling good about dispensing even a modest amount of largesse to a friend. He would then catch the late train—a 12:20 a.m.—back to the city, where he'd spend the remaining dark hours riding aimlessly on the subway. He was certain this would be his final night for so doing; fortified with a stash of walking-around money, he could begin to put his plans in motion.

He reflected on his *tete-a-tete* with his wife. Did he really need to go out to the house tonight? Yes, he answered himself. I had to have what was there, and there wasn't any way I'd gain entry without confronting her unless she simply wasn't at home, and he had no way ahead of time to know if she was or wasn't. Anyway, he wanted to hear about the insurance, and with the settlement in her hands momentarily, it pretty much iced her silence on the matter of Evan Callman. Then he thought back to her accusations regarding the women in the office, smiling to himself as he did so. *I shouldn't underestimate my wife*, he mused, *there isn't much she's going to miss.* He allowed for a touch of flattery that she suspected him of carrying on perhaps two affairs. Noemi, well, that would be all right—had Georgina met her twice when she had reason to come to town, that would have been a lot. But she surely remembered the boobs. *The firm, bronzed legs. Don't forget about those, Georgina.* Noemi would have been poison, though. Even had he tried and met with some success, Evan might have found himself close to the edge of one of her brothers' switchblades.

Mary Ellen Dunn was an altogether different story. The girl should welcome a go with anyone. He often wondered whether she had a boyfriend at all, or maybe did have in the past, that being in high school, he guessed. Mary Ellen had little of a life beyond Integrity and ongoing care for an elderly and ailing mother. An only child, it had become her calling to serve only those two masters, to the exclusion of all else. From what he could discern, loyalty of an unquestioning nature was her foremost quality. But would it stand up under pressure? He harbored some doubt, recalling her talking about needing money the other day. It was the first time she had approached him so directly. Maybe the mother had an unexpected need. At any rate, he would have to face the issue of Mary Ellen, and soon. *Do I call her?* he wondered. *If so, that's one more person who will know the truth about me.*

He concluded he would have to contact her. She was a part of what had been going on, and he would need to rely on her loyalty big time. He reasoned that her future at Integrity was uncertain, with him out of the picture. He was assuming that Trulett Maddox would assume his work and Truly Mad (as he was called around the company) would want his own crew to come in, and that would not likely include Mary Ellen. Maybe she would leave Integrity altogether and arrange to disappear, but such action would in and of itself arouse suspicion. With all these thoughts whirling around in his head, Evan let out an involuntary sigh, closed his eyes and tried to sleep through the rattle of steel wheels and steel rails. *Yeah, we're going to have to talk*, he thought before nodding off.

Callman was at the Port Authority Bus Terminal shortly after dawn. Only the late-night junkies seemed to be resident, stirring around on their wooden benches, some of them beginning to shed their worn-out blankets. He was on the way to Washington, D.C., which would be the first leg of a longer journey. Oddly, he did not think to be in any hurry—not just yet—and the nation's capital was a place he could lose himself in, at least for a day or two. Besides, it had been years since his last visit, and he planned to take in some of the attractions like any other tourist—maybe the Holocaust Museum or that new American Indian (Native American? Whatever.) Museum. There's lots to see. He was on his own time, as they used to say in the military.

The bus left at 6:35 a.m. Rolling out of the city, he had a cup of McDonald's coffee in one hand and an Egg McMuffin in the other, and he was working up an appreciation for the rising sunlight on that pristine vista that was the New Jersey meadowlands. He allowed himself a feeling of relaxation that bordered on detachment, like being a kid on a trip all alone, and nobody knowing where you are, and thereby unable to intrude on your life.

Hotels would be an issue. They all required credit cards and sign-ins at the front desk, cash being unorthodox. Thus far he had done everything (so he believed) to not disclose his identity. In a town like Washington, there was always the Y, but that presented risks of a different nature. Once he arrived, he found a budget motel that was more accustomed to hourly guests than overnight ones, but cash was just dandy, and no questions were asked. No matter—by the following morning he'd be back at the bus station to resume his trip in a southerly direction.

He would now call Mary Ellen Dunn, using a prepaid phone card from a public telephone at a nearby shopping mall.

It was 7:00 p.m. The phone rang in the two-bedroom cape on a tree-lined street in Massapequa. The old woman in the wheelchair shouted for her daughter to pick up, much like the tone Stanley Kowalski used when he called for Stella. Mary Ellen Dunn fairly ran from her kitchen chores to do her mother's bidding. "Mary Ellen?" the somewhat muffled voice at the other end inquired.

"Yes, this is she," came the tentative response.

"Uh, it's me, Evan, Mary Ellen."

There was a pause. Had the acoustics been better, Evan might have heard the woman drop the receiver momentarily and then clutch it back before it would have hit the floor. "Evan? I don't know any Evan—the only one I did know died recently. I'm sorry, I'm going to hang up—"

"No. No. Don't. It is me, Evan Callman, your Evan, Mary Ellen. Stay with me on the line."

A tone of anger now welled up in Mary Ellen's voice as she spoke. "Is this some kind of sick joke, you—whoever you are. Evan Callman is dead. Leave me alone."

She hung up. *All right*, he figured, *I suppose I should not have been surprised. The lady's going to need some convincing.*

He redialed, she answered again, and this time he held her attention by spelling out details of the events of the past few days. Although still skeptical, she had little recourse other than to hear this man out. She harbored the hope that it was him, that Evan Callman alive would mean that goals could be achieved; in fact, when she first learned of Callman's death, the first thoughts that crossed her mind were what could she do from that point forward, suddenly isolated. As Mary Ellen listened, composure was returning. She elected to engage in the conversation. "You know—Evan—everyone called on Georgina, while she was—what do you call it?"

"Shiva. Sitting shiva. It's traditional," he said, his own curiosity building, "so who all came out?"

Mary Ellen went on, "Oh, a lot of the execs, naturally your own staff. Besides me there was Trulett, Tommy, Douglas, Noemi, of course; the house was full. Mr. Grader even showed up."

He was impressed with the roster of VIPs. *I should do this more often*, he thought. *It's a grand goodwill gesture, like Jimmy Stewart in It's a Wonderful Life.*

"What do we do now?" she asked.

Ah, it's "we," isn't it? he thought. *Okay, the girl is back on the page.*

"Here's what I think ..." Evan answered, and he proceeded to lay out immediate plans for the two of them. Mary Ellen concentrated on what he wanted her to do. He then asked about the situation at the company as it related to the organization in light of his sudden departure.

"Things are starting to happen, Evan. You should know that Maddox has taken over your work. That's not good for me. He'll want to bring in his own people."

Callman said, "That's what I would have figured. Look, you may have to sit tight. I know you're at risk, ought to get out of there, maybe even get out of Integrity entirely, but any sudden moves will invite attention. Play along for a while. We will meet; I'll tell you when and where. You have some vacation coming, don't you?"

"Yes, Evan. You should know that I've always got some days banked."

He said to her, "Then it would hardly be unusual for you to say to—whoever—'this death has taken a toll, and I'd like to take some time.' That would be understandable."

She agreed that it should be a workable approach.

"Good. I'll be in touch."

He was once again in motion the next morning, this time toward the next destination, that being Atlanta. A full day and evening ride, he would arrive just in time to locate a bed for the night. Through the past few days he had done little to mask his appearance—the hair coloring, dark glasses, and a pulled-down baseball cap being his principal artifacts. He was letting a beard and mustache grow in, which would help, at least in time. Then again, he was less concerned about recognition the greater the distance from New York. However, he took care to keep to himself as he traveled, electing to speak to no one and seeking out seating where he would not have a companion alongside.

Mary Ellen Dunn was having a hard time effecting an exit from the office. As expected, Trulett Maddox was officially placed in charge of Callman's responsibilities, and in initial meetings he bade all of the staffers to remain in their jobs. When Mary Ellen came to him, pleading emotional distress surrounding the death as a reason for time off, Maddox evidenced scant sympathy and became insistent that she not take any leave yet. "Hey, Mary Ellen, I've had to take all of this over, and I don't mind tellin' ya'll I don't know diddly scrap about the stuff you did with Evan, like them systems. So, I'd like to have you hang for a while till it sorts out."

She said to him, "I don't do systems, Mr. Maddox. The IT people do systems. I do business procedures. IT takes my process work and translates it into code so they function as designed."

Maddox allowed a toothy grin to expand his round, florid face. "See, I love the way you said that. Ya'll just told me that I don't know from shit, pardon the expression. And now you understand why I need you on deck."

It wasn't hard to grasp; Truly Mad was Evan Callman's polar opposite. Whereas Callman was a "Mr. Inside," Maddox was Integrity's man for bringing in business. They were known as the company's dynamic duo, Blanchard and Davis, Csonka and Kiick. Maddox carried a larger than life reputation. By his own admission one of the smallest men from Texas, standing all of five feet four in elevated heels, Maddox overrode his height with outrageous marketing practices which were tolerated because he consistently captivated and captured the customer, all to the benefit and glory of the corporation. Down home in south Texas, he drank Maker's Mark from a Tony Lama boot with the prospects when hustling accounts, and then he took them out to Gilley's, where he did a spin on the mechanical bull. In Florida, he would arrange for his clients to join him on a late-night alligator shoot-em-up. On one such occasion, armed with AK-47s that he had purchased in Miami from a Cuban arms dealer, the group had bagged six of the creatures before being apprehended by the local sheriff. No one cared about the gators, but it seems that the hunt occurred on conservation marshland. A hefty fine was paid before the corporate gunmen were freed, but it was worth every penny, as the contract ultimately was one of the largest in Integrity's history. Only when he showed up in a Hell's Angels getup to pitch a motorcycle manufacturer did he come in for an icy reception. It seems that the cycle people were more straight laced than would have been expected, and they felt that his demeanor denigrated their product. "Only one ah evah lost; failed to do my homework," he would later say.

Evan Callman was nothing of the sort. Thought to be cerebral, introspective, perhaps seeming aloof to some, he rarely worked alongside of Maddox; they each did their own thing, the typical pattern being that once Maddox &

Co. brought in a new account, it was handed off to Evan to set up, process, and integrate it into Integrity's ongoing business services.

Men like Trulett Maddox have a knack of picking up enemies along their way. One such person at the company was the chief auditor, Alexi Petrova. The animosity stemmed from a dinner two years prior when Maddox, at the time in between wives two and three and having consumed a jug's worth of Jack Daniels, turned to Petrova's statuesque blonde wife and asked, "What's a looker like you doing with a devil-ass commie like him, anyway?"

"Ex-commie, darling," Yanna Petrova replied flatly as she blew smoke into Truly's crimson face. "In case you've been away from earth for a while, they've been out of favor for some time now." Her husband merely sat and smoldered throughout the dinner.

Nobody save the CEO knew that not only was Alexi a communist, he was a former KGB operative, which was precisely what endeared him to Lowell Grader, who believed it to be a most applicable background for audit duties. Still carrying a torch for the good old days, Petrova still held on to his party documentation, just in case the old guard ever returned to power.

Thus it was that, hardly a week after the accident, Trulett Maddox found Alexi Petrova at the front of his desk. (Following the blow to the building, what remained of Evan Callman's office furniture and accessories were shipped off to the basement, presumably to gather additional dust for an indefinite period. Maddox was running things from his own office.)

"How's it going so far, Truly?" Petrova asked with the widest smile he could generate. The auditor had a talent for taking on a broad array of speech patterns and personae, a chameleon-like skill that he had developed in his former profession. He could spread charm that masked a iron-bound resolve and could intimidate when the situation called for it. With Maddox, he would begin with the charm, an attempt to out-Tex the Texan.

Petrova did not wait on a response. He continued, "Look, I will not waste your time, which I know to be under pressure. I want to audit your department. It has actually been … ah … (and here he pretended to stare down inside a manila folder that in actuality was empty) three years since we have examined these operations."

What Petrova failed to tell Maddox was that he wasn't in his office on a whim, not at all; he had been briefed by Lowell Grader to ready a review of the unit as a prerequisite to its impending sale. The CEO did, of course, swear Petrova to secrecy, which the latter warmed to immediately with the comment that "secrets are my business."

"So?" Maddox tried a poker face.

"Can I take that for a 'yes'?" Alexi was still in a light mood with Maddox, when the latter leaned over his desk and said, "You know, Alexi, ah've just taken over; why don't you let me get situated."

Petrova moved for the close. "Actually, I think we can help out, here. I realize you aren't familiar—yet—with all of what Evan did, and a current review will identify any control weaknesses, set up priorities, get your staff focused. We'll be constructive." Maddox chuckled and squinted at him, simultaneously.

"Constructive? Ya'll mean like the IRS is constructive?" Trulett Maddox leaned back in a chair whose back rose at least a foot over his head. "Aw, what the hell; go ahead, Alexi. This ole boy caint go toe-to-toe with auditors. You got all the leverage. Just cut the bullshit. Who ya planning on sending in?"

That question was anticipated by Alexi Petrova, who was quick to throw out the name of Leroy Brown, a name not familiar to Maddox. "We call him the audit department's junkyard dog," Alexi said. "It's our little joke."

The aptly named Leroy Brown was indeed a joke of an auditor. In the "gotcha" culture that defined the auditing profession, Brown would have ranked in the bottom quartile when it came to nailing suspicious and/or inept behavior. He had still to uncover anything significant of the sort in his investigative work that would bestow an "atta boy" on him in a public venue. Petrova was affording him a last chance to do something special and was betting this assignment would motivate him accordingly. Having gotten what he came for, Petrova was leaving. Truly was about to ask after Yanna Petrova in a parting effort at cordiality, but for once an involuntary tinge of discretion arose, and he demurred. For the rest of the day, he busied himself with other projects. *Let nature take its course*, he thought, *they'll call me when they want to start.*

On the following morning, they did.

Four

Callman was in Atlanta. He was becoming experienced at locating no-star motels that were relatively clean and were happy to accept cash from the man who this time signed the register as R.E. Lee. He would take a day off, noting that the Mets were in town to play the Braves at Turner Field. He bought a third-base side, field-level box seat ticket and enjoyed the warm, if somewhat humid, Georgia afternoon. The home team battered a succession of Mets pitchers, much to the delight of the sparse chop-wielding crowd. In the bottom of the eighth inning, a foul pop fly drifted toward the third-base side of the stands. In all his life he'd never caught a major-league baseball, but here came one floating down within reach. He leapt up—instinctively, partially in self-defense—and had three fingers on the ball just as a foreign hand came over his shoulder and speared the prize. As a vocal reaction, he blurted out an, "Oh, shit," followed by, "I nearly had that sucker—story of my life," and then looked behind at his competitor, one among a party of three business types out for the day, who was being high-fived by his companions. One of them, catching sight of Callman, said something about quick hands and in a second breath said to him, "Hey, you seem familiar. Do I know you?"

Evan shook him off. "No, I don't think so."

"You're not from Atlanta, are you? Sounds like you're from up north. New York, maybe. Am I right?" The speaker turned to his friends for validation of his assumption, and they were nodding in agreement, while Callman returned to his seat, a bit hunkered down. The inning ended, and with the Braves on top 9–2, fans began streaming out of the park. His best chance for a foul pop having come and gone, he rose as well to make an exit. As he did, his questioner said, "Did you work for a big company up there? I could swear we met at a conference a few years back. Could it have been Integrity? My outfit was doing some business with them."

Trying to make nice with the guy, he effected a smile and said, "No, sorry, it must have been someone else."

Once Callman was out of earshot, the man said to his friends, "Damn, I'm sure I met that guy. I wonder what he's doing here—lookin' a bit scruffy, I do believe."

"Sure didn't seem friendly, did he," one of the others chimed in. "Hell, you jes' took that little ole horsehide outta his Yankee hand, what 'n hell ya'll 'spect? Thas' what I like about the South." The group laughed and took a long pull on their beers in unison. The prober didn't want to let go. "I remember," he started, to no one in particular, "there was this character sent down to see us; he was decked out in confederate grey—we thought it was so funny, and we kept him around. Next thing we were up in the Big Apple, the character was gone; but here's this other guy, the one I talked to, he and his team, well they really knew their stuff and the price was right. Jew-boy, if I recall. Smart."

"Come on Yancey, give it up," one of his buddies said. "Anyhow, Braves got this one sewn up; let's go."

The ballpark incident was a close call. It was foolish on Evan's part to be in such a public place as a stadium, even one nine hundred miles from New York. He didn't remember the man, conferences with clients being a daily routine for him. He easily could have been one of Maddox's prospects; Truly had them brought in and then left him the nitty-gritty. Nonetheless, he found himself trembling as he repaired to his motel room, unnerved by the afternoon's incident.

That night, he called Mary Ellen and got nothing more than the answering machine message; he broke off the call. He believed that to be a bit off-kilter, Dunn being a *numero uno* homebody in the evening, but he'd try again tomorrow.

She was working late and the expectation was for a continuation of extra hours for so long as the audit was in progress. Under Leroy Brown's supervision, a team of three had encamped themselves in the administrative department, and Mary Ellen and several other associates were assigned to work with the auditors. Knowing of Leroy Brown's record to date, Alexi Petrova had stacked the deck by including Charlique Stevens in the group. He was confident she would cover any inadequacies that Brown might exhibit. They set a goal to wrap up the project in a week, or sooner. They employed a routine of examining each business function, using guidelines and checklists to organize the work. The standard they would shoot for was one of complete accounting and adequate controls, such that the reported results were an accurate portrayal of the business. The work required in-depth sit-downs with the managers, whose obligations were to demonstrate clear explanations of their work.

Mary Ellen's part of the picture involved banking and payments. Once an account was absorbed by Integrity, she managed the files and processes that allowed for the flow of payments to customers, in almost all cases a fixed monthly amount. Of course, new names would be added, changes would occur, and payment instructions would follow suit—all part of the day-to-day minutiae that was demanded and which consumed Mary Ellen's time. Having thirteen years of experience at Integrity, the last nine of which she worked for Evan Callman, she was always evaluated to be competent in her job.

Two days into the audit, Brown and his team randomly had tested accounts for accuracy, in accordance with original instructions. They also surveyed customers to determine the reliability of periodic payments. Mary Ellen was obliged to outline procedures for posting entries for payment.

He was disinclined to hang around Atlanta any longer, especially after the interrogation at Turner Field. The next part of his journey was to take him to Fort Myers, Florida, for which he boarded a southbound bus the next morning. Any contact with Mary Ellen Dunn would have to wait a bit longer. Before leaving, he bought the *Atlanta Constitution* and the *New York Times* at the depot's newsstand. He went through the Atlanta paper quickly and then turned his attention to the New York paper; all the while, the bus was making rapid headway on a clear day straight down I-75. Callman figured he had to make the newspaper last him time-wise—the market pages, Metro, Sports, The Arts, Dining In/Dining Out and then the crossword puzzle, hoping the latter was challenging enough to stimulate him for at least an hour or so. Approaching the Georgia-Florida border, and thumbing through the Metro section, an article in the lower left-hand portion of the page caught his eye.

Widow Files Multimillion Dollar Suit

Citing wrongful death, the widow of a prominent New York business executive has filed a $400 million suit against the A&G Construction Company of Manhattan. Mrs. Evan Callman, 46, was left widowed last month when her husband was killed in the collapse of a portion of the building in which he worked. At the time of the accident, a considerable amount of construction activity was taking place in the area, and one of A&G's cranes slammed its wrecking ball into the Integrity Investment building at a spot where Mr. Callman was working. He is said to have died instantly under tons of debris that rained down on him. Mrs. Callman contends that the crane operator missed his target, was intoxicated at the time, and, further, that he was incompetent because he had logged only four hours of prior experience on the job. Moreover, he was alone in the cab at the time, and A&G had failed to provide adequate supervision, so the action alleges.

At the time of the accident, the crane operator, Muhammad Al-Omani, was briefly held for questioning, but no charges were brought against him or the

A&G Company. All of the required permits were found to be in order. The A&G Company had no comment to make upon learning of the lawsuit.

Hey, Georgina, he thought, *you want it all, n'est pas? I guess a mil isn't good enough for you.* He was sure that the A&G Company (which stood for Anastacio and Genovese), one of the largest contractors in the city, not only did a lot of buildings and property work for Integrity, but that they were a client as well. He remembered that Truly Mad closed the deal with them while wearing a trademark A&G royal blue hard hat throughout the proceedings. The A&G guys loved it.

Well, wifey, you are swimming in infested waters, he thought.

His bus continued on its route and reached Fort Myers in the early evening. Now into the south Florida off-season, the town seemed as sleepy as the heavy, grayish humidity that enveloped it. At this time of year, there would be little difficulty in finding a nearby cheap motel. He bought the local paper, ate at a neighborhood place, and then repaired to his room to try once more to get hold of Mary Ellen Dunn.

This time she answered on the third ring. "Yes?" the voice, tentative, picked up.

"Mary Ellen, it's me; I've tried to reach you. Where have you been?"

Dunn told him of extra hours at the office in light of the audit project. Hearing that, Evan was momentarily startled. "What audit?"

"They started a few days ago."

"Who's 'they,' Mary Ellen?"

She listed the players. Callman knew that the chief auditor, Alexi Petrova, carried a thing for Trulett Maddox; he didn't know why, but it was there. Callman always maintained an easy relationship with the audit group, and, in fact, they had not bothered his area for quite some time. But now that had all obviously ended with his demise and, he surmised, with the prospective sale of the unit. New brooms.

He continued, "See, Mary Ellen, I think you're going to have to get out of there. I'm on my way to … well … you know where; I'll be there soon."

She asked, "And then what? When will I see you?" The woman sounded nervous.

"I'll wait for you," he answered in a tone that fell short of conviction.

"You'd better, Evan. I know you hold all the cards, but right now I'm the one with feet to the fire. Don't make me blow a whistle."

The lady could be a little toughie, or a little uptight, Evan thought, yet he believed there was scant risk of whistle-blowing; it would be like calling in artillery rounds on your own position.

He chose to ignore her threat, telling her there wasn't much time to waste. "Try to make a getaway on a long weekend. You can't stay there, you know."

A pregnant silence, then, "Yeah, I know."

Finally, "And as for any turnabout, that wouldn't do either of us any good, now, would it?"

Click.

Detective Bruno Kiel was slouched behind his fully depreciated desk, trying to hide in plain sight behind an in-box exhibiting severe overflow, when his partner came over to him. "What is it, Em?" he asked.

"Lady wants to see you. Says it's about that exec guy in the building smack-down, you remember, the other week."

Kiel was not even looking up from his desktop. "You think I'm into early Alzheimer's, Em. Sure, I remember. Do *you* remember that we closed that one? You see her, Em."

Hamilton was persistent. "Insists on you. You're the man."

Kiel relented, choosing the path of least resistance, and bade Hamilton show her to his desk. "Better hang around, though, if I need you."

A not unattractive woman somewhere in her forties entered the room and sat alongside of the detective's desk. She was wearing a shirtwaist dress in a shimmering coral fabric, a bit retro and a bit covered up for a summer's day, and her streaky blonde hair was pulled back in a tight pony tail. All of her body language indicated tautness. "Thank you for seeing me, Detective," she started. "I'm Wynne Flanagan, that is spelled W-Y-N-N-E, and Flanagan with all As, that is, if you choose to write any of this down. I live in Manhattan and want to discuss my brother with you."

"Who would be …" Kiel was faintly amused and off-put by her formal manner.

"Oh, forgive me," she said as she emitted a muffled laugh, "it must have sounded as though you knew him—I don't believe you would—his name is Cameron Wynne III. Yes, you see, he's been missing for some ten days or more." She extended a weak smile.

As though that explained everything, Kiel thought. "Lots of folks missing in New York, ma'am. Would you care to elaborate? No offense, Ms. Flanagan, but it's hectic around here," he said while waving off-handedly at the frenetic motion that was a constant condition around the station house.

She got on with her story, which was that her brother had been living inside the Integrity building, and that when she learned about the accident there and had not heard from him since that time, she began to suspect that he might have been injured—or worse—in it.

Kiel was puzzled yet intrigued by her tale, which he processed internally as bizarre, but he didn't mind bizarre at all if it brought color to an otherwise boring day. "Okay, let's just go through this. You say he was living *in* the building?"

"He was a homeless man, Detective. I can understand how this must be coming across to you … but we did talk to one another often, even as he was cut off from the rest of our family. They all thought of him as insane—perhaps that is too harsh, eccentric may be better, wouldn't you say—and wanted no part of him, but I never accepted that." She shifted gears in her tone. "Do you know if he was there at the time? In the building?"

"Whoa, now," Kiel was signaling across the room for Hamilton to join them, figuring by now he needed a witness. After a hasty introduction, Wynne Flanagan told Hamilton that he was a dead ringer for Samuel L. Jackson.

"Ringer, okay. Dead, not just yet, ma'am," he commented, beaming all the while. They all laughed.

Kiel went on, "First of all, we don't have anything to tell you about your brother—now—but let me ask you, if he was there, what was he doing?"

She answered, "He worked for that company for a while until he was let go in a staff reduction. He always told me the bosses had it in for him, and this just set him off. Oh, he would write letter after letter to them; he complained about their policies to the shareholders, all to no avail. I advised him to give it up, but that merely seemed to strengthen his resolve. Then, he worked his way into the building somehow, created a kind of living space for himself, and obviously found ways to come and go without restraint. Moreover, he'd tell me that sometimes he'd listen through the walls to a meeting going on, and he would whisper suggestions. He even believed some of his ideas were put into effect."

The policemen had listened intently to Wynne Flanagan, and Kiel subtly indicated that Hamilton pick up. "Mrs. Flanagan," Emshaw was saying, "there was only one body recovered in that wreck, and it was a positive ID, a man who actually worked for Integrity and was in his office at the time"

"You are referring to that—uh—Mr. Callman," Wynne smiled again.

The lady was certainly up on the news reports.

"Yes, ma'am."

She persisted, "And he was indeed identified. By whom, may I ask?"

Kiel was emphatic in telling her she was at liberty to ask, but he was not obliged to divulge such information to her. Undeterred, she asked about the autopsy and the disposition of the corpse. Again, the officers demurred.

"You see, I have my doubts that an adequate investigation took place, officers. I may be forced to take steps—legally—to see if it can be reopened."

"That would, of course, be your right," Kiel said as he leaned back in his chair, a posture that declared his weariness and the interview at an end.

She rose to leave and politely thanked them for their time. "That—Mr. Callman—was the only body found?"came as a parting shot.

"The one and only. Goodbye, Ms. Flanagan."

Hamilton spoke first following her leave-taking. "Crazy-ass story, boss."

"Yeah, so crazy that you couldn't invent it. I still think there's something screwy about the whole case, Em. But, the case is closed."

Hamilton saw that Kiel had returned to his desk work. "Weird friggin' people in this town," he muttered as he walked away.

Evan Callman was on the day boat that ran between Fort Myers and Key West. In high season, the boat would be full of vacationers and snowbirds who would make a long day out of a four-hour voyage each leg, with time in between for harried shopping and a quick lunch in the town. However, this day it was lightly populated, maybe half full, he estimated. The boat itself was a ferry with few amenities save for a coffee shop and restrooms. He carried his belongings, which might make him conspicuous to other passengers, most of whom were armed with little more than a camera and a light jacket or a sweater should the air turn brisk on the trip, which it did not. No one paid any attention to the dark-haired, lightly mustachioed and bearded man with the straw hat and the aviator glasses quietly reading his newspaper at the stern of the vessel. The contrast in hair color top and bottom was troubling him as he consulted his bathroom mirror before embarking that morning, and he made a mental note to do something about the facial hair. As it was, he thought he was starting to look like Leon Redbone.

The seas were mild, and their brackish-green hues merged with heavy grey cloud cover to present a kind of monochromatic setting for the trip. The boat docked more or less on time, shortly before noon. Once on land, he melted with the strollers along the town's main artery. Wall-to-wall gift shops were selling T-shirts, boogie boards, and little else. Tiki bars, bed-and-breakfasts, and art galleries were around corners and side streets. He ate a grilled grouper sandwich and washed it down with a Beck's (apologies, Harry, gotta spread the business) at an outdoor café, after which he arranged to take a room at a B&B on a quiet side street, The Master Gator it was called. He liked the name and the lavender bougainvillea climbing the whitewashed façade of the place. The front desk was pleased to accept cash in advance, and the room was fine. It was, after all, off-season and availability was ample. After settling in, Callman did what he rarely did, which was to take a nap. The days on the road had caught up with his body, and he quickly nodded off the afternoon.

Five

At Integrity's offices in New York, the review of Evan Callman's old work units was drawing to a close. Mary Ellen Dunn had seen little of the audit team leader, Leroy Brown, since the projects' commencement, having to work instead with Charlique Stevens. Among other things, Ms. Stevens held an MBA from NYU's Stern School of Business and was a statistics freak. For relaxation, she would pore over publications such as *The Statistical Abstract of The United States* and *The Baseball Encyclopedia*, the latter being her primary source for concocting her personal major league Hall of Fame, based on incontrovertible cases for players bypassed for admission vis-à-vis those already enshrined who should never have been.

For the last several days, Charlique applied her dogged statistical approach to a pile of payment streams, bank records, and customer feedback against a sample of accounts selected for testing. Sitting down with Mary Ellen and presenting several number lists for review, she was preparing to ask some questions in a wrap-up interview. "Mary Ellen, look at these accounts," she said as she pointed to a set of tables with an exquisitely lacquered cherry-red fingernail. "The frequency of bank account changes greatly exceeds the norm for all of the company's customer accounts. Many of the changes happened after the initial bank account was in place for a lengthy period. It seems odd." Charlique was dressed right out of Versace, her caramel-toned skin was nearly flawless, and recent LASIK surgery had allowed her to ditch a long-term relationship with a strong eyeglass prescription.

Mary Ellen examined the data for a moment and then said to the auditor that people changed their accounts all the time. She was thinking, *Why is that so hard for Ms. Auditor-fashionista to understand?* "And you do request documentation for when an account changes?" she was asked.

"Well, in most cases, we only receive notice from the new bank telling Integrity that so-and-so has opened this new account and that future payments from the company should be directed there." Mary Ellen managed a half smile, a form of influence she hoped would satisfy the auditor.

Charlique seemed to file her response away, and then she asked if the payments were made to the customer's account electronically. Mary Ellen answered in the affirmative, adding that electronic money transfers were instituted by Mr. Callman some time ago, that they were standard in the financial industry, and that it was a process that had saved Integrity a lot of expenses. Stevens nodded in comprehension, if not acceptance, of the answer and continued on. “All right, then, here’s another tabular display,” she was unbundling a printout ream, “that shows the number of months that these new accounts remained active.”

“Your point?” Dunn was again poring over numbers, fidgeting with the strand of pearls above the neckline of her white sweater.

“The life of those changed accounts was, for most of them, quite short. Look …” and here the auditor was running her ideal fingers down the pages, “anywhere from 2 to 14 months, the average being 7.3 months and the median being 6.8 months.”

“Proving?”

“I thought *you* might be able to tell *me*. One of the typical causes of the closure of an account in the business we have on the books is the death of the payee. The pattern here suggests that someone changes a bank account and then dies soon thereafter. I don’t know that it proves anything, but it gives me the impression that switching your bank account could be harmful to your health.”

Charlique’s cell phone was ringing to the opening bars of “You’ve Got a Friend.” “Leroy, yes, I had called earlier. I’ll be right over,” she answered, then said to Mary Ellen, “Gotta go. We’ll pick it up later.”

The auditor had a thing for Leroy Brown, and she had every hope that the combination of her new eyes and the germination of cool audit findings would impress her boss. Up to now, Brown had evidenced little interest in anyone other than himself. A former running back at Michigan and a near Heisman Trophy candidate, Leroy Brown was courted by any and all corporate recruiters, some of whom dropped out of the hunt when his grade transcript arrived. At the end, Integrity offered the best starting salary, with the added benefit that he could serve as a de facto poster boy for the company’s affirmative action program. Always dressed impeccably in conservative designer suits, English shirts, and Paul Stuart ties, and with a ready and blinding smile, Brown made an impression wherever he went. He was steadily moved around to numerous jobs at Integrity, the current assignment being auditing, for which he had no aptitude whatsoever. Fortunately for him, there were assistants like Charlique Stevens who would feed him useful information, even though much of it would not sink in for quite some time. Nonetheless, he was content to proceed on a path of his own choosing, pausing to stop at mirrors from time to time. He checked himself out in the men’s room and then departed for the meeting with his assistant.

Evan was awakened out of a sound sleep by the rumble of the seasonal afternoon tropical storm. As if mechanically, the late-day clouds laden with hard rain moved through and continued eastward; the sun reappeared and dried the streets of Key West. He put on a Cutter and Buck golf shirt over a pair of khaki walk shorts, items he remembered to take from home in anticipation of warmer climates as he progressed in a southerly direction. The B&B host recommended dinner at an indoor-outdoor café, Blue Heron, where he ordered a bowl of conch chowder, pecan-crusted yellowtail snapper and a decent-grade Sonoma County chardonnay. After dinner, he walked the waterside streets, observing the nature of the boats docked alongside. *God, there are all shapes and sizes of craft; funny how there always seemed to be so many boats at idle and so few out on the water,* he thought. *I should be able to find what I need here.*

He considered giving Mary Ellen Dunn another call but believed that it could keep. It was a Friday night, and with the long holiday weekend coming up, he'd try the following day. He wandered into Cane's Mutiny, a bar that faced the Gulf, and, looking every bit the *turista,* took up a perch and canvassed the room furtively, as though he had expected to meet someone there.

"If you think Jimmy's here, you're in for a disappointment. You just missed him. This time of year he's usually up north, on the Vineyard or maybe in Sag Harbor."

"Jimmy who?" was Callman's rejoinder to the bartender, which elicited a round of guffaws and titters from those in earshot.

"Aw, shit, another wise-ass, right, guys?" the bartender, a totally head-shaven man with a pinkish mustache (in the garish light, Callman could swear that was the color) and a silver earring, bellowed to any who would listen. Then, his breath hot as he leaned in at his new customer, he said, "Actually I like your style and sense of humor, fella. What'll it be?" A rum-and-tonic was ordered.

"Make sure Otis pours you a Mount Gay," his stool neighbor chimed in. By now Callman was sorely tempted to bolt, but he sensed that he was in one of those situations where a graceful departure could not be managed without risk, however undefined. It was only when the bartender placed the drink before him and inquired if there was anything further he could do in his behalf that Evan decided to take him up. Maybe this was as good a time and place as any.

After a long pull on the drink, he said, "Well, there is. I'm wanting to hire a boat and a captain."

A few heads turned in his direction. Now the stool mate became animated. “A captain! Oh captain, my captain! Why, don’t we all long for a captain to guide our passage?” Callman figured the man to be a twenty-something, wide eyes, flat black hair and redder-than-average lips, slight of build, and barely able to maintain his balance on his perch, obviously well sloshed. “Otis, help this wayfarer find his captain,” he implored the bartender.

“Lots of boats in Key West,” Otis offered. “What you want depends on what you need. Deep-sea fishing, just a little spin around the shore, see what I’m saying?”

“I may need a bigger charter than any of that.”

Otis went on, seeming to effect cooperation, “Well, there’s old Pete Simmons; he’s got a big Luhrs, maybe forty foot, flying bridge … then you may want Captain Jerry Squires, he’s got three boats out for hire, one of ’em, it’s this cigarette, must be fifty foot, can’t miss it if it’s in port …”

“That’s helpful.” Callman was noncommital.

“What we try to accommodate here in old KW, mister … ah …”

Callman answered, “Ed.”

Moving away now, Otis laughed and said that it was remarkable how many men named “Ed” he met every day. “Name’s common as hell.”

The stool mate now made his own introduction. “Oh, by the way, my name is Matthew.”

A tepid handshake. “Glad to meet you, Matt.”

“Oh, no, it’s Matthew, never Matt.”

Otis the bartender was serving others at the bar’s terminus, muttering something about leaving Ed and Matthew to their own devices.

Matthew said to him, “You have such tender hands. Are you a doctor, by any chance? And I adore your beard with its hint of grey. May I treat you to a refill, Ed?”

“Uh, perhaps another time. I really must be on my way.” Evan climbed down and away from the barstool.

Unabashed, Matthew said jauntily, “I hope you find your captain, but if not I’m usually available. I so despise second fiddle, but I think you’re special, and I’d wait.”

“Yeah, well,” he was out the door and into the languid night air. He thought about a stroll along the wharf in search of the seafarers Otis had mentioned, but the area looked to be tucked into bed. The sooner he got out of this place the better; his work would have to hold until the following morning.

Otis was right. Captain Jerry Squires's cigarette boat was the only one like his description in port, visible for a couple of hundred yards from where Callman was starting out the next day. He walked up and approached the man who was busily polishing the chrome fittings on the sleek red-and-white craft. "Morning. Are you Captain Jerry Squires?"

"Who wants to know?" The man did not look up, intent on his modest task. He was paunchy, maybe a little older than Callman, and he sported a red bandana holding back a free-range growth of reddish hair going over to grey, along with a walrus mustache, looking every bit of what any KW visitor would expect to encounter along the wharf.

Choosing not to identify himself, he answered that he was looking to book a charter out into the Caribbean. Now attentive, Squires observed this man with eyes squinted tight by a lifetime of weather and said, "Now, could you be a bit more specific? There's a lot of sea out there, Mr.—"

"Ed. Yeah, okay, here's the thing. Could you run me over to Grand Cayman?"

Squires put down his polishing cloth and invited him on board. "Look—Ed—I don't just "run over" to the Cayman. It's a long way from here, and it's not a direct route, which I suppose you know if you've looked at any kinda map lately. However … it can be done, but it'd cost ya. Now tell me …" he beckoned him closer, where the lingering aroma of Beefeater emanated from Squires's breath … "ya not runnin' drugs or anything, are ya? Cause that I won't do, mister. I'd need to search you and everything you bring along before we set sail. Capeesh?"

Callman said that would be fine with him, and he proceeded to ask about the boat and the time it would take to complete the trip. Squires said, "Not this boat, it's my fastest, for sure, can do seventy-five knots, but it's too goddam conspicuous. Naw, I got an old fisherman docked twelve slips from here. Big enough to get there with all the toys, radar, sonar, GPS—slower—but won't get noticed."

"Noticed? By whom?" He was having trouble suppressing a bout of nerves.

"Oh, Coast Guard, Cuban navy, pirates of the Caribbean, could be anyone out on those waters. Have to take care, man. Hey, don'tcha want to know my price? You may not be able to afford me, so let's not waste each other's time. I'll tell you straight out, man like you, voyage like this, I figure you must be runnin' from something, so's it'll be five thou. Sound okay?"

"It sounds like a ten-day cruise in an outside cabin."

"Yeah, don't it, now. So get your butt over to Fort Lauderdale and get on the first Carnival ship you see. Be a damn sight more comfort than my old tub," Squires bellowed and laughed.

In the end, they negotiated a price of $4,500. Evan insisted on making landfall under the cover of darkness, so Squires had that requirement in mind when timing out the trip, which he would run mostly at night anyhow, and told his passenger to be ready at sunset that very day, if he was so inclined, which he was.

That afternoon, there was one more call to Mary Ellen Dunn using a prepaid phone card. Again, there was no answer, but it was early into the holiday weekend, with the expectation that lots of people would take extra days off from work, and she could have used the time to make her getaway, or she could be anywhere else. The invalid mother never picked up the telephone, but had Mary Ellen taken off, she would not have done so without arranging for home care, so it seemed odd to Callman that there was no response whatsoever. Before collecting his sparse belongings and leaving The Gator, he opened the now-worn manila file he had taken from his office desk on that fateful day, which in his present mind-set seemed like ages ago. The file was slim, comprising a few pages of number lists and codes that were significant only to him. He then dialed a number that he had committed to memory, waited for the automated menu of options, and began to speak a handful of codes on his sheet, one at a time, each followed by a voice response at the opposite end. He ended the call. *Good,* he thought, *it's all intact, undisturbed.*

Back at the dock, Squires, true to his word, patted Evan down and rifled through his Knicks duffel bag and satisfied himself that the mysterious passenger known as Ed wasn't carrying contraband of any sort. They pushed off at 4:00 p.m. Evan was indifferent to the appearance of the boat—of an uncertain age, somewhat worse for the wear, but sturdy enough, at least to his untrained eye. "Nice and calm today, Ed," the captain said, "looks like we'll be lucky with the seas, and the night will be under a half moon, which is okay because I don't want to run any lights at all." Having his passenger fork over the agreed-upon fee before Squires turned the engine over had put him in an expansive mood.

Callman, inquisitive, wanted to know about the route to be taken. "Well, Cayman sits behind the west end of Cuba," Squires said, "and I intend to take a wide swing around that island, so it won't be the fastest, but it'll be the safest."

"What are we worried about, captain?"

"Oh, all them things I mentioned earlier. Look, the U.S Coast Guard, we lose them the further we get from Florida, but then it's the Cuban gunboats, such as they are, which there ain't many of, but you don't want to meet up with them at all." Evan asked him why the Cubans, if they were out there, would be troublesome. "Hell, man, they're always looking for boats leaving the island or anyone else picking up the greasers when they try to escape. That's why I'm swinging wide. Most of the escape routes leave Havana to the northeast. Miami, that's where they're bound for. But then some of 'em have been known to get lost." Squires laughed a little boy's laugh and offered up a swig of gin.

"Don't mind if I do," Evan replied as he reached for the bottle.

On the eve of the weekend, Charlique Stevens was in Leroy Brown's work-station cubicle, some 120 square feet, which was standard for an Integrity manager of Brown's status. He, of course, awaited the day when he'd be awarded an office with floor-to-ceiling walls. Impatient, he asked his auditor for a summary of her work before he made ready to meet with friends at their summer rental in Quogue. He was already in his business casual mode, an aqua Faconable lisle shirt over black silk-and-wool Brioni slacks. A college duffel bag lay at the foot of his desk. She rapidly reviewed the items that had been put in front of Mary Ellen.

"So?" was Brown's response.

"So, Leroy, I think there's some hanky-panky going on here." *What an archaic term for an auditor to use*, she thought. *Better regroup, girl.* She continued, "This thing with the bank account changes. I researched some of the cases and found discrepancies between our payments matching up with the death, or a *reported* death. Our contracts call for such payments to end with a death. Sometimes it takes a month for insurance, if there was any, to settle, and papers to cross, so Integrity could have an extra month's payment out there."

Brown smiled. "We're paying dead people?"

"In theory, only a month, and Integrity has the right to recall those overpayments."

"How many of these did you look at?" he asked.

Charlique was sheepish, "Six, Leroy. But the patterns were consistent."

Brown rose, glanced at his Rado watch, grabbed the duffel, and headed out the door. "That's not much of a sample. It sounds promising, but you have a lot more work to do, girl," was his parting comment.

Never noticed me at all, did he, she thought.

The auditor had no plans to escape to the Hamptons for the weekend; she worked away on the ongoing project. She selected another batch of accounts that had been reviewed with Mary Ellen and began to contact the associated family members. Her success in reaching any of such people was low: families move, phone listings need to be tracked down, and, when they are, the majority aren't available to talk. After a frustrating evening, she did reach a name on her list at around 9:00 p.m.

"Yes, I'm trying to reach the family of Alan Washnick," Charlique began. "I'm with customer service at Integrity Investment, and I'd like to talk to you about a satisfaction survey."

The woman on the other end remained on the line. "I'm the Washnicks' daughter, Marjorie. I kind of remember that my parents used to get payments from your company—they're both deceased now—but they looked forward to that check every month. Actually, it wasn't a check—"

"I know," Charlique chipped in, suddenly energized by the conversation. "We went over to electronic payments several years ago. My records show that your folks' payments were made to an account at the Third Community Bank. Is that right?"

"I can't help you there. They managed all their own money. But it makes sense. That's a bank near where they lived. Of course, that would all have ended when my dad died; see, my mom predeceased him by six years, and I'm the only child. It came to me to settle the estate, which was pretty small. The house and a life policy; that was about the extent of it."

The discussion is developing, Charlique thought. *Keep it rolling.* "Well," she said, "here's where our records get a little fuzzy, Ms. Washnick. Your dad died when?"

Marjorie threw out an exact date.

"Okay, then. We show that about that time a new account in Mr. Washnick's name was opened at the United County Bank with instructions to receive Integrity's payments to him, and that the account went on for five months thereafter, at which time it was closed. Can you help me there?"

At first, Marjorie Washnick was silent. Charlique probed for a response, hoping she had not signed off. "Uh, I never heard of that bank, and I have no knowledge of anything further from Integrity after Dad passed. Sorry, I can't help you. Hey, what's this all about, anyhow? You told me at the beginning it was about customer satisfaction, and I haven't heard you ask me questions about all that."

"Oh, but you have helped me, Ms. Washnick, and our company appreciates your time. I realize it's late. All the best to you." She hung up the phone and took a deep breath.

The next morning, she persisted with more phone calls. It was again frustrating, just like the previous evening, but she was able to connect with a widower of a woman who was listed on one of the selected accounts, and she heard a story that was identical to what Marjorie Washnick had told her. It was little to go on—far too little, it seemed—but she was becoming persuaded that an image was coming into focus, like the protrusion of an iceberg that was cold and deep. She wanted another meeting with Mary Ellen Dunn.

Mary Ellen wasn't in the office the following morning, having told her coworkers the previous afternoon that she was taking an extended weekend and would return the next Tuesday. No further information was disclosed to any of them. However, she did leave an itinerary at home with her mother and her caregiver before departing, and Charlique Stevens, on a hunch and falling into some luck, was able to learn of it when she called the Dunn home. She was told that Mary Ellen was en route to Grand Cayman and would be staying at a resort called the Royal Palm Gardens. "And tell my daughter to get back here right away to take better care of me," she could hear the old woman rasping in the background. True to character, Mary Ellen Dunn would never, ever, leave her mother in the hands of in-home care without detailed forwarding instructions.

Charlique scooped up her files and left the office; within three hours she was waiting to board a flight from JFK to Grand Cayman. Being off-season in the Caribbean, there was availability on all flights headed in that direction; she knew from reputation that Cayman had some of the finest reef diving in the world, so she packed some of her dive gear. *What the hell,* she thought, *I had no other urgent plans, and worst case is I'll see some very colorful fish.*

Therefore, that very same night she was able to call up Mary Ellen's room from the lobby of the Royal Palm. Hearing Charlique's voice close at hand, and in person, Mary Ellen, appearing shaken and not a little surprised, joined her downstairs. "Why, Charlique, fancy seeing you … here."

The auditor tried unctuous charm. "Oh, I just thought it would be nice to visit and treat you to an elegant dinner. I know the cutest outdoor place around the corner that serves the yummiest jerk chicken on the island." Arm in arm, she said, "C'mon, Mary Ellen, we'll dine and talk."

Six

Captain Jerry Squires was concentrating on a persistent green blip on his radar screen. The seas were quiet, inky-black yet illuminated sufficiently by the yellowish half moon so that there had been no need for running lights. Callman had been on-and-off catnapping since sundown, and he was jolted out of his reverie by Squires saying, "Hey Ed, or whoever you are, looks like we might have some company out here. I been looking at this marker on my screen for a while now, and it may be somethin' moving toward us."

"What do you think it could be?"

"Dunno. Not yet close enough, but—now let's not get alarmed—we're not that far removed from where some of them Cuban patrol boats could range."

Within the next ten minutes, they could see another craft with lights on moving fast toward their boat. At two hundred yards by Squires's reckoning, he could see with his binoculars that it was indeed a Cuban navy vessel. A moment later, they announced their presence with an arcing shell that gave off a *wooosh* before slamming into the sea, sending up a high plume of water close enough to bring a shower of droplets onto the deck.

"Holy shit!" Callman yelled.

"Get under the bulkhead, mister. I'll deal with this. Gotta hove to—I can't outrun 'em at this point."

The gunboat drew alongside of Squires. He could see a machine gun mounted on the deck of the bow, and mortar-like weapons midport and starboard; these were evidently the type that had fired the warning shot. An officer appeared on the bow with a megaphone. "Hola … Subire a nave para la inspeccion en aguas Cubanos."

"How's your Spanish?" Squires asked.

"Nonexistent. I took French, but I think I heard something about an inspection and Cuban waters. He's approaching us."

"French, ah? Lotta pissant good it'll do us out here." Squires shook his head and went on to mutter under his breath that he was so far beyond the Cuban sovereign limit that he might as well be in the Pacific Ocean, but he answered that, all right, they were welcome to come aboard; he had nothing to conceal—if that was the concern of the Cuban navy.

The two boats were still, bobbing gently at one another, rubberized bumpers against each hull. The Cuban captain, a small man in khaki fatigues and a rumpled sailor's peaked hat, climbed onto the *Chicken of the Sea* (that was the name of Squires's craft; Callman having been in such a rush, so intent on his escape from KW, that he had not even bothered to ask his captain the name of the boat).

"Soy Fuentes Escobar del capitan y subo a esta nave, arte bajo autoridad marina Cubano. I am Captain Escobar Fuentes, and I board this … ah … ship … ah … craft under Cuban marine authority. You are?"

"Captain Jerry Squires."

"De que peurto?"

Squires figured that one out and told him Key West.

"Ah, Americano, Yanqui. You are alone, no?" The Cuban officer knew more English than he let on; he had a flashlight and a drawn pistol as he moved about the boat and wore a small metal nameplate with "Fuentes" on a soiled shirt.

Squires believed it to be futile to hide his charge effectively from an inspection. "No. I have one passenger." At that point, Callman, hearing the dialogue, emerged with hands up and shaking uncontrollably.

Fuentes regarded him and started to laugh. "You need have no fear of me—you, passenger. You can relax, provided you are not a Cuban refugee and carry no drugs. Do you have papers? I'm going to search you." The Cuban officer was certainly bilingual, and he was delighted in switching back and forth between the languages, as it happened to suit his fancy.

He'd been had. Through his journey, concealing his identity, he was careful not to hold anything that would give it away. Fuentes fished a Mastercard from one of Callman's pockets and examined it with amusement.

"That is all you have?"

Callman nodded in the affirmative.

Fuentes scowled and shook his head from side to side. "Ah, that is most unfortunate because it does not allow me to make a definitive ID on you. Anyway, I will have to confiscate this as evidence. How much credit remains on this card?"

"About four thousand—U.S."

The Cuban shook the little plastic card, as if to see if anything would tumble out of it, and sighed, saying "Eso podia alimentar a una familia en Cuba por un ano. That could feed a family in Cuba (he pronounced it *Kooba)* for a year."

"If you had kept it, I'm sure you would have bought some girls with it, so we will apply it to the betterment of the revolution. Now I will complete my inspection."

With that, Fuentes motioned for two sailors to join him, and they hopped aboard, each toting an AK-47. "You, *capitan,* show us around," he motioned at

Squires. Within minutes, they emerged from the hold of the vessel, carrying nothing other than Callman's duffel bag. Squires called Evan to his side. "They will overlook your lack of ID proof but want money before they let us go. What've you got in there?"

He had the remainder of his original stash in the bag, other than a few dollars he kept in his pants pocket. He told Squires there was about ten thousand dollars left. "Give it to them," Squires said.

"Damn, Jerry, I need that money for when I get to the island."

The captain was in his face. "We ain't gonna get to no island unless we pay 'em off, capeesh?"

"I'm waiting," Fuentes said melodically.

The cash was handed over. The boarding party was ready to exit, the sailors leaving first. Fuentes turned to Evan. "Oh, one last thing, *Yanqui,* would you be kind enough to write a sample signature for me, so your credit card purchase tickets can be forged?" (The officer had reverted to fluent English, an indication that he wished to get this episode over with as quickly as possible.) He obliged without comment. When Squires walked alongside the Cuban as the latter left to climb back on the gunboat, Callman could swear he saw an envelope pass from Fuentes into his hand. Then again, the experience had been draining, and tired eyes could have been deceiving him.

Back at the helm and under way, Squires said, "Well, at least he didn't say 'hasta la vista, baby.'" Evan failed to see the humor in the comment, wondering what else could happen out here—maybe an interdiction by Jack Sparrow was next—and then he mentioned that Squires wasn't asked for ID. Squires said, "Hey, no one gives a flying fart about me," and then, after a pause, he changed the subject. "Okay, Ed, the good news is that we're closing in on our destination. Now where exactly do you want to go?"

Callman answered that he wanted to make landfall about a mile from the west end of George Street, the main thoroughfare in Georgetown that bordered the sea on the north coast of the island.

The night carried on; then at about an hour before dawn, there rose the first appearance of harbor lights toward the port side. "Okay, Ed, we're closing in, so grab up your personal belongings," Squires instructed, "and … uh … you're gonna want to roll up them deck pants you're wearing."

Once more, Evan was taken aback. "What do you mean, Jerry?"

"What I mean is, I'm gonna cut the engines, coast on in, and put you in a little rubber dinghy a hundred or so yards from shore. I got it on a long winch.

You tell me 'sayonara' and then wade on in the rest of the way. We wouldn't mean to arouse attention by any noise after all this, now would we?"

"Yeah, I guess so, but is it—"

Reading his passenger's mind, Squires answered, "Safe? Oh, yeah, this spot is real shallow out aways—mebbe a five-par—but we're rolling in as far as I dare go so's not to run aground. In case you don't know, this crate draws four feet."

Evan readied himself and climbed into the dinghy when they approached. He paddled straight toward the shoreline, and when he was confident that the water's depth was a mere couple of feet, he exited and watched the captain quietly reel in his little craft. Before the parting, Squires genially wished him luck in finding whatever it was he was looking for. Having reached land, and now under the lifting blanket of darkness, he scrambled away from the narrow beach and its bordering scrub brush to the coastal road that would run eastward into the town. He reckoned the distance to be between one to two miles, and he would walk it carefully, trying to stay out of sight of the occasional vehicle that would be on the road at that early-morning hour. He had reached his intended end point, journeying a distance of nearly two thousand miles anonymously and using cash only, not under the best of conditions, but still in one piece. (He had a fleeting thought that the whole thing would make for a good vignette on one of the morning TV shows.) No stranger to this island, Callman had journeyed there at other times, in first class, even economy class, but this—this was no class at all. *Hey,* he thought, *they're just different ways to come to the same address.* He could feel the resurgence of energy, having completed his personal odyssey.

While Evan was in the midst of his adventure, Bruno Kiel, on his own volition, went to Integrity's offices to meet with Tippy Worthington, who was the company's vice president for community relations, neighborhood relations, and public relations.

A willowy blonde with tanzanite eyes that were partially occluded behind particularly ugly designer glasses, she came off with well-honed effervescence. "Detective Kiel, it is a pleasure to make your acquaintance. I cannot recall when Integrity has had a visit from our esteemed police force. I hope, Detective, that we remain on our best behavior."

Kiel smiled wanly and waved indifferently. "Oh, of course, Ms. Worthington—no, my visit has to do with one of your former, or I believe former, employees. May I call you—"

"Tippy. Please do so. It's actually an abbreviation for my given, which is 'Tippecanoe.' See, I'm a descendant of William Henry Harrison; you know, our ninth president. He carried that sobriquet along with 'Tyler Too,' but he died after only a month in office from pneumonia, following his inaugural in inclement weather. So it passed to Tyler."

Kiel had grown antsy with the history lesson, and he felt like telling her he was descended from Admiral Doenitz but thought better of it. "Yes, well, I don't want to take up your valuable time, but I'm here to ask you about Cameron Wynne III."

Integrity's online systems allowed Tippy Worthington to punch up a file on Cameron Wynne III instantaneously on her screen. Squinting at the images and talking to Kiel at the same time, she began, "Here it is. Mr. Wynne was at Integrity for about three years during the 2000 to 2003 period. He started in our treasury bond compliance unit, then on to municipal bonds …"

"May I see that?" Kiel asked. Worthington was printing out the file and advised Kiel that he was welcome to examine what was there, but company policy would not permit him to take notes or retain any hard copy. Not overly pleased with that reaction, the detective nonetheless held back any complaint; in police business, there was always the opportunity for a comeback later on.

"There's not a whole lot, here," she concluded.

"Do you know why he left?" Kiel inquired while he pored over the pages, which provided no reasons for his departure.

"The file wouldn't say," she responded. "I suppose you could say those reasons could often be … uh … somewhat subjective, and whether he was let go or he resigned, I do not know. I can tell you that the company did not have any mass layoffs under way at the time of his leaving, so it was unlikely he'd been caught up in one of our periodic rightsizings." There was a patrician smile coming across the desk at Kiel as this last commentary was offered.

"All right, then. Let me go in another direction." Kiel continued, "Can you tell me about his physical features, what he looked like?"

"Looked like?"

C'mon, lady, don't jerk me around, he thought. "Yeah, you know, height, weight, hair color, and so on.

Tippy Worthington sought refuge in her screen. "Why, I don't think I've ever been asked that sort of question in a personnel search, but let me look further … ah … here's something from his entry into the company. All prospective employees must take a medical exam and a drug test." More printouts, and Bruno Kiel saw that Wynne was a man of five feet eleven and weighed 172 pounds at age thirty-five, when he applied for a job at Integrity. The record was silent as to any other physical characteristics. He rapidly scanned the pages and picked up a footnote back on an early page that had been marked at the time of his departure. It read, "Personal property remains in Integrity's possession, awaiting Mr. Wynne's claiming such in the near future," which he called to her attention.

"That's not as unusual as it might appear," she commented. "We have been known to hold on to an employee's … things … for time immemorial. We're not called 'Integrity' for nothing." She gave a light chuckle.

Kiel was being tenacious. "So, what was it? Did he claim it?"

Worthington was gravitating from perky to huffy. "How would I know that, Detective?"

"Can you find out?"

"Well, I suppose, but I really need to get to a meeting …" Tippy stole a glance at her Michele watch.

Kiel persisted, wanted to find out, and was willing to wait around while she put the search in motion and went off to her meeting. He went across the street to Starbucks, ordered a Sumatra Grande and perused the *Times* before returning to her office an hour later.

Having returned from her meeting and reclaimed her desk chair, the charm switch was back on. "Well, Detective, now I can understand why you are so adept at your *métier*, look what has been found …" And here was the vice president handing over a wire basket filled with a gym ensemble of stiff and threadbare shorts, a jockstrap, T-shirts, socks, and sneakers. Kiel could hardly believe what he was seeing as his meaty hands reached in to fetch the pair of fully depreciated Adidas, circa 1998.

"It seems our man was working out at the company health club. As I said, we keep things forever."

He wasn't even listening. The sneakers were worn out to the extent that the size posted inside had long been obliterated, but he could tell they were either an 8½ or 9.

"Detective?"

Pushing the basket back across the desk, he commended Integrity for a generous policy of minding its ex-employees' personal effects. "Tippy, one more thing. I'd like to see the spot where the construction accident happened."

Worthington made the connection. "Oh, now I realize where I heard your name previously. You were in charge of that investigation. Poor Mr. Callman. We are still in shock over it here at Integrity. As for the site, I'm afraid it's all been bricked over, as the reconstruction goes forward. There's really nothing recognizable from that awful event."

Kiel was surprised by the rapidity with which the company was moving to repair the damage. "Well," he said as he was rising to leave, "I understand. Tell me, did you know Evan Callman?"

"Certainly. He was well known throughout Integrity. I would, you know, attend meetings when sometimes he was present."

Kiel asked her what he looked like, not disclosing that the mutilated body in the morgue precluded an accurate rendering of appearance in everyday life. She said, "He was, oh, I'd say around six feet tall, perhaps a bit less, nice bearing, by that I mean not especially heavy or thin. Sandy hair, with flecks of grey, somewhat curly. Always very well dressed."

The detective once more thanked her for the time spent and made his leave-taking.

Seven

Evan was sitting at The Mask and the Tube, an outdoor café on George Street in Georgetown, Grand Cayman. It was the morning of his third day there, and he was enjoying a croissant and a cappuccino while observing the growing stream of human traffic funneling into town from the tenders of the five cruise ships that were moored in the harbor like a kind of nautical parking lot. It looked to be a busy day in the little port town. After he made landfall, he came into Georgetown as the morning sun was beginning to appear. Once there, he ordered up a breakfast in the same café where he was now seated. Not all of his cash was confiscated; while below decks on the *Chicken*, he stuffed as much paper money as he'd dare risk in the bottom of his Topsiders, which Fuentes (or whatever his name was) declined to check after having hit pay dirt in the duffel. It wasn't much, but it would keep him for a few days. Once on shore, he set out to find lodging. The large resort complexes were mostly on the south coast of the island—he would avoid those in any event—but there were any number of smallish rooming houses on the side streets of Georgetown. Once you turned the corner from the town's main drag, where all the commercial activity took place, the streets and alleys behind it offered up a different world where the real people, the islanders, lived. He settled on a place called Aunt Dinah's Inn, a nondescript but clean place managed by Auntie herself, a tall and slender lady wearing a tropical print muumuu and a bright blue turban. She flashed a full row of gold teeth when she smiled, and she moved fluidly. Evan paid her for four days rent, which he fervently hoped would be more than enough time to accomplish what he came for.

As he sipped leisurely at his coffee, his thought was that Mary Ellen Dunn had yet to show; she was on the island, he knew, having easily tracked her down as registered at the Royal, and left messages on her phone, a risk he felt he had to assume, and was toying with the idea of a cab ride out to the hotel and waiting around. Something did not feel right, however, and he decided it was better to invest a little more time staying put. What with the onslaught of tourists, no attention would be paid to a man and woman having a pleasant interlude at a restaurant they had long ago agreed upon as a meeting place.

Callman's next thoughts turned to the establishment of a new identity, something he had neither the time nor the opportunity to work on after his unexpected demise. Within recent months, in one of those idle conversations, the origins of which could not be recalled, he'd heard about one of the premier forgery artists in New York known only as Van Eyck, whom, it was rumored, was formerly known in younger days as The Master of Graffiti for his flamboyant signature and creative images on the subway cars of the city's Number 7 line. It was said that The Master came close to having the façade of one of his pieces severed from the train's corpus and mounted in the Whitney Museum, but for various reasons that never came to fruition; thus disheartened, he turned to what he liked to call "documentation art." In Callman's case, not having followed through promptly on this connection was, he now concluded, an oversight—for in the weeks leading up to the accident he had been increasingly coming to believe that the time frame for the realization of his work would be diminishing. However, no exit strategy had been formulated. This time, the issue would have to be resolved.

Which was where Mary Ellen Dunn came in. She would have to get the job done, and whether it was to be Van Eyck or someone else, the completion of a new identity might involve a considerably longer stay on this island than he anticipated, a disturbing feeling.

I am a man without an existence, he thought. *How does such a man get away from where he is? I am starting to feel discomfort, a writhing in this chair and a pronounced quiver of my hand as I reach for my glass.*

Then he looked over at a bank which was in view of his vantage point at the café table. He forced a masking of the onset of squeamishness with a pleasant thought over the prospect of such proximity to his personal holy grail.

Banque Huite de Geneve came to Evan Callman, or rather he came to it, unexpectedly, but it was to become the catalyst in a plan that would evolve. The bank and a plan would come into concordance, the moon and the stars in perfect alignment, so he believed.

Several years prior, he had been on a summer golf outing, one of those corporate events that bring clients, service providers, and assorted hangers-on together for an afternoon of gamesmanship and lies, followed by a rejuvenating cocktail party and dinner, at which time prizes would be awarded all around and nobody would escape a roasting in the process. Trulett Maddox was there, naturally, but Callman saw little of him that day. The idea was to spread the Integrity people around so as to mingle and schmooze, all in the interest of the company's business. Evan's foursome included three bankers, only one of whom he was acquainted with. Out on the course there was in place an unspoken rule prohibiting business discussions; the focus was on Nassaus, gimmes, mulligans, and scorekeeping, a heady stew of intellectual effort for the time span of eighteen holes.

However, at the nineteenth hole, after play was completed, there were no rules. Drinks were washed along in rapid progression, hair was let down for those with any to spare, and tongues wagged freely. Evan, generally a reticent person and having been trained to think before speaking, thought most bankers to be just the opposite. In their drive to impress and sell, they talked too much, he felt, and when several were together, the conclave would often turn into a game of who had the best info, the juiciest dirt, as if it were a competition, the winner being the one with the best stuff to unload on his compatriots.

After the third round of preprandial gin and tonics, banker one, who managed the U.S. business for a large British organization, was asking after the whereabouts of a mutual friend. (That was another thing about these guys, he opined, they all seemed to know one another and relished nothing more than tracking the ups and downs of their peers.)

Banker two said, "Oh, he's a managing director for a fairly new offshore venture."

Banker three, from Canada, contributed, "I know old Whitfield from his days at Pinckney's Trust. What's this all about, eh?"

The subject was Banque Huite de Geneve, a lately established Swiss company with offshore branches that practiced the kind of confidentiality that the Swiss banks were known for. Banker two continued, "It was started a few years back by two Europeans, Karl-Erik Ollendorf, a Swiss, and Rene Benoit, French."

Callman's ears were tuning in, and he elected to jump into the conversation. "I've never heard of it," he said, thinking an innocuous comment may prompt additional information.

"Hardly surprising, old sport," banker two said, now fully loaded to show off his knowledge to his drinking pals, "very hush-hush. They out-secret even the most secretive of Swiss banks. You remember that some of that tradition has come under fire recently—at least for some of the big boys there—like the brouhaha over the Holocaust money, but till now these guys have stayed under the radar."

Banker one added that he'd never heard of a Swiss and a Frenchman cooperating for more than an hour, and he forecast an early demise for the Geneve, generating hearty laughter among the group.

"Not so," banker two picked up. "So far as I understand it's been quite successful. It's numbered accounts, of course, but no identities are shared with the bank when accounts are opened. Geneve doesn't want to know anyone by name. I hear they rely on codes and sophisticated DNA testing devices to determine who they're dealing with."

"You seem to know quite a bit about them," Evan offered, generating still another round of laughter.

The banker said to him, "Evan, it seems as though this has caught your attention. Has Integrity got some gold bars or priceless artworks it wants to salt away?"

"I'm afraid that's not my department," Evan said.

"Well, it's not for corporate anyway, now is it," banker one added, "but I hope Whitfield's doing okay. I may just look him up one of these days."

"So you're the one with the assets to be hidden, eh," the Canadian banker said to him.

The dinner chime beckoned all to their tables, and the foursome drained their glasses, let fly a few more chuckles, and made their way to the dining room.

In the weeks immediately following, Callman researched the Geneve and learned that it was more visible than the bankers' conversation had led him to believe. It maintained an office in Geneva (but not in Zurich, Switzerland's principal financial center), yet most of its facilities listed were in the Caribbean, including Grand Cayman, Nevis, and the French portion of St. Martin. Soon after, he and Georgina happened to arrange a winter vacation to the islands; while there Evan took time to scope out the Banque Huite de Geneve. He saw that the bank occupied a prominent location in the principal business districts and that it offered a full range of banking services in attractive but understated surroundings. It was more typical for offshore banking to have little or no physical presence, mounting a brass plate on a wall somewhere as evidence of their legal existence. Not so Geneve, which was out there for all to see. Recalling what he'd heard from his golfing partners, he could only speculate on what lay behind and below the gleaming teller's counters, platform desks for the well-groomed executives, and rows of ATMs for customer convenience.

While on Grand Cayman, on a hunch, he entered the branch there and asked after Owen Whitfield. "Are you here for an appointment?" the slender receptionist asked.

"I am not, but a former colleague of his suggested I look him up if ever I was on the island, and here I am," Callman said, flashing his most genial smile. "I'm here on vacation and realize this may be a long shot, but I wanted to try anyway."

The woman was not especially impressed with his pitch. "I gather, then, that you are not a client of the bank?" After confirming that he was not, he was asked to wait while she ascertained whether Whitfield was presently in the bank.

While she was making the call, Evan, trying to appear nonchalant, scanned the bank's personnel on the floor and observed that none of them seemed to be island people; they were more on the order of well-turned-out Europeans. "Ah, yes, I'm Owen Whitfield," said a rangy man of six feet plus, wearing a black suit and having dirty blond hair middle-parted and fashionably long, as he approached Evan from an oak door. "Can I be of some assistance to you?"

Callman allowed as how he had brought greetings from a former associate of his (the banker's name escaping him) in London—"a Canadian, as I recall."

If Whitfield was miffed about the man's faulty memory, he did not show it, saying, "Oh, I bet that was Oliver Dawson. Yes, we were at Pinckney's there. Is he well?"

"Very much so."

"So. It must be more than a 'hello' from old Dawson that brings you to the Geneve, sir." Whitfield appeared to be a man who had a very strict time budget.

"I would like to open an account."

Hardly listening, Whitfield busied himself with multitasking while he proceeded to tick off the bank's requirements for its accounts. Callman assumed that the banker would be off to a meeting soon or that the request had been posed to him so often that Whitfield's tone came off as a bit world-weary. Much of what Callman was hearing was a continuation of what he'd gotten from his golfing group.

"Geneve functions mainly as a deposit-taking institution—we do offer standard retail services, but I assume you would have no interest in those."

"You assume correctly."

Whitfield went on, "We provide secure safekeeping for just about anything a client chooses to deposit. Well, perhaps not anything. One potential client wished to park three antique cars with us—one being a 1935 Bugatti supposedly worth three million U.S., and while our deposit vaults are more than ample, that we could not accommodate. Now, everything is done with confidentiality—anonymity, really. Clients are assigned a code. Deposits can be made in a variety of ways. There are no written account statements, ever, but clients can check daily with a dial-in call on a separate code. Oh, and once a year, we do require an on-site visit—which is verified through a DNA sample and voice pattern recognition—to assure that we are dealing with whom we think we are. Any physical visits to the vault are subjected to the same checks. Are you interested?"

He asked about the bank's fees. "It's all based on the space contracted for, sir; they range from $75,000 to $300,000 annually, U.S., of course, everything I quote you will be in USD. Shall I go on?"

Callman gasped, not inaudibly, and told the banker to continue.

"Fees, codes, forms of voice and biological recognition, I think we're covering most of it. I am authorized to open an account immediately upon the payment of one year's fee." Whitfield showed a quasi smile. "Oh, one other consideration, the bank pays a modest rate on deposits—currently 2.10 percent."

"That's all?" He was taken back.

Whitfield stood up, "I really must be going on to one of our other branches. Actually, you're quite fortunate to have caught me here today. To answer your query, we find with our client base that the preservation of the deposit in strict confidence is paramount. Had any of them cared to optimize earnings, there are numerous financial companies available to satisfy their needs. From time to time, we do assist clients with regard to the conversion of certain assets on deposits to liquid instruments such as bearer bonds, but those transactions are processed by other financial institutions." His hand was on the doorknob, and he was hesitating merely to see that Callman was up and following him out. "Let me know if we can be of service, and give my regards to Oliver back in the states—it was in the states that you met, wasn't it?"

There was no answer.

"That's perfectly fine. You aren't obligated to answer. Ta-ta, now."

It was not until two months later that Callman opened an account with Geneve. Reaching Whitfield on a secure line, he found that the banker did not recall his visit—"I see many people, sir, you must appreciate that"—but, nonetheless, the bank would be pleased on his next visit to open an account for him at a yearly fee of $100,000. When that payment was made in good funds, and the agreed-upon safeguards were set up, instructions would follow, and he would be free to place deposits within the bank's vaults. Evan and Georgina cashed in a lot of frequent flyer miles and took an extended weekend back on the island. Everything that Geneve demanded was satisfied. The couple had come to love Grand Cayman.

Eight

Edgy at the lack of activity and tired of thumb-twiddling, he left the café and took a long stroll up and down George Street. The harbor was still packed, with the cruise ship passengers combing the shops for whatever would catch their fancy. He had ventured into many of them himself and was impressed at the high prices on the luxury goods that the Caribbean was noted for. Jewelry, fine porcelain, crystal, and the like were on display in gleaming stores so over-air-conditioned that it gave one thermal shock upon entry, and then the price tags added sticker shock. He surmised that the efficiency of the global economy had brought the value of all such things into a kind of retail equilibrium, and a hail and farewell to duty-free bargains.

He wandered into Pieces of Eight, a restaurant only a block away from his morning station at the café, wanting to grab a table before the boatloads descended on the place. Off in a nearby courtyard, a reggae band was performing:

> … When the wicked carried us away in captivity
> Required from us a song …

Ordering a well-done burger and a bottle of Red Stripe, he knew that he would have to do his business with the Geneve, and soon. He recalled Owen Whitfield's comment (it was some years since he'd seen the banker, and Callman wondered where he was nowadays) that the bank would suggest references for other institutions where clients could convert assets on deposit to other instruments such as bearer bonds, which would be portable and easily marketable. Planning on doing some of that, it would require the opening of a new account and the placement of the bonds in another depository. Unlike the Geneve, that would require an identity—a new one, which, of course, he did not have—and that's where Mary Ellen came in. He would instruct her to see Van Eyck back in New York and work up the papers ASAP while he remained in Grand Cayman awaiting her return. Yes, that was it, a straightforward plan, the way out of the island, with the lady happy to oblige out of loyalty and just compensation for her work. The burger arrived, which was wolfed down with gusto.

Afterwards, settling the bill and in the process of departure, Evan glanced from the restaurant along the busy street. *Well, lookee here, I do believe my date is in town,* he thought; out of an eye corner, he was certain he spotted Mary Ellen Dunn, walking briskly away from where he was positioned. Dressed rather too smartly for the turista crowd, the woman was wearing an oxford grey skirt, a sheer white cotton top, and basic black pumps. Not very islandlike. He began to follow, concentrating on the rear view up ahead. One of his high school buddies held a philosophy that every woman has at least one outstanding feature, even if the total package is less than ideal, and it was the quest for that feature that kept him in the hunt. Callman never fully bought into the theory, but it came to his mind as he maintained focus on Mary Ellen's sternward assets. She came across to him as a mousy kind of woman, yet carrying a lovely geometry of butt, and the black high heels complemented very shapely calves.

She stopped at the café where Evan had been earlier and scanned the entire area before sitting at a small table to one side. "May I join you?" he inquired of her in a faux nonchalant tone, and plunked down alongside of her, not waiting for a response to his question.

"So, it is you, isn't it?" Mary Ellen leaned back in her chair and took him in with a quizzical expression. "You … Uh … seem different, Evan, but those who know you can still tell who they're looking at."

He said that it was the best he could do for a man who died without advance notice and then, miracle to behold, rose from the dead and went on the run for almost two weeks now.

Mary Ellen pulled meekly on her skirt, draping it to cover her knees. "So?"

"So, Mary Ellen. I thought you'd be a little more punctual. You've been in town a while now, I assume. Anyway, let's move on. What have you brought down here for me?"

She answered, "I have the ID—"

He jumped in. "Which isn't any good anymore, kiddo. Evan Callman is dead, remember. I hope you at least have a bag of money, and depending on how we close this out and divvy up, it's going to require you to get a whole new package for me."

Dunn said, "Yes, I kind of anticipated you'd say as much. While we're still on the subject, am I in for a share, Evan?"

He shot her a toothy grin. "Of course. I've been waiting patiently for you. Hey, lighten up. This turn of events is our way out. I'll ask again, do you have a deposit with you?"

"There's about forty-eight thousand in a bag."

"Which may be the end of it, you know. Too bad we can't keep it going, but then it's time, isn't it, to settle up. We'll negotiate a slice of it for you, Mary Ellen, then you take half of what is agreed to and claim the remainder when you return with my new persona. Trust, trust above all. Deal, kiddo?"

Mary Ellen, suddenly appearing weary, said in a flat way, "Whatever you say. Maybe you are right about closing out. I'm tired of the whole sham we've been running all these years. That audit got me spooked, Evan. They're coming on to us. I may need a new ID myself. At the least, I'll have to get out of Integrity, maybe move somewhere with my mom where she can get quality care."

Callman was silent, believing that she *was* at risk and would need to deal with it in her own way. Hopefully, it would not call for more than he had in mind, which was likely to be an amount less than what the lady would feel she was entitled to. Sure, he held the codes and the access to the account status, but she performed double duty as the system manipulator inside the company and then as bag lady, bringing periodic deposits to the Cayman branch of the Geneve. Callman had her establish handprint and voice recognition IDs, which allowed her to bring deposits to the bank: a messenger. If anyone around Integrity's office in New York had paid more than cursory attention to Mary Ellen, they might have wondered why such a woman would be making from eight to ten trips annually to Grand Cayman at holiday times and on extended weekends, but, then again, she was hardly noticed at all.

They ordered drinks, a Mount Gay and tonic for Evan and a Long Island Iced Tea for Mary Ellen. "Whoa, kiddo, that's potent stuff—we've got business to do," he said.

She was fidgety, glancing around from side to side, and merely offered the comment that it was he who had the silver key to the treasure chest, and that while she waited she may just as well enjoy as many LIITs as she cared to. He bore in on her leaden brown eyes and said, "Are you okay, Mary Ellen? You seem all on edge."

"I have to let you know about one other thing."

He was at full attention. "Which is?"

"There's someone else … someone who'd need to be paid out … who's been involved."

He asked who that was. She continued. "Better you do not know, but it's … uh … someone responsible for taxes. We had to fix that problem. I had made arrangements with this individual to stall tax reports or bury them altogether. Still, some customer inquiries have been coming in lately."

He took a deep breath. "Okay, I get the picture. Now, let me guess. Your … uh … confidant … it's a woman."

Mary Ellen gave him no indication.

"You are lovers. Am I right?"

Again, no response.

"One more question. Is that it? Was there anyone else?"

This time, an answer was forthcoming. "No, Evan. I swear, that's all. She can be trusted if I take care of her as part of my share."

Before he could manage a subsequent comment, turning the street corner and claiming an unoccupied chair next to them was Georgina Callman. "Well, hello there, my dear," she said and sidled up to her husband. "What a pleasant coincidence to run into you so far away from home. The 'small world' cliché proves to be apt once more." Her eyes fixed on his. "Nice try with the progression of your altered state—that is you, isn't it, Evan? Actually, on concentrated sighting, your disguise isn't so bad after all; if we were not such intimate partners, I wouldn't be certain. In fact, the resemblance to the mangled body I had to identify—"

"Georgina, what the hell is this all about?" He was flustered and not a little angered by the surprise intrusion. The spell was broken momentarily by the appearance of a waiter; Georgina ordered a chocolate martini. Mary Ellen leaned back and, for the first time, seemed to be enjoying the show.

"We always adored this island, Evan, you do remember, do you not? I just thought it would be nice to return, you know, to revisit some of the old haunts that I was fond of when my husband was alive." Georgina's gaze turned in Mary Ellen's direction while she went on to ask Evan which of his girlfriends she was, "the mick or the spic?" Now addressing the woman directly, she said, "Oh, by the way, let me introduce myself. I'm the wife, but you already know that."

Callman muttered, "This is one of my … uh … former associates from Integrity. I mean I'm former, but she's not."

"I'm Mary Ellen Dunn." A hand was extended to Georgina.

A nod of recognition. "Ah, so you are the mick. I would've guessed as much, but who knows, there may be others as well."

"What do you want, Georgina?" Evan said, now exasperated.

The martini was served in a ten-ounce goblet. She dove at it like a pit bull after an ankle. "Want? Why only to reconnect with you. It's been oh so lonely at home. You haven't even noticed my new clothes and perm, all for your benefit, my sweet." Now that the lady had called attention to herself, he observed that she had a new do, shorter, and she wore white linen slacks and an apricot tank top. *New wealth, new outfits,* he thought.

"Come on, you're full of shit. So lonely that you've got a monster lawsuit out against the company whose crane did me in."

She countered, "Such vulgarity, Evan, not at all like Integrity correctness. So you've learned about my action; well then, I suppose you do have access to newspapers in these remote locations."

By now he felt he'd heard enough and moved to rise from the table. "Let's go, Mary Ellen, we've got some work to do across the street." She remained fixed in her position. Georgina was looking at each of them in turn, grinning broadly. She was halfway through the martini.

"Mary Ellen?" Callman was standing.

"Sit down, Evan," Georgina was direct.

He ignored her command. "Mary Ellen?" he asked once more.

"Uh, I'd follow her command, Evan," Mary Ellen said, looking up into his eyes. "We don't appear to be finished here just yet."

As if on cue from offstage, Trulett Maddox joined the group and pulled up a chair at Evan's right hand. Maddox was wearing a Tommy Bahama tropical shirt over cutoff jeans, and he had a calico bandana around his forehead. His left eye was occluded by a black patch. "Hey, good buddy, how's it hangin'?" he addressed Callman in a jaunty manner.

"Why Truly, you seem to have lost the parrot that belongs on your shoulder," Evan replied. "What brings you to the island?"

Maddox rifled in on him with his free eye. "Why, just to visit with you, my man." He was taking in the bustling sidewalk activity all around them and caught the waiter's attention, whereupon he asked for a Corona; Georgina wanted a refill on the martini and made a statement that it was nice that Evan had so many friends and family who would travel all this way to look in on him. Callman, seated again, and Mary Ellen wore stone faces in silence.

"Well, actually," Maddox began, after taking an extended draw on the beer, "I thought it fitting that I personally welcome you back to the land of the living. Perhaps you can tell us something of the other side, but you don't seem to have spent very much time there."

"You can cut the crap, Truly," Callman retorted, now testy. "You can't tell me that this conclave is some kind of spontaneous party," he said, talking to the table occupants as a whole.

Maddox started to respond, and two others came around to join in the fun. They were Integrity's CEO, Lowell Grader, and a spiffy-looking black man who Evan did not know but who may have been vaguely familiar to him, someone he had passed by in the corridors around the office building.

"May we be included?" Grader asked in a casual tone, a rhetorical question, as though any of the Integrity people would deign object to his request. The younger man pulled up two vacant chairs from a nearby table, and everyone else made a bit more room to accommodate the group of six. Comfortably seated, Grader surveyed his table partners and declared the meeting on. "Our time is valuable, is it not?" the CEO opened, in a commanding mien, "so we ought get on with business. Firstly, well, Evan," he said, smiling cordially, "I'm delighted to see you in such robust appearance. That is you, isn't it, behind the dark hair and the beard? My, this island must cast a youthful effect on its visitors, if I gauge it right."

At the moment feeling anything *but* robust, he acknowledged the salutation with a grim nod and an "Evan Callman died, Lowell. I'm puzzled as to why you all traveled all this way for an off-site, and that I seem to be the focus of everyone's attention. I suppose I should be flattered."

"Well, I am the chief exec, and it is my prerogative to schedule a meeting at a time and place of my choosing. I thought this would be a delightful location. As for flattery, that is hardly my intent, but we thought it important that we come together to resolve some issues that demand resolution, and if this was the venue, well, so be it." He gestured in Leroy Brown's direction and said, "Oh, for those who may not know this gentleman to my right, allow me to introduce Mr. Leroy Brown of the company's audit staff."

"As in bad, bad, Leroy—" Maddox was draining his Corona while signaling for another.

"Trulett!" Grader shot him down. "We need to get on with it." He spoke to Evan, "We have reason to believe that *you* have been a bad boy, Mr. Callman, and that we stand to be most disappointed in you." Grader was speaking much like a chastising middle-school teacher, which is precisely what he was before seeking his fortune in financial services. "I'd like for Mr. Brown to relate to the group what we've learned and then check on its authenticity with you and," he faced Mary Ellen Dunn, "Ms. Dunn, as well."

He ceded the discussion to Brown, who brought forth a thick file and several sheets of talking points that at a glance seemed to come out of a Power Point presentation.

"What, no colorful brochures to hand out?" Callman inquired, grasping a sense of what was coming and deciding to abandon a deferential attitude for the time being.

"Hey, none of that sass, bast—"

"Truly!" Grader said, reestablishing control.

Brown began, head down in his notes, literally reading the talking point words on the page. "We have found that Integrity employees Evan Callman and Mary Ellen Dunn have been engaged for several years in a scheme to steal from and defraud Integrity by virtue of manipulation of its systems." Brown looked up to see all pairs of eyes riveted on him and felt confident in the cadence of his exposition.

"Leroy?" Grader interjected, "move along. Explain for everyone's elucidation what was done and how it was done."

The auditor returned to his sheets for guidance as he went on, "The company's contracts stipulate that payees—the individuals—are paid monthly and electronically, that is, their funds are automatically transferred into a designated bank account. These payments are the same, month after month, and they remain lodged in the system until some event triggers the need for change. You might say at that point the process is on a form of autopilot."

"And what might trigger such a change?" asked the CEO, being a coach to his player.

"Well, any number of things," Brown said, "such as the passing of the customer ... ah ... this payee, in which case the payment would cease. Or the closing of an account or a new address following a move and most likely a new bank account, those sorts of events."

The group maintained its attention on the presentation. It heard that Callman's unit was responsible for the process described. They did all of the setup, which was much of the work required—getting it going. "We pay many thousands of people on a regular basis," Brown said. "What happened was that in some of these cases where a cessation was called for in the payment stream, they would, instead, create a new account in the customer's name—at a different bank, of course—and direct a continuation of payments. This would go on for a matter of months, and then the account would finally be closed."

Grader prompted him again. "Okay, Leroy, so they extended the money flow, and it sounds like Integrity was giving the payee a free ride."

"Not so, sir," Leroy responded, their one-on-one routine coming across as having been well rehearsed. "See, the documentation for cessation had already been in-hand. There was information that so-and-so was no longer entitled, and that our obligations were satisfied. What *did* happen, of course, is that payments were redirected to new bank accounts."

Evan squirmed in his chair, Mary Ellen averted her eyes from everyone else's, and Georgina and Truly were on their next rounds, beaming and hanging on every word.

"Can you tell us how that could be?" the CEO asked in a hushed voice laced with sarcasm.

"Well, they sat on the info. Originating the protocols that made the processes accurate and efficient, they also carried the authority to post changes to systems and dispense funds."

The shit has hit the fan, Callman thought. *They had to have gotten to Mary Ellen. Now I know that only one person can keep a secret.*

"Talk about the new bank accounts, Leroy."

Brown moved ahead. "It seems that they—Callman and Dunn—opened them up using the names of the original payees."

Grader nudged his presenter again. "You mean they just walked into a bank, pretended to be so-and-so, and started an account into which automated payments from Integrity would flow. I'd think that it'd be hard to do, particularly for a large number of accounts—which, I assume we're dealing with."

"Yes. At any given point in time, there were about sixty of them active. As for opening bank accounts, you'd be amazed at how easy it is. There are banks that let you do it over the Internet or by mail. The two of them had all the vital numbers like Social Security. Evidently some banks just take down the data and don't bother to verify a lot of these things. They came to know which banks were easy, and those were the ones used."

"Does everyone understand so far?" Grader was talking to the group. "You're doing just fine, Leroy. Proceed."

"New mailing addresses were given, always post office box numbers. There were normal retail services associated with the bank accounts, including checkbooks and ATM cards, which is how they made most of the withdrawals. As everyone knows, ATM cards can be used just about anywhere. Apart from possibly an initial visit, these two never set foot in any of the bank premises."

Mary Ellen conveyed her need for a bathroom break. Grader declared a hiatus, and everyone stood and stretched in place with the exception of Georgina, who accompanied Dunn.

Eyes fixed on his associate, Callman thought, *she'll be back to claim her reward for turning state's evidence. Not to worry about her skipping out.*

With all present once more around the table, Lowell Grader asked the auditor how it was that the company could have been bleeding from unauthorized disbursements all this time. "Remember that movie *Cool Hand Luke* where Paul Newman said, 'What we have he-ah is a failure to control.' Well, that's the situation we face."

Georgina spoke up. "Uh, sir, the line was, 'What we have here is a failure to communicate.'"

"Well, that too, now that you mention it," he said.

"And it was Strother Martin, not Paul, who delivered the line."

"As you wish."

It was an opening for Leroy Brown to continue. Evan envisioned him as a puppet dancing on a string every time Grader goaded him on. "Audit had not looked at this operation in more than three years," Brown said. "It seems the company's priorities lay elsewhere, so this turns out to be an oversight."

Indeed. Integrity, along with every other financial house in the nation, had been under scrutiny about its practices in the early years of the twenty-first century. While answering voluminous queries from regulators, the company revamped its internal audit efforts, which took the form of a shift in emphasis away from traditional and mundane business processes and into the areas that had garnered all the attention.

Georgina, animated by her display of movie knowledge and another chocolate martini, interjected, "Okay, I guess we get the picture, guys, but what I'd like to know is how much my husband and his … shanty little friend, here, stole."

Grader solicited volunteers. "Anyone?"

Callman asked if he was eligible for a lifeline.

"You sumbitch, you don't even get to phone a friend," Maddox spat out.

Leroy Brown turned in Georgina's direction and in a smooth tone said, "Ma'am, we believe it's on the order of $21 million."

"You … think? On the order?" She laughed heartily. "You call yourselves accountants, or whatever. Don't you know?"

"Members of my staff are finalizing the numbers back in New York as we speak," Brown responded evenly, demonstrating a high-level command of corporate jargon.

Georgina continued, "Actually, the estimate is close enough for me, Leroy. I'll never see any of it. But tell me, what did they do with it? Where is it?"

"Ah, the $64,000 question," Grader said, showing his appreciation for ancient quiz shows and, by association, his own age. "Well, Mary Ellen and Evan, is there something you would like to share with us?"

How much do they know? Evan wondered. *What did Mary Ellen tell them?* He was uncertain. She did not have access codes for the account at the Geneve; only he held those. However, she of course knew the identity of the bank, and it was highly likely the name was wheedled out of her in return for—

"We're waitin' on you," the CEO said.

Callman, perhaps playing for time, answered him. "Lots of banks in Cayman, Lowell, as I'm sure you've already noticed."

"Evvy, don't try to play some goddam game with us," Maddox pleaded. "It's too late for that, man."

"This reminds of that scene in *The Godfather*," Georgina piped up, "the one where Tessio's duplicity is outed; he's confronted by the family, and he turns to Tom Hagen and asks, 'Tom, can you get me off the hook?'" She surveyed her audience. "And what was his answer, folks? All as one, now."

"Can't do it, Sally," they responded in unison, except for Evan.

The CEO had listened enough and sensed that the meeting was getting punch-drunk, or actually drunk, and had exhausted its value. "Evan, let's you and I take a little stroll," he said. "The rest of you can stay put. We won't be long." The two men proceeded down the main street, Grader up to his tall and spare frame with arm gently around the other's shoulder, the latter offering no resistance to the gesture; Callman in full cringe but having to go along for whatever awaited. Afternoon shadows were gaining length across the little harbor area, and activity was winding down as the cruisers stood in long lines for the bumpy tenders that would run them back to their mother ships.

"You know, Evan I've always liked you and believed in the job you had done for Integrity, but I suppose that's beside the point now," Grader said, all the while focused straight ahead as they walked. "In a way, I have to hand it to you. All that hard work for so long a time, and—for what? Steal a little, steal not really a lot, not by today's benchmarks. It reminds me of that Johnny Cash song, the one about the guy on the auto assembly line who takes a part every day, and years later has enough to assemble a car at home. Hell, he'd a been better off just leasing one. But look, y'all have some leverage; I hate to admit it, but the truth is we're pretty sure which of all these banks you've got your stash in—but it's not 100 percent, and no one wants to waste any more time. And then, only you know what's there, which we will all learn in due course. So, I guess you could stonewall us a bit more but not much."

"How'd you ID the bank," Evan wanted to know. "Mary Ellen spill the beans?"

"Negative. Above all, she's remained true to you, which you might find surprising in light of the discussion we just had. I always admire loyalty—other than to an unworthy cause, which isn't loyalty at all. No, it was your wife, Georgina."

He seemed dumfounded. "Georgina?"

Grader pushed on, warming to the conversation. "You both went to Cayman several times. On more than one occasion she got, well, a little curious when you left to play golf or some such thing in the afternoon while she wanted to nap or maybe engage in what you young'uns call a matinee. She thought that behavior to be out of character, and it seems a couple of times she followed you and watched you go into this Geneve bank here in town. It appears that you weren't quite dressed for golf, in a tropical suit and toting a large case. She figured that something was up, that there must be some money lying around, and she evidently wasn't in on any of it. Some greed knows no boundaries. I would have believed you to be more careful, Evvy, given the way in which you've planned everything else out."

They came to a bench recessed in between a duty-free liquor store and an antique shop. "Let's sit down. Now, here's *my* leverage. I am certain you do not have a passport, and even if you do, it's in the name of a dead man, and if the authorities around here don't know that Evan Callman is deceased, they will soon enough. Therefore, you have no way off this little Caribbean paradise unless you can arrange for a forger who can somehow get you a new ID. Otherwise, assuming you do have all that dough, you'd have to live off of it here. In any event, you'd be a target upon attempted departure."

Callman didn't know if he was calling a bluff. "You're speculating, Lowell. I could probably work my way off of Cayman and disappear somewhere."

"Maybe. Ah'll grant you some slack on that one, Evan. However, I don't believe life as a fugitive would suit you. Allow me to go on, though. We aren't finished. Tell me, do you know a Bruno Kiel in New York?"

Evan said he did not. The CEO went ahead. "No, you wouldn't. Bruno Kiel—Detective Kiel—was in charge of the investigation that followed on the industrial accident that led to a death in the company's office building. He has kept the inquiry alive, even asked to meet with me the other week, this after more than one interview with the personnel department. It was a very illuminating talk. It appears there was another man in the area besides yourself when that wrecking ball came across. And Kiel has identified him—knows all about him."

Evan sat transfixed, his eyes straight out toward the water and the massive cruise ships that lay in the distance.

"Now, there's good news and bad news. The bad news is—to cut to the chase—you're wanted for murder in New York."

"That's bullshit, Lowell, why that guy was—"

"Was what, Evan? You're gonna tell me he was killed by the ball?"

Callman was silent. Grader lay a hand gently on Callman's hand and intoned in a quasi whisper, "Maybe so, but, Evvy, the police don't know that, and you'd never be able to prove it to them. At the least, you'd have to endure a painful and costly trial. And even if'n you beat the charges, you'd be scarred big-time."

"So what's the good news?"

"Kiel and company do not know anything about the embezzlement. I figured they have no need to know."

He did not want to accept all of what Grader was spelling out, but he was feeling increasingly cornered and ready to make a deal. Grader rose and said that it was time to rejoin the rest of the group. They started to make their way back to Pieces of Eight. "Now, Evvy, here's what I propose …"

The players were once again seated around the table. "Now," the CEO began, "in just a little bit, Evan, here, and I are gonna take another little stroll, this time across the plaza to that bank over there," he gestured in the direction of the Geneve building, "where he will transfer the account that has been maintained to my control. His codes, voice, and print imaging will be deleted. Mine will supplant his, and the bank will record his consent to all of the foregoing and authenticate it, providing assurance that the transfer is entirely consensual."

With bated breath, all awaited his next words; and the CEO, proficient in meeting management and presentation, was relishing his role.

"Then, it will be revealed what is actually in the bank's vault for that account, and, when it is validated, here's what'll be done. Mary Ellen, (he was looking squarely at the young woman whose head had been virtually in her lap but who suddenly snapped to at the mention of her name) as you might surmise, you would be in a heap of trouble back in New York. However, we're going to arrange for you and your mom to be relocated to a place of your choice—somewhere in south Florida may have appeal, I think—and we'll set up a new identity for you, probably as a young widow, so you can live without lookin' over your shoulder. We'll buy you a house—within reason, of course—and spoon you over a quarter mil as a transition to a new career in your adopted town. My advice is to stay clear of the financial business. Sound okay?"

Mary Ellen Dunn murmured a tenuous affirmation.

"May I make a suggestion?" Georgina interjected.

"The floor is yours—but make it quick," Grader said.

"I think she should use some of that money to get an extreme makeover to protect her new identity. Lady," Georgina was locked in on Mary Ellen, "that shit-brown hair has to go, and furthermore—"

"Point well taken, Mrs. Callman," Lowell jumped back in, his top teeth firmly on his tongue, "and since you've spoken up, let us deal with you. Firstly, there'll be no contest over the death benefit with the insurance company. As far as they are concerned, the case is closed, and our long-standing relationship with them is such that even if something were to come up, we'd settle it out. But you *will* drop the wrongful death action against the A&G Construction Company."

"I will? Why should I do that?"

"Here's why. A&G is a client of Integrity's, and pursuit of this suit is embarrassing all around. This is what'll go down for you. A&G has built, and manages, lots of luxury buildings all over town. They will offer you a selection of a good-sized apartment on an upper floor at a prestige address in Manhattan—rent free."

"For how long?"

"Indefinitely. This is a sweet deal. You'll have a view of the river and have room for your own studio. I understand you like to paint."

Georgina, for once, seemed satisfied, though it was not in her nature to show her cards. But her wheels were turning. She had a million dollars in her kick already; she could sell the suburban house and move into the city, and she'd be independent, free as a bird to indulge her every spirit.

"Truly," the CEO honed in on the completely smashed Trulett Maddox, "you have been a trooper, stepping up throughout all of this turmoil. There is a recommendation to be put to next month's board meeting for your promotion and a salary of $800,000 annually with an expanded bonus opportunity. You are a keeper, son."

Truly Mad barely lifted his head from the table, merely enough to wave faintly in the wake of Grader's announcement. His eye patch had slipped to a position alongside his reddened nose.

"Mr. Leroy Brown will also be promoted to head up our audit department," Grader said.

Hardly surprised, Brown grinned in a facetious manner.

The CEO added, "The control breakdown in this matter is shocking and unacceptable, and I'm glad that we had in our midst an exemplary young man like Leroy Brown to have gotten to the bottom of it all. Good work, son."

Brown was applauding himself.

"Lexi Petrova has been let go. This scandal occurred on his watch."

At the hearing of Petrova's name, Maddox, whose head was now at rest sideways on the table, stirred. "I always hated the commie bastard, anyway."

"What can I say?" Leroy Brown asked.

Nobody responded.

Silent until this point, Callman weighed in. "Well, that has covered everyone attending except for two of us. What about you, Lowell?"

Grader hesitated a moment, reviewed the faces around him, then said, "I was going to get to you next, Evan, but since you asked, I'll tell you and everyone else about me and save you for the end. I think that's appropriate. This whole episode will not be well-received back at ole' double-I. $21 mil? It's not a lot for a company of Integrity's size. Hell, we can win or lose those amounts hourly in our portfolio operations. However, that's part of the game we play. What you did wasn't in anyone's game. It was stealing, pure and simple."

"Lowell, you're pontificating."

Unfazed, the CEO said, "Perhaps a bit, Evvy; I guess that's a bit of the former teacher in me, but allow an old man his moment. After the board listens to all of this, yours truly will be—to use your generation's epithet—toast. So, I'll elect early retirement. Lillian and I had always planned to move back south someday, so we'll merely move our schedule up. I will negotiate a severance package with the board. It won't be as much as I had hoped for, had I stayed on, but then I'm not a greedy man."

Callman asked, "Aren't you forgetting something?"

"Am I, Evan?"

"Yeah. The money."

"Ah, the money," Grader answered. "Well, since we have arranged to dispense some of the shares around the table here, I'm confident that the residual will be sufficient for my needs. Let's see. There should be close to $20 mil available if the accounting proves out. That will be more than adequate to buy a place somewhere in one of those fancy golf communities and then maybe another in New England for the summer when the South gets too hot, and there is the risk of hurricanes. There's golf up there too, boating, whatever you want to do. The wife and I, well, we don't need any more than that. Does that answer your question?"

"It sounds a little pat to me. What are you going to tell the board about the alleged shortfall?"

Grader continued. "Alleged? I'd not use that word, Evvy. There will be a loss. Mr. Brown, here, will make a presentation much along the lines we're gone over today. In fact, we might consider today's discussion to be a kind of dress rehearsal. He'll say that the investigation is not final, but we're giving them an estimate as a kind of 'heads up.' He'll add that Integrity will make a claim under the liability protection we have against fraud, misdeeds, and such. So, Leroy—"

Brown was at attention.

"You'll calm their fears by saying that we'll get most of it back. And another thing—"

"Yes, sir?"

"Make sure when you present that you've got a couple of other audit issues for their consideration, so that this becomes one of a group. Sort of insulates the blow, wouldn't you think?"

Leroy Brown's head bobbed in the affirmative, a signal that he understood his marching orders. His attentiveness to the CEO's instructions was in competition in his mind with what his raise in pay would open up for him—perhaps the lease of a Porsche and an open ticket at Paul Stuart for starters.

Throughout, Callman had hung on every word. He saw that everyone around the table was being taken care of by something he'd made possible. "So what about me?" he asked.

Grader's voice was laden with syrup. "How forgetful of me not to include you, so let's make up for that. Evvy, what is—was—your salary at Integrity?"

Evan told him it was $275,000.

"Including any bonus?"

"No. Another hundred-and-fifty would be added, based on last year's results."

"Ah. Now, Evan," Grader leaned in until they were virtually nose to nose, "if you were let go, your severance package would pay around a year's salary."

"Cut the bastard," Maddox warbled, now awash in his own saliva. Evan could see where this was heading.

"With or without the bonus?" he asked.

"Stuff the bonus up his keister."

"Truly, I think we can offer a *soupcon* of generosity here," Grader said. "Let's throw in a little bonus and round it up to 300 K." The CEO glanced at his Timex watch and stood up. "We are done here. It's time to go." Beckoning to Evan, the two walked off in the direction of the Geneve building. The plaza held a stillness; the day tourists had repaired to their cruise ships and resort hotels in advance of the evening's activities, presumably without a care in the world.

Nine

"Hello, gentlemen." Bruno Kiel, alongside of his partner, Emshaw Hamilton, cordially greeted Grader and Callman in the lobby of the bank building, "Mr. Grader, it's nice to see you again and … this …," the detective was gesturing at Evan while Hamilton made a stealthlike move to bracket the two men, "must be the elusive Evan Callman."

Lowell Grader forced himself to appear unruffled. "I'm sure this is more than a social call, detectives. Would you care to tell us what this is all about? We have some business to attend to here."

"As do we," Kiel said. "We'll not waste one another's time. You see, we know all about your little scheme. I guess you didn't notice that Kia parked across from your meeting place. That was a most informative meeting we listened in on."

"What do you mean, 'listened'?" Grader asked.

"Emmy," Kiel motioned at Hamilton, all the while keeping his left hand deep in his jacket pocket—perhaps gripping a concealed object. His partner moved deftly to Evan's side, whereupon he removed a listening device from the latter's pants pocket and handed it over to Kiel.

"Thanks, Emmy. Didn't know it was there, did you?" said Kiel, addressing Evan.

"Who—" was all the stunned Callman could blurt out.

The detective responded. "Your wife. She slipped it into your pocket while you were occupied with your mai tai, or whatever you were putting down. My, the lady is versatile, to say the least. You see, gentlemen, we never thought things were quite kosher, so to speak, from the beginning. Later on, we put a tail on Mrs. Callman; then when we learned of her plan to come down here, we began to put some of the pieces together. We *are* detectives. Then we approached her with a proposal, and this," he held the device for effect, "is the end result."

Hearing it all spill out, the picture was beginning to clarify to Lowell Grader. "Well, here's the man you want," he said to Kiel while gesturing at Evan.

Callman turned to leer at Grader. Kiel smiled broadly, paused a moment, then told the Integrity CEO that that was not necessarily so and that it was now time to proceed with the business at hand. "Oh, we want him, but not in the way you're thinking. He is going to transfer the account here to me and my loyal sidekick."

Grader made what seemed an involuntary feint toward Kiel, and Hamilton stepped in between the two. "There's an example of loyalty," Kiel said. "I'm sorry about all those houses you aren't going to buy, Mr. Grader, and as for your associate, well—" he faced Callman. "Better *you* remain dead. We could bring you back to New York to face charges, but we figure it would take a lot of our time with no assurance that a conviction would prevail. Besides, we may not be with the police department much longer, and we'd hate to be recalled for what could be a lengthy investigation and trial."

"Lotta friggin' paperwork, too," Hamilton volunteered.

"You said it, partner," Bruno added. "Now, shall we get to it?"

Some forty-five minutes later they were all on the street. Kiel placed a document in Callman's hand. "Here's something you will need. There are two options included. It's your choice. And there's a little going-away present tucked inside as well, a token of the NYPD's appreciation. After all, it was you who made it all possible. And now, our business concluded, we bid you good evening, or, as they might say on the island, 'don't worry, be happy, mon.'" They left the area with surprising speed.

Callman and Grader were standing alone. "Well, Evvy, we were had," the boss said. "Easy come, easy go, I suppose."

"What's this 'we,' Lowell?"

The question elicited a smile and a shallow laugh from Grader. "That's right. You're dead, so it's up to me. Well, I suppose I can convince the board to do something for me. What am I to tell the barflies?"

"Oh, you'll think of something. You're still the CEO."

"*Cara mia,* I'm back," Evan Callman greeted Noemi Lorca as he opened the door to the room at Dinah's. Noemi was propped up on a lumpy and concave mattress, sucking on a cherry lollipop and watching a limbo contest on a twelve-inch TV set. She was wearing cutoff denim shorts and a lime-green tank top that intermittently clung to her full breasts. In his regard, this was hardly the same woman who, seemingly only hours past, had slipped away from her post at Integrity Investment; perhaps Noemi was rapidly reverting to an inherent version of herself. *Funny, I guess no one ever shucks their roots entirely,* he thought.

"It's about time, Ev-vie," her words rang out plaintively in a rhythmic faintly Hispanic tone, "so don't try to sweet-talk me with the 'cara mia.' That's

Italian, anyway. Why don't you try *mia del cara* next time." She took a massive slurp from the lollipop.

Noemi rose from her bed, approached him, planted a lubricated cherry-flavored kiss full on his lips, and rubbed fingers along the nape of his neck. "You shouldn't leave me so stranded for so-o long," she fairly cooed.

So much for my initial consternation, he mused. *The emotions change so very quickly, don't they?* He stepped back momentarily from her embrace, the better to admire her form as she turned to shut down the blaring TV with a graceful bend. *Yes, she is a risk and a challenge. I just hope we get out of town before her brothers start looking for us.*

"Ev-vie, do you have the money?"

Callman, now energized, dropped in an Austin Powers-style "yeah, baby."

"So, when are we out of this dump?"

"As soon as we can get to the airport. Hey, Noemi, you didn't ask me about my new identity," he responded to her question.

That was true. He told her he was "working on" a new personna which would get him out of Grand Cayman, but that was pure speculation; he did not know where and when it would be coming, and certainly not from the handout that Kiel had left with him.

He pushed two newly minted passports across the motel room's highly distressed coffee table for Noemi's inspection.

"Let me know what you think," he said. "It appears I've got a couple of options."

She flipped through the passports, the first describing Noel Taylor, a citizen of New Zealand residing in the capital city of Wellington, and its alternate, one for Edward Mansfield, a Canadian from Toronto. The photos on each were identical, portraying the Evan Callman of several weeks prior, *sans* dark hair, beard, and big glasses.

"Um … I don't know." Noemi was about to go into an eeny-meeny mode before she said, "I think New Zealand sounds nice—it has a certain exotic character to it, and we might want to go there someday. I also like the 'Noel and Noemi.' Did you come up with that?"

"Sure. New Zealand it is, then." Evan was definitive. *Thank God for English-speaking countries,* he thought.

"Should we pack?" Noemi asked.

"Might as well. I'll settle up with Dinah; call the airlines for flights, and then we'll be on our way."

"To St. Bart's, Ev-vie? Or do I call you Noel, now?"

"Why not. Noel always said it was a classy island."

Noemi continued. "And we'll build a villa overlooking the water. Can we have a boat? (She lapsed into the Caribbean pronunciation *boad.*) I've wanted one ever since I went out on the water with my City Island friends."

"When we get settled," Evan said. "First, we'll check into a hotel. I've got the guidebooks. You can choose one. Then we'll look around. There's no need to rush into anything."

"I know, *mi amor,* but with what we've got to spend, we can have one of the best places on the island. I'm anxious. Also, when we've moved in I want to have my *mamacita* and one of my brothers—Raffy, the one with the clean shirts—visit. They'd be so proud."

"As you wish." Callman's voice was showing signs of exhaustion.

Expending little time, they packed, checked out, and were on their way to the airport, where a commuter-type plane would whisk them eastward to the tiny island of St. Barts. Once there and awaiting departure, his eyes darted around the lounge for sightings of his Integrity associates and Georgina. (Was he still married to her? No. Evan was gone. He was now Noel Taylor. Therefore, nothing to worry about.) He had told Noemi to stay out of sight at the airport, a precautionary device, he said, overruling her gathering pout; but with no indications of their presence, it seemed as though they had already left and that the coast was clear.

Or so he thought. There, emerging from the bathroom, was none other than Mary Ellen, and it was a no-blood wager as to who spotted who first. "You double-crossing bastard," Mary Ellen shouted as she headed straight for Evan, with Noemi all of a sudden coming alongside of him, "and you too, bitch. I might have known it would have been you all the time."

I suppose Grader went back to deliver the news, Callman thought. *Actually, I'm a little surprised he did. They probably left him dead on the sidewalk afterward.*

"You took my money, you bastard. Now what am I and my mother gonna do." She lunged at Callman clumsily, and he could see the flash of what appeared to be a gold-toned letter opener in her hand. She took a swipe at his arm, but he reacted with agility and forced it out of her hand; it clanked to the floor. He gripped her forearm and led her to a seat in the small lounge. She put up no resistance. By this time, a small crowd was forming around them, and a security officer was running up to the scene. Before anyone could notice, Callman retrieved and pocketed the letter opener, which had a large red 'G' logo on its blunt end, which he recognized as that of the Geneve bank. *Funny, the bank never gave me any souvenirs,* he thought.

"What seems to be the commotion here?" The security man was nonchalant, as in the island style.

"No commotion, officer," Callman said.

"Like hell," Mary Ellen piped up. "The bastard screwed me out of everything I worked for."

The officer came up to her. "Now miss, calm down, please. I can see you're stressed out." Upon close examination he concluded that she had had way too much of some island treat and was not in a rational state. He turned to Callman. "Do you know this woman?"

"I've never laid eyes on her until minutes ago, officer."

Mary Ellen, in a voice lowered but still laced with venom, said, "He's a liar as well as a cheat. That's Evan Callman. Search him."

Resigned to her request, the security man requested that Callman hand over his passport. He read it and handed it back. "This is not who you think," he told Mary Ellen. Back to Callman and Noemi, he told them they were free to go, whereupon they moved toward the gate for their flight, for which they had only minutes to spare. The security man had not referred to "Mr.Taylor" when he returned the passport; that was a piece of luck, for Mary Ellen, drunk as she was, might have picked up on the name and tracked him down. As it was, it could not be disguised that the pair were headed off to St. Barts, and who knew what a now unbalanced Mary Ellen might try. In one last surreptitious move, Evan wiped clean the letter opener and tossed it in the waste can nearest the gate. It seemed to go unnoticed. *OJ revisited,* he thought.

The New Zealand passport worked without incident. Once in flight, Noemi brought up the Mary Ellen incident. "Did she think you were going to be hers, Evvy? I often wondered, when she'd be at those meetings—with you—if she had a thing for you. But I was the winner. I came away with you, and nobody gets to share." She took an exploratory direction. "What was she doing down here, anyway?"

That was the last thing he wanted to get into with Noemi. "I don't know. Do you think she got on to you coming down here and followed?"

"Evvy, how could that be? I kept it quiet. *Mi dio,* I can't imagine how. She sure was pissed. What money was she screaming about?"

"Look, she had a lot to drink. Tee many martoonis."

They both laughed. Noemi held his hand as she gazed longingly at the tantalizing waters beneath. She was thinking about her prospective life of ease. It made her feel giddy. As for Noel Taylor, he gently rested his eyes. There would be things to disclose to this fine-looking woman, but later on. As an example, she would need to know that St. Bart's is French-speaking, so her Spanish would hardly become her there. On the other hand, he could practice his college French. *How d'ya like that, Captain Squires?* he thought.

For now, he could play at relaxation. After all he'd been through, he surely could do with a vacation.

William Goes to Town

"Hey, Shakespeare, table three needs a refill on the flagon of mead, forthwith," the innkeeper shouts at me. Hurriedly, I put down my quill pen and parchment folio and move to comply with the master's order.

"Writing again on break, eh, what-ho," master Robin-A-Brew chides. "William, be mindful of your work now or you will lose your situation." Discarding the reprimand, I proceed to bring a round of refreshment to the table of goatherds on the far side of the room. Hmm … "forthwith" and "what-ho." Well now, those words can be used in a new play.

The Serf and Turf is Stratford's leading tavern—truth be told, it is the only tavern in town—and I toil there to support myself and my growing family at those times when not immersed in the theater trade. Allow me to introduce myself. I am Will Shakespeare, playwright and sometime actor.

Closing time: after having dispensed innumerable rounds of oxblood Marys and venison wings in the tavern, I trudge wearily home to Anne and our children. "Hi-ho, my sweet, I'm home," I offer with forced cheer upon entry to the small thatched-roof cottage, where I must bend down to avoid bumping my head in the doorway. Already in a balding state, I am in no humour to risk additional loss of hair by dint of scraping of the pate. Later on in the evening, as we prepared for bed, she told me that the Elizabethan Express came today with word that I am to meet Dick Burbage in London to review my latest work. She adds, "Be sure to ask for an advance. We need some roof work, and I must summon the village thatcher lest he become booked up."

Ah, my dearest Anne! Ah, lovely maidens! I have written of them. As wooing them is all springtime, the seasons oft turn wintry when they become wives.

Shortly after sunrise, your intrepid playwright embarks by wagon to London, a journey of two days. Robin would, of course, wonder where his young charge had gone off to today; he would have to fill the position through Peon-Power, the temp agency, and Will will likely be out of a job once again. No matter. If this new play were to be a smash, I'll be buying the rounds instead of serving them.

The trip was halted only once, at Charing Cross Road, by a highwayman-in-training. *Could not have been a day over twelve.* The youngster brandished a rusty dirk with trembling hand as he stuttered repeatedly, "St … st … stuh .. and de … de … liver!" By the time he had finished, the coachman whipped his horses and sped on, leaving this novice in the dust, still practicing his lines. I had to laugh out loud. Prithee, it seems there must be a new crop of these louts, and this one won't last the season. Lack-a-day, what are we coming to?

London City was reached around sunset, had there been any sun. I step from the coach into a chilly rain at the doorstep of The Ground Hound Tavern, striding into a brawl between two drunks that was spilling out onto the prevailing mud that posed as a street.

"Knave!"

"Varlet!"

"Two crowns on the varlet."

"Against you, sirrah, and I'll back the knave.

Screams emanate from the front of the tavern as the gamblers alternately jeer and spur on the two combatants, at this stage hopelessly covered in slime and mutually indistinguishable. I resist the temptation to participate in such folly and push through the crowd and climb to the second floor of the establishment where the meeting is to take place. "Ah, Shakespeare, welcome indeed," Dick Burbage, actor, producer, and tavern master, calls out upon my entry. As wide as he was high, Burbage's round and florid face was engulfed by a disheveled blonde beard. A fragment of mutton dangled lazily from one side of his mouth. "Finishing a meal," he continues, "come forth, and I'll have Mistress Jolly bring a schooner of my finest brew. Canterbury Ales, it is. This morn's vintage." A massive fist to the table summoned a large-eyed buxom woman, who left straightaway to fulfill the master's wish, but not before he laid a meaty hand around her waist. "Will, is not my mistress of the tavern a sweet wench?" he asks of me. I seem to recall penning that line myself in some long-forgotten play. *Zounds, is there no integrity remaining?*

The drink brought to us, I offer appreciation for the tonic after a tiring journey while not appearing overly eager to get on with the business at hand, lest I loose my anxious emotions to disadvantage.

"Well now, Will Shakespeare, I have slaked my thirst and am once more refreshed," he says. "Tell me what you have in that folio you clutch so firmly."

Opening the portfolio, its contents remov'd, 'tis a mound of scripted sheets placed on the table. *Did he notice the tremor in my hand? My whole life is bound up in these pages.* "I have been hard at it, as you can see, and can present dramas, comedies, fantasies, whatever is in demand. I propose a play about two young lovers in Italy who come from families that despise one another—a quite emotional tale."

Burbage took a long pull from his drink and I watch with amusement as the mutton slides into the amber ale. Then, with a sudden snap-to, the outer door flies open and in breezes a young dandy, dressed head-to-foot in rich burgundy velvet topped off with a plumed hat cocked jauntily to one side. His vee-shaped faced sports a manicured mustache and a goatee. He is known to me, and I care not a jot for him, a popinjay if ever was. Our host leaps up to embrace him, as would a martinet greeting a prince, saying, "Marlowe, my good fellow, come along and bid hello here. I think you know young Shakespeare."

Turning to the new entrant, I greet him with little effort to conceal a tone of disdain. "Hello … Marlowe …" I consider Christopher Marlowe arrogant, lazy, a rounder, and not above the theft of goods or ideas. In short, bad news.

The conversation continued. "Marlowe, we were discussing a new play," Burbage says.

Marlowe addresses me. "By the by, Shakespeare, how do you wish to be called, Will or William?"

"Actually, I prefer bard these days … Chris," I respond. "I believe I held the floor prior to your dramatic entrance, thus I ask your attention to our discussion."

Marlowe weighed in, "Yes, I overheard you describing a new play. Now, bard, you say there are five families …"

"No, just two," I corrected him. "There were others but they were whicked …"

"You mean 'whacked,' don't you?" Marlowe said.

"As you like it. Whatever. Anyway, it is set in Verona, and the young lovers meet a tragic fate. It is a highly charged story, full up with swordplay and passion, and sure to raise the hackles of the most jaded theatergoer."

Burbage solicits Marlowe's opinion. He appears truly obsequious in his approach toward this man, as though I am a cipher, an afterthought. *I* am the playwright here. Have I not senses and affections?

"Well, now," Marlowe goes on as if he were the cock-o'-the-walk, "all of the elements are mix'd in .... what if we produced it as a musical?" He added, "You know, bard, that last season's play about the duke and the two daughters—those wenches—flopped. Too confusing. Music might have helped. I know of this effete but wonderful songsmith, a coal porter by day, but he writes the most delightful music by moonlight."

A-squirm in my chair, I say, "They were not wenches—they were shrews. If you want wenches, I can do them, too, and as for the music, Marlowe, why the lute players were on strike."

"Lyre players, Will, and they are back to work."

"Not exactly," Burbage said. "Now they're talking about forming a guild. Can you imagine? Well-a-day, let us move on. Leave the manuscript, Will. We shall be in touch."

All rose, as it seemed the meeting was concluded. Marlowe left to return to the tavern below to see a villain about a duel.

I call to him on his way out. "Oh, Chris, next time you see your friend, the coal porter, tell him to brush up on his Shakespeare." There. The bard has the last word!

Alone together, I say to Burbage, "How can you be a friend to that man?"

"Ah, bard, I can take care of myself, as you know. Yon Marlowe, well-a, I am privy to the rumors surrounding him such as the murder implications, and I have witnessed first-hand his fiery temper. Yet I value his talent. I am, after all, a man of business, and of necessity reliant on multiple sources of advice. You are not the only wordsmith on this isle."

"But, Dick, he is known to be a thief. Observe his finery. How can you believe they were purchased with his own currency? It strains the imagination. And surely if he pilfers raiment, what of plays and poetry as well?"

"Now, Will, you transgress a fine line. There is no evidence presented. As for his lust for fashion, he claims to have patronized the tailors, Brothers by the Brook, with his own treasure. Come to think of it, Will," Burbage now in close examination of me, "you could do with some new threads yourself; presentation and image is important for a man of the stage."

"So be it, Richard. You have made your point, as have I, and momentarily I must take my leave. Yet, pray keep Christopher Marlowe in close proximity. He has a lean and hungry look, that which befits a blackguard."

At the tavern's door, a sallow-faced and spare-looking man garbed totally in black sheep's wool brushes against me while entering the establishment. He is known to Burbage. *By the hounds of Saint Dominic, is there anyone in London that Burbage does not know?* "Why, Donne. Tarry here a moment. There's someone I would like you to meet." Could it be that he was seizing on the chance encounter to move away from the contentious discussion over Marlowe?

The stranger came to a halt and stood erect, aiming a piercing gaze into my eyes while the balance of his face remained mute, frozen, and expressionless. Dick was making the introduction. "Will Shakespeare, this is Johnny Donne, an up-and-coming poet." We clasp hands, his grip as icy as hoarfrost, and this poet says, "Thine hand in mine 'ensconced, and gentle fingers join as dual souls' choir in song comprehended."

I am at a loss for words, a rarity if truth be outed, and a threat to my livelihood should it occur again. Donne's words were delivered in a cadent and melancholy tone, like the tolling of a church bell, yet Burbage waxed ecstatic upon hearing him. "Such eloquence, Johnny. Come, sit with us, and do tell of your writings." They were at a table and Mistress Jolly was summoned to bring flagons of mead. Again, I was made the very image of a fifth wheel on a wagon in these interchanges. *What do I get from him? Leave your manuscript, Will.*

Donne goes on. "Alas, I am a troubled fellow, somewhere between the renunciation of a dissolute life and an embracement of faith."

Burbage cleared his throat. "Well spoken, Johnny, but your tribulations are not my concern; our mutual interest is in your latest poetry. What have you done, Donne?"

"I'm working away, but I'll offer a preview." The poet was in full recital.

While intertwined flesh do quiver, eyes and minds in poor pursuit
And pale moon casts tenuous ray upon this lovers' haven
Pray wouldst' these hearts endure natur's inconstancy
And outlast realms' fleeting glory.
If that, the very air we breathe canst spur our love
And transcend the dropping of time's steely end.

Burbage turned to me. "What say you, Will?" *Finally, I am being consulted. Perhaps Dick is on to the wiles of these fops.*

"Methinks he is having difficulty ridding himself of dissolution."

Donne took a long pull on his flagon and sneered at my comment.

"And what do you do, good fellow, so sharp with yon wit?"

"I write plays."

"I'd 'ave wagered as much. A guttersnipe's trade. Burbage," Donne addressed him, "as befits your station, I see ye must contract in disparate means of expression, even tho it oft calls for you to wallow in the depravity of a stage play. But then, a man cannot distance himself as an island from the main now, can he?"

With that, Donne drained the last of his mead, executed a solemn bow, and bid us a good day.

"What was he all about, dear Burbage?" I plead.

"I've taken to represent him. He has promised me a series of poems and to read them in the new coffee houses that are springing up in the city. The younger folk will be most attentive: they will fail to understand a word of what he writes, which is the very reason they will deem him to be profound, and why his work will sell. In his strangeness lies his import and my fortune."

"Are you referencing that drivel we just listened to? 'Sblood, I'll grant you a better effort than that."

"Then go forth, Will," he tells me. "There's a growing market for this stuff, verily."

I become pensive. "Verse, you say? Perhaps. It could be a supplement to our other endeavours, and I must admit I did like that line about the island."

Burbage was seeing me out the door. "Ah, bard, forgive me for neglecting to ask the name of the play you are proposing to stage. I will need it for our handbills."

"I call it *Chuck and Diane*, after the thirteen-year old lovers."

Taken aback, he said, "Master Will, thirteen? They are much too young. The theater scribes would brand us a wanton breed."

"I was married at eighteen," I say emphatically.

"Eighteen is not thirteen, and as for Chuck and Diane, why I don't know of any one on this sceptered isle or in Verona, for that matter, by those names. Alas, Will, the play may need revision. Make them at least … fourteen … and then be of good cheer—all is well if it ends well. You do plan a happy conclusion, do you not? This season's audiences have begun to express disenchantment over such ponderous dramas as have been produced recently."

Here I will hold my counsel and forsake revelation of my plan for the time being. In my folio, I have alternative endings for all of the plays, equally joyous and tragic, and any one subject in its employment to the prevailing winds of the theater trade, *viz* what it takes to sell tickets. Thus, I'll tell Dick which is to be used when the time is propitious. Perchance I have him!

The return trip to Stratford was uneventful, the fledgling highwayman nowhere in sight. "Heigh, ho, honey, I'm home," I call out as I open the door.

"What news have ye, husband," Anne inquires. "How about that play about the Prince, Omelet?"

"Prithee, my sweet, the correct title is *Hamlet*, and, no, we did not talk about it."

"I hope you did not suggest that downer about the child lovers," she said, "Will, you know it needs work, and besides, the names are all wrong. Not even Italian. What about calling them 'Rodrigo and Gina'?"

"Perhaps," I respond, "I can be flexible. Dick Burbage made much ado about the names himself, and yet I fail to understand the hurly-burly over someone's name. What's in a name, anyway?" *Hey, that's a clever phrase.* "Now, tell me, wife, did you seek an estimate on our roof?"

"Yes, and it is an issue of to thatch or to patch."

"Is that the question?"

"That is the question."

And it certainly is. I rush to a writing table and draw out quill and ink and hurriedly write down dearest Anne's thoughts, lest they be forgotten. I am neither a lender nor a borrower of words—well, most of the time. Above all, to mine own self I am true. Once a playwright, always a playwright.

The Last Parking Space

The airplane buzzed lazily in the white sky over the coast, almost hanging there as though in a pause mode and undecided where to turn next. An ancient DC-3, unmarked, nicked in the skin, it was today's preferred means of transportation for the White House.

"There, Mr. President, the platform is coming into view now, just off the left-hand side,"Chief of Staff Arthur Vandotti alerted his boss to the emerging scene below. Thad Morgan, the forty-sixth president, shifted in his seat and craned his neck to look at what appeared to be at least a partially burned-out hulk of twisted steel and concrete that seemed to be arranged in a surrealistic position.

"Hey, Art, get Mufti and Derek over here; let 'em look at it," Morgan said. His chairman of the Joint Chiefs, General Mufti Hakeem, and his Energy secretary, Derek (Oil) Wells, rose from their seats and ambled over to the president's window. "See, guys, this one's the last one to do, the final piece. What do ya think?"

"I'd say 'Amen,' Mr. President," Wells said, and cracked a broad grin on an even broader face.

"Been a long time coming, sir," General Hakeem added without any expression, his deep-set dark eyes focused on the platform below, his body, as always, looking tightly coiled as if to pounce at any one or any thing.

"Indeed, gentlemen. Now we'll look forward to the work crews getting that sucker up to speed, and let the good black stuff flow. Then it's all restored, and the job's done—this part anyway." Morgan turned back to Art. "Let's get on, then. Where do we stop? New Orleans?"

Vandotti paused a moment before saying, "Mr.President, I don't think so. We hear there's still the possibility of some resistance in Louisiana, and even though we're unmarked here, they'd pick us up on the approach. No, best to turn north. Maybe to Little Rock—there's enough range to get there. Besides, you always like to visit the Clinton museum, don't you?"

Vandotti smiled, as did the president. "You know me too well, Art. Okay by me."

Resistance in Louisiana? Guess that shouldn't be surprising, and maybe we're not all the way there, after all.

So why was the White House flying around in an unmarked retrofitted DC-3 anyway? What had become of Air Force One?

The end of the war was coming up on its first anniversary. President Thad Morgan had become the beneficiary of peace, perhaps all's fair, given that he had inherited the messy situation in the first place. In any event, it ended on his watch, and he meant to make the most of it when he ran for reelection next year. Could he have avoided the whole thing if he had been in the chair when it began, instead of his predecessor having to deal with it? *We'll never know, but I've got a hunch it wouldn't have made any difference,* he thought; *it's like Lincoln believed, that events often overwhelm men despite all of their efforts to influence them.*

Events that gain momentum until they become unstoppable take on a life force of their own. The unyielding instability in the Middle East was, in hindsight, destined for catastrophe rather than the status quo of nothing but trouble, but something you came to live with. What the social scientists like to call the "tipping point" was the overthrow of the Saudi royal family by the radicals and their immediate enactment of a policy for selling oil—in reality apportioning the oil—only to those who were deemed to be sympathetic to them. The United States was at the bottom of that short list: the nation didn't have to waste its breath seeking any kind of confirmation. Other neighboring countries followed in close order, most of them already having in place Islamic theocracies, although few had the Saudi resources. Some outliers continued to supply the hated West, because even Islam needed to feed its followers. The Saudi revolution ended any easy oil flow and forced the United States to turn inward for its energy needs. Since the country had never been able to climb down from a nearly 60 percent reliance on imported oil, the Mideast cutoff would prove to very painful, for certain. There was hardly any oil to be had east of the European landfall.

The southern fields, inground and offshore, were the principal source for the needs of the United States, along with expanded production out of Alaska. Moreover, the dwindling group of the nation's friends who were net exporters—Norway and Scotland—took up some of the slack. Still, as time went on, the supply-demand relationship put continuing stress on the energy situation, and, despite the maturation of technologies such as hybrid cars that were helpful, the voracious needs remained. The southern fields were depleting in a meaningful way: some geologists predicted a run-out within fifteen years at the rates of extraction that were forecast.

The state of Texas elected a governor whose primary campaign issue was the preservation of energy resources for Texans. Houston Oakes, heretofore little known outside of his hometown of New Braunfels, where he was the collector of taxes, was voted in in a landslide. Within one year of his term in office, he proposed secession for Texas and put it up for a referendum. It carried with an 80 percent majority. In the next four months, similar actions took place in Oklahoma and Louisiana. There was talk of a confederation among the states, and when Mississippi and Alabama wanted in, the Gulf Nation was born. The GN then adopted a self-sufficiency policy for the development and consumption of its oil supplies, with any excess left over to be sold to the highest bidders among the states (now down to forty-seven, what with the secession and the prior years' acceptance of Puerto Rico and Israel into the union). Since the GN was expected to cease to be a net exporter after the next two years, the policy would become moot. The United States, more starved for oil than at any time in its history, could look only to Alaska, Mexico, the North Sea, and its strategic reserve for its needs.

President Megan Sandra Munro was ready to act as soon as GN came into being, and its attitudes surfaced. She believed GN had blundered badly in its energy policy because it left the United States with no alternative, no room for negotiation even if the atmosphere had been conducive thereto—which it was not. Had GN offered up any kind of solution toward its neighbor, it might have forestalled action, bought time, made use of the recipe of delaying tactics that adversaries often find attractive.

As she convened her Cabinet, she made her opening statement brief. "Ladies and gentlemen, I'll offer a cordial good morning to you all, despite the fact that this morning is anything but. The good news is that we all know what we are here to do, so you will all be free for your lunch appointments. I will seek a unanimous support for national policy and with that proceed to carry out the tactical actions that will flow from it. Are we all clear?"

The secretaries, each in a politically correct aura of somber or somberer, all nodded in the affirmative.

"Then, let us proceed," the president continued. "I propose that we go to our Congress with a resolution seeking a state of war between the United States and this so-called Gulf Nation, which I prefer to term breakaway states, or BS. I will, of course make the presentation to a joint session, and ..." She paused, surveyed her audience, focused on Vice President Thad Morgan, and went on. "Mr. Vice President, I want you to accompany me to the Hill. We will go there no later than tomorrow—provided that we are all as one here."

The grimmest of smiles crossed her resolute face. "Is there any discussion?" Munro surveyed the locked-in expressions seated around the well-varnished oval table. One hand went up in a boltlike move. "Ah, Camille, I knew you would not disappoint me. Ask away, Madam Secretary," said the president, having recognized the dashing Treasury secretary, Camille Gates.

"Well, Madam President," Secretary Gates spoke up in her trademark singsong tone, "I am certain as to our outcome here today, but I see that General Hakeem is at your right hand, and I'm wondering whether he might wish to weigh in on our capacity to carry out our campaign to a swift and successful conclusion." The president made the merest of body shifts in the direction of the general while maintaining a steely gaze at her Treasury secretary, all designed to elicit a terse response to the question.

The general, picking up on the situation, turned to Treasury and said "No."

"All right, then," Munro went on, "let's not waste one another's time. Are we okay with this?" Hearing no dissent, no sound of any kind, she rose and thanked the Cabinet for its support and declared the meeting adjourned.

The resolution passed without any argument whatsoever in front of a wildly enthusiastic Congress, replete with flag-waving, shouts of "Amen," stomping feet, calls of "you go, girl" from the California legislators and a chorus of "never again" from the (for now) forty-seventh state, Israel. President Munro had her marching orders. The declaration was made to the GN and the United States began a massive mobilization organized by General Hakeem.

While the opposing sides were preparing for conflict, an eerie and tense calm overcame Washington and, for that matter, the rest of the nation. Everyone was waiting for the proverbial shoe to drop, yet silently wishing something would occur to cause the whole mess to go away. Then something did happen, but it was not on anyone's radar screen, even that of the most devout Monday-morning liar.

Two weeks after the fateful Cabinet meeting at which the declaration was approved, Treasury Secretary Gates was being interviewed by a veteran White House reporter for the Washington Post, ostensibly on the subject of fiscal policy in the wake of impending war. As the interview was winding down, Gates said, "You know, Eloise, I must tell you that although I support our actions wholeheartedly, I have issues with this president." Eloise Drake lifted her head from her notebook, thrust her glasses on top of her auburn brush-cut, and bade the secretary to go on, asking if what was coming were to be on or off the record.

"You know me, Eloise, if it's off the record, I won't do the interview. Look, she—the president—dissed me, that's a fact, in front of the full Cabinet. I was the only secretary showing enough concern to seek an analysis as to our preparedness, and she turned immediately to the general, Hakeem, with a subtle but definite cue to offer a one-word answer according to her wishes. I consider that to be an affront and let it go at the time. What else could I do? But I haven't forgotten it. If you ask me, she is an arrogant—"

"I have not asked you, secretary, but I … have come to accept that your relationship with the president has always been … ah … frosty," Drake said, "so what can I print?"

"Whatever you wish," Gates said while rising from her desk chair to declare the interview at an end.

Camille Gates, ex-supermodel cum-investment manager, waltzed into the Treasury post in a flourish of money and with the recommendation of Megan Munro's father, Brian Munro, the former governor of Ohio, when the administration's first choice turned out to have several numbered accounts in Swiss banks that represented accumulations of fees skimmed from the investment firm that he had led for twelve years. Gates was deemed to be "clean," from a money point of view, but she brought to Washington baggage of another sort. She wallowed in the glow of press conferences, interviews, and guest appearances on talk shows, all fully understandable, given her combination of brains, beauty, and wealth, but it was of a dimension that continually seemed to upstage the president. It was an unmanageable situation, and the less-than-glamorous President Munro had already been on the verge of asking her Treasury secretary to resign, and was stopped cold in her tracks only when she learned that her father had been carrying on a love affair with the woman for the last three years. So she lived with it, chafing all the while.

Nonetheless, when this latest interview with the secretary in the Post hit the newsstands, the president, forever feisty, blew up in outrage and called for Chief of Staff Vandotti—to vent, if nothing else. "Arthur," she howled as the chief stood at her desk at modified parade rest, "what am I to do about this bitch? We're off to war, and here she is fighting with me and undermining my command in full audience of the Cabinet and the whole nation, for that matter. Know your enemy, goddamit."

Vandotti had been privy to some of the gathering tension between the two, but never at such a screeching level. He sought to lighten the atmosphere somewhat with a comment he would later regret. "Well, Madam President," he began, "I suppose you could settle your differences by challenging her to a duel."

Munro stared at him, boring in with wide sky-blue eyes. "Why, Arthur, how novel. I can always look to you for creativity, can't I?"

"I was only trying to defuse things," Vandotti pleaded. "You wouldn't seriously think I was … uh … being serious."

"Try me," she answered.

For the next week, the media was full of the unfolding story of the blood-feud between the president and her Treasury secretary. War-related news was relegated to the inside pages of newspapers and, for the TV commentators it averaged item number four, with the first three being takes on the Washington dustup.

"I won't recant my statements!" vowed Camille Gates.

"Treasury Secretary On A Slippery Slope, White House Says"

Arthur Vandotti ran around trying to mediate the quarrel by talking to the two women, but to little avail. Then, on an afternoon show hosted by the daughter of Oprah Winfrey, Camille Gates said that she was insulted on a national basis and demanded an apology from the president. Upon hearing that, Megan Munro commented to her chief of staff that she had had enough; no apology would be forthcoming because no personal attack had occurred, it was all in the secretary's mind, and so forth. "And Arthur, if she wants to come out, you go over and tell her so. I'm ready to settle our differences once and for all."

"Madam President, you can't be serious," Vandotti said, realizing the implications of what he had just heard. Munro smiled, looked his way, and offered that the remark he'd just used was a favorite quote of John McEnroe's. "Very appropriate, Arthur, so go ahead and make the arrangements."

So it came to pass that a duel was scheduled, the first major one since the days of Burr and Hamilton, between these two bitter adversaries. Secrecy was the order of the day, but it was a ludicrous hope in the era of everyone knowing everything before anyone else knew it. Gates favored a return to Weehawken, New Jersey, for historical reasons, but she subsequently learned that the site was now occupied by three competing Starbucks' cafes and was thus unavailable. Vandotti heard an offhand idea from someone in the West Wing who, recalling the president's long-standing love of paintball, suggested a paintball duel in the woods surrounding Camp David. It was readily accepted by both sides, and the chief of staff was breathing easier, recognizing such a solution to be non-life-threatening and to be a way that might, after it concluded, allow the two to part ways with a minimum of damage to either.

At sunrise, under chill and misty conditions, the two opponents donned camouflage jumpsuits, goggles, and baseball caps, and they loaded up paintball rifles to begin their adventure. They were given the full swath of the terrain, with no witnesses within sight. Even the Secret Service hung back beyond the fields, sipping coffee and otherwise attempting to stay warm in a parking lot. After an hour, with nothing seemingly going on, the Secret Service agents—there were three of them—got fidgety and talked among themselves as to whether they should move into the brush to see if anything was happening. It had been assumed, though not via any formal understanding, that the ridiculous episode would last about a half hour, and then the two would emerge, kiss, and make up, figuratively, anyway, and go on their respective ways.

As the three men proceeded into the wooded area, they came upon Camille Gates coming their way. She approached them and said, "You can pick her up in there, fellas, about two hundred yards or so," never breaking stride or looking back as she headed rapidly toward the road's end, where a stretch limo was waiting to take her back to her Georgetown house. The SS guys, sensing something afoot that would not be to their liking, quickened their pace and soon enough came upon the supine body of President Megan Munro, her face looking up to the brightening sky, arms akimbo, but in other respects not appearing to be in distress. From a few steps away, she seemed to be at rest, much like a hiker on break before returning to the trail.

"Madam President, are you okay? Can you get up now?" asked the SS leader as they drew closer. When no audible response was forthcoming, they observed for the first time that a paintball was firmly lodged in the president's throat, much like a golf ball in an impossibly plugged lie in a bunker. She made barely perceptible gurgling sounds, but that was the extent of her sound capacity. The paintball was yellow, and the men noticed a growing ring of blue and purple surrounding it, colorful concentric circles having ugly implications. The SS called in backup and medical help, and the president was taken out of the Camp David woods on a gurney, placed in an ambulance and driven to an emergency hospital facility in the basement of the White House. Arthur Vandotti was informed of the situation. He cleared Munro's schedule for the remainder of the day and swore the Secret Service and anyone else in attendance to secrecy. “We’re going to tell the media that the president has decided to take a couple of well-earned days off at a location of her choosing before grappling with the critical issues facing our nation,” he said to no one in particular.

The story could not hold. Within hours, Press Secretary Jack Helms was onto Vandotti, demanding to know where President Munro was. “Arthur, as usual, I’ve got a pack of hungry wolves in the briefing room not buying a word of this. You know as well as I that our national security meeting was damned important; no way can she take off unannounced. So what gives, my friend?”

It was late afternoon, more than eight hours after the fight had ended. Vandotti saw no choice other than to let Helms in on the events that had unfolded. “You’re not shitting me, Arthur?” Helms asked as he listened to the chief’s presentation. Vandotti nodded so as to indicate “I’m not. How could I fabricate something so bizarre?” in a resigned manner. “Okay then,” Helms said, “I’ll stay with the away-for-a-short-time story, but can I tell them she’ll be back at her desk tomorrow? That should keep them at bay.”

“Sure, tell ’em that,” the chief of staff responded.

In fact, Vandotti was checking in on the president’s condition every hour. As evening fell, he once again descended to the basement facility where he conferred with her doctors. Through the day, her vital signs had been deteriorating, and the trend had yet to be reversed. “Look, Arthur,” the surgeon general was telling him in the hallway, ‘I don’t think this is very good at all. As we found hours ago, not only did this paintball crush her vocal chords upon impact, as it lodged in her throat it gave off a deadly toxin that started to spread throughout the body. We are doing all we can to stabilize her and treat her for a poison that has thus far proved to be elusive to control. So, I am sorry to say there is no progress to report.”

Vandotti looked away for a moment and then turned back to the doctor, asking if the culprit paintball had, in fact, been removed, and if it was being sent to a forensic lab for testing. “Yes and no,” the surgeon general answered. “I know you don’t want any of this to get out … yet … so we’re still holding the … uh … missile in the room, but actually I don’t believe there is anything but loaded paint in and around it. I find it hard to accept that she went out there leaving such a vital part of her body exposed; still, it took one lucky shot in a million to have had this occur, and there are people who can have a lethal reaction to the introduction of chemicals, such as are found in paint, to their bodies. She may be one of them.”

For once, Vandotti was speechless; there were no further questions for the physician. He went on to keep an all-night vigil at the White House but was careful to stay out of sight of anyone who might be prowling the halls. Awakened from a fitful sleep at 4:30 a.m. by the jingle of his cell, it was the SG on the line informing him that despite the efforts of the medical team, President Munro had died some ten minutes previous.

Paintball? Who the hell would believe the story? And, even if you got past that one, who the hell would believe that Gates had not used a poisoned bullet, like the darts of some Brazilian savage dipped in a kind of deadly elixir, in her passion to exact revenge? Hell, maybe she did, after all, but the evidence was not there, and it was unlikely to get there. Better get with Helms so that a story can be fashioned.

The news broke simultaneously with the actions required in Washington to ensure the orderly transfer of power. The Cabinet met in emergency session. The chief justice administered the oath of office to Vice President Thad Morgan. Congressional leaders were summoned to the Oval Office to learn of the tragic events, so that they could spread the word among their fellow legislators. Everything was being reported around the clock by all forms of media.

As for (soon to be former) Secretary Gates, she was nowhere to be found. Ex-Governor of Ohio Brian Munro had also slipped away, and it was thought by all that it was outrageous that he would be incommunicado in the wake of his daughter's death, but it would be a long time before any connection between the two lovers was made.

Thad Morgan addressed the nation and promised to do his best. To some it seemed like a scene out of *Dave*. He spoke with effusive praise for his predecessor and said that he would carry out her programs. The speech took all of four minutes. The following day, Arthur Vandotti offered up his resignation, but President Morgan rejected it, saying, "Arthur, if there's anyone around here I need, it's you. Who else is going to show me around? You know, vice presidents don't get over here very often. So, I'm telling you, don't even try to leave the building."

He was lucky. The war against Gulf Nation, or the BS, as it was referred to in Washington, had been under way now for several weeks and was going well. The Air Force had kept up a campaign of pinpoint strikes on the GN's energy sources on the ground and in the Gulf of Mexico, interdicting the movement of its oil supplies. The Texas Air National Guard proved no match for the USAF, and over the course of two days, substantially all of Texas's planes were destroyed on the ground with precision bombs. The GN also had no Navy except for some retrofitted offshore gambling steamboats and was ultimately isolated by a blockade of its ports by the U.S. Navy. There was no movement of army and marines to take any of the GN's territory, on General Hakeem's theory that "if we box 'em in, cut off their oil, and close off access to the sea, they'll get the message." Still, the GN, pride at stake, did not capitulate right away. Their president, Houston Oakes, looked south to Mexico for resources and political support, trying to come across as a neighbor and with a veiled threat that this thing could spill over the border, but the Mexicans weren't buying it, claiming that they too remembered the Alamo. The GN began to search elsewhere for help and found it in Saudi Arabia, of all places. Based on their hatred for the United States and Texas, the Saudis flipped a riyal, decided that a North American civil war was, God willing, to their best interests, and offered to come to the assistance of GN for replenishment of lost oil—at a tidy markup, of course—if some practical way could be found to deliver it. A handful of tankers left Saudi ports, bound for the Houston ship channel, but when two of them were sunk by nuclear missiles from submarines, the others turned back home.

The GN even approached Cuba for help in countering the sea quarantine, but Fidel Castro, now in his sixtieth year of rule (if, indeed, it was truly him), politely begged off, saying he was no longer in "that business." The GN hunkered down for a protracted siege, living off what resources were in place; a tense stalemate emerged. In the end, two factors came together to close it out. First, there was intramural squabbling among the GN states. Their relationships, never particularly firm to start with, frayed when the governor of Louisiana, Napoleon Pierre, decided to go his own way and thought he could sell the place back to France and once again be part of a greater Gallic empire. The French, intrigued with the proposal, made numerous field trips to consider the deal. They were impressed with the chefs in the Vieux Carre, the gambling boats in the river, and the semitropical atmosphere along the bayou, appealing to their love of ennui and je ne sais pas quoi. At the end of the day though, France, strangely enough the wealthiest nation on earth, took a pass and bought Canada instead for about the same value Pierre had put on Louisiana.

But what really brought the GN to the table was a force of nature. A searing drought enveloped the entire Sunbelt for upwards of a year, and it played into the U.S.'s hand, as it was able to cut off a considerable amount of GN's water, which was dependent on hydro facilities to the west. Thus, it was a fundamental tradeoff of oil for water, although neither side would admit to that as the basis of settlement. President Morgan, emboldened to appear conciliatory, allowed the states back into the union under a general amnesty, provided their leadership under the GN was ousted and each state held new elections. The only condition imposed on the various candidates was their fealty to union; otherwise, all the essentials of southern politics were fair game, including payoffs, gravestone head-counting, multiple voting and an occasional assassination. Other than some lingering opposition in Louisiana, it all came off, although there remained sour feelings among all parties for some time.

Afterwards, the work of rebuilding what had been destroyed commenced. Once again generous, Morgan and his administration worked out a sharing of the costs between the rebel states and the federal government. By now, he was being labeled a wimp and an appeaser by many in the greater USA, especially a now-militant group of liberals from the northeastern establishment that once and for all wanted to tame Texas and saw its golden moment tarnish. In other quarters, he was held in high disrespect by Sunbelt reactionaries, some of whom saw the war's end as a mere temporary truce in what would turn out to be a long-range conflict. For in fact, the country's total energy situation had not changed at all.

Two

"We'll be landing in Little Rock in another fifteen minutes, Mr. President," Vandotti said to Thad Morgan, having conferred with the flight deck, "and will you be wanting to visit the Clinton Library? We will have some time to spare before refueling and flying back to DC."

Morgan looked … wistfully … at his chief and asked, "Do you think, Arthur, the man himself would break bread with us, that is, if he's in town?"

Anticipating his boss's question—de rigueur for an effective chief—Vandotti told him that no, he had checked and the ex-president was, in fact, on a speaking tour in Las Vegas, but that the library would remain open for as long as he might care to stay. He was quick to add that the leg back to Washington would run over four hours, the speed of the old DC-3 being hardly half of what the precursor Air Force One 797 had been. It was only when the war got under way that the White House opted to ground the racy jet plane—after being fired on twice—-for an unidentified antique craft that was lucky to poke along at three hundred mph. Believing that such a deception would remain undiscovered was the kind of self-delusion given over only to presidents and their staff, but it worked to some extent because the plane never came to be in harm's way. After peace broke out, one of the exiled GN leaders allowed that they knew about it but agreed that it was too pathetic to bother with. Morgan continued to fly in it because he liked the old-fashioned two-by-two plush seating, but he told the press it represented his gesture of national sacrifice.

Having paid his respects in Little Rock and gushed to the library's staff as well as his traveling companions that he had once again come away recharged with inspiration, the president once more boarded the DC-3 for the flight home. "Did you get enough of the saxophone, sir," General Hakeem asked him as they were airborne. "Never get enough of it, Mufti. And the Elvis section, too. Do you know he had Fleetwood Mac perform at his first inaugural?"

"No, Mr. President, I did not," Hakeem responded. As Arthur Vandotti moved to join in the conversation, Morgan said, "Well, Mufti, you should study up on your American history. You may have more time, now that hostilities are over."

He turned to his chief. "Yes, Arthur, sit across from us. What is it?"

"I thought, sir, we might go over tomorrow's agenda, while we have some free time."

The president smiled. "No bedtime for Bonzo, then. Okay, let's go over what we have." Vandotti opened his notebook and reeled off a number of ceremonial events—a reception for a team of dwarfs who had won a national cheerleading competition, Ms. Monica Lewinsky about an NEA grant for her handbag museum that mysteriously has become stalled, and Senator Trump from New York concerning his proposal on the sale-leaseback of the Washington Monument.

"Whew, a heavy day. Jeez, Arthur, can't you take it easy on me? Do I dare ask if there's anything else?" Vandotti, furrowing his thick black brows, said, "Just one more so far, sir. The Transportation secretary needs to see you."

Morgan seemed puzzled. "Toshi? What does he want?"

"It's about the parking, Mr. President. He says this time it's very serious."

Morgan leaned back in his seat. "Here we go again," he said with a faint sigh.

During the energy supply crisis that had enveloped the nation, Americans continued to travel the way they had always traveled, in cars and derivative vehicles. The evolution of hybrids and the high cost of fuel did little to alter old habits; at best, such trends held back the degree of the problem. There was some anecdotal evidence that longer car trips were being curtailed, but that merely resulted in an uptick in local driving. Global car manufacturers went on to supply whatever they perceived the market would demand. Simply put, there were too many cars. Even while the war was on, the Morgan administration had expressed concern over the pincers of short gasoline supply and the steady growth in vehicles to consume it. In addition, related issues came into focus. The condition of U.S. roads seemed to deteriorate daily, despite huge budgets for repairs and construction. It all only served to exasperate the public even more. Slow going everywhere, or so it seemed.

Within the last year, another developing problem had emerged; parking was increasingly hard to come by. Now it was painfully evident that there was inadequate room for all of the cars. The administration did what any right-thinking government would do—it formed a committee and empowered it to produce studies at great cost. The committee—it had no other name—was comprised of experts in engineering, geology, physics, hydraulics, equity-fund management, and real estate. It was chaired by a retired psychologist, Dr. Phil McGraw, and was answerable to the secretary of Transportation, Masatoshi Fujiama.

Among other recommendations, the committee proposed that there be a strict quota on the quantity of new automobiles produced. The proposal was adopted by the administration, and it was delegated to the secretary of Transportation to deliver what was, unsurprisingly, a most unpopular decision. The heads of the overseas manufacturers and the chief executive officer of the one remaining domestic car company, CryForGen Motors, sat stony faced at a meeting where they were mandated to cut back production by 40 percent—until further notice.

"Why, it's … it's … un-American," the head of Toyota USA stammered, which about said it all for the group assembled in Fujiama's office. "This is really gonna hurt Japan, and you, above all, should be against that," said Al Spokes, CryFor's president and CEO. Fujiama had said his piece, had little else to add, and was sitting back behind his desk, listening to the onslaught of invective from the automakers. As far as he was concerned, it was a done deal, and he had to push himself to stay awake as, one by one, the businessmen took turns at venting.

Fujiama himself was an interesting case. He was—and this was authenticated in the Guiness Book of World Records—the last remaining survivor of the Japanese Imperial Army in the South Pacific. Discovered by a triathlon biker who had lost her way on the tiny atoll of Kukua, he had rolled out of a cave he had been living in since 1945 with a rusted hand grenade and the cry "Banzai and screw Babe Ruth" before collapsing at the biker's feet. For over sixty years he had lived on and off the island, waiting for the marines to invade once again. The only thing he had to show for his time there was the preservation of the wreckage of a single-engine plane on the northern tip of Kukua that was ultimately proven to be the long-lost plane of Amelia Earhart. When asked about the fate of the airwoman's remains, along with those of her navigator, Fujiama clammed up and reverted to his diatribe against the Babe. Nevertheless, he was brought back to the USA, where he became an instant celebrity, featured on every talk show available. He was held up as a symbol of friends forever after the war and was staked to new clothes, a scholarship to UCLA, and a guest shot on Senator Trump's Megabux Review, where he promptly walked away with the grand prize of $11 million. With little time to lose, now in his eighties, he parlayed his stake and his college degree into a nationwide chain of taxis and limousines, took it public, and on his eighty-fifth birthday was splashed all over the cover of *People* magazine. From there, it was not much of a leap to see him in the Cabinet of the Morgan administration as Transportation secretary. Under the Diversity In Government Act of 2012, it was law that the President's Cabinet must reflect every aspect of American society in terms of gender, religion, age, and ethnic background. Fujiama met every criteria: he was a Japanese-American senior who practiced the B'hai faith. In fact, President Morgan tried to claim a one-for-four in appointing him to the Cabinet, but the White House lawyers told him that such would not reflect the spirit of the law. "You mean, then, that I have to retain my Ag secretary?" Thad Morgan asked plaintively of his White House counsel.

'That is correct, Mr. President," came the answer, which was in reference to twelve-year old Harald Soderstrom, a 3-H winner in giant onions from Nebraska and the aforementioned secretary, "the act envisioned the reasonable bands of youth and age being represented, so, yes, you have to keep young Harald. But look on the bright side, he may grow into the job."

The automakers left the meeting bloody and bowed. They threatened to kick the issue upstairs to the White House, and when Fujiama was roused from his doze-off he managed to say to them, "Go ahead, you'll get the same answer. Let them take cabs."

As events turned out, auto production was indeed limited; the American public had become ever more infuriated, and the edict did little, if anything, to alleviate congestion on the roads and the crowding of idle cars into increasingly fewer parking places. Now it was time for the Transportation secretary to meet with the president. They were soon huddled over cups of latte umber at the Starbucks across the street from Pennsylvania Avenue. In keeping with the Executive Frugality Act of 2014, the Oval Office had been turned into a fee-based museum on daily White House tours, and the president was directed to conduct his business in local coffee shops and fast-food restaurants: a by-product of the act was to ensure that the chief executive got out of the house more often—it was thought to be good to mingle.

"Well, Toshi," Morgan said, "what is so urgent that it couldn't wait?"

Fujiama removed his Santo Domingo Yanquis cap and squinted at the president. "It finally happened, boss."

"What happened, Toshi? I don't have all day. The latte is getting cold."

Fujiama was the only Cabinet member allowed to refer to Morgan as "boss" without reprimand. He said, "The parking is, how you say—pfft—gone, boss, no more."

Morgan slumped in his cane chair. He peppered his secretary with questions, to which he received terse answers.

"Could we build more?"

"No room."

"Up? Basement garages?"

"No, everything is taken. At least for the foreseeable future."

The problem had actually been building for some time. Along with the reductions in auto production had come additional requirements for parking privileges. Only licensed drivers had been granted parking stickers. Then, as spaces continued to constrict, no cars were allowed to be sold unless parking rights transfers accompanied them. Thus, autos and parking were joined; it was illegal to sell parking stickers by themselves. Of course, this did little to avert a booming black market in parking permits. As yet, government policies had failed to ease the situation. Fujiama reviewed recent events with the president. "Here's one, boss. A week ago, in Atlanta, a man suffering a heart attack died on the way to a hospital because there was no room in the parking lot."

"So," Morgan replied, "why didn't he just get a drop-off at emergency?"

"Too big a line. Stretched all the way to the GeorgiaDome. They were all looking for parking. The Falcons game was on that day. The lots for employees were the closest, and they take up 90 percent of the room. The sickos—ah—patients and their ilk have to fight for what's left. Then, you know about the steep rise in car thefts?"

The president effected a blank expression. Evidently he did not know about it, so the secretary went on to tell him that car thefts had been rising for the last several months on a nationwide basis, the principal cause of which was believed to be the attached parking rights. The insurance companies were starting to become alarmed.

"How about you, Toshi? Where are you able to park these days?" the president asked.

Fujiama broke into a smile, the first of the day. "Oh, me, boss, not to worry. I take cabs everywhere since you slashed my department's budget last year, and I had to turn in my limo. Actually, in the current circumstance it's much better for me. Besides, I still own the cab company."

"Oh."

"So what do you think we should do?" Fujiama asked the president.

Morgan lifted from his latte and answered, "What do I think, Toshi? Why, I think you and I ought to leave town, maybe go down to Vegas, put in to one of Wynn's hotels, find some girls. What d'ya say?"

The secretary wore a broad grin, "Oowee, boss, like cool. Can we take the DC-3?"

"Absolutely, Mr. Secretary. I still have first dibs on it. The Pecking Order Act of 2013 left this office with the first hour for phone-in reservations. But do you think you're up to it? You look pretty tired to me."

Fujiama exclaimed, "Let's give it a shot. Banzai again!" Then, returning to the issue on the table, he said to the president, "Look, about this parking problem, I have an idea. Here's what maybe we could do ..."

Thad Morgan then listened to his secretary and from there took his ideas to his next Cabinet meeting, where a plan was approved. On the Wednesday next, President Morgan would address the nation about an "urgent matter of concern to all."

The venue was Madison Square Garden, the time frame being an hour before the scheduled WNBA game. Masatoshi Fujiama would share the podium with the president. At the appointed time, network cameras ablaze, the two men mounted the stage, the president decked out in NASCAR driver's garb, the secretary wearing his Yanquis cap but otherwise looking sedate in a grey pinstripe suit.

"My fellow Americans," Morgan intoned, "I come into your homes tonight with—as the late, great Lyndon Johnson used to say—a heavy heart, for we are facing a matter of the utmost urgency, which is the absolute lack of any additional parking to be found in this great land of ours, amber waves of grain notwithstanding."

"Looking good so far, boss," Fujiama whispered encouragement to the president.

Morgan glanced back quickly at his secretary. "Toshi," he whispered, "don't call me boss in public; here I'm Mr. President. And stand at attention, remove that cap—oh, never mind ..." He continued with the speech, "And we are here to lay out certain actions that must be taken to stabilize the situation and, ultimately, we believe, to improve it. First, I am ordering a temporary stoppage to all automobile production and importation, including any vehicles that might be through the various lines of production and destined for dealers' lots. Second, we have found that the previous system of stickers has not worked effectively. There has been a disturbing increase in car theft across the nation which is directly linked to the availability of parking privileges. Therefore, we will institute forthwith a program to imbed microchips in licensed drivers—ah, those who already have the right to park. The risk will thus reside with the driver, rather than with the car, which, I am pleased to say, will meet with the unanimous approval of all insurance companies. Finally, we remain committed to increasing parking capacity, although this will take some time. Among the measures under consideration are the narrowing of handicapped spaces—a special interest group having surplus room—the dismantling of bike racks, wherever they may be, and the opening up of federal properties such as national parks to park-and-ride facilities. Now, I realize that many of you do not live near the parks, but we are looking into shuttle bus service between the proposed lots and whatever your destination might be. For example, it is only four hours from Yosemite to downtown Oakland and, by golly, there's a lot of land at Yosemite. Besides, it'll do you good to get out of your cars and into nature a little more often."

Morgan turned to Fujiama and asked, "Are you ready, Mr. Secretary?" The secretary nodded in the affirmative. Once more facing his television audience, the president continued, "My fellow citizens, we feel your anxiety, and we think a bit of good will might be constructive, so to that end the Transportation secretary has developed an idea to raffle off the last available parking space and the rights to own a new car to one lucky American. So, here we go. Drum roll, please." Fujiama, flanked by two former Rockettes, wheeled out a massive glass bowl filled to the brim with folded index cards.

"Now, Toshi," Morgan directed, whereupon the secretary reached into the bowl with eyes shut, this after grazing the right breast of one of the Rockettes, for which he muttered an apology in Japanese, and plucked forth one of the cards and handed it to the president. Morgan looked at the card, then returned to the cameras and jubilantly announced that the last parking space would be going to Ms. Annabelle Dortmunder of New York City. He then closed his address with the traditional blessing and hurried from the podium in a violent sweat brought on by the heat of the video lighting and the entry of the WNBA players, as game time was at hand. Fujiama followed after the president, and they were soon joined by Arthur Vandotti. "So that was your solution, Thad?" Vandotti was incredulous. "A goddam parking privilege—for one person? What friggin' good could that possibly do?"

"Hey, Arthur, lighten up. We're just trying to have a little fun with it, aren't we, Toshi?" Morgan answered while looking at the secretary. "Hell, if goes over, we'll do another each month as spots become available, or if they become available."

"Yeah, it'll go over, as likely as an ant jumping over the Washington Monument," Vandotti said. "Just wait'll you see the *Post* tomorrow."

"Are you done for now, Arthur?"

"I guess."

"Good. Because I want to invite this … what's her name—"

"Dortmunder!" Toshi chimed in gleefully. "Maybe an ally."

"Right, Helga Dortmunder," Morgan said. "I want her invited to the Oval Office, and then one of those car honchos with the keys to whatever she's getting from them; we'll make a big presentation out of this. People will feel good. Trust me, Arthur, I know people, just the way Clinton did. You follow?"

Three

The bus stopped at the corner of Queens Boulevard and Sixty-fifth Road. All eight passengers departed into the blue gloom of a humid November evening, including a tall, somewhat stooped woman of indeterminate age concealed under a wraparound grey woolen coat and scarf worn in the old New York babushka style. Rangy and fast on her feet, Annabelle Dortmunder traversed the beckoning six city blocks she knew so well in her usual pedestrian pattern, having come from teaching an evening class entitled "English for Jihadis" at PS 102. *How do I reach them*, was the thought she kept carrying along, although in last week's sessions she believed a sort of breakthrough may have occurred. Borrowing from an old World War II song, she had the class—all male, of course—sing, in unison, "God is great and pass the ammunition," with improving diction and enthusiasm. But enough of that; she was hungry and anxious for home and reheated pizza. One block in front of her apartment building she saw the scene of a traffic accident, or so it seemed, with yellow police tape cordoning off a section of the street, three cop cars parked at angles, sirens blaring, and lights whirring around. As she approached, Annabelle recognized the officer. "Good evening, Sergeant Mulroon. Whatever has happened here?" she asked the beefy cop plunked squarely within the scene.

"Oh, hello, Ms. D," said the officer, now looking up from his pocket-sized ring notepad to greet her in a neighborly manner. "Not to worry, just a little flap over a parking space, smashed windshield with a crowbar, but we got it under control. Too bad; there's more of this all the time, it seems. I'd rather go back to drug busts."

Determining it to be none of her business, she hurried on to the doorstep, saying "Thanks anyhow, Sergeant, and you take care now." Mulroon called after her as she opened the front door, "Oh, and congratulations, Ms. D. We all heard the news before we got the call at the station house." She glanced back, puzzled. She thought, now what in the world have I done to be congratulated for; lord knows I don't even buy lottery tickets, so there was nothing to win. Once inside her one-bedroom apartment, Annabelle flicked on the hall light and, before turning on her oven to preheat for three pizza slices, stopped to check her answering machine, a daily ritual. The answering machine was one of a handful of concessions she had made to current technology. "You have one message," the box was singing out. She pushed "play" and listened to an atonal speaker:

This call is for Ms. Annabelle Dortmunder. This is the office of the president calling to inform you that you have been selected by lottery to have the last remaining parking privilege in the country. This is a great honor, and President Morgan himself wishes to invite you to the White House to make a formal presentation to you. Please call the following number—1-800-us-tunes—and ask for Andy so that the arrangements can be made. We look forward to hearing from you as soon as possible, day or night, because operators stand by around the clock. On behalf of your federal government, it is my pleasure to extend our heartiest congratulations to you.

Crank calls, that's all I ever get, she thought. *Shit, it might have been one of the jihadis, but none of'em was smart enough. I don't even know why I listened to the whole thing*. The aroma of overdone pizza wafted through her dimly lit hallway, and she hurried into the kitchen.

It was only the following day—after the morning TV shows, and the news reports on AM radio, which Annabelle put up with in between the programs featuring the most strident talk show clerics, which she never missed—that she became convinced something was up, when they all reported the result of the drawing for the last parking spot (as it was now dubbed) and named her. *Me! Hot damn*, she thought, *guess I'd better call Andy*. And so she did, Andy being code for something or other, because all she wound up doing was speaking to a machine and punching up number one on the phone in response to the menu, push one for English, two for Spanish, three for Hebrew, four for Arabic, and so on, and all of it resulting in a meeting at the White House for Friday at 3:00 p.m.

Annabelle Dortmunder, retired school teacher, dressed in a new royal blue boucle suit purchased the previous day at Penney, was being escorted through the chambers of the White House to meet with Thad Morgan, the nation's president, in the Oval Office. "Ah, there you are, Hel—uh, Annabelle, may I call you Annabelle? We're all informal here these days, aren't we?" Morgan said with a broad grin as he rose from behind the presidential desk as she entered the room. "Now don't be intimidated by all the cameras and the folderol, my dear, and let me introduce you around." He proceeded to introduce her to the office stand-ups, which were Vandotti, Toshi Fujiama (whose resignation as Transportation secretary was fresh on Morgan's desk that very morning) and Al Spokes, of CryForGen, whose role in the play was to present Ms. Dortmunder with the keys to a previously owned UGRY four-door sedan (the company having ceased production of said model some eighteen months prior), deemed a suitable car for the honoree to be driving. After the obligatory photo ops, they settled down to business. "Well, now, Ms. Dortmunder, what's the first driving you'll be doing with your car?" asked Morgan, still all smiles as he played talk show host.

"Oh, go to the mall, I guess," she answered, and then, surveying the conferees and the assorted hangers-on around the room, added, "My, you're all so young. Except for him—" She was referring to Fujiama.

"Flattery will get you everywhere!" the president responded, and all those assembled laughed heartily. "What, no Disney World for you?" More peals of laughter.

"When can I get my car?" She stole a glance at her watch as if she had an appointment pending.

"Toshi, Al, let's not keep the lady waiting," Morgan said. Spokes fished in his pocket for the keys to the UGRY and presented them to Annabelle with a flourish, and, as if on cue, cameras clicked all around. Annabelle, sensing closure to the meeting, car keys firmly clutched in her arthritic right hand, rose from the golden sateen sofa on which she was seated. The president said, "Ah, Annabelle, there's just one more formality," and in an imperceptible gesture signaled to Vandotti, who advanced toward her with a large hypodermic needle, "We want you to be the first person in America to own the Individual Parking Molecule, or IPM, as it will come to be known."

Arthur Vandotti plunged the long needle into Annabelle's spare left shoulder in an inelegant way. Eee-ow-eey! Annabelle screamed as she leaped at least a foot off the ground. "You hit my damn bone. Damnation, did you boys have to do that?" she said.

"All for country. God Bless America," the president answered. More cameras clicked.

As they exited the office, Annabelle turned to the president and said, "You know, sonny—ah, Mr. President—I have this feeling we've met sometime in the past. You didn't grow up in New York, did you?"

They were walking briskly through corridors. "Why no, Florida was my boyhood home. Now as you know, nobody from New York could ever become president, or even, as in my case, vice president. But Florida, well, that's a different story, and I'll be elected in my own right next year."

She seemed unimpressed. "Mr. President, indulge an old maid a little. Walk a bit ahead of me, if you would." Morgan, in between amusement and annoyance, complied. "There, that's it now. I see," Annabelle said as she observed the chief executive ambulating, a kind of bobbing gait favoring front foot weight and a slight listing to the left side.

"See what?"

"Your walk. It's very distinctive. You know everyone has an individual walk, a little like fingerprints. And I've seen yours before; I'm sure of it."

They were at the portico, where a car was waiting to escort Annabelle Dortmunder to Reagan Airport for the shuttle back to LaGuardia. All said their good-byes. She refused to shake hands with Vandotti, for fear he harbored yet another needle. The presidential party went inside. On the way back to the Oval Office, Thad Morgan bade his chief walk alongside. "Arthur, stay a few minutes. We need to talk."

Monday morning at ten o'clock sharp and there was Annabelle Dortmunder driving her (newly washed) UGRY into a front-row parking space at the Mall of Long Island. The space itself was bordered with pink ribbon, and overhead were banners announcing the welcoming of Ms. Dortmunder, "America's Parking Sweetheart." A handful of retail executives rushed out to greet her and provide escort to the air-conditioned reaches of the shopping complex. "My, oh my, I haven't been here in a coon's age," she remarked as she toured the glittering storefronts. "Well, we're here to make your shopping day a memorable experience," the center's general manager said. "Where would you like to go first?"

"I've always favored Penney's," she answered. The Nordstrom store manager, strolling with the group, gagged in an audible fashion. "Penney's, then, it is!"

"Are the towels on sale?"

As they moved along to the store, she noticed—just about everywhere—clusters of people, families in most instances, huddled together outside of the stores. Blankets, laundry bags, and ragged Starbucks coffee cups lay strewn around the little areas that they had seemed to stake out, like squatters in abandoned buildings. Many were calling to her from their encampments. "Hey, Annabelle, good luck, baby." "How's the outside world?" "Did you really get a parking spot?"

"Who are those people, Mr.—ah?"

"Muckenstein, Annabelle. I'm Arnold Muckenstein, and these folks are, well, they are living at our mall. You see, some got caught here when the parking spaces shut down. They were worried that if they left, they might never get back inside, so they stayed."

"But … Why would the mall be that important to them?"

He continued. "Understand that our mall is a most hospitable place to be because there is everything here that anyone would ever want. There are clothing stores featuring fashions for each season. The food court provides a full range of cuisines—fast foods of all ethnic groups, hot dogs, cinnamon buns for breakfast, and on and on. It is a way of life."

"What about money, though? Haven't some of them run out by now?"

"Certainly. However, for those people, we have banks throughout offering personal loans at competitive rates along with credit cards carrying substantial lines for these valued customers, which, of course, are welcome at our retailers. And there are ATM kiosks sprinkled all over the premises—seventy-five in all. I counted them myself one day." The mall manager seemed pleased with the opportunity to educate his guest.

"Then, they have everything they need," she said.

Muckenstein adjusted his hand-sewn regimental tie (Forty-seventh Hussars) and said as sincerely as possible, "Now you get the point, Ms. Dortmunder. The Mall of Long Island constitutes its own economy, a world unto itself able to sustain life indefinitely, and at a high-ticket level, I am happy to report." They were approaching the interior entrance to Penney, where the entire sales staff was massed, poised to greet Annabelle. "Let's go in and buy our brains out!" he exclaimed.

In the days immediately following her mall shopping experience, Annabelle took short trips in her UGRY. Living alone, having no remaining immediate family and in possession of acquaintances rather than friends, she was a woman who had no one close to share her notoriety and good fortune with. It was of little concern to her, since she'd lived the greater part of her life in a solitary way, in which she was fully acclimated. The car trips were a means of escape from the media onslaught that had been cascading upon her. Offers, some firm, some tenuous, for talk-show appearances, calls from reporters, tabloids seeking photo stories (some lost interest when they learned she had no celebrity cellulite to provide), were each in competition for an exclusive or an angle on the Annabelle Dortmunder story. There was particular interest in her reaction to the IMP injection ("painful or not, Annabelle?") so as best to prepare the nation's drivers for the mass inoculations slated to begin momentarily. One afternoon she drove to Jones Beach, sparsely populated in the off-season, but a cafeteria was still open serving chowder and sandwiches. To her delight, she was not recognized and was content to gum down her modest lunch while bundled up in a new faux shearling coat from Penney ("*Tres* stylish, Ms. Dortmunder," the saleswoman said) while watching the ever-present sea gulls flit and swoop around against the day's iron-gray sky.

Evening closing in, and on her way home, not four blocks from her apartment building and waiting for the light to turn green, she was suddenly aware that all the doors of the UGRY (except hers) were pulled open at the same time. She turned around in a kind of spasm to see four people climb into the car and proceed to shut all of its doors. "What the—"

The man now alongside of her, facing straight ahead, poked her firmly in the ribs, the light now green, and commanded, "Drive!"

"Who are you? What do you want?"

He answered her. "I said … just drive. I'll talk for now. Allow me to introduce myself and my family, Ms. Dortmunder. Yes, we know who you are. Doesn't everyone? There now, go up that ramp to the right and get on the LIE westbound," he said, motioning in the direction he was ordering her to take. "Good. Okay, so we are the Stackwold family. I'm Henry, and in the back seat we have my wife Rosalie and our two children, Svetlana and Leonid. Say hello, Rose."

Mrs. Stackwold, flanked by her children, smiled, managed a little wave, and uttered a baby-doll "hi-ya." They were halfway to the westbound entrance to the Queens Midtown Tunnel. "Do you have an E-Z Pass, Ms. Dortmunder?" Stackwold asked. Annabelle concentrated on her driving with trembling hands on the wheel and declined an answer. "Look, this can be nice and easy all around if you cooperate, Ms. Dortmunder … uh … Annabelle. I hope we can call you by your first name. Friendly will be better than not, since we expect to be together for a while," he went on.

Through the tunnel and across Manhattan on 34th Street, Stackwold directed Annabelle to take the Lincoln Tunnel and proceed south on the New Jersey Turnpike. "Where are we going *together*, Mr. Stackwold?" she asked in a frozen tone.

"Please, call me Henry." Twisting to the rear, he said "Children, where are we going?"

They responded in harmony. "To Disney World!"

It turned out that the Stackwold family had carved out vacation time three weeks prior for a trip to the mecca in Orlando. Having packed up and flown down on InkJet Air (offering seats for $7.95 apiece, plus another thirty dollars in taxes and fees) they arrived only to learn at the car rental counter that their reservation had become null and void, there being no cars available because the rental companies were unable ("temporarily," the agent explained in a cheery voice) to provide customers with parking privileges.

"And that's when Dad shot the counter agent," Leonid blurted out.

"In a manner of speaking," Henry said, addressing Annabelle. "It was merely a stun gun. Nonetheless, I was detained overnight and only released because of the amnesty provisions of the Justifiable Rage Act of 2012. The following day we retuned to New York. Needless to say, we were heartbroken by the turn of events. You only had to look at the children's faces to understand the true depths that sorrow can sink to. Then we watched the television speech of President Morgan and learned that you had won the parking drawing. Luckily for the Stackwolds, we are virtually neighbors, so it was only a matter of time before we connected with you."

She said, "You expect me to drive to Orlando?"

Rosalie Stackwold chimed in, "We'll all share the tolls, won't we, Henry?"

"Of course, my dear. We want everyone to enjoy the vacation."

They stopped for the night at a motel outside of Norfolk. The next day, Henry decided as a precautionary measure to have the UGRY repainted, should anyone be on the lookout for the Dortmunder car. They located a six-hour paint shop in an industrial section of the city, and by late afternoon the flint-grey car had become cobalt blue. To complete the transformation, he exchanged Annabelle's New York license plates for a pair of South Carolina tags he'd been saving for this very occasion. Anyone looking for Annabelle's car would be sorely frustrated.

Cruising south on I-95, the Stackwold children sang a relentless chorus of "are we there yet?", more loudly when their parents were in front and Annabelle was trying to sleep.

Standing in front of a recently sponged vinyl table at McDonald's, Arthur Vandotti saw that President Thad Morgan was preoccupied with affixing his veto on a bill that would have closed down the Open Poppy Skies program. "Can't do this; it would not be prudent," Morgan muttered. "It's the whole of the Afghan gross domestic product. How can we put these loyal allies out of business? Yes, Arthur?" He was looking up now.

"Annabelle Dortmunder has gone missing, boss," Vandotti said, his voice rushed and anxious.

"What do you mean?" The president matched Vandotti in angst. "Is this your doing, Arthur, like we talked about the other day after her visit?"

"No. Actually, I haven't yet worked something out. I found out about this an hour ago. From Senator Trump.

The president was cranky. "Trump. He thinks he knows everything. And he's responsible for all the empty office towers that took away half our parking lots. All right, keep me posted, and, Arthur, refrain from addressing me as 'boss.' I don't know when you started with that. Understand that it was a factor in my firing of Toshi—which, by the by, we need a replacement for him. Get me a short list of candidates for Transportation. You think Trump might want it?"

Vandotti executed a form of pirouette and exited the golden arches.

The UGRY, with its precious cargo, was closing in on Orlando, and as it did, an atmosphere of hush enveloped its passengers along with a palpable air of anxiety. What would happen when they rolled into one of Disney's fabled color-coded parking lots? Would Annabelle's presence secure their rightful place? The final legs of the trip had proved uneventful: one more road night, somewhere in south Georgia, everyone tired, and even the children taking an intermission. It was late afternoon the following day, and they sailed through the number four lot with ease, Annabelle's new IPM providing access through the concrete pillars and three-foot-thick steel gates that guarded America's most coveted entry point. The Stackwolds smiled amongst themselves, exhaled in relief, and prepared to enter the realm of this national holy grail.

"Well. Here we are, Stackwolds," Henry said expansively. "It's time to get it on. Let's storm the booth and pay our respects to Walter E. and all he has created." Rosalie and the children hung on every word.

Annabelle, stirring about, said, "Okay, you've all had your jollies; you got here. I want to leave now, go to a hotel, get some sleep."

Henry's eyes met hers at an angle, given that he was seven inches shorter than her. "Not just yet, lady. You're our meal ticket. What do you think would happen if we let you go? We couldn't park anywhere. Oh, no. You're with us all the way. Besides," he grinned, "it's time you got a life, anyhow. Hey, babe, it's the Magic Kingdom!"

Even Henry Stackwold was not prepared for what awaited them once they'd gone into the park. Just beyond the gates stood a phalanx of reporters from all the national networks, mikes in hand and backed by their respective video technicians, all jockeying for position. "Here they come," shouted Fox. "Get outta my space," CBS yelled as she muscled into a better attack spot. "Get behind the parking lady and drop the damn boom mike in her face!" barked

NBC. Their little group was surrounded. ABC jumped in, facing his cameraman and going into his spiel. "In Orlando—and I should point out that ABC's parent company owns this magnificent facility, the entertainment center of the universe—we have finally caught up with the missing parking sweetheart of America, Annabelle Dortmunder. Tell the audience, Annabelle, what motivated you to grace our presence here today?"

Annabelle, already exhausted from the trip and flustered by the microphones in her face, could only muster a, "Look, I just want to sleep. These so-and-so—"

Henry Stackwold, sensing that perhaps this was not going down well, pushed her to the side and puffed up all of his five-foot-five frame to address the correspondent and, by implication, the nation. "America, this lady is the dearest person in the land, someone we can all be proud of. She, out of the charity of her heart and the inner reaches of her wallet, took our family to Disney World when we were down and out, unable to take our children here without assistance. You see, I'm on disability from the post office. I need a new left-foot operation, which I cannot afford, therefore I couldn't drive. Furthermore, my wife was laid off from her job a month ago, and—"

NBC leaped in. "You, sir, are—"

"Henry Stackwold, and this is my wife Rosalie, and these are our children, Svetlana and Leonid.

CBS could barely contain a wry smile. "Leonid?"

"Named after Chairman Brezhnev," Henry said proudly.

"My husband is a communist, you know," Rosalie added.

"I always told you I hated my name, Dad. I'm gonna change it when I'm eighteen," the boy said.

The newshounds returned to Annabelle, not sure of how to handle the Stackwolds any longer. "Is that true, Ms. Dortmunder? Did you really do this out of the goodness of your heart?" Fox asked.

If you can't beat 'em, play along with 'em, she thought. "Well, actually the way it came about …"

Not allowing her to complete her thought, Henry again bust into the conversation. "Annabelle here is entirely too modest. Do you know that she's treating us to a week in Orlando? If more people were like her, we wouldn't have all this conflict in the world …"

The tapes from the interviews made for highlighted features on the evening news broadcasts, and the networks readied invitations for Annabelle and the Stackwolds to appear on the morning shows when they returned to New York.

Park management hastily threw together a ceremony bestowing The Freedom of Disney World on them, and there were photo ops with Mickey and Goofy along with the executive director. Rooms were provided at the newest park hotel, the Everglades Lagoon, along with a weeklong meal plan at Donald's Duck Pond Grill. Annabelle's favorite ride was "Small World," which she went around on fifteen times. None of the people who endured the hour-plus wait for that ride minded as she went immediately to the front of the line. Some even applauded.

"Annabelle, we're leaving early in the morning," Henry told her as the week was drawing to its end.

"All right, I'll be ready whenever you want," she said.

"Well, that won't be necessary, dear," Rosalie Stackwold said. "We're flying back on InkJet. They gave us free tickets. We won't be needing you any longer. Isn't that right, Henry?" She fluttered her eyelids.

"You bet, baby. Have a safe trip home. One thing, I know you'll be able to park when you need to." Henry wore a broad grin.

Annabelle was dumfounded. "You mean we're not returning together? I'm having to drive that bloody car back thirteen hundred miles by myself?"

After a momentary silence, Svetlana Stackwold piped up. "Kinda looks that way, you old hag."

"Svettie!" Rosalie shouted.

"See you on the morning shows," Henry said.

Four

So she drove, five days and nights on the road, stopping at nondescript motels along the way, eating forgettable food and reading newspapers when she was not cramped behind the wheel. The news that week centered around the final vestiges of opposition in Louisiana being quelled, and as that state returned to the fold the country was a union once again. There was a report on the accelerated government program to inoculate drivers with the IPM device. The program was being conducted at DMV offices, and there was plenty of trouble to be had: people jostling one another on endless lines; stolen IDs reported; muggings, and even a number of unconfirmed abductions. The National Guard was called out to put down disturbances in as disparate a group of cities as Beverly Hills, East St. Louis, and Cambridge.

Annabelle was physically exhausted upon her homecoming, but not so exhausted that she delayed opening up a steel case file drawer in her clothes closet, an initial act upon her apartment entry. There had been ample time to think on the trip north. She thought about the Stackwolds and how perhaps they did her a favor by flying back. Sure, it was a bear driving that distance alone, but she came to realize the joy of never having to see them again, not if she had anything at all to do with it, all the media attention linking her and them be damned. She thought about the White House visit and not being able to purge a *déjà vu* impression of President Morgan from her mind.

She retained class records, however far back in time they were. Estimating a time period, it took Annabelle hardly a matter of minutes to pull a manila folder from the 1991–92 school year, a sixth-grade class, home room number 127. The folder contained individual files for each of the thirty students in the class, along with other assorted items from the year. Thumbing through the papers with a rush, Annabelle lifted out a thin file on one Roberto Goncalves and began to read its contents. There were the usual scholastic disciplines listed for the fall and spring terms, English, math, social studies, science, phys ed and geography, accompanied by the attendant grades for each shown in her handwriting in a right-hand column.

Goncalves was a below-average student according to the record: a C-plus in math, a C-minus in English and social studies; somewhat better grades for the rest. There was a line item for conduct, which had been marked "u" for unsatisfactory, a harsh judgment and one reserved for less than a handful of her students. Moreover, the file held explanatory notes, among them commentary that Roberto was an indifferent student—at best—often unattentive, talking to other students while she demanded full attention towards the day's instruction, that is when he deigned to attend class, which was not always, to say the least. At the bottom of the page there was a footnote to the effect that Roberto may be disadvantaged by his foreign upbringing, a memory jog that caused Annabelle to check the front of the file once more and view the lines on a sheet containing personal information. There she saw a birth date of May 15, 1979, for Goncalves, Roberto, and the place of birth being Santo Domingo, Dominican Republic.

What else? Another page of notes. Maybe. Yes. That could be it. Again, in her own hand.

"Roberto responds poorly to constructive criticism. For example, I've noticed a pronounced bounce in his gait and a lurching from side to side when walking, which I do not believe is due to a genetic condition but to poor posture and lack of motivation. I have repeatedly asked him to stand up straight and walk in a balanced way, which he persists in ignoring. I've also recommended a doctor's visit as a check on any inherent disability."

The notes ended there above a date of May 29, 1992. Annabelle reconstructed a conversation she held with Goncalves, a request that he apprise his mother (a single working one, she remembered) of her concerns and to look into appropriate remedies as needed.

There was one other item in the file, a late 1992 newspaper clipping dealing with the arrest of a juvenile for robbery and attempted murder, name withheld, but a description of the accused "shuffling into the courtroom" to be arraigned. Then she lost track of Roberto Goncalves. She would continue to meet former students around the area from time to time, but not him. But—that walk—it returned to haunt her memory. *I'd know it anywhere,* she thought.

President Thad Morgan was a fabrication. That very year—1992—Roberto Goncalves left (fled would be a better word) New York for south Florida, where he arrived unannounced and uninvited at an aunt's house in Miami, this after withdrawing five thousand dollars from his mother's savings account for his trip. His mother screamed ultimate revenge at both he and the aunt but relented when he agreed never to see her again or ask for further support, which, when Mrs. Goncalves did the arithmetic, she figured it was only a three-year payback, not a bad rate of return. Roberto did even better; he invested the money, most of it anyway, in tech stocks and the occasional sports book, and the money increased rather nicely for him. It would come in handy.

In high school in Miami, and not an especially good one, his studies continued at about the same level they had in New York. He grew and worked out enough to carry an eventual 195 pounds on a muscular frame. He ran track in the spring and played football in the fall; the team never cracked a record above .500 and his skills as a running back and free safety went unheralded, which did not seem to bother him. It was about that time that his infatuation with President Bill Clinton began to emerge. He understood they shared a common height of six feet two, but little else; yet, he aspired to be "just like Bill." He worked for the Clinton reelection in 1996 at the local party headquarters. In one instance, when the great man was campaigning in Miami, he got close enough to shake the hand, and he felt the president look him square in the eye as if to say, "*By God, this is one handsome Hispanic stud. Hell, he's what America is all about.*"

Then Roberto Goncalves disappeared for a while. He had money and had made some contacts in the Latino community in Miami—enough of both to get him to Sao Paulo and the office of one of the most eminent plastic surgeons in Brazil and himself one of the wealthiest men in a nation obsessed with appearance.

When he resurfaced, it was within the strapping body of a striking young man with a square jaw and wavy ash-blonde hair, as well as a skin tone that was decidedly more white than someone carrying the olive cast of a Latin heritage. In addition, when he landed back in Florida, he held a letter of acceptance to Florida State, based on a contrived secondary school record. He played varsity football at FSU, having made starting free safety as a walk-on, no small accomplishment there. His cause was rumored to have been helped when a heavily recruited black player at the same position was suspended for having seven stolen Armani suits found in his dorm room, along with five kilos of crack cocaine, nobody quite believing the young man's claim that the items had been planted there. As one of only two white stars on the FSU defensive team, Thad Morgan (for that is who he had become) received more than a relative share of attention and praise during his college years, including a shared cover on *Sports Illustrated.* Although he was drafted in the NFL's third round by the Denver Broncos, Morgan elected not to play professional football, but to embark on what would be a lucrative career as an investment banker and venture capitalist in West Palm. From that base he slid, naturally it seemed, into politics and was elected Florida's governor at a younger age than when Bill

Clinton was elected to the same office in Arkansas. From there, he was awarded the vice presidential nomination as Megan Munro's running mate. His role was to deliver the state of Florida, which their ticket handily won in the election.

Annabelle had several messages that had piled up on her answering machine during her unplanned trip to Disney World. There were three from representatives of talk shows; she listened to them all, pondered a few options, and then picked up the phone to make a call.

Many of the talk shows had been reconfigured in recent months. The most popular morning program, hosted by ex-golfer Tiger Woods and ex-tennis champion Maria Sharapova, was too bouncy, not quite the right venue for what she had in mind. The afternoon program, long Oprah's province, was now in the hands of Angelina Jolie, and with an emphatically sharper tone; guests appeared at considerable risk. At night, following the retirement of Larry King, that show's new host was L'il Kim, a surprise choice in a way—but not really, as the network's decision to hire her was heavily influenced by the tons of monogrammed items bearing the initials LK, including seventeen cases of suspenders in a variety of colors. The cost savings in taking on Ms. Kim were significant. Moreover, Kim carried on the tradition of Larry's softball style of interview. It was the offer that she chose to accept.

They came out suddenly from cover behind an ancient hemlock guarding the front entrance to the building. They swiftly assumed positions on either side of Annabelle, looking like little bookends, each dwarfed by her six-foot frame. The shorter of the pair spoke in a clipped, deliberate manner. "Please walk toward your car. This will not take long at all. We need you to perform a service for us."

Oh, no, here we go again, she thought, not getting a good look at either of them in the early evening dark. At least there's only two of them, not a family like the Stackwolds.

They held her elbow, strangely in a gentle way, as she was leading them to her UGRY, which was parked outside the front of the building in its preferred space. "Who the devil are you two?" she asked.

"I am Mr. Tambourine," Shorty said. "My associate is Mr. Cloud. Here we are now ..." Turning to his partner, he added "Mr. Cloud, would you be so kind as to place Ms. Dortmunder in the vehicle once she opens it."

"And if I do not, Mr. Tambourine?"

"Ah, but you will," he responded confidently, now applying a higher notch of pressure on her arm. Cloud smiled lightly (he reminded her of Dr. Shand in *Rosemary's Baby*) as he extended a welcoming open hand toward her. Annabelle unlocked the car doors with the remote and a sigh of resignation. Tambourine, more agile than she would have thought, immediately popped the trunk from the driver's side and, within seconds, the two grabbed the remote, swooped her off her feet, placed her in the trunk, and shut it tight.

Inside her dark chamber, she was aware of the car driving off and then, after perhaps twenty minutes, coming to a stop. She could hear their conversation. Cloud was asking Shorty if the IPM device would work for parking, what with "the lady being in the back."

The latter answered. "No problema, my friend. These homing chips are good within a range of at least a hundred feet, and they go through steel, anything. I studied up on it, you know. We'll be able to park anywhere."

All was quiet until Annabelle picked up on a muffled sound—a firecracker, no a gunshot, maybe, then another—and silence once more. She heard footsteps approaching. The trunk sprung open. She looked up into the ebony sky for a moment and then a man, or a body that had once been a man, was thrown in, rolling a quarter-turn to rest against her side. The trunk was slammed shut again. Doors closed, the engine started up, and there was a push to higher speed; it was a new ride pattern, one with a feeling of urgency.

The man was not quite dead, a surprise to her since by now she had processed what had likely gone down. "Ooh … uh … urghrr …" were the sounds emanating from the mass of clothed flesh against her. "Are you all right?" she asked hesitantly, a rhetorical question really, and all that it prompted was a spate of moaning directed at nothing in particular. Annabelle began to sense warmish liquid seeping around her. *Blood?* she wondered. *I suppose so. Can't see anything here.* Her car continued in motion. A few sharp turns were apparent to her, no room to adjust her position, and then the car stopped. She heard doors opened, hurried footsteps on pavement fading away and—after an interval—back again, doors closed, car started up and moving forward once more. This time the ride was quite brief. After a stop and the engine shut off, she heard the now familiar ritual of door operations and footsteps diminishing into silence.

Somewhere amidst the slop that increasingly surrounded her, she noticed a small object that must have slipped out of body's pocket at a point where the car had made a lurching turn. It was a cell phone, and it was fully illuminated. The body was either nodding off or quite ready for death at this point, expressions of life having left him except for weakening sounds of breath. She picked up the phone, wiped off traces of blood on its screen, and managed to punch in 911, evidencing a presence of mind that she didn't know could be summoned up. When a respondent came on, she explained her situation in a rational way and added—of course—that she was unable to pinpoint her location. The technician said, "Just keep talking to me, ma'am. These new models are powerful, and we are able to latch onto the origin of the signal with satellite positioning, despite what barriers may be in the way. There, I've got it … within a half square mile, anyway. Now. What kind of car did you say you have?"

The trunk was pried open with a crowbar, and a flashlight was beamed in. Hit in the face with a blinding shot of light, Annabelle instinctively covered her eyes, but then opened them up to look at the cop on the other end of the light. "Why, Sergeant Mulroon, it is you, isn't it?" she said. "What took you so long?"

Mulroon was expansive. "Annabelle Dortmunder, as I live and breathe, why I should have guessed ahead of time, with all that's been going on with you lately. But then, when I recognized the car, I knew, just knew, it would be you. Had some more adventures, haven't we?" He placed his attention on the car. "Have you changed the color on this? It's an improvement over what you had."

"Well, that's another story, officer. Now get me out of here." His charm commanded no staying power with her, and she began to stir around and then accept his hand to help pry her up and out of her metallic cell. By now Mulroon had his backup crew around her. Easing her onto the sidewalk, they did their best to sop up the blood on her clothes and then moved on to do an on-site postmortem on her erstwhile companion. Although unable to make an immediate ID, one of the cops opined that he had been a small-cap punk, while another said that he was too old and too well dressed, which probably qualified him as a midcap punk, but a punk in any event, they reached agreement.

Annabelle looked up and down the streets and was happy to find orientation in a familiar vista. "Why, I'm only around the corner from my building," she said, "and to think I could have died in that … tomb."

"Right you are, Ms. D," Mulroon said. "There's not much air in those trunks, not for long anyhow, but all's okay now. Say, can I get you a coffee and donut at the Dunkin' Donuts?" he asked.

"I'd prefer Starbucks."

"You got it," he said, and they started walking toward the commercial lights ahead.

"Take care of the stiff, would ya, boys," he called back to his men, "I'll take Ms. D's statement over a latte up the block." Turning to her, he told her that he'd have to impound the car. "Evidence, you know."

She halted for a moment, then looked squarely at him and said, "Officer, you can impound and *impale* that car, for all I care. Take it anytime you want."

Inexplicably, the media was on hand at the Queens Boulevard Starbucks as soon as she and Mulroon sat down with their coffees. *Eyewitness News* was the first to thrust the mike at them, cameras behind whirling away. The "incident," as it was referred to, was soon a matter of video record, wrapped for the next morning's shows.

Five

Thad Morgan was not pleased. "Arthur," he wailed at his chief of staff, "just talk to me, *mano a mano*, about what happened up there in New York. Vandotti was standing sheepishly in front of him at a table for four in the back section of an IHOP on K and Twentieth streets, this week's venue for the White House, the policy being to move around the District so as to afford each local business a share of the presidency. The president was about to attack a steaming plate of German pancakes, which were covered in a mist of confectionery sugar.

Vandotti remained upright, steeling himself against the aroma of Morgan's breakfast, not having been invited to sit. He gulped once and explained. "The people we hired … well, they were highly recommended by the Bureau of Extreme Prejudice, but it developed that they had taken on another job and thought they could handle both together, and that's where it fell apart. Multitasking. If it had not have been for the other contract having a cell phone and Helg—I mean Annabelle—using it to call 911, we'd have had a better result. She would have suffocated in there."

"But she didn't."

"That is correct."

"And I suppose our agents never checked to see whether the other body had such a phone with him?"

"I don't know the answer to that question, Mr. President, but we are in the process of finding out as required under the Hitman Accounting Practices Act of 2016. That is, if we can find them."

Morgan was incredulous. "Find them? You mean, you let them get away?"

"Apparently, they got right down to the R—that's the subway line in the neighborhood—and the station was on the corner where they finally parked. Don't worry. We'll never use them again."

Morgan was temporarily unable to respond, an occurrence as rare as an eclipse of the sun.

"Will that be all, Mr. President? You have Senator Trump waiting at the counter. He's finished with his Belgian waffle and is becoming just a bit antsy. He wants to talk to you about developing the Capitol Mall into a par-three golf course. He thinks that the pool fronting the Lincoln Memorial would make for an exceptional water hazard, and that the greens fees would be among the highest in America, a real moneymaker, if I say so myself."

"Yes. That will be all," the president said.

Leaving the table, Vandotti added in parting, "Sir, if you don't mind my saying, your hair could stand with a little coloring touch-up. I see an imposition of grey at the temples. I'll arrange for the stylist, if you wish."

Morgan regained a sunny demeanor. "By all means, Arthur. Try to get that *zaftig* redhead in Arlington, if you would. Ask the senator to approach."

The taping for *In Deep With LK* took place the next day. An odd duo across the desk were they—host L'il Kim, not so little anymore, sporting fuschia LK suspenders and not much else, and Annabelle Dortmunder buttoned-up in an oxford grey tweed suit. "So, Annabelle," Kim said, "let America know how it was for a common citizen like yourself to be in the spotlight and in front of the president. What's he really like?"

"I object to the implication that I am common."

Kim seemed taken aback. "I meant—well, you know, ordinary, regular. You know what I mean."

"Yes. I believe I do. Apologize to me."

Kim fairly leaped from her swivel chair, suspenders flapping into a glance of a malfunction. "Now, look here. I don't have to take this kinda crap from you." Kim caught hold of her emotions just in time and retook her seat. "Okay, Annabelle, I am sorry for any misunderstanding. Please, go on."

Annabelle, apparently buoyed by the outcome of the little squabble with her host, assumed control. "Well, I'll get to your question, Kim. But first, I would like to provide some background. You, see I knew him—when. That's right. Once upon a time, President Morgan was …"

Thad Morgan was not nominated by his party to run for the presidency the following year. To spare the nation further turmoil, a hastily patched-together Ad Hoc Forgiveness of Presidential Omissions Act allowed him to complete his term without threat of impeachment. He received a warm note from California's ex-governor, Arnold Schwartzenegger, which said, in part, "now you feel my pain," himself a foreign-born presidential aspirant and sponsor of a failed constitutional amendment that would have allowed those of Teutonic heritage to run for the nation's highest office.

Arthur Vandotti left his job following the L'il Kim interview to become the host of *Family Feud* on afternoon television.

Masatoshi Fujiama returned to Japan to a prodigal hero's welcome and went on to develop all of Japan's former island conquests in World War II into tropical resorts, several featuring scuba dives to sunken warships of the Japanese Imperial Navy.

The next presidential election is shaping up to be a contest between Senator Donald Trump, running on the Rich Man's Ticket, and Camille Gates (having made a triumphant comeback), who will run under the banner of the I'm Rich Too party. Both are pledging increased parking as the nation's top priority.

Annabelle Dortmunder signed a multimillion-dollar book deal for her biography and received a hefty fee as executive producer for a Lifetime movie based on the book. It is rumored that Nicole Kidman would like to play the Annabelle character. Ms. Dortmunder has put some of her money toward the hiring of a car and driver on a permanent basis. The driver has—naturally—an IPM for parking purposes.

The Stackwold family left Queens for parts unknown, but there has been a recent sighting in and around Lenin's tomb in Moscow, where there are plenty of places to park. Sergeant Mulroon still patrols the old neighborhood; he keeps a dog-eared description of Messrs. Tambourine and Cloud in his wallet, should he come upon them. They remain unaccounted for.

The Summer Intern

They were not called summer interns in those days. In fact, the term had not yet been invented; it was a phrase awaiting coinage. Then, it was merely a "summer job," but a coveted one at that, an opportunity for a young man or woman to experience a career appetizer and not always easy to come by. Students looking for money when their school terms end need to go for seasonal openings, the guys working construction, but in New York City, construction jobs were held by union old-timers, not Ivy Leaguers and their ilk hoping to bulk up in the sun at a scale wage. So, he had a downtown job, not nearly as much money as the other, but you kept your hands clean anyway.

The Rudder Agency (nee Rudder and Mast) occupied prime quarters on Madison Avenue and Fifty-sixth, nicely situated for whatever action that might take place along New York's adverting row. Not a soul paid attention to Davey Wharton as he emerged from the depths of the Lex at Fifty-ninth every morning and walked the blocks to the office, the distance being sufficient to dry out from the subway steam, and more the better should there be a north-to-south tailwind. A soon-to-be senior at W-, he was in the early stage of the job, yet would before long hone in on deciding between an entry-level in the ad game next year or grad school (assuming the draft board did not block the way), choices not at all for the worst in this time of promise and abundance in the great USA.

"Hey Davey, you'd better hop-to in that art library, because Mr. Perry Jamicco is looking for you," said Dale Margolis in a faux cheery tone. Margolis was Rudder's all-around nosebody, and had taken it upon herself to serve as Wharton's mentor-confidant over the long, hot, summer days. Hardly in the door and over to his All-Steel junior desk, he'd barely had a chance to shuck off his tan cord sport jacket before hot-dog account executive Perry Jamicco stood ready to pounce upon his compact frame, just as Dale had warned.

"Wharton, I need that mock-up of the new Nash hardtop from the library bin now," Jamicco barked as he chewed hard on his wad of Blackjack gum, mournful eyes half covered by droopy lids, and change jangling in the pockets of his Hammonton Park sharkskin suit.

To Davey, Jamicco came off as more Times Square hustler than an ad agency executive, but then again, what did he know, being in his fourth week in the industry and there to observe and to learn enough to fix up the business once and for all, maybe not right away, but certainly by the time he got out of graduate business school. Should Jamicco deviate from change manipulation to steel ball rolling a la Captain Queeg—Humphrey Bogart in *The Caine Mutiny* which he'd seen the previous year—he would not have been surprised. *Suppressed masturbation, Davey thought, wasn't that the explanation in Queeg's case?*

"Right away Mr. Jamicco." He responded in quite a subservient manner, straightening up to his full five-feet-nine height and giving an involuntary toss of curled reddish-brown hair as he disappeared into the inner reaches of the art library. Not much more than a warren of stacks and bins in a cavernous alcove, reorganizing and categorizing Rudder's disjointed advertising art was one of Wharton's assignments, something no self-respecting full-time Rudderite would deign to do, but an ideal project for a summer guy.

It did not take long for Wharton to locate three mock-ups of the forthcoming 1957 Nash Rambler for the account executive; he emerged from the stacks with the artwork on illustration board, a slight patina of dust and the start of back perspiration, but otherwise unscathed. He handed the pieces to the exec.

"Ooh … this is hot. Nash is gonna overtake GM, and I'm gonna see to it. Thanks, kid. Nice work." Jamicco's eyelids never moved. You couldn't tell whether he was awake or ready to nod off. He clicked his spit-polished Florsheim tasseled loafers, turned at a right angle, and left. *This business is a snap*, Davey thought. *Hand over something and you get a star. Maybe grad school would be a waste of effort.*

The intern's day had begun. In the few weeks that he had been at the agency, he'd assembled a coterie of friends and characters. Not being able to distinguish between the two categories, he judged it unnecessary, but kept mental notes of his experiences along the way. Dale was one of them; she sauntered over to his desk soon after Jamicco departed, curious as to the outcome of their interchange, and when he shrugged the episode off, she repaired to her own desk, which was strategically placed in the mainstream of the office traffic where she could concentrate on ongoing people movements and on where to go for lunch. On a path to a matronly look, auburn hair pulled back from her forehead and sporting bulky, black, horned rims, Dale possessed a prominent upper body, and, it being summertime, she'd often wear tops showing ample cleavage when bending to address him from the side, a move undoubtedly perfected over time. He did not mind the glancing peek, even if it arrived wrapped in the pungent aroma of whatever was selling at Bonwit's cosmetics counter. He thought Dale to be one of his friends.

His immediate supervisor was one Duncan Bruce, who regarded his young charge with a blend of amusement and ennui. Supervising Davey throughout the summer, the task of showing him the ropes seemed, to outward appearance, to leave Duncan Bruce with a quasi "Why me?" look, as though the assignment was the final burden to an overloaded plate. Which was a significant distance from reality, since Bruce had very little to keep him occupied other than to portray an attitude that he was the most harried man in the place. Most of the time his act worked successfully.

"Davey, I trust you'll be with us in a week's time for the summer outing?" Duncan Bruce said laconically.

"You mean I'm invited? I'm only a summer employee."

Bruce showed him a patrician grin with a full set of pearly whites in high symmetry and answered with majesty. "Why, of course, you're part of us now, aren't you? Besides, the office is pretty much shut down that day, so I'd classify your presence as a done deal, old chap."

That was the way Duncan Bruce talked. Early on in the summer Bruce revealed himself as several things to Davey: a man of a multigenerational Scots heritage, an occasional polo player, patron of bespoke tailors on Jermyn Street, never married, and, perhaps most seriously, a T-man. It would be Davey's luck to work for a graduate of his college's archrival, but he had come to like Bruce quite a bit, found his imperial manner a unique joy, and held some admiration for his natty dressing. Bruce, with his acerbic wit, longish blonde hair and a six-feet-two frame clothed in perfectly tailored silk blend summer suits, English spread collars, and bold shantung silk ties, cut an impressive figure at Rudder, probably another reason why he was tolerated around the office, seemingly on a cruise as a free agent. Bruce could have stood for the graven image of the *Playboy* bachelor, pulled right out of the pages of said magazine that he rolled up and carried from time to time on his jaunts to the men's room, or the "loo" as he referred to it. Davey Wharton, never having crossed the Atlantic, had previously understood the word to refer to an aging wrestler.

"And, Davey, you must take part in the music and dance. Who can tell, you might even get to interact on the floor with Renee Robbins."

With that and a blend of grin and smirk, Duncan left him to whatever tasks were pending that day as he mentioned something about a client meeting he had to attend. Renee Robbins? She was someone who'd be noticed in an office of any size within a New York minute. With raven hair that fell to her shoulders and bobbed in a sensuous way when she walked, or rather glided, Renee was blessed with a star's figure, which at that point in time was comparable to the one and only Marilyn's. Which is to say a touch voluptuous by subsequent health-club standards, but some people believe there are certain standards that never face obsolescence. Her eyes, a deep cocoa, evinced fire, complementing a sultry look of the Latina or the Semitic, take your pick. Renee's demeanor around the agency was one of wariness, of being on alert, of a don't bother me attitude. That was perhaps her only failing in Davey Wharton's mind, but he attributed that posture to his belief that she'd probably been set upon relentlessly by the male species since the age of twelve. No more than nodding her way when their paths crossed in the office, he did look forward to the outing and maybe an opportunity for more than a hello.

That summer was uncommonly hot, even for New York City. The day of the Rudder Agency's outing at the New Century Country Club in Scarsdale was true to the pattern, held on a genuine 3-H day: hazy, hot, and humid. It was an event much the stuff of legends, like the song "Once a Year Day" in the musical *The Pajama Game*. Stories would be told and retold around the agency in the days leading up to the outing of previous gaffes and mishaps, unplanned happenings, whose careers blew up in the course of those hours, who keeled over at cocktails, who pushed over who, which nabob was insulted, and so forth. The week prior, sheets were circulated inviting all the employees to sign up for organized games and activities. Davey chose to play golf at Century's heralded and manicured course.

He had one problem, or so he thought, which was not owning a car, thus having no way to transport his body and his bag to the club. Not to worry, Duncan Bruce came to the rescue. "Look, my good fellow, I will come to pick you up at a convenient location in the Bronx on the way to where we are going," he said. So that morning Duncan found Davey Wharton dutifully standing by his golf clubs in front of a Howard Johnson restaurant hard by the Whitestone Bridge.

"Now there, you have a knack for the elegant entry, I must say." Duncan Bruce was facetious as Davey loaded himself and his bag into the former's car, which turned out to be an aging Citroen, one of the models with the automatic seats that rose and fell in tandem with the passenger's body movement. Only the French would offer a product like this, Davey thought, and why shouldn't I be surprised anyway; Duncan would never drive a prosaic Nash, undoubtedly because Nash was Rudder's automobile account.

"What, Dunc, you mean the Ho Jo location?"

"My favorite, young man, the orange roof and all. Did you know that I have sampled all 21 flavors? I found the chocolate chip to be the best around."

"Me, too."

The Citroen sprung forward with a throaty roar, and they were on their way to the outing. Arriving at the club, Davey checked the activity sheets and located his golf tee time, which was within the hour. He also saw that he was paired with another summer guy, Jimmy Fleece, and the suddenly dreaded Perry Jamicco. He did not know Jimmy Fleece very well, only that he was starting at P- in the fall and lived in Queens. What little he did know was that Jimmy chewed gum as aggressively as did Perry Jamicco and had what New Yorkers referred to as "a mouth on him." Until proven otherwise, he represented all of the characteristics that Davey Wharton was trying to distance himself from.

"Hey kid, how about a Bloody Mary before we tee off? There was Jamicco in his face, dressed in luxurious cream-colored slacks with a knifelike crease, topped off with a shiny royal blue golf shirt, curiously buttoned to the neck and with back collar turned up despite the oncoming heat of the afternoon. Reflecting for a moment on the paucity of his plaid button-down shirt and rumpled khaki pants, his attention turned toward Jamicco's overflowing inventory of gleaming Wilson clubs in one of those billowy stand-alone pro-style bags of polished leather, an instrument of golf intimidation.

"No, thanks, Mr. Jamicco, but I'd like to go to the practice range and tune my game up a little."

"Trying to get one-up on me already, are ya? Well, suit yourself, kid. Hey, today you call me Perry, okay?" He was lifting his eyelids ever so slightly. "We're all equals here. Before you go, though, what do ya shoot? We need the handicaps for the tournament. I play to a seven."

Golf was another of the day's problems for Wharton. He played to a seven also, as in a seven on most of the holes. "Uh, I dunno … Perry … maybe I'll shoot a 95." The lying was starting early. He was likely to exceed 110, and it would take a sports miracle if he broke 100.

As he turned to go to hit some balls, Jamicco called after him, "You know your pal Jimmy signed up too, and we have a late entrant, Harvey Madrid. See ya on the first tee."

Madrid. He had heard the name. The man worked somewhere on the other side of the office. So we have a foursome, he thought.

An intense player, Perry was out for blood. His drives found the fairway, carrying well over two hundred yards and looking good in the process, the kind of ball rising effortlessly on a taut line and falling to ground at a shallow angle that delivers extra yardage on the hole. He hit most of the greens in regulation and played to his handicap. Davey was, true to his own game, entering lots of sixes and sevens on the scorecard. "Yo, kid, ya told me you were around a twenty five," Perry called over at one point as he was attempting a hack out behind some high grass. "Maybe it's an off day for ya. Did ya think it was only for nine holes, huh?" It was clear that Jamicco was not fooled.

Harvey Madrid, who had joined the others just in time for their tee-off, was a hacker as well, although he could produce sporadic excellence within his inconsistency. He recorded three pars on the front nine, which brought a faint nod of recognition from Perry, about as much deference as the man seemed capable of. Then there was Jimmy. After the third hole, he admitted to having played golf only once before; he had rental clubs, wore a T-shirt over shorts and torn Keds sneakers, and, by Davey's reckoning, did not land more than two shots on any given fairway. All of this did not interfere with his consumption of green bottles of Ballantine ale from the courtesy cart that made continual stops all along the golf course. As the sun rose higher in the sky, Jimmy's game, such as it was, declined even further. On the baked fourteenth green, he spun around twice before ejecting a massive flow of vomit along the line of Perry Jamicco's potential birdie putt. It did not assist Jamicco in taking in an accurate read. A moment later, Jimmy himself collapsed at about a forty-five-degree angle across the projected line of the golf ball's roll.

"That's it. I'm walking off. You guys do what you want, but I've had it." Perry was in full snarl.

"Aw, come on, let's finish. We're still in this." Madrid, decked out in a yellow shirt and shiny black pants and looking like a forlorn bumblebee, was pleading to no avail. Jamicco never looked back; he signaled to his caddy (this was—you must remember—in those simple days before golf carts were prevalent) to follow and headed in the direction of the clubhouse. This left one prostrate player wallowing in his own vomit and two temporarily stunned compatriots along with an unabashed caddy and three sets of bags. They lifted Jimmy with the utmost care and positioned him to stand upright. Davey and Madrid finished their round carrying their own clubs; the caddy limped back with the still woozy young Mr. Fleece.

"That was laughs, wasn't it?" Madrid was saying to Davey back in the clubhouse over a large dirty martini, his third.

"You bet. That's what I love about golf. No matter how often you play it, there's a new experience every time you're out there." Spoken like someone who'd played the game for an eternity.

Madrid, in the process of spitting forth fragments of olives, grinned and said, "Same as in advertising, but you kept cool. I like your style. Wharton, you'll be okay."

Duncan Bruce sidled up to their table. "Ah, my young charge, I see you've found the clutches of the notorious Mr. Madrid, "he said.

"Notorious and glorious, that's okay, cousin Bruce," Madrid chortled in between pulls on the martini. Duncan was a bit unsteady but declined an empty chair when offered. They asked him what he had done all day; the afternoon's blazing sun was finally slipping into an evening haze and the dinner event was about to start.

"You know, mates, I can't recall very much. That means it must have been a profitable day," Duncan said as he wobbled off in the direction of the buffet table.

After dinner a small combo was playing dance music, and a cadre of brave souls took to the floor. Brave in the sense that the seated audience would as a totality focus in on who's with whom, who's grab-assing, and which couples are maintaining a social distance between themselves. Davey Wharton had the stares for Renee Robbins, who had shown up at cocktail time in tight black shorts, an off-shoulder bolero top, and high heels—red—that amplified the shapeliest set of legs he had ever seen in a three-dimensional way. "G'wan, Wharton, give the girl a tumble." Duncan Bruce was slobbering in his ear.

The combo was playing "Cherry Pink and Apple Blossom White" to a cha-cha rhythm, and Davey, seeing Renee unoccupied for the moment, moved with agility to her side and invited her to the dance. Somehow it didn't matter that he could not dance the cha-cha, another one of the day's problems presenting itself. "Okay, okay. It's Davey isn't it?" she said, those eyes now flashed at his and the whole impression on him being marred (but only slightly) by Renee snapping away at a stick of Juicy Fruit gum.

"Yes, that's me, for sure, Renee."

"Uh, so you know me, huh?" she replied. "You like to cha-cha-cha?"

"I do, indeed," he answered, his confidence escalating with no supportable basis.

They managed through the dance, front to back, back to front … ahh … uh … cha-cha-cha. Davey was oblivious to the multiple pairs of eyes feasting on their dance as it progressed. When the music ended, they were the only couple remaining on the floor, and there was—from more than one quarter—a smattering of applause, whether in appreciation or relief, or some combination thereof, who could tell. "Hey, great, Renee. Maybe we'll dance again, could we?" He was, for the moment, *con brio.*

"Yeah, maybe not a cha-cha, but look for me," she said before turning away from him.

He sauntered over to the bar for a beer, vowing that it would be his last for the evening. Duncan Bruce appeared again and said, "My gawd man, you are multitalented I must say. Renee Robbins! You could do far worse, far worse. Not bad for a summer employee."

They did dance again. The song was "Unchained Melody," the summer's big hit; this one he knew how to handle, so he virtually propelled himself to Renee before anyone else could get to her, and off they were on the floor. Initially at a chasm of a distance, he, with hands lightly on Renee's back and sensing a faint line of perspiration as a symbol of communion, her spine nearly concave to his touch, began to move closer, dipping his hand now to Renee's fleshy hip just at the top of those black shorts. Renee moved an assortment of fingers around his neck.

"… lonely rivers flow to the sea, to the sea, to the open arms of the sea …"

As the music entered its final phase, Renee, intuitively sensing enough of the burgeoning closeness, moved definitively apart from him toward a separated position.

"I need you love, I need your love. God speed your love, to—ooh—ooh—me."

There. No applause this time. He was slow to let her go, with fingers resting lightly on two of hers before the parting.

For the buffet dinner, Duncan Bruce had changed into full highland regalia, the kilts, the *sporran*, the abbreviated formal jacket over a ruffled shirt. All in the clan tartan of the Bruce, or so he told anyone who would listen, and the authenticity of which was closed to challenge since no one had a book of Scottish clan tartans with which to check. It bothered him not a bit that the early evening temperature persisted in the mid-90s and that the rest of the Rudderites remained in their day clothes; perspiration never made an appearance on Duncan's brow. As for the others, their attire becoming somewhat fetid; you wanted to keep your distance.

The outing came to an end, and Duncan drove back to the city, depositing Davey and his golf bag at his apartment building in the Bronx. Exhausted, Davey came to the conclusion that a day in the office was less demanding than the kind of day he'd just gone through. He advised Duncan to leave the Bronx with all due haste; it would not do to have the wrong people meet up with him while he was still in his dinner garb.

Two

Duncan Bruce was on vacation. He didn't alert Davey or anyone else, for that matter. His status was simply in absentia. Dale Margolis thought he may have gone up to Provincetown or, then again, maybe Tangier. No one really knew, but Dale said he'd be back when he returned; it was the sort of statement that may have been attributed to Yogi Berra. In the meantime, she advised and supervised Mr. Wharton. "Hey, I hear you and sweet Renee are an item," she said to him in a hushed monotone one morning.

"You mean just 'cause we had a couple of dances at the outing? No, I don't think so," he answered.

Dale was already walking way from his desk with a grin. "Summer romances can be as gossamer as the season itself, but go and make the most of it. Oh, just a change in subject. Harvey Madrid is out for your body. I'd advise you to be careful."

What did all that mean? he wondered. Soon he found out. Madrid did indeed want him (maybe because Bruce was gone), to be in on a client conference. "Look kid, A to Z Industries is coming in. I want you in on it. Take notes. Look important." Those were his instructions, barked out while leaning over Davey's desk and dribbling a few beads of saliva on his shirt cuff as he did so.

"Harvey, you look tanned up, you can't be working too much ads for me," Stanley Goldrunner, the president of A to Z, said to Madrid in an opening salvo across the bow, kidding but perhaps not. Goldrunner, around five feet six, sporting an obvious rug in Van Dyke brown, and drawing on one cigarette after another, was accompanied by his marketing vice president, a pencil-thin and dour-looking man wearing a black silk suit, white shirt, and coordinated black tie. He was Colin Rum, and he said nothing throughout the meeting. He took notes at a frantic pace, though, even when there wasn't anything to write down, while Goldrunner did all of the talking in between puffs on his Chesterfields.

Davey had had all of ten minutes to bone up on A to Z Industries, which was a conglomerate in an era when that form of business structure had yet to find a name, let alone become the rage of corporate America. Its retail division ran chains of men's and women's clothing stores; there were manufacturing businesses for outdoor furniture, powerboats, and golf equipment; there was a soda bottler and distributor; and there was a network of resort hotels in Florida and the Caribbean.

Goldrunner chose to ignore the young man who had been introduced as Madrid's account associate and an expert in media analysis and selection. In fact, Goldrunner didn't believe a word of whatever it was that Harvey had ever told him. He continued, saying, "I'm just pullin' on your hairy legs, Harv. Let's see the campaigns ya got for us."

Madrid seemed ill at ease, somehow unprepared for the presentation. He brought no papers in to the meeting and, fidgeting with his shirt collar, was showing evidence of inner stress. Suddenly, with a start, he jumped out of the swivel chair he was spinning around in, looked away from his audience, and spouted out, "Excuse me, Stan, gotta get the paperwork, the mock-up, gotta get … out … of here." And he bolted for the door to the conference room they were seated in. Following the leave-taking and pausing in a moment of silence as though in remembrance of someone who'd gone before, Goldrunner said, "Rum-dum, write all this down, would ya, otherwise I may not remember it." *Write what down? Madrid bolting for parts unknown?* Colin Rum nodded and proceeded to pitch his balding head toward a pad in front of him and started to write furiously, happy for the activity in the atmosphere of weighty silence.

Further moments of quietude progressed, the stillness's only competition being Rum's frenetic scratching. No sign of Harvey Madrid. Davey, who had brought his own notes to the meeting, glanced furtively at the material in front of him, then looked up and asked Stanley, "Uh … Mr. Goldrunner, how is your … boat division doing this year?"

The A to Z president was jolted out of an apparent reverie by a question from—who—this … young tyro? He locked in on Wharton full-on for the first time and said, "Hey, we sold that shit bag six months ago. Don't you know anything about our company, cap?" Colin Rum placed his pen down with utmost care, folded his arms, and smiled.

So, now I have a name … Cap … hey, maybe that's a good thing in advertising, he thought. "Well …" he said, clearing his throat, "then can we talk about the retail business?"

Here Goldrunner seemed to warm to his subject, saying, "That *shmatta* we still got. Styles change, ya know, the women's ain't too bad, but the men's … I see a trend away from this Ivy League shit into like, European. The ivy is too goddam conservative, it makes guys look like they can't force a crap no matter how hard they try." He continued on, evaluating Davey. "For example, look at your clothes. You got on a tan cord jacket and a striped tie, for Chrissake, why they went bye-bye with spats and garters. It's crapola. You oughta upgrade yourself kid, here ..." Goldrunner was thrusting an orange card at him that read:

Special Discounts
For Special Customers
Walk Up One and Save Ten
A to Z Men's Shops
Tell Them Stanley Sent You

Rum continued his writing. "Hey, what happened to Madrid anyway? Rummy and me ain't got all day. What we really want is new ads for the soda company; Pepsi and Coke are hosing us big time. Bet you didn't know that either. If we don't get these new ads soon, I'm taking my business up the street to Y and R or Compton." Goldrunner said.

Y and R or Compton? Davey thought. Those white-shoe guys would throw him out on his ass, commission or no commission. Still no sign of Harvey Madrid. He started to take his own notes ... need new campaign for soda bottling company ... while offering to Goldrunner the comment that he would visit one of A to Z's shops at his earliest convenience.

"I hope so, son," Goldrunner said, showing a more conciliatory tone, "'cause what you wear won't cut it in this business, or any other business that I know of, and won't help you pick up any gash either, and from what I can see there's some stuff to be had around here—although in my humble opinion, not as much as some other places."

Now it was his turn to leave the table. "C'mon, Rummy, put your pen down; we're wasting our time here." Addressing Davey one last time, Goldrunner said, "You give this message to Madrid. Either he comes up with an ad campaign for all of A to Z's businesses within ... shit ... I dunno ... days, weeks ... or we're putting the account up for review. Got that?"

"It's loud and clear, sir."

"Good, you tell him, hear, and ... ditch that jacket."

They were out the door, not looking back. *So that was my first client conference in the advertising industry,* he thought. *It didn't go too badly. At least they didn't dump us right then and there. Harvey will be pleased that I handled it so smoothly. I asked some penetrating questions, didn't I?*

"Uh ... I had a nature call, Wharton," Madrid said when he showed shortly afterwards. "I ate some runny eggs for breakfast and they just gave me the shits. Had to stay in the men's room. But that's all behind me now. So how'd you do with Goldrunner? Great guy isn't he? He's a charmer, really smart too. One of my best accounts."

Davey was momentarily stunned. "Harvey … I mean, Mr. Madrid … how well do you know him? He's rude, crude and … hey, look, it's a good thing we didn't lose the account. I started by asking him about his boat business."

"The boat company?" A to Z sold that shit bag last year!"

"I know now. Funny, he said the exact same thing."

"Oh God, what else went on?" Madrid was pumping the intern franticly. Davey reviewed the remainder of the meeting with him, including the demand for new ads right away. Hearing all of this, Harvey Madrid appeared to be sinking ever so slowly in his desk chair, his suit jacket hanging tiredly on sagging shoulders. Davey felt half inclined to hand over the orange discount card but thought better of it. *Sometimes the finest decisions are the actions not taken*, he thought. "I … uh … could take a shot at the soda company ads," he said.

Madrid continued to descend further in his seat, just staring ahead, glazed eyes fixated on space. "Anything else he told ya?"

"Well, yes, one more comment. He said if he didn't get new ads right away, he'd put the account up for review."

Harvey Madrid raised his creaky body out of his chair and grasped the younger man by the lapels of his summer jacket. "Up for review! Do you know what that means?

There are no three words that strike fear into the heart of the ad industry with the force of "up for review." It meant that the account was in play, open to any and all competitors who would make a pitch to secure the client's business. For the defending agency, it meant long days and nights of brainstorming and new ideas to be floated, and then preparation for a do-or-die presentation, all this in stark contrast to the halcyon days of lavish lunches and self-congratulatory speeches about ongoing campaigns. Madrid slumped down once more and waved a weak hand, a motion of surrender. "Could you help, you there, ya think?" he asked blankly, to no one in particular.

A few minutes after five o'clock: it was an era when most office workers in most businesses were more or less programmed into a clock that might as well have had a face that read only the hours between those numbers. As Rudderites were drifting out of the building, and herself on the way out, Dale Margolis stopped by Davey's desk, leaned down closely to him … enough that he could inhale a dose of Chanel, some portion of which emanated from the hint of cleavage lightly guarded by a V-neck blouse … and passed across a piece of paper with the scrawl TA 6–9593.

"Night, night. See ya tomorrow."

Hmm … the second message passed to me within the last four hours, he thought. *This must be my lucky day.*

Davey Wharton's gilt-edged education came in handy in this instance, for he knew without a doubt it was Renee Robbins's number. He had heard she lived in the Bronx too, but had not asked her about that or anything "personal" while they were together at the outing. He had certainly by now looked her up in the book, but there were lots of Robbins listed, none under the name Renee. He assumed she lived with her parents. Okay, so here it was; a door opening, maybe. Before tucking the scrap of paper into a pocket, he committed the number to memory.

The city remained enveloped in a series of steamy nights, and he was hardly in a hurry to go back to the family apartment. Residential air-conditioning was nonexistent in the buildings in his neighborhood, such that all the tenants suffered through the summer on an equal footing, equipped with electric fans of varying power that chugged on valiantly; a few fortunate places boasted cross-ventilation, said to bear one's body through the summer a bit more comfortably. On some nights a peaceful sleep was hard to achieve, still and heavy air and saturated bedsheets being standard fare.

Vacations and summer retreat homes lifted a noticeable percentage of New York's population during these months; the city could, from that standpoint, become more available in its slowed pace. On these kinds of nights, he would often walk around Manhattan, content in his privacy, grabbing a meal on the run and sampling the current entertainment available under the neon lights. Bars, jazz clubs, and theaters were all welcoming in the summer, doors perpetually open to the street beckoning one and all passersby into their darkened and smoky interiors. These places were often air-conditioned to a maximum level; there would be an instant of thermal shock upon entry that would linger until the human thermostat made its adjustment.

He sought out the Metropole for its traditional jazz, and then sometimes, for a 180-degree turn, there was Birdland, where everyone sat on hard benches and effected an attitude of deep concentration while they listened to the Modern Jazz Quartet and watched Percy Heath lean on his bass and marveled when they witnessed Percy actually strum a chord—a significant action. The Metropole demanded little or no intellectual effort; it was a raucous environment situated in a long corridor perpendicular to the street. The musicians perched in a row high above the seemingly endless bar; for a quarter you could linger over a glass of beer in a nondescript nine-ounce glass as long as you wished. Henry "Red" Allen played lead trumpet, but the star of the show was drummer Cozy Cole, the de facto chief executive of the ensemble. Cozy had merely to nod and show off a set of bone-china white teeth in a wide smile, and the band was off on "Tin Roof Blues," "Muskrat Ramble" or another of the old-timers in their catalog. The crowd would be into the music, often being bunched up two or three deep, putting the barstools at a premium. He did not care whether he was seated or not. To him, the place was a joy on any level.

Cozy Cole had even played up at college the previous year during fall parties at the Delta house. Davey was a Kappa himself, but at fall parties all of the houses were open, and there was a variety of music for the asking between the Friday night kickoff and the Sunday afternoon letdown. His Delta friend Arch Thompson took Cozy for a campus tour in between sets. He told Davey that the musician was especially impressed with the massive Case Memorial Library, imposing enough in its Colonial brick and white-pillared façade, but renowned for its obscure and eclectic collections, though rarely read and more rarely dusted. "So what did he think, Arch?" he remembered asking Thompson.

"All them books, man, all them books," was what he said, Arch told him.

"That's all?"

"Well, you have to remember that Cozy is a man of few words, but when he speaks, it carries an impact," Thompson said.

Indeed, Davey thought, as he admired Cozy Cole's effortless precision with the drums. Never show any stress or uncertainty; now, that's what I like. On this night, he waved knowingly at Cole from his barstool. Hey Coze, it's me, Wharton, you know, Arch's buddy from the college concert. Mouth in motion, the words were inaudible to all but himself, yet Cozy took an instant to glance toward him and wink back without relinquishing a drumbeat.

Three

He called Renee Robbins. Their conversation went something like this:

"Hi, Renee, it's Davey Wharton. You know, from near the art library."

"Davey? Yeah, I know you. Hi yourself."

"You remember our dance at the outing?"

"I guess (silence). "Hey, how'd you get my number anyway?"

"Oh, I have my sources (a pause, then a forced chuckle)."

"I'll bet it was Dale Margolis. Was it?"

"Uh, Renee, can we skip that. I … uh was calling to see if we could get together." *There, it was out on the table*, he thought.

"Ya mean a date?"

"I'd call it that. Yes."

"Well, maybe but …" Then, after an obligatory pause, Rene asked him, "What did you have in mind?"

"Oh, whatever you'd like. A movie, maybe dinner like at City Island. Hey, we both live in the Bronx, you know?"

"You know that too? Huh. Jeez, what else do you know about me? Where do you live anyways?"

He disclosed his address. She knew the area and made the observation that it was where all the "rich" people lived, which in those times and in Bronx terms was a euphemism for the Jewish community. "So. Will you … go out with me?"

She, maybe out of curiosity or an opening on her calendar, agreed to a date with him.

This was work, he concluded, suddenly aware of his soaked-through shirt.

They went to see *La Strada* at a small movie house that showed foreign films on 180th Street. Renee wore toreador pants and a cinched-in white blouse that rode faintly above her waist, exposing a rounded couple of inches of midriff. He had bought a madras shirt in summer colors expressly for the date, which he wore over newly pressed khakis. Renee made no comment on his clothes. Afterwards they shared ice-cream sundaes at Krum's, that palace of sweets on the Grand Concourse. Renee did not care for the film. It was black and white, she expected color; she didn't relate to the story and said Anthony Quinn was ugly, to boot.

Had Peter Pain, the little green Ben-Gay guy with the hammer, come up to Davey, he'd have said, "Schmuck, you don't take a girl like that to some high-brow foreign movie on the first date. You oughta know better. Now I'm gonna hammer you!"

Moving past the poor film decision, Renee perked up over the sundaes and at evening's end submitted to a perfunctory good-night kiss, although he was not invited to her apartment. She lived with her parents and a younger sister in a small building off of Fordham Road, the sort of location his own neighborhood friends would refer to as "the West," or that vast panorama of multistory structures that permeated the often windy streets of most of that borough; to them, anything beyond minutes of Pelham Bay Park was "the West."

They continued to date. He took her to dinner at a restaurant on the edge of City Island, a New England-like boating community that was one of New York's better kept secrets, and to other movies, including *The Seven-Year Itch*. He was somewhat sheepish escorting her to Marilyn Monroe's latest, male worship of the Hollywood goddess inviting comparisons with real-life women being an inevitable and common affliction of the day, but Renee laughed as much as he did at the summertime comedy. He thought about a Yankees game—the team was well on its way to a pennant once Bill Skowron and Elston Howard returned to the lineup from early-season injuries—but eschewed that option because he knew that, arm-in-arm with a beauty like Renee, the attention of the adjacent fans would be aroused, and not in a constructive way. She wasn't a Yankees fan anyway; it turned out that the Robbins family had moved to their present quarters from a smaller place in upper Manhattan hard by the Polo Grounds, so their loyalty belonged to the Giants.

"When are you going back to school?" she asked him over pizza and beer one night after a movie. He was into the final weeks of his job, and the oncoming new college term was looming larger in the mind's eye. Renee heard that he would be leaving soon, and although she was invariably in an up mood when they were together, there were periods when she appeared to place distance, an invisible wall, between them. This was one of them. She was not always available when he called; mostly their dates were on Friday rather than Saturday nights and once or twice during the week. On one of the weekly dates, they went to see *Fanny*. Renee loved the show; it appealed to a sentimental side of her that he'd had not seen before, and she said it was only the third time she had gotten to a Broadway theater.

Duncan Bruce had returned with a deep tan and in need of a haircut. Vowing to visit his stylist soon, for a while he opted to show off his flowing dirty-blond mane, a departure from the short military and crew cuts worn by most of the men in the office. But then again, Duncan would be nothing if not for his little deviations from the prevailing social conventions. "Wharton, you must go to Cuba," he said to Davey, who had a hard time believing anyone would go to Havana in August.

"Oh, I like it warm anyway," he said, "if you catch my drift, my good fellow. It's just marvelous—the nightlife, the shows, casinos, open all the time, and the girls, ooh, so overfriendly. It is a playground for all the senses, Wharton. And, I hasten to add, the off-season rates are very inviting. "Anyway, I'm back to the hardscrabble world of advertising. Bring me up to date on what's been going on here. I don't want to be blind-sided, you know."

He told Bruce about the conference with A to Z Industries and Madrid's inexplicable behavior.

"It's what the man deserves Wharton. Justice will be served. I bet he loses the account."

"Will he blame me?"

Bruce answered with a broad smile, "Oh, sure, I'd bet he will, but you're merely a summer employee. You didn't seriously covet a career in this business, did you?"

Later that same day Dale told him to expect a call from Jack Rudder: it was Rudder's practice to have summer people sit down with him toward the end of their tenure; the meeting was either an exit interview or an impression for the future. Forewarned, he was ready to respond when Rudder's secretary arranged for him to see the agency head two days following Dale's alert. In anticipation, Davey had taken himself to the nearest A to Z men's store and purchased a basic gray suit. For the time being, the maligned cord jacket was remanded to his closet.

"Ah, young Mr. Wharton, come in. Visit, will you?" Rudder motioned him to a plush leather chair at an angle to the chairman's desk. Behind the dense block of rich walnut, Rudder was visible only from the neck up. Davey took a moment to scan the office environment; the furnishings were of a university or gentlemen's club style—wood paneled walls, bulgy chairs, a domineering bookcase holding rows of antiquarian volumes with polished bindings. Atypical, he thought, for the leader in a business supposedly as forward looking as advertising to have an office so steeped in traditional trappings.

Davey had seen Jack Rudder only a few times and mostly from a distance. He was short, thick, and florid, the sort of man altogether standard issue at leafy country clubs in Connecticut or the north shore of Long Island. At the agency outing he was never without a hand surrounding a fresh Beefeater and tonic, as portrayed in the photographs snapped that day (which were on display the succeeding week for the entertainment, embarrassment, and ultimate enlightenment of the Rudder tribe), a man fully in tune with his bearings.

The agency began as Rudder and Mast, and Jack Rudder came to run it by himself five years previous when he arranged to buy out the Mast interests following the untimely death of his partner. For his vacation in that fateful year, Gallant Mast had decided to retrace Teddy Roosevelt's trip down the Amazon River. Setting forth in a small motorized boat with a crew of three Brazilian Indians, Mast and his compatriots disappeared within two days and were never found. Rudder waited for a respectable amount of time before making his move to assume control of the agency. In tribute to his erstwhile partner, Rudder commissioned the agency's art department to design a new corporate logo incorporating the nautical elements of a sailboat's mast and rudder. Done up in '50s *moderne* style, most observers believed it more resembled a cocktail frankfurter speared by a toothpick than a boat's appendages. Rudder paid little mind, though; after all, he was now in charge.

Far from an imposing presence, Rudder was easy in his mannerisms and conversation, sometimes a deliberate approach propounded by supremely confident men. He spoke in a soft cadence, maintaining a free-form attitude born of an inherent assumption of superiority. Not knowing what to expect of the discussion (Dale had not volunteered preparation, as if there was any to produce), Davey found that he was put at ease, able to say the right things (so he thought) without hesitation. Rudder seemed pleased that Wharton liked his summer work and that he'd welcome a career in advertising.

"You know, this is really a simple business, Wharton," Rudder offered, in the kind of statement that is designed to be an obvious deviation from the truth. "It's about imparting knowledge. All we need to do is to educate the marketplace, and the products that we promote will succeed. And if we do that with skill and honesty, those products will lead their competitors."

"But, Mr. Rudder, what about the cases where the market … pretty much knows all there is to know about a product?"

"Ah, but it's never a totality," Jack Rudder replied. "Look, let's take an industrial ad, for example, where you are informing a technical audience. There you want to emphasize capability, specs, and the like. Your question probably had in mind a consumer product. There we have to find the critical mass that differentiates it from the competition and … by God … drum that into the public's psyche and in the process tell the consumers something about themselves."

Rudder stopped there, eyes half closed, hands folded on an ample middle, a thorough captive of his own rhetoric and appearing somewhat drained. *How I love instructing the young,* he was thinking.

Man, he believes his own BS, Davey was thinking . 'Well, uh … I was working on some potential campaigns myself … in my spare time, of course," he added.

Rudder perked up momentarily. "Were you, now? Ah, splendid. Wharton, I admire initiative, yes I do."

"I am nearly finished. I'd appreciate the opportunity to present …"

An incomplete sentence. Jack Rudder bade the meeting to end. He rose stiffly from his chair, motioned the young man off, and said, "Right. Yes, when you are done, feel free to bring them to my office. All right now, good work, Wharton, and above all …" and here he was leaning across his desk with eyes locked in like a duck hunter eyeing his target, "where did you get that suit?"

"Uh … at one of the A to Z stores."

"Ah. Madrid's account. Well, I should have known right off the bat. Next time, go to Brooks Brothers."

He was treated for lunch during his final week at Rudder, nothing more than an excuse for the agency group to steal away for a leisurely repast. Not quite in the three martini category, but not far short of it either. At Romero Blanca, an uptown eatery adorned in fuzzy red wall paper, wrought iron lighting fixtures, and high-backed peasant-style chairs, a lunch could be had in 1955 for around four dollars that leaned more in the direction of gluttony than fine continental cuisine. Abundant cocktails and a generous washing of Chianti wrapped in straw bottles raised the cost by another two dollars, but who in hell worried about that. The house specialty was manicotti Bolognese, prepared al dente and served with an unlimited supply of garlic bread. They ordered zabaglione for dessert and were merrily satiated by 3 p.m. All toasted Mr. Davey Wharton and wished him well.

On the walk back to the office, the head of the personnel department, Don Helms, invited the group to participate in his favorite lunchtime Manhattan game, the ass of the day. It was early in the *Playboy* magazine era, and Hugh Hefner had, if nothing else, stimulated American males' fixation on the female body to heights heretofore unscaled. Helms claimed to have invented his game in the *Playboy* spirit and said that he was considering pitching it to Hef. Toting his Harvard MBA around several of the agency's departments, Helms was known to be an up-and-comer. He would offer a rating as they shuffled along

Madison Avenue—"The pearl gray skirt, snug around both globes, rhythmic motion, I give it a nine."

"Nah, too low-slung for me," Bill O'Dowd chipped in. "Now check out the one in the khaki poplin, a perfect arc from the back to the cheeks, slim waist opening up to …"

Even Jimmy Fleece tried his hand at the game, but was hooted down when he zeroed in on a girl with a billowing print sundress that revealed little of her lower anatomy. "Hey, at least gimme points for imagination," he said.

"Not a chance for a prize," Helms responded with an air of authority. "You can't even dream the contours of her ass in that kind of dress. If you want to play, Fleece, concentrate on the tight skirt, or slacks, if no skirts happen to be available." And on it went.

They walked on, coming alongside the sundress. "Don, Don Helms, that is you!" Sundress called out in recognition.

Helms turned in her direction; she was a pert blonde with gray-blue eyes. "Why, Annie … yes it's me all right," said. "Haven't seen you since college." They stopped to converse; they exchanged basic information about jobs, apartments, and whatever else was included in the checklist of essentials for a chance street corner meeting.

"Hey, call me sometime," Annie Richmond (which was she) said as they parted. Helms jogged to rejoin the Rudder strollers. "So, cap, aren't you glad I hit out on that one?" Jimmy Fleece exclaimed in between gum chews and lip snaps, to no one in particular, but in reality the comment generated for Don Helms, game-wizard.

Entering their building, Fleece took Davey aside. "Hey, top," he said in a half whisper.

"What is it, Jimmy?"

"Did you hear what he said to that babe?"

"No, Jimmy."

"He told her she had a great summer dress—it suited her figure. Can you believe that shit?"

Back at his desk, Davey Wharton expressed puzzlement to Duncan Bruce as to why Fleece had been with them at lunch to begin with. He had had minimal contact with Jimmy since the outing debacle. "Oh, I thought you laddies were buddy-buddy, old sport," he offered, "Rumor has it Jimmy may even be staying on at Rudder, as it seems they like his work."

What work would that be? Davey thought. "Really?" he replied to Duncan. "I thought he was going on to a … local college," "local college" being a pejorative term in his lexicon.

"The Rudder grapevine also has it he may get some help with that, as well. Are we done with *l'affaire Fleece* for now? Good. On another subject, your friend Madrid is trying to rescue that A to Z account. It's a good thing you're heading back to school soon, or he might be after you again. In fact, he would have been with us today, but for the fact that he's had to work on some proposals for the account."

Sounding annoyed, a departure from the sunny demeanor he had maintained all along, Davey said, "Come on, Dunc (he was on a limited list of those allowed to refer to Bruce as Dunc), you know Madrid isn't any friend of mine. What's his story anyway?" He was mystified by Harvey Madrid's staying power in the first place, placing him within the culture of the agency to be at best a lone ranger and at worst a virtual pariah.

"I suppose I never related to you the episode involving Harvey and Milton Berle, did I?"

Laughing at an instantaneous image he conjured up of two such unlikely characters, he cheerily admitted, "Oh, no you have not. I'd have remembered that one. Sensing one of Duncan Bruce's fantasies aimed his way, Davey bade him to continue.

"All right, then it is new to you. Forgive the omission on my part. Well, it seems that some years back, when Berle was all the rage, Mr. Television and all that, he had occasion to be in the agency's offices. I can't recall what for. In fact, his show, *The Texaco Star Theater*, well I don't even think Rudder had any Texaco advertising. Not that it mattered. Berle was leaving, being seen to the door by an account executive. It was early evening. Anyway, he spies one lone employee hunched over his desk, lit only by a dreary one-bulb lamp. There's nobody else around him. Berle cannot resist playing the showman for laughs, so he proceeds to crack jokes, directed at this guy. By now, my good man, you can guess that employee was …"

"Harvey Madrid."

"Ah, no wonder you'll graduate come loudly or whatever. Anyhow, Madrid never lifts his head from his desk work. Berle delivers one joke after another, increasingly in strident tones. No recognition and no response from his audience of one. Finally, the great man approaches this desk and its occupant and virtually screams at him, "Laugh, you son of a bitch, everyone laughs at my lines."

Here Duncan pauses for effect, much in the way Berle had behaved, awaiting a reaction.

"And ...?"

"Madrid slowly lifts his head from his paperwork, turns to Berle, looks him in the eye, and says ever so delicately, "F--- you, Uncle Miltie!"

"No sh--?" Davey said.

"It's the stuff of legend around here, young Wharton. That account exec, the only witness, claimed later that Berle stood speechless for a moment, with feet of clay, so to speak, and then proceeded to vacate the premises as fast as he could."

"But ... not ... how did Madrid keep his job after that? You couldn't flush Berle like that and get away with it."

"Ah, but he did. They loved it around here. See, anyone who knew Berle in those days thought he was the most arrogant ass they'd ever run across, and here was this little ... uh ... what's a word you Bronx inhabitants might find fitting?"

Davey said, "Maybe *meshugeneh*, it means like, crazy, but sounds more colorful."

Duncan continued, "Right. That's the very word I was searching for. So, Harvey assumed the *cachet* of the little man that could. Of course, right after that, they had to move his desk to a remote corner of the floor, near the broom closet, just in case, you know, Berle ever showed up again. I don't believe he ever did."

That weekend, Davey and Renee double-dated with Duncan Bruce and (Duncan's term) his *inamorata*, Paige Jessica Bradley, who wanted everyone to call her Jessie but was more of a Paige. Tall and angular, with honey-blonde hair in a swept-back cut that framed chiseled patrician features, some might see in her a resemblance to Hepburn, circa 1938. Straight up, she matched Bruce in height. She wore a teal silk blouse and high-waisted navy-blue slacks that emphasized what may have been a set of legs of indeterminate end. Renee looked stunning, so Davey thought, in a sleeveless deep coral shantung dress, tight to the hips and with a high neckline.

They were off to dinner and dancing at a club called Way Down There, in the basement of a small midtown hotel on Madison Avenue. Dark and a bit edgy, the club was a favorite for Duncan and Jessie. Dinner was basic, hardly memorable; the place was set up for structured intimacy with its banquette seating, muted lighting on deep-toned walls, expensive drinks, and a trio that played well-known tunes for close dancing. In between there was opportunity for conversation full of innuendo, if the participants had the creativity, or, better still, introductory groping. Davey and Renee danced often, to songs such as "Where or When," "Isn't It Romantic" and "I Can't Get Started," the latter performed a la Bunny Berigan with a trumpet solo and a graveled vocal by the bandleader.

"… I got a house, a showplace, still I can't get no place with you …"

Duncan and Jessie spent most of the evening woven in advanced cuddling. They danced hardly at all, laughing softly on the plush banquette, both sets of hands hidden from view, as though anyone would have been able to see very much in the dim atmosphere. Later, as couples were beginning to drift out of the club, Duncan decided it was time to move along as well. "Here, young Wharton, you get to drive the fabled Citroen," he said as they surfaced again on Madison Avenue. "You do drive, don't you, old chap?"

"Now, Duncan …" Jessie started, Bruce interrupting, "Shhh, Jessie dear, the young lad will be just fine. Why we'll have a chauffeur, my lady." Jessie had said very little to anyone all evening. *Chauffeur indeed*, Davey thought as they pulled away into the heavy summer night, and the mighty Citroen snorted and phased into its seat adjustments, sounding like a steam presser laying on a crease.

"Hey, where are we going?" Renee asked, a tone of impatience in her voice. "I really want to get home."

"Home, then, it will be, "Duncan said magnanimously. "But this is such a lovely evening, let's, as they say, take the long way home …"

"And what would that be?" his fledgling driver asked.

"Why, have you never circled all around Manhattan?" was Duncan's response. Both he and Jessie giggled. It was Duncan's idea to embark upon an around-the-borough tour of Manhattan, a sort of Circle Line on land. Heading southbound along the FDR, Davey knew that Renee was antsy, pissed about the seating assignments, and now was primed to fold her femininity for the night. Hardly halfway down to the Brooklyn Bridge, alternating clothing swishes, throaty murmurs, and giggles wafted from the back seat. Citroen's seats may have been fully set in place, but the occupying bodies were anything but. Rounding the southern tip of Manhattan, the city still valiantly putting on a light extravaganza over land and water, the muffles continued as the route took them north toward the West Side Highway. The rear seat activity intensified into an "aargh … oooh … ah … oh, God, God …"

Enough of this, Davey thought (Renee was now a frosty distance away from him and wrapped into a ball hard by the passenger door, her body position and silence sending a leave-me-alone message), *we'll do Manhattan another time, possibly the Bronx and Staten Island too, but I've got the wheel, and I'm cutting right across at Canal to go straight home, and then Duncan can reclaim possession of his French passion pit.* It wasn't until they negotiated the Willis Avenue Bridge and were well onto the Bruckner that Duncan and Jessie, by this time evidently unbundled, woke up.

"Hey, what happened to the Cloisters?" Bruce asked.

"Sorry, Dunc, but I had WINS on, lightly, of course, but a news bulletin came on to say that it keeled over and fell into the Hudson. Had to make a detour." Renee interrupted her icy funk to laugh. Once safely back in the Bronx, he relinquished command of the car in front of Renee's apartment building; she, out in quick time, was already at the entrance. Jessie, climbing around to the front passenger seat, was making final tugs at her silk top (down) and slacks (up). Duncan, now behind the wheel, saluted Davey and Renee on the sidewalk, and the car huffed its way in a downtown direction.

He looked at Renee. "Oh that … that man," she started. "You're leaving Rudder, but I'll still be around him at the agency."

"Look, can we just talk about us? I had a great evening with you, dancing and all, and you looked gorgeous. You put what's her name …"

"Jessie."

"… to shame. Maybe that's why she ignored us all night. I think she looks kind of, well, horsy."

"Yeah, I think," Renee said. "They go well together but." In the Bronx tradition, Renee often left her sentences unfinished and hanging on the word "but," somehow inviting expectation of a follow-on thought that never emerged.

Then they both laughed, Renee on the doorstep to her apartment building entrance. "Renee, can I come up?" he asked.

"You know I really like you."

He smiled at her. "Somehow that doesn't come across as a ringing endorsement. It wouldn't fly in the ad trade at all."

"You can guess, Davey. We were good together, real good, but we were different."

Were. He effected a puzzled look, not knowing what he would hear next.

"Hey, you're smart. I know that, and you do too, and that you want something. Thing of it is, you don't know what. You're looking to see where you fit. I'm just a girl from the Bronx, but I know where I belong. I just think you're always gonna be reaching out for something else, something you don't have. So …"

"So, you're blowing me off, Renee? Was it just the summer? Was I a diversion for you?"

Renee was still talking. "The thing is, well, you heard what I said about Bruce, but you have more in common with someone like him than me. You guys talk about your colleges, you dress alike …"

"Wait a minute. I don't wear kilts and tartans," Davey said, taking umbrage at her last comment.

Laughing, she said, "Oh, I'll give you that, although I bet you've got the legs for it. Anyway, I've said my piece. I'd better go now."

"Kiss?"

"Yeah, sure, sweet friend," Renee said, relenting as they kissed lightly on the lips. They were parting. "Okay, I'm walking away now, Renee. You take care."

"The bus stops on the corner, Davey. Safe home." And with that, Renee turned into her building.

City bus service operated around the clock, albeit with less frequency in the early hours. He heard the beginning rumbles of thunder, signaling the arrival of rain. It would be a fitting end to the evening if he got drenched before the bus arrived. Luckily, he saw headlights of a bus approaching the corner. As he boarded, for the moment still dry, he looked up at Renee's building and was certain that he saw her light come on and Renee moving in silhouette against the curtain. He also believed her darkened figure gave a little wave down to him on the street below before the lamp dimmed, but then again the impression could have been imagined.

Four

Davey had worked up advertising proposals for A to Z's soft drinks, which were branded, not surprisingly, A to Z sparkling sodas. *No wonder it was a laggard, with such a boring banner. Maybe I can help*, he thought. His proposal envisioned a print campaign in popular magazines such as *Look*, *Life*, and *Holiday*, and he developed copy, roughed out illustrations (though hardly an artist, although he had always had drawing ability), and shaped a strategy for media positioning and timing. Having completed his efforts in the final week of his stay at Rudder, he brought everything to Jack Rudder's office.

Recalling his prior meeting with Jack Rudder, Alison Joust, the ooh-so-prim secretary, greeted him warmly. "Mr. Wharton, how nice of you to stop by," she said. "We (supposedly speaking for Jack Rudder, or perhaps all of the agency) will miss you as we toil on."

"Likewise on my account," he replied. "I'm glad to have had the opportunity. Now. I promised Mr. Rudder I'd bring an ad proposal to him, and I'd like to do that. Is he available for a moment?"

At that, Miss Joust rose from behind her desk and informed him that, no, that would not be possible inasmuch as Mr. Rudder was away on a very important client conference. Seeing a look of disappointment begin to take hold on Davey's face, she added, somewhat mischievously, "And would you like to know what it is about?"

"Well … uh … I suppose so." It occurred to him that perhaps because he was leaving, Alison Joust was disposed to break ranks and pass on a confidence to him.

"So, then," and Alison lowered her tone several decibels even though there was nobody but the two of them within earshot, "Mr. Rudder is playing golf at the Hippopotamus Club in Westchester with Mr. Madrid and … Stanley Goldrunner of A to Z and … Milton Berle himself, along to keep them in happy spirits."

There, the news was out and Alison seemed delighted to have imparted the information to someone, as though it was a mighty burden that had to be lifted from one's shoulders. Davey thought it was one of the stranger golf foursomes he could imagine, and for a fleeting moment he wished he could have caddied for them.

She added, "You can leave your work with me; I'm sure Mr. Rudder will be pleased to review it upon his return," quickly reverting to a professional mode as he left the office.

Duncan Bruce was wearing the following outfit: navy-blue Bermuda shorts, high socks in charcoal gray, polished black tasseled loafers, a gray striped seersucker sports jacket, a pale-blue button-down shirt, and a regimental tie bearing the colors of the Twenty-fifth Guards Grenadiers. It was a particularly uncomfortable day in the city's now mature summer season, so the choice should not have seemed shocking apart from the fact that even Duncan Bruce would have to make a brief appearance in said attire on the Lex at rush hour, which would entail some risk. Still, Davey was curious about it. "Hey, what gives with the clothes, Dunc?"

At this time he could go ahead and be flip with Duncan; it was his final day at work, and he had only to straighten out his desk before the leave-taking.

"It was my fervent hope that you'd notice, dear Wharton, and take inspiration," Bruce said to him. "But, I'll let you in on my true intention. You see, the agency is pitching the Bermuda Tourist Bureau account, and I just thought, well, it would help us along if their reps would see one of our executives who was … shall we say … bedecked for the occasion. If you happened to consult the July Playboy, you would have found a very favorable article on the Bermuda style, well illustrated, I would add." Bruce was as smug as a pelican who had just speared the seafood special of the day.

"Dunc, correct me if I'm wrong, but isn't that Jamicco's pitch?"

"The one and the same," Duncan answered.

He went on. "If Perry sees you like that with those guys, he'll have you for lunch for stealing his thunder."

Assuming a pose of noblesse oblige, Bruce said, "Then I'll say to Sir Perry—come and get it!"

A toss of his curly hair while laughing out loud, Davey loaded the last of his meager desk belongings into a large manila envelope and said to Duncan, "You are a pisser, without question."

"On that note, my young charge, I bid you adieu until we meet again. It's been swell."

He said, "Oh, on that subject, I … was going to talk to you about getting together in October for the homecoming game—it's at our campus this year. In fact, it's on the twenty-fifth. What do you think?"

"I think—fabulous, I'd love it—assuming you guys are prepared to lose the title to us again, as usual. Let's do it."

They agreed to meet before the game, and then Davey would host dinner at the Kappa house.

"You'll bring … Jessie … or a reasonable facsimile?"

Duncan Bruce nodded in the affirmative. "So long, then, Duncan. Just watch your back on the subway."

Now on free time before fall semester started, he saw the Yankees play the Red Sox on a gray and humid afternoon, and from his bleacher bench witnessed, with escalating aggravation, Boston center fielder Jimmy Piersall kick up manhole-sized divots during the half innings when he patrolled his position; whether out of boredom, psychosis, or a calculated plan to wreak havoc on Mantle's knee (once again) when the Mick took his turn on the field was anyone's guess. The season was headed into its final three weeks, with the Yankee pennant all but a formality; the game was a yawn job and it ended rather peacefully, no harm befalling Mickey Mantle that day.

He also took in the film *Pete Kelly's Blues*, directed and starring Jack Webb of *Dragnet*. An attempt to recreate the 1920s jazz scene, an era that Davey found entrancing, the movie opened to less than stellar reviews, but he liked it all the same.

Dale Margolis called him. On vacation the week he left Rudder, she did not have a chance to say good-bye and wished him luck back at college. "Don't be a stranger, Davey," she said in signing off. He called on Duncan's home phone a couple of times, but there was no answer. *I guess he's away on another mystery voyage*, he thought.

Five

The football game was tied at 7-7 as the first half ended. On this brilliant October afternoon, Davey Wharton kept scanning the smallish stadium for signs of Duncan Bruce; he had hung back before the second-half kickoff, hoping to spot the man, but to no avail. Prowling the area and not finding him, he began to get down on himself for failing to track down the elusive Mr. Bruce beforehand to remind him of their plan to meet. He had been primed to show Duncan off later on at the Kappa house, believing his presence would delight the brothers with tales of his misadventures, and, had he brought Jessie, add a touch of New York sophistication to the postgame party. His own date for the evening, Sarah Codd, from E- in Boston, was arriving around cocktail time, and he thought that she would find his new-found business associates impressive as well, which just might help his chances with her later on in the evening. He had only dated Sarah twice before—an initial blind date on a weekend run to Boston and another time two weeks thereafter. He had wished his date could have been Renee Robbins, but no, the relationship was long gone, and he believed that a girl like Renee, despite her urban sexiness, would not pass muster with his peers on campus. Invariably, the majority of the dates at parties were of a more conservative bent; they tended to come from homogenous suburban towns, did not wear tight skirts, and could discuss James Joyce with the best of his classmates. Sarah, a befreckled redhead, probably met most of the preceding criteria, save for the James Joyce discussion, which he certainly would not initiate. Upon her arrival, and based on his discerning eye, he speculated that her pleated plaid skirt cinched with a gold safety pin (the part of the outfit she had worn last time) concealed shapely territory—of which he harbored hopes for exploration.

"Hey, Wharton, you hanging for the second half?" It was his pal, Arch Thompson. 'You looking for someone, man?" Arch went on, picking up on his impression that Davey appeared to be distracted.

"Uh … no … well maybe, but not yet," he replied.

"I hope she doesn't crap out on you," Thompson said as he laughed and began to move in, "Hey we got Cozy Cole back at the house; drop over." *Yeah, the Coze himself. Maybe I'll go up and say hello between sets,* Davey thought; *maybe he'll remember me from his summer stint at the Metropole I was the guy with the rumpled cord jacket and the red challis tie.*

The remainder of the weekend played out uneventfully. The home team won in an upset; Davey and Sarah enjoyed the house parties together, and when he approached Cozy Cole during a break, the drummer didn't know what the hell he was talking about but nonetheless flashed him a mouthful of perfect teeth with an enormous grin.

"Hey, I thought you said he knew you," Sarah said, looking on, oddly crestfallen. "And what happened to your New York friends?"

"Oh, the main guy, he knows me all right but just doesn't remember. There's a lot on his mind, you know."

"And the other ones?" she continued.

He thought about Duncan Bruce and wondered what had happened. "I guess they … uh … had other commitments," was his unconvincing answer.

Soon after, Peter Pain paid him a return visit. 'How often I gotta tell ya? You blew it with the body last summer. Now you have this one, maybe there's a body, maybe not, there's too much cloth in the way to make an assessment, but you have to come up with better lines than that. You need help, kid. I'm not even gonna hammer you—it'd just be a waste of effort'.

It was December, and he was waiting for a haircut, a final grooming before the Christmas break. After two years of crew cuts, which never worked with his genetic curls, he'd made a significant decision (so he believed it to be) over the summer to let his hair grow out; he was after all, a senior, and it was high time to show a little maturity. Besides, all the town barbers were butchers, and the less surgery performed on his head, so much the better. The radio was playing Gail Storm singing "I Hear You Knocking." Rock 'n' roll was coming on in an undeniable movement that left him distraught in a musical way, he being a traditional jazz fan. Not very avant-garde at all, he tried but found wanting the merits of modern jazz as well. Some of his friends would listen to such as Dave Brubeck, Paul Desmond, Chet Baker, and Gerry Mulligan for hours, hardly stirring, seemingly enveloped in a strange cerebral trance. It never appeared to be much fun, in his opinion. Rock, of course, wasn't in the same game; you could, if you wished, identify a beat and even a melodic character to some of the songs. He was beginning to concede a future for it.

He was thumbing through a recent issue of *Holiday*, when he found it. A full page, the illustration in vibrant color, the ad was for Glacier Ice Colas and portrayed a family exiting a car at a roadside eatery under the banner "Brake for Glacier Ice." The copy extolled the refreshment and taste superiority of the beverages. Reading the text rapidly, he recognized his work right out of the very same portfolio he had submitted to Rudder at summer's end … for the A to Z soda line, "A to Z Softies." So here were his ads in full bloom for a competing brand; Glacier, like the A to Z products, was among the handful or so of brands fighting for a spot just beneath the two big hitters, Coke and Pepsi. He fumbled through the pile of magazines strewn over the adjacent table, locating the latest issue of *Look*. There, within the magazine's first third, was another full-page ad for Glacier Ice, this under the headline "Refreshment Is Just Around The Vend" and illustrated with a happy group of office workers convened around a hall vending machine enjoying cans of Glacier Ice soft drinks. That was his creation as well, virtually word for word, as best as he could recall.

"Hey, kiddo, you're next. You want a haircut, or ya here for a reading room? In case you were looking, someone pinched the holiday *Esquire*. So don't bother." The barber, Antonio or something close to that, was motioning in his direction. "Dat book you got so important, take it, my compliments."

"Yeah, sure," Davey said, suddenly disoriented, as he slipped into the cracked and worn burgundy leather barber chair.

"College kids, who can figga them?" Antonio said to his compatriot operating in the next chair.

"Hi, Dale, it's Davey Wharton, you know from the summer." Now back in the city, he had called Dale Margolis for the express purpose of finding out what was behind the Glacier Ice advertising.

"Why, Davey, I'm glad to hear from you," Dale said cheerfully. "In fact, I was thinking about you; our office Christmas party is coming up, and I was going to be in touch with you for an invite."

When he told her the reason for his call, Dale paused for a moment and then suggested they get together for lunch, about which he readily agreed. A week later they met at Romeo Blanca. He had spent a significant percentage of his summer earnings at Bloomingdale's on a senior-year wardrobe; for the lunch meeting with Dale, he trotted out the best of his selections, a muted olive herringbone jacket with a subtle blue window pane over oxford gray slacks, blue straight-collar shirt, and hunter green knit tie. Dale had dressed for the occasion as well, with a soft wool black turtleneck over a gray glen plaid skirt, the top accented by a twelve-carat opal on a pendant surrounded by diamonds, an island of color against the ebony background. He could not help but appreciate the way in which the top hugged every contour of Dale's full breasts, but he kept that thought tucked away and limited his expression to a compliment on her jewelry.

"Oh, thanks," she said. "My splurge. October's my birthday, and opal is the birthstone for the month. Did you know it's bad luck for anyone else to wear it? Makes it kind of exclusive, I think. But we're not here to admire one another, however gratifying that may be. Let's order, then we'll talk."

He savored a three-olive martini while Dale nursed a glass of Soave as they awaited their lunch order to be served. He asked her about the Glacier Ice ads.

"That's ours, for sure."

"So?"

Dale picked up. "So … Davey, here's what took place. Madrid lost the A to Z account shortly after Labor Day and before he had any chance whatsoever for making a proposal, including your work. Goldrunner moved his business to BBD&O, which some people would consider an upgrade, but I'm not going to get into that. Okay, so Jack Rudder decided to pitch the competition—which was Glacier Ice."

"With my ads," Davey chimed in in an aggravated tone.

"Enough already; try not to be so possessive," Dale said. "Yes, your ads, but you also should remember that when you joined Rudder, even as a temp, any work done while there becomes their property. There's probably some clause in whatever paperwork you signed in the beginning of your job that says that."

Not letting go, he went on. "Okay, Dale, but someone could have contacted me acknowledging my work …"

"Well, look, I'm not apologizing for the agency, but even though you recognized your creative ideas when you saw them, they'll say, one, that it was Rudder property, two, that it's only a start for a much larger campaign, and, three, that it was hardly a finished product that you turned in. The end product reflected all of the finishing touches edited, tweaked, and so on by agency personnel. You had intended it to go toward another account, and you had no role with the eventual advertiser. So, at the end of the day, is it entirely yours? Hard to say; hard to say. Look, maybe you can parlay the thing into a job offer from Jack"

"Come on, Dale, you're spouting the party line. Can you deny that those ads were mine?"

She turned pensive. "I can understand your feelings, Davey, but I wouldn't take …"

Their food was being served. Dale was enjoying a turbot oreganato with broccoli rabe, and he was digging into the pasta special—farfalle with diced smoked salmon in a velvet pink sauce. Blanca had recently hired a new chef, direct from Siena (or so the maitre d' had informed them) and had begun to move its menu more in the direction of classic northern Italian cuisine, priced accordingly. The place still had the red-flocked wall covering.

"Finish your thought, Dale?" he asked.

"Oh, I was going to say that if I was an attorney, I'm not so sure I'd take your case."

"But you're not a lawyer."

"No," Dale responded. She looked squarely at him and said, "You know, Davey, I … I really like you when you get riled up, like now. I could go for you myself." A mischievous smile (that may not have been a total fraud) occupied her face.

"You're changing the subject."

She laughed. "You bet I am. I'm tapped out on the other one. You shouldn't rule out older women, especially any whose waists haven't thickened too much. What I mean is you ought to be willing to expand your horizons."

He laughed too. *Maybe that's not such bad advice*, he thought. *A martini, a sumptuous lunch, and a woman like Dale Margolis in that huggy knit top looking better and better.* He continued. "Since you've introduced the … uh … category, how's Renee?"

"Since you're asking, I guess you haven't stayed in touch."

"No. I must have been a summer romance, if you could have ever called it that. You know, Dale, I never got a solid reason for why she broke off so, so … abruptly. I suppose nobody ever gets a satisfactory explanation, anyway."

Dale said, "Okay, since you brought it up, yeah, there's a story there—you might as well hear it. First of all, Renee had this old boyfriend who had been in the Army and was set to be discharged after the summer. You were an interlude in anticipation of his return. But the boyfriend did not come home alone. He showed up nonstop from Germany with a new bride—a pretty fraulein. Renee, of course, never knew before the fact and went kinda nuts. For a couple of weeks I thought I'd be reading about a murder in the Bronx, but then it all seemed to blow over."

"Is she available, then?" He was showing interest in a rekindling while completely skipping over any concern over the degree of hurt that Renee may have experienced.

"Davey, let me finish," Dale continued. "Last week she and Perry Jamicco announced their engagement, so the answer to your question is 'no'."

"What!"

"Yeah, I know. Weirdsville, isn't it? It turns out there was some history between Renee and Jamicco, but it picked up much speed after her thing with the boyfriend."

He was dumfounded. "Jamicco? I can't believe it."

"Wait, there's more. Renee got a promotion to assistant account executive and she's enrolled at Columbia part time at the company's expense."

"Columbia?"

Dale hastened to elaborate. "General studies, Davey, but its still Columbia."

He managed a smile, "Hell, if it's good enough for Pat Boone, I suppose it's good enough for Renee. Hey, Dale, can I go back to the Glacier stuff for a minute? What about Madrid? He loses a big account, he pisses off Milton Berle, and the next thing I know these guys are all playing golf together. How does he manage to keep his job?"

"Oh, so I see you know all about the Berle episode."

"Yeah, Duncan told me."

Dale continued. "Sure, but Duncan has that knack for disseminating selective information. What he probably didn't tell you is that Madrid is Jack Rudder's brother-in-law. See, when Jack led the buyout of the Mast interests in the agency, he needed the last dollars from his wife, who has some family money of her own. She went in on it, but demanded that the agency hire Harvey—who just happens to be her younger brother. So here's the infamous Harvey Madrid, a washed-up car salesman, all of a sudden an ad executive, and bulletproof to boot.

"And there's more. They played golf last summer, as you know. It's a last-ditch effort to rescue the A to Z account. Jack says to Harvey, 'Look, under no circumstances do you beat Goldrunner at golf. It's customer golf.' So what does he do? Shoots the game of his life; he's totally on fire. Embarrasses Stanley and laughs at every cornball joke Uncle Miltie tells all day long. The next day A to Z goes down the tubes."

"And?" Davey asked, by now totally immersed in the tale being told.

"And," she proceeds, "for the first time in years Jack is this close," Dale squeezes thumb and forefinger, "to throwing Harvey out, wife or not, but he catches his breath, gets the bright idea to pitch Glacier with the gestation of a new print campaign in the can, so to speak. Moreover, having just been with the great Berle, he makes an approach about TV specials under Glacier sponsorship if it turns out that Rudder lands the account. Berle says, 'Sure, I even drink the stuff. Oh, and Jack, if you bring it in, I'd love to see that guy Madrid handle the business. He's got a hell of a sense of humor and a great golf game besides. Dynamite combo, my man.'"

"Therefore, Madrid's back on top and in everyone's good graces," Davey offered, with not a little disgust coating his voice.

They had finished their main course, and the busboy cleared the plates from the table. "Maybe not everyone, but, yes, he's riding high right now. Even Jack's okay with it. You wanna hear about your friend Jimmy Fleece?"

I don't know why I got tagged with being his friend, Davey thought. "Oh, sure. Tell me, Dale, is he in line for Jack's job?"

"Not quite, but you remember Don Helms, don't you?"

Recalling Helms, the grad school hotshot with curly blond hair, a permanent smile, and an oily personality who concocted the lunch hour ass-of-the-day game, he nodded in the affirmative, and Dale continued. "Well it seems that on one of his lunch-hour strolls where Fleece was along, Fleece had singled out this girl—from the rearview mirror, of course—and when they all pulled alongside, she recognized Helms from back in college. A chance meeting, but the two reconnected and are seeing each other."

Davey chimed in, "I remember it, Dale, I was there. It was my farewell lunch day. And Helms was playing his …"

"I know. Favorite ass, or something like that," Dale said. "Anyway, Helms was so beholden to Fleece that he took him under his wing and moved him into media, which Helms is slated to be running next year, as his personal assistant."

Davey mentioned to Dale that he understood Fleece was returning to school, and she said that Fleece was combining school with his new job at Rudder and that the agency was also sending him for golf lessons to bolster what was being termed his "potential for interpersonal relationships." Dale checked her watch, indicating their luncheon was winding down, and asked if he wanted any more Rudder updates. "Actually, Dale, yes. What's Duncan up to? I've tried to reach him, to no avail. In fact, we had planned to meet at a football game back in October, but he never showed up."

She turned quiet for a moment and then went on in a flat, lower voice. "That one is not too good."

"What do you mean?"

"I mean … well, he's sick Davey," Dale said, placing a hand over his. "Nobody knows what's wrong, and if some people do, then they aren't saying much. He took a leave of absence about a month ago."

Assuming that Duncan would be still in town in his apartment, he expressed surprise no one was checking in with him. It was an incorrect assumption; Dale told him Bruce had left New York with no forwarding address. "That's why you couldn't reach him. I hear he has some family in San

Francisco; that's probably where he's gone, but I can't give you an address or a number. If I come on to one, I'll let you know. I promise."

The waiter served each of them an espresso. He ordered another martini. Dale said, "Davey Wharton, maybe you will make it in this business—the old pros can do a triple play at lunch, and you're two-thirds on your way."

He managed a smile, even though he admitted being quite shaken about Duncan Bruce. What could have gone so wrong?

She checked her watch, he taking in its classy gold casing. *Bonus payments must be good this year,* he thought. "Hey, you know, I need to get back for a meeting. I'm a full-timer, and you're on holiday break. You enjoy that martini. I got the check."

He became somewhat sheepish over the fresh drink. "Well, Dale, I needed it after hearing about everyone and everything at the agency. I gotta tell you, though, that it's a lot of crap."

"Not really, Davey. That's advertising."

Dale got up from the table and started to leave. She turned one last time to him and said, "Oh, and consider what I told you. I expect you to stay in touch and will be damn mad if you don't." A parting shot.

He watched her walk away. Yeah, maybe the waist was a little thicker than he would like, but the impression from behind wasn't all that bad. He reached for another pull on the martini. You never can figure it out, can you?

Santa Cashing Out

She found him fast asleep, slumped over a pile of letters and a legal-sized yellow pad, pencil in hand. "Nick, Nick, wake up! Are you all right," she wailed. He shuddered momentarily, then came around and smiled her way.

"Oh, liebschin, I must have dozed off," the jolly man said. "I was going through the mail to see who's been naughty and who's been nice." He gestured at two stacks of letters, the nice ones far outweighing the naughty.

Brunhilde Claus moved her considerable bulk alongside of the rustic worktable behind which Santa was wedged. "You know, Nick, there are hardly half as many letters as there used to be. They're all e-mailing you these days, and I haven't seen you touch that computer in a week," she said.

"Computer? Ach, to me it's just a confuser, mein frau. I cannot get the hang of it and, besides, I'm too old to be insulted by messages on a screen," he answered with a sigh and a twinkle.

"Well, Nick, I've been meaning to talk to you about the big picture and maybe this is as good a time as any," Mrs. Claus began in earnest. "Have you given any thought that possibly times have … er … passed us by and perhaps we should sell the business?" She stroked his full beard and went on, "Why don't we retire while we can?"

"Retire?" Santa appeared incredulous at the idea. "Whatever would we do?"

It was the cue she was looking for. "For starters," she answered him, "we could get away from the North Pole in the winter. Up to the holiday it's all preparation, and then from January through March you work on returns and ninety-day warranties. All of our friends are in Florida for the winter. Why, the Burgemeisters just bought a condo in Bonita with a view of the gulf. They're not freezing their tushies off like we are."

"Not everyone is gone. The Snowmans are still here—Frosty and Freida."

Mrs. Claus said, “Nick, you know full well we can’t even see that couple indoors. All of our dinners are alfresco, so they won’t melt. What good are friends like that?” She stood and added, “I see I’ll have to take the initiative. I’ve invited the firm of Gold and Max to come in here and give us an evaluation—you know, financial planning and what a sale of the business would bring in. We’ll have ourselves a merry little Christmas. You’ll see.”

A pair of investment bankers arrived the next day and were whisked into Santa’s office. The old man pushed his girth away from the worktable and rose to greet them. For the meeting, he was decked out in full regalia, red suit, wide sash, and polished black boots. The only deference he made to the indoors was the doffing of his stocking cap, which lay across the chipped and battered table. “I’m Claus,” he addressed his visitors, “although my close friends call me Nick, which is actually short for Saint Nick. And you are …”

“Booker Addington,” answered the tall, gaunt young man with slicked-to-the-skull dirty blond hair and wearing a tightly fitted black suit in the bespoke tradition, “managing director of Gold and Max, and this is my associate,” he gestured in the direction of the Asian man alongside, “Pao Kung Fou, who graduated magna cum laude from MIT last year and does all of my number crunching.” The associate also wore black, but to the trained eye his suit would be instantly recognizable as a Far Eastern-manufactured knockoff so not as to upstage the senior man. Addington regarded his host and fairly gushed, “Love your suit. Is it designer?”

Santa appeared puzzled. “Could be,” he responded. “I have three such red suits and they were all made by Eddie the Elf, so I guess you might say so. Everything we sell—everything we have here at the Pole—we manufacture. Shall we get started? I thought you both would enjoy a tour of the workshop.”

As far as the eye could see around the cavernous factory, there were little people in green uniforms working feverishly at long tables, hammers banging, wood chips flying, saws and metal cutters buzzing and grinding away, all to meet the holiday demand for toys. Santa pointed out that they were observing a peak busy period in advance of high season. The Gold duo looked on impassively, posing questions along the way. “What are you principal raw materials?” Addington asked.

“Oh, wood mainly, some tin, fabric for the dolls,” Claus responded.

“What about electronic games, Nick?”

“We don’t make them. It’s all kept basic here. These are wholesome toys that have stood the test of time.”

The banker was aghast. "You don't make Pre-Teen Internet Robot Blasters? You don't make Slaughter Station? That is what's all the rage in the toys and games space. You're missing a huge market, man. This … uh … stuff you're turning out is old hat, a joke."

Some of the elves overheard the last remark, as the banker had become increasingly agitated. A growing murmur enveloped the room as the tour group was noticed; the elves gradually ceased their labors until a heavy silence prevailed. Sensing anxiety, Santa Claus quickly moved to address his workforce. "It's all right, munchkins. These are our guests from New York, where, as you may know, some citizens are given to outlandish statements as a means of expression. No ill will is intended. You may all carry on with your duties. Ho, ho, ho."

Leaving the factory floor, he added, "They get nervous when strangers show up, especially men wearing black. Some of them think they're the immigration authorities. I always shoot them a ho, ho, ho for reassurance. Then the union leaders calm them down."

"Is this a union shop?" Addington asked. Fou was busily tapping away on his Blackberry.

Santa answered, "Yes, as a matter of fact it is. They belong to the UFT—the United Federation of Trolls. It's a very small union, and our labor relations are cordial. We've never had a work stoppage."

Addington seemed perplexed and somewhat dissatisfied with what he was hearing. "You need to modernize," was all he offered to Claus, shaking his head simultaneously.

Repairing to his office to catch up on the incoming mail, Santa was aware of the opening of his door. He looked up, saw nobody, then heard a high-pitched voice saying, "It's me, chief," coming from somewhere close to the ground.

"I'm sorry, Eddie, I should have recognized you," he said, adjusting his focus at a downward angle.

"Yeah, how would you feel if everyone else looked down at you all the time, especially someone like you, mister global goody two shoes—or two boots."

Santa sighed and in a placating manner said, "Eddie, this is the season of good will toward men. Let nothing you dismay and all that."

"How about good will toward elves? Word is out on the street that something's going down, and it does not bode well for us little people." Eddie the elf was the UFT local leader and spoke for the workers. His tone became conspiratorial. "My sources inform me that your wife was seen packing swimsuits—size 3 XL—in a garment bag. There's no outlet for that around here now, is there?"

Santa Claus's great weakness of character was an unwavering honesty in his dealings. He told Eddie about the possibility of his unwinding the North Pole operation and retiring, while being quick to point out that any such plans had yet to be made.

"Aha, big fella, I knew those shifty-eyed guys walking around this morning were not here just for a joyride. I know the drill. Downsizing, outsourcing, reduction of benefits, reengineering of work. That's what the black suits live by." He paused to catch his breath. "Well, no more custom-made red suits for you," Eddie went on.

Santa's patience was being tested. "Look, Eddie, where the missus and I would be going, I'll not require any red suits. So there. Why don't you just return to the floor and sit tight until things clear up."

"You just think I'm a pushover 'cause I'm small. Well, you'll see who's got the power if I order a work slowdown just before Christmas."

"You wouldn't!"

Eddie remained in a state of high dudgeon. "Try me, you … bowl of jelly. Elves aren't gonna take this sitting down. Come to think of it, you never let us sit down anyway. That'll change, for sure."

With that, the elf slammed the door upon departure. Santa was left with the impression that the conversation did not go well at all.

That evening Santa Claus served his guests a sumptuous repast of roast partridge from the North Pole's lone pear tree, washed down with wassail, and then a dessert of mashed candy canes over chestnut sorbet. The Gold and Max people asked to see the wine list and were met by yet another ho, ho, ho. Santa told them the wassail was of the prior week's vintage, Vixen '07, which he judged to be excellent.

"Gold and Max has analyzed your business model, Nick," Addington said as they sipped cups of eggnog after dinner, "and while we see potential and intend to maximize the value to you, there are several problems which require attention."

"Such as?" Claus was about to become thoroughly bored with the trend of the conversation.

"This is a high-cost operation. Look at where you are—the North Pole is remote and bitterly cold, demanding high energy costs, and you're clearly overstaffed. Moreover, this place is likely to melt into oblivion in the future. You're aware of global warming, aren't you? Any of the buyers that we target are going to pick up on that right away. Have you considered relocation, like to the South, or, better still, outsourcing to China?"

Fou nodded happily. "China can manufacture all your toy needs, and all at the best quality."

Addington went on to tell Claus that Fou's family owned the biggest factories in Shanghai. "That's why we hired him," he said, "for deals like this. Of course, it doesn't hurt that he's in Mensa and works ninety-five hours a week. By the by, Nick, we had a devil of a time just getting here. We had to leave the corporate Gulfstream jet back in Labrador, and there are no hotels. You know, old man, you could really do with a Ritz here for your guests—that is, if you could entice them to visit.

Santa said, "Well, we don't entertain very much, and as for the transportation—"

"That's another talking point, good fellow. Your distribution system is completely antiquated. We understand that you deliver your products via reindeer and that you personally place the toys in each residence. Am I correct?" Fou was busily checking his laptop for validation of the statement.

"Why yes, gentlemen, it is true," Santa answered with pride, "and I accomplish that all over the world in one night."

The bankers looked at each other with skepticism. Addington said in a hushed tone, cadenced for dramatic effect, "You don't expect in all seriousness we'd believe that, do you?"

The old man shifted in his chair, then leaned forward and locked eyes on his guests. "I most surely do," he answered in a confident voice. "Belief is what we are all about. It has been our mantra, if you will, since the beginning of the enterprise."

They were not persuaded. "Well, it's not us you'll need to convince. It's the eventual buyer. We are just your agent—at a big fee, of course."

Fou poked him in the ribs. "Can I tell him about the focus groups, boss?"

"Yes, please do," Addington replied with a trace of a smirk.

The associate cleared his throat and nervously ruffled through a sheaf of computer printouts that he plucked from a four-gusset briefcase. "You see, there has been a significant drop-off in those who believe in you. Your most recent approval ratings are hovering around 30 percent, which is at about the level of American presidents and only slightly ahead of lawyers. Extensive interviews with children show that you are down to three-year-olds, where once you had control of the entire market up to age eleven. Your once solid image has been compromised by all the pretenders and the wannabees on the street corners and in the discount department stores."

Addington chipped in, "So, now you can understand the challenging task ahead of us. We may need to reexamine our fee structure and retainer."

Santa had heard enough. As he rose from his chair, Fou's cell phone rang to the tune of "If I Had A Million Dollars," and the young man listened intently to the message coming across with a gathering frown. "Boss," he said to Addington, "that was our pilot. There's a big storm on the way, and he doesn't think we can get out of here for days."

"You are welcome to stay," Santa said.

"Afraid not, old chap. We need to get back to work on the City of Pyongyang international bond deal." Addington was terse. "I bet that little guy with the red nose can guide us out."

Santa was all smiles. "Ah, now you're having to believe, aren't you! If you are referring to Rudy, he's not available. Actually, he's in your town at the celebrity tree lighting and afterwards appearing with Regis and then *Animal Planet*. He gets a nice little fee for it—not as much as yours—but it helps pay the utility bills. Anyway, I'll see who else is around to help you both out."

He called the transportation department and was informed that most of the team was out of town, competing in the reindeer games in Helsinki. He told the bankers that Dasher and Vixen would be able to take them back. "They're old, but they know the route, and you can borrow my sleigh."

Within the hour they were standing on the North Pole's tarmac in the teeth of a howling blizzard. Observing the uncovered sleigh being hitched to the two shivering reindeer, Addington said, "Look Claus, that … conveyance … has no top. It is, as the French would say, en plein air."

"Well, as we North Polers would say, it's any port in a storm. Gentlemen, you'd best be on your way—oh—and please leave me your Christmas lists before takeoff," Santa replied.

"We don't do lists, Nick; we do year-end bonuses," Addington said, effecting a haughty manner.

"But boss," Fou chimed in, "a Christmas list would be nice—"

"You got a signing bonus when you were hired, Fou. Let's not be greedy. Furthermore, I'd advise you to refrain from referring to me by such a salutation in the presence of clients. You could find yourself on thin ice, and not only here, where it's all a bunch of thin ice."

Turning to Santa as they climbed into the sleigh, he continued, "We'll be back to you with some numbers, ballpark figures at this stage, but at least an indication of value. Oh, Nick, would you want to attend our holiday office party? We do Christmas, Hannukah, and Kwanzaa all at the same time. It builds diversity, you know. You could represent all the constituencies. You'd be a big hit."

Santa's grin seemed to pierce the harsh weather. "Sorry, Bookie, I don't do corporate events. There are no chimneys in the buildings, and riding in the elevator would be bad for—what did you call it—my image. But thanks all the same. Happy Christmas now, and be sure to bundle up for the ride. Believe, and all will be well." He offered them a parting ho, ho, ho and waved merrily while he watched them fly off into the storm and vanish from his sight into the ebony skies. *How I love this kind of weather,* Santa thought as the snowflakes swirled around his ample body. *I can hardly wait until the twenty-fourth.*

Later that evening, at the end of their dinner hour, Mrs. Claus asked her husband for a recap of the meeting with the Gold and Max team. "Are we going to get top dollar for the business?"

He was reflective and not all that forthcoming. "We'll see."

"Do I detect a reluctance on your part?"

Santa answered, "You know, I still kind of like it around here. And liebschin, I have my eye on that warm strudel of yours. Would you pass me a plate? Then afterwards we could sip some schnapps and settle down for a long winter's nap. What do you say?"

"Why, you old rascal. Husband, wait'll you see my Christmas list!"

He put an arm around her. "Frau, I'm able and ready to fill your stocking. Ho, ho, ho!"

Allie Fair

He woke early on the Friday after Thanksgiving. He was dressed, ready to go, when his mother came into the bedroom he shared with his younger brother. "All right, Allie, we're going to leave after breakfast," she said. "Rob will stay with Grandma. Remember, though, we're only looking."

This was to be a big day. They were headed downtown, Manhattan, that was, to both Lionel and American Flyer. The only obligation Allie had to fulfill was to suffer through the selection of a suit at nearby S. Klein's. *Just looking, huh? Well, it's at least a start*, he thought.

The Lionel exhibit was located in an office building on the north side of Madison Square Park, and the American Flyer showroom was a short distance away in an odd triangular spot where Broadway and Fifth Avenue converged at Twenty-fifth Street. Lionel had a room taken up by an enormous train layout that displayed their full line—in both O gauge and its more compact 027 gauge. Freight lines, sleek passenger cars, black locomotives with whistles, diesels, bridges, tunnels, signal crossings, everything in motion. They had been there not an hour when Allie's mother said, "C'mon, son, time's up; let's go over to the other place."

"Wait, Mom, just a little more, I want to see the milk car unloaded," he answered. This was one of Lionel's latest innovations, a white boxcar able to dispense milk cans onto a platform siding. Satisfied, more or less, he reluctantly left the railroad paradise on Twenty-sixth Street and walked with his mother over to American Flyer. There he was less impressed, for Flyer was S gauge, slimmer, slick, and fast but not as brawny, gritty, and, in his eyes, as authentic as Lionel. Yep, that was it.

On to Klein's, where Florence Fair, finally in her rightful element, selected a double-breasted flannel suit for Allie in a color she described as cocoa, but he thought it bore a resemblance to something quite unmentionable even for an eleven-year-old. "Yeah, it's okay, Mom," he said, "but how about the trains?"

"Like I told you, we were just looking. You're going to look so grown-up in that suit. Maybe a nice burgundy and gold striped tie to set it off …"

Trains had been on his mind for some time. Following the excursion downtown, as the countdown to Christmas accelerated, he sucked it up and asked his parents for a Lionel train set. This was after dinner on a weekday evening. "Well, you know your father will have to decide about that," his mother said. Turning to his father, she asked, "What do you think, Donald?" Allie's father sucked vigorously on his pipe and then looked squarely at his son and said, "Allie, that would be a major gift—an investment, almost—but you see we each have a Christmas budget for gifts which goes for you, your little brother, and for your parents as well."

"And how much is that, Dad?" Allie asked in trembling voice.

"Eight dollars," Donald Fair replied in a confident tone.

Allie gulped once, twice, then said, "Dad, Mom, the Lionel sets are at least twenty-nine dollars, and that means I could never get one. I'll give up my allowance—or most of it—next year. That would help to pay for it."

"Son, you can do the calculation. You're taking math this term, aren't you?" his father asked. "Geometry, Dad; next term it's algebra," Allie answered. Although he was in all advanced classes, he had his distinct likes and dislikes among them. He related to geometry, which was mostly visual—shapes, angles, and the like. Not unlike the track layouts for train sets. You could see things develop, which was much more satisfying than mere numbers. *Totally impractical*, thought the father. W*hat could anyone do with an isosceles triangle*? "Well, then, next term you'll get into compound interest and understand the problem," his father said.

"There, you see now," his mother chimed in with a gleeful countenance.

His friends at the schoolyard were none too helpful. Pitching pennies against the curb didn't generate a lot of cash, even when he won. "Eight bucks, that's all you get?" asked Steve Gross when Allie told the boys about his problem.

"Yeah, that's what they said," Allie answered.

"Jeez, I do better than that, and I'm Jewish," Gross said, laughing.

"Ah, c'mon, you celebrate Christmas, Steve? I don't believe you."

"Do too, World's Fair. Hannukah, Christmas, we got the tree, the menorah, you name it, and the presents just keep on rolling in," Gross said.

They filed in to class, the ringing of the bell in the morning chill breaking up penny-pitching and other games of chance. Mike Cochran joined them, saying to Allie, "Hey, Fair, you'll get your trains; your parents are just ball-busting. I heard the same thing went on with Conrad Harrison last year. He just kept holding out, and they came through; of course, he's a lot richer than any of us."

He remembered going to Conrad's apartment last year. His family had a four-bedroom jobbie, a rarity in the high-rise development they lived in, and they even had a woman—a stranger—there to clean up. Conrad had half a room devoted to his train layout, the crowning feature of which was back-to-back diesel locomotives in the flagship colors of silver, red, and gold of the Santa Fe Railroad. He didn't really know Conrad very well but figured to find him and ask what his strategy was that produced the end result.

When alone, Allie would break out the Lionel catalog he got at the exhibit downtown and thumb through it, the vivid four-color pages now becoming worn. He wasn't going to get the Santa Fe diesels, or even that Pennsylvania R.R. articulated engine, but he had hopes for a basic freight ensemble in O gauge, and maybe some accessories such as the beacon tower. On late afternoons Allie would walk ten blocks over to Castle Hill Avenue at the corner of Newbold, where there was a hobby store that had a large train display. There he would press his face to the plateglass of the front window and stare at the train sets displayed in all their glory. He would wait until the blue gloom of mid-December settled in and then head for home. On the third of these visits, the store's owner, acting more out of curiosity than anything else, popped out the front door and asked him, "Hey kid, something I can sell ya? I've seen you here more than once. Bet it's the Lionel sets you're interested in."

"Well, I guess so," Allie replied, "I'm pretty sure I'm getting some for Christmas only I don't know which ones yet."

"The O gauge is the thing to have," the man said, "but I suppose you know that anyway. How about that freight set in the middle of the window? Comes with the milk car and powered by a 110-watt transformer."

He looked up at the man, who was as wide as he was high, with frizzy salt-and-pepper grey hair, and said, "Yeah, and I see a fifty-dollar price tag as well. Hey, you ever lower the prices?"

"Not a chance, kid. These babies fly outta here as soon as I stock 'em, or, I shoulda said, they roll out."

"Okay, then, but I had to ask. Gotta go, now," Allie said.

"Next time, bring your father," the man said and laughed."Hey you don't believe in Santa anymore, do ya?"

"Nah. Wish I did."

The owner laughed again, then returned to the warmth inside and said, "That's too bad. Still, ya might give him a try. Ha. Ha."

Allie trundled home, feeling dejected by the interview, and becoming even more so when his mother inquired as to his whereabouts for the last couple of hours, and on other afternoons as well. He provided the standard kid's response to "where did you go?", which was "nowhere."

The mother stared him down sternly. "That won't cut it with me, young man. Maybe from now to Christmas you'd better stay closer to home."

The next week at school Steve Gross approached Allie and said, "Hey, Un-Fair, you don't look so good. What's going on, my man?"

"Christmas blues, Steve," came the reply.

"Well, cheer up, buddy, I just got my third Hanukkah gift—there's supposed to be eight of 'em—and if they happen to give me any trains—which I seriously doubt—I want you to know I'd sell to you at a most favorable price."

Gross looked across the street at the local deli—it was lunch hour—and continued, "Harrison is buying knishes at Glazer's. Let's go."

"What's that all about?" Allie asked.

"Oh, his family won a quiz show jackpot—*Stop The Music*, I think. So he's treating. But it's today only," Gross said with a knowing grin.

Swell, thought Allie, *he'll add to his Lionel layout for sure. If trains were Monopoly, Harrison would have the four railroads, Boardwalk and Park Place to boot.* He suddenly experienced a drop in appetite, but he went along anyhow. Gross could always eat another.

Two

The next Saturday, Allie found himself in the vast and ornate central reading room of the New York Public Library on Forty-second Street, having made a case with his parents to complete needed research for a term paper on famous shipwrecks.

"Here's enough for the subway and lunch," his father said, "and be home for dinner. Your mother has you on a short leash these days."

"Home for dinner, right," Allie answered tonelessly. In his hand he clutched a single dollar bill.

Not in the library but an hour, surrounded by three massive tomes on the lives of the great explorers, he bolted from his chair, put down his fountain pen, donned his plaid mackinaw, and headed out, south and east to Polk's. On the west side of Madison Avenue, just below Thirty-fourth Street, Polk's was a three-story cathedral of hobbies with a specialty in model railroading. It was inhabited by customers and employees alike who were hobbyist aficionados, many slovenly in appearance, with unkempt hair and extreme body styles, just the hallmarks of those too busy with their hobbies to devote time to any degree of personal care. Still, he was feeling much at home whiling away the hours among all manner of train gauges, model layouts, railroad structures, and all the materials one would need to construct them. He sprang for the latest edition of *Model Builder*, the magazine with plans for making stations, factories, platforms, and just about any kind of rail accessory imaginable. Returning to his library chair before closing, he managed to squeeze off a page and a half about his subject before lifting the weighty books and plopping them on the front desk. "Did you find what you were researching for, young man?" the matronly librarian inquired .

"Sure did," he said. *Not here, though*, he thought.

"Well, Merry Christmas," she said. "Oh, by the way, what did you think of this one?"

The large, illustrated book was entitled *A Century of Sea Disasters*. "Great," Allie answered. "I'll do my report on it."

"Well, I can help you out, I think. Would a good grade improve your chances for a bright Christmas?" This graying woman, hair turned back in a dated kind of bun and wearing a dark green print dress with white collar up high now showed some sparkle in the eye. Allie considered the offer and stood waiting to hear more.

"There are a lot of sad tales in this book, as I am sure you can see. The battleship Maine in Havana harbor—started a war with Spain, you know. And mysterious to boot. The cause was never fully determined. The Fort Slocum, such a loss of life right outside our door, so to speak, and on a pleasant summer day."

He concluded she was well-versed in this particular book for sure and said, "I looked … a little at those, I did … but the one that I read the most was the Titanic."

The librarian leaned over her desk and stared at Allie for what seemed to be an eternity to him. She said, "It is, of course, the most famous of them all. It happened … more than thirty-seven years ago. It's been written about every which way, made into movies and all that. I know something about it. I was there."

"You were there?" Allie asked incredulously. "Most of the passengers died in the water."

"Well, not there, there. I'll explain." She went on, "I was a young girl at the time—well I'm sure you can figure that out. I expected someone who was sailing on that ship. When word of the … uh … disaster reached New York, people gathered at the steamship's office downtown to wait for news. Passenger lists were posted outside the building. This went on for a matter of days, some of the watchers relieved at the end, others fast losing hope before the rescue ship docked. I was one of those. I was turning for home when a little girl—about your age—approached me. She asked my identity, then explained that she was told to look for someone of my description in New York when, and, I guess, if, she reached the city. 'I have something for you,' she told me, and then handed me this ring I'm going to show you."

The librarian pressed into Allie's palm a dull, plain yellow band and told him to look at the inside inscription, which read "From TT to MC, my love forever."

"See, he did not survive, and before the evacuation that took place he handed this ring to the girl as she was about to leave in a lifeboat. I always thought it was fortune, or something beyond it, that brought this girl, the ring, and me together that day."

He had listened patiently to this story, trying to understand how this would help him in his project. Finally, he asked her how this might relate to his work. "It is a true artifact of the Titanic. Show it to your teacher as part of your report."

"Okay, I will, and then I'll return it to you," he said.

She talked to him a soft tone. "No. I do not want it. Look, I have held it to my heart all these years, and now it is time to let go. You came along today and have given me a reason to do so. Now … the library is about to close; run along, and good luck. I believe you will do just fine."

Allie seemed nonplussed by all of the preceding and was grateful for the wind-down. "Well, thank you, and Merry Christmas," he said. "You know, I don't even know know your name. I'm Allie, by the way.

"Allie, that's so … boyish … I think. It suits you well. My name isn't important. Merry Christmas to you." The conversation was over.

As he descended the enormous front steps he came to think how everyone seemed to be more open to one another at Christmastime. Of course, he neglected to follow through on his theory at home, simply reporting that the research was well under control. He even had a dime of change left from the day's activities. Perhaps hope was alive after all.

He was riding with his mother on the Westchester Avenue bus, on their way home from heavy-duty shopping at "the Hub" in the south Bronx. Florence bought winter coats for herself and Rob and treated him to a charlotte russe. Allie was disappointed that time did not allow for a quick look at the train display at Hearn's, the department store across from the elevated tracks. His face was buried alternately in an issue of *Model Builder* and the Lionel catalogue, as his mother was asking him, "What's so special in those magazines, Allie?"

"Oh, just lots of plans, Mom. This issue has one to make a downtown passenger terminal." He flipped to the now dog-eared pages of the glossy train brochure to reread a favorite paragraph:

Just imagine this scene: the black signal light glowing green as the fast limited streaks over the main line rails—the distant wail of a freight train whistle—the giant crane boom swinging over to the scrap pile—the switch engine rumbling out of the yards with a string of empties—lights winking on in miniature houses as night settles over the town!

She went on, "You know, those trains you want, well, they really take up a lot of room. They're really for people in houses, all those cutesy pictures they show you. We live in an apartment." Allie, of course, was well aware of that and asked her, "Mom, do you think we'll ever live in a house?" She hesitated a moment, "You'd have to ask your father about that, but I don't think so. We have a great apartment. It has southern exposure." This was true. On sunny days, there was a corner in their master bedroom that opened to a panorama extending from the Whitestone Bridge in the east to the George Washington in the west and with an unobstructed look downtown at the skyscrapers of Manhattan in between. Allie had often spent meaningful time at those windows, dreaming about worlds beyond his own and trying to figure out what some of the odd-shaped buildings down below were.

At the Soundview Avenue stop, a small, darkish man of indeterminate age entered the bus. He was dressed in a faded cotton jacket with collar pulled up around his neck and wrinkled pants with what looked to be embedded paint stains. Passing the Fairs in search of a seat, the man offered Allie a nod of recognition. "Hi ya, kid, didn't know ya got this far down in da Bronx." Allie, sheepishly, returned the nod and then proceeded to bury his face in the magazine. As soon as mother and son left the bus later on at 177th Street, Florence Fair turned to him. "Now what was that all about?"

"About what, Mom?"

She continued, "You know perfectly well; that … that … man who knows you. What is he, a drug dealer? Don't tell me you're on drugs, Allie."

In a wavering voice, he answered, "No, Mom, he's the pin boy at the bowling alley. Ray. He's nice to us guys."

"Bowling alley! So now you are hanging out there," the mother went on in an increasingly frantic tone.

"Only once in a while, Mom. Me and Steve and Mike."

"I don't know what to do about you, Allie," she muttered and stared straight ahead as they reached their building. Allie was beginning to think his Christmas window was closing. Better now to get the holiday over with.

That night as they were in bed, Florence told Donald of the day's events with an emphasis on Ray, the pin boy. Donald suppressed a smile and said to his wife, "Actually, bowling is a good outlet for these boys on cold winter days. I was a championship bowler myself, you may remember. Even did a 300-game a couple of times."

"But Donald, it's the influences … you should have seen this man. He was frightening, to me at least. These … people … are starting to come into the neighborhood; you don't see it because you're not here all the time."

Donald answered, "Well, dearie, I'll be on the lookout for him when I am around. Meantime, let's put the boy on a tight schedule." With that, he rolled over and fell asleep immediately.

Three

Allie Fair was on a schedule, to be sure, but he still squeezed some time a handful of days before Christmas to walk back up to the Castle Hill hobby store, expecting to press nose to the cold glass display window once again. As he approached the shop, he could see activity around its entrance that appeared to be out of the ordinary. Several men were milling about, including the odd-shaped proprietor, and there was a police car parked alongside. Facing the front window squarely, he saw that the glass had been broken; a large crack ran diagonally across the entire pane, there was a large hole in its center, and it appeared as though some merchandise had been removed. He thought for a moment about bolting out of this scene but became rooted to a spot, half-frightened and half-intrigued.

The owner was talking rapidly, gesturing and prancing about, while another man, taller, spare, and bundled up in a dark overcoat and wide-brimmed fedora, was with him and taking notes down on a small ring-binder pad. *Must be the detective*, thought Allie. I've seen enough *Man Against Crime* shows to recognize them .

"Okay then, Solly, you came in this morning and found it like this," the detective said. "Do you have any ideas as to who might have done it?"

The owner, whom Allie now understood to have a real name, Solly, said that he hadn't a clue, other than the fact that the thief didn't know what to take. At that point, both men noticed Allie, who was still fixed in a position on the sidewalk. Solly made a nod of recognition in his direction, which the detective picked up on. "You know this kid?" he asked the store owner. "Yeah, he's just a neighborhood kid, comes up here and looks through the window at the trains, ain't that right, kid?" Solly said, focusing on him.

The detective whirled around and faced Allie, who by now was beginning to quiver on the spot. Allie looked up into a craggy face and watery, world-weary pale eyes and then down at long fingers poised to write into the frayed little pad. "You know anything about this, kid? Sounds like you're a regular around this place."

"Uh … me?" he replied in a halting voice.

"Yeah, you. I don't see anyone else around here to talk to, now do I, other than the store owner here," the detective said in a biting tone while shifting his head from side to side for emphasis.

Before Allie could respond, Solly chipped in, "Nah, Lockbonder, this boy don't have anything to do with it. As I said, the guy didn't know the value of what he was taking. I lost three sets of Lionel trains out of the window, two little Scout sets, run around twenty bucks apiece, and an 027 freighter. Now the kid here, he knows what the good stuff is, the 0 gauge, which wasn't taken. Isn't that the truth, kid?"

"Yeah, I guess so," Allie said. He was beginning to think he might get out of this after all. A glass repair truck pulled up to the curb and parked behind the police car. The window would be back in its frame in no time at all. The detective, still considering pressing further, asked Solly if he wanted him to take the boy's statement. Solly declined, at this point more interested in the window repair than the ongoing investigation. "Like I said, he's only a kid, and if he did it, the good stuff woulda been taken. Look through the hole. The big black New York Central diesels are still there on their tracks, waiting for somebody to take 'em home for Christmas."

Sensing that his business was reaching its conclusion, Detective Lockbonder stuffed his pad into the slant pocket of his overcoat and said to Solly, "All right with me. I'll do a sheet on it back at the precinct house, which you can use for the insurance. How much you want me to write up?" With that, the two men huddled out of earshot and conversed. As the detective broke away, Allie thought he heard, faintly, the words "usual cut" as he shuffled off to the police car while Solly turned his attention to the glass repair. Still transfixed, Allie endured Lockbonder fixing his rheumy eyes on him and saying, "Get lost, kid before I change my mind about you. Lucky for you Solly stuck up for you. Guess there's a Christmas spirit after all, hah, hah."

The crime scene calmed down, the principals all having departed. As Allie started for home and turned the corner of Castle Hill and headed south onto Westchester, he ran smack into a fight that was well into its final rounds on the middle of the street. The combatants were going at it with all they had, bare fists, a bloody nose, a sliced lip, and half an eye, the scene surrounded by a circle of fans, well-wishers and taunters. It was a moving tableau along the street, spilling at once to the curb, then back again against a storefront. Allie had the misfortune to show up just when the combatants, a tangled mass of ripped shirts and sweat, rolled into him at the corner. "Hey, watch out for the little kid, Jimmy," one of the watchers yelled at the bigger of the two fighters. This had its intended distractive effect, as Jimmy turned his head for just an instant and caught a right fist into the mouth. A small fountain of blood spurted into the chill, then cascaded onto Allie's winter coat. "Way to duck, Jimmy," the same man continued, "the kid'll have to send you the cleaner's bill, that's if you got any face left to see it." Everyone else laughed. Allie, finally realizing the risks facing an innocent bystander, bobbed and weaved around the makeshift bout and proceeded to take himself and his now blood-spattered coat home. Mom would sure have something to say about this.

Evening had arrived like an early guest as he reached his apartment building, the shortening of days turning late afternoons the colors of ever-deepening blues. To Allie, the air at holiday time felt like an enveloping mist, a climatic cocoon that would surround the family and draw them together. As Christmas would approach, he would often look out his kitchen window in the early evening to the street below and await the return of his father from work; when he was identified in the parade of men in a kind of march up the block, Allie knew his entire family to be secure in that immediate time. This day, though, it was Allie himself who was late. It turned out that Donald Fair had broken free of his office a bit early and was already home and in a content mood, via some holiday cheer. In keeping with the atmosphere of good will, Florence Fair greeted her son warmly, instead of with the usual "where have you been?" which preceded a "what am I going to do with you, Allie?" He was even able to stash his bloody coat in the closet before anyone saw him. Hopefully he could keep the garment away from close observation until after Christmas. Perhaps his luck was turning up.

"Allie, Dad's home early; say hello," she said with a lilt. He gladly complied, and the conversation between father and son turned to holiday plans and remaining obligations before the big day. In a hushed tone, Donald Fair asked his son if he had presents for his mother and brother. Allie replied in the affirmative, for he was proud of his present-buying prowess. He had spent almost all of his saved allowance on Christmas; well, he needed a bit of help at Macy's when the bejeweled pin for his mother that had so caught his eye was over budget, and the saleslady actually kicked in a half-dollar to seal the purchase. "It's such a pretty pin, young man, and the one I would choose for your mom, myself. Look, I'll give you fifty cents, so you can buy it," she said across the counter to him.

"Would you really do that for me?" Allie said, looking up at her, somewhat in disbelief.

"Hel- … sure, son, it's Christmas, better to give than receive, dontcha know?" she said. Allie was never in complete agreement with that adage, but he took the deal. He bought a mixed bag of comic books for his little brother: *Batman and Robin*; Classics Illustrated's *Moby Dick*, and *Crime Does Not Pay*. He was skittish about the last title, as it looked a little gory, featuring the gunning-down of John Dillinger. For his father, an inveterate pipe smoker, he bought a large can of his favorite tobacco, Walnut. "Ya know, Fair, if I didn't recognize ya from the neighborhood, and your pop wasn't such a regular customer, I couldn't even sell ya this stuff. I could catch a load of crap, so take it quick and get out," the candy store owner down the block said to him last week when he went in for the tobacco. *So much for the Christmas spirit in that place*, he thought as he hightailed it out of the store, the contraband tobacco safely clutched to his chest. Hey, what's Christmas shopping anyway, without a little intrigue?

"Well, good, Allie," his father said. "I'm glad that you have something for everyone … you know, boy, you look … a little frazzled to me. Is everything okay?" Donald Fair was viewing his young charge more closely now.

"Uh, sure, Dad. I'm just fine."

The father continued with him, "I think there's something on your mind, though."

"Maybe, Dad. You know, I'm not so sure I really want those trains I asked you for." *There. It was blurted out.*

The slightest smile came upon Donald Fair's face. "And why would that be? You've been pretty insistent about this all along."

"Oh, I guess it's that limit you talked about. I probably ought to ask for presents that stay within it. Like, there's that new game, Clue; it's only $3.50." Allie believed that this kind of money talk would put him on common ground with his father. He was not certain what his father did for a living, knowing only that it had a lot to do with numbers and that when it came to numbers nobody could challenge him.

"We'll have to see about that. After all, the holiday is almost here and time is getting very short. Besides, it should be fun to be surprised, don't you think?"

Allie said, "I guess so, Dad. Can I go now? I still have to study to give my report to class tomorrow."

For once, Allie was forthcoming. He was up against a deadline to present an oral report on his research project the following day, the last major hurdle between him and the Christmas break from school and all of its demands.

"Attention, class. Allie Fair is going to deliver his talk on the research project he has chosen," the social studies teacher, Miss Harvey, said the following morning, "which is …" And here she turned to him.

"Sea disasters," he virtually shouted out.

"Yes, sea disasters." Miss Harvey sat back in her chair.

The presentation went well, though Allie felt it was the longest five minutes of his life to date. He emphasized the Titanic and illustrated it with the ring that the librarian had given him, which he thought would represent a kind of dramatic coup and bring in an A. The class was unimpressed, as was usual, most of the seated bodies squirming around, but the teacher remained alert, said a few nice things afterwards, and, although she was noncommittal, Allie had a good feeling about the ultimate result. At least it was over, finito.

"Hey, State-Fair, where'd you come up with that gimmick?" Steve Gross asked, somewhat out of envy because he, Gross, possessed the minimalist's share of imagination. "Uh, like I said to the class, Steve, the librarian gave me the ring. It's real, you know."

"You believe that? Hah. If you think so, let's take it over to Rabinowitz at the pawn shop. I bet there's no value in a grubby old ring anyway."

"Nah, Steve, not now."

"Okay, then, let's go bowling," Steve continued. "They got a special today, like only fifteen cents a line."

"I can't go anymore … at least for a while … I told you that story about meeting Ray with my mother on the bus."

"Don't you know, man, Ray's out."

That was news. "What happened to him, Steve? My mom thought he was a drug addict anyway."

"It wasn't that. No. He cut his hand, bad, on some glass. Not too good for a pin boy, is it? Hah, hah."

Allie stared straight ahead and said, "Still don't wanna bowl." He did not know what he wanted to do.

The Fairs had a low-key approach toward Christmas Eve, using that occasion to decorate their tree, with little else going on. Presents were to be exchanged on Christmas morning. An elusive sleep came for Allie in fits and starts; when he appeared in the morning he found his family already gathered around the tree, gifts in garish holiday wrap piled alongside of its base and awaiting their distribution. *Certainly looks like more than eight bucks each*, Allie thought.

Florence Fair oohed and aahed when she gazed upon the pin Allie presented to her; Donald added the can of tobacco to a growing inventory of the same and heaped praise on his son for his acumen in gift-giving. A long rectangular box remained. "There, Allie, open that one," his mother said with a knowing smile. He reached, pulled, then tore at the wrapping with a strength he did not know he possessed. It finally yielded the revelation of the trademark orange and blue color of what he was hoping to discover. Then came the final validation, the art-deco style "L" of a Lionel train set.

"What do you think, son?" asked Donald Fair.

"It's … just great, Dad," Allie exclaimed in the process of probing and authenticating the contents inside.

"One of Lionel's finest."

"Yes, yes, a freight set, I see, that's it …" the tone of the boy's voice displaying just a hint of … misgiving? The parents moved closer to the enfolding scene.

"Allie, thank your dad. He went way overboard this Christmas! Isn't that right, Donald?"

The father turned somewhat coy. "Oh, I suppose so, dearie, but … that's what the day is for. Meeting—no—exceeding expectations." Then Donald Fair asked his son for a reaction. Was he pleased, or better still, bowled over?

Allie, looking up from the now disheveled box at his feet, said, "Sure … it's 027, right, Dad?" The set was a three-car freight powered by the No. 2026 locomotive and a 90-watt transformer.

"Lionel's newest model. And look, I even threw in the lumber car and its platform," Donald said.

Not O gauge, thought Allie. *Now I'm forever locked in to the 027 and it means I'll never catch guys like Conrad Harrison.*

An inexplicable, perhaps divine, revelation came upon him at that very moment that caused him to wax diplomatic. As a result, he did not communicate a deep-seated disappointment over the failure to have the top-of-the-line ensemble (his dad wasn't getting the point) but chose instead to express heartfelt gratitude for this most wondrous of Christmas presents that any boy in the mid-Bronx in 1949 could ever have wished for.

"Dad, Mom, it's all I ever wanted," he said, with a bit of lump in the gullet.

Everyone hugged and embraced, the parents breaking away in their robes for the ritual of morning coffee at their modest dining table, Allie busily unbundling the rolling stock, tracks, and power plant for the trains, and little Rob tearing up two of the three comic books from his brother—he liked the crime one—all the while wondering what he did to tee off Santa Claus.

Oh, well, it's a start, Allie thought.

Four

During the Christmas school break, Allie busied himself with the variations of track layouts, which at times took up most of the living room's square footage. He was allowed to travel by himself downtown to go to Polk's on one of the days. Before going to the store, he went back to the library to find his librarian friend, the "MC" of the ring, for he had decided to return it to her. It had served its purpose nobly, getting him through his class presentation, and rightfully belonged with her. Returning to the great reading room, Allie saw that she was not at the front desk there. "Uh, pardon me, I'm looking for the lady who was here a week or so ago," he said, looking up at the woman who was sitting behind the desk.

She, like MC, was a steely-haired, bespectacled woman of uncertain age—the library seemed to have a supply of them. "Oh, you must mean Marion Clover, young man. Why she is no longer here. In fact, her last day was Christmas Eve. She retired from her job, and now it is mine. My name is Miss Pimm," she answered.

"Do you know where I might find her? I need to return something that she gave me."

"Ah, I am sorry that I can't help you. You know, Marion is a very private person. Why I have been here more than ten years myself—she was here long before that—and I never learned where it was she lived. Funny, isn't it. You can talk to somebody every day for the longest time and still find out little about their lives outside of the job. Just out of curiosity, what was it she gave you?"

He mentioned the ring and the story associated with it. "Well, I know Marion was always giving things to people she took a liking to—small items, mostly—I think sometimes they were made up, though. That could be what you call an occupational hazard around here; all the books and all the stories within the walls stimulate one's imagination," Miss Pimm said.

"So she left no forwarding address," Allie said, being insistent and skeptical. "What if the library needed to get in touch with her?"

"It's unlikely. I know she was entitled to a nice pension—that was one of the things we'd discuss—but she chose to take it all at once, cut all ties with the place. I can't help feeling she managed everything to shield her privacy." At this point, he was worn down. He thanked Miss Pimm—for what, he could not fathom—and left. Feeling glum, he even bypassed a run at Polk's and went home.

The following day, he caught up with Steve Gross, who was all ears about Allie's train set. "So, you got what you wished for, huh?" Gross asked.

"Yes and no. I was kinda hoping for the O gauge, but it's okay."

Gross continued, "Hey, I hear Conrad Harrison is expanding his train layout another six feet to make room for all the new tracks and cars he got. Wanna go over to his place and see it?"

"No, but there is one place I did want to go with you. Remember the other week you wanted to go to Rabinowitz to pawn that old ring I got? Well, I'm ready."

"Yeah, cool. I'm always game for the pawn shop. You never know what the old guy has there for sale. I got some extra holiday cash and was planning on spending it anyway," Steve Gross said.

The pawn shop was in the middle of a nondescript block along Boston Road, not far from the boys' school. Steve cautioned Allie that old Rabinowitz was a tough trader, but sometimes you could bargain with him. The shop was, not unexpectedly, musty and disorganized, and with the heat cranked up to at least eighty degrees, it was a steam tank in the midst of the winter chills. Rabinowitz, right out of a casting call, with stooped shoulders, a lone strand of wispy white hair, and wrapped in a stained brown cardigan sweater despite the stifling heat, ran true to his billing as he appeared to examine the ring with a critical eye. One thing the pawnbroker was sure of was that underneath the tarnish it was gold, but beyond that had no clue as to its worth. Naturally, he could not let uncertainty play upon his audience. "Vell, I am not so impressed with this, but I'll give you twenty for it," he said.

Allie, taking Gross at his word, tried his luck at negotiation and asked for more. "Look, kid," Rabinowitz eyed him coldly, "ya think I got all day for you? Now, it's eighteen." Gross nudged his friend in the ribs. "'Take it; it's a good price—before he goes any lower."

Turning to Steve, he whispered with a scowl, "You said to bargain; this isn't bargaining."

Rabinowitz, leaning over his dusty countertop, said, "Look, I ain't got no more time. It's on da table; if you don't want, take the ring and go."

"Deal! Allie shouted.

Out on the street, Allie was eighteen dollars to the good but feeling at a loss. "Jeez, thanks for all your help, Steve," he said with a tone of sarcasm that was lost on his friend, "and you didn't buy anything, either, like you said you would."

"Yeah, well, that's his technique. He starts high, then goes lower. I've seen him do it. You gotta know how to jump in. Anyway, I was checking out that guitar in the window. I hate my clarinet lessons and think I ought to change instruments," Steve said.

For the first time that day, Allie laughed. "You got to be kidding me, Gross," he said. "Nobody plays guitar I've ever heard of except for Les Paul."

"Maybe, but it's the coming thing."

"Never happen, Steverino, but I'd still like to see you blow your dough."

He was back at Solly's hobby shop, the front window new and crystal clear. "Hey kid, how're ya makin' out?" Solly greeted him. "Did ya get any trains for Christmas?" The shop owner was seated behind his counter, munching a bagel dripping with egg salad that was falling in globlets to the floor in front of him.

"Well, I got the 027 freight set," Allie answered in a flat tone. "I would have liked the 0, but it's okay."

Solly, offering counsel, told him that he had a lot to look forward to and that he could build on what he started and someday trade up, if he wished.

"So, I see you got the window replaced," Allie said. "Did that detective ever find who broke it?"

Solly grinned, revealing a mouth still occupied with egg salad. "You mean old Lockbonder? Hey, he couldn't find an elephant in a bathtub, but they did bring in a guy for questioning, some little squirt from a bowling alley with a cut-up hand, but he had an alibi so they let him go. I guess I'll never know, but it's nice ya remembered. Anyhoo, what can I do ya for today?"

The front door opened and in walked Conrad Harrison. "Hiya, Fair, how's it hanging?" was his greeting to Allie, who nodded to him in return, a grudging acknowledgment of his presence, really intrusion, on his time with Solly. For his part, Solly ditched his bagel and immediately sprang to alert upon seeing Conrad, assuming a retailer's position to serve a valued customer who was known to have money. Allie proceeded to pore over the contents of the train accessories in the counter while Conrad began a series of transactions. "Hey, Fair, I came into some extra scratch at Christmastime," he announced, and then turning to the shopkeeper said, "Yeah, Solly, I want the passenger set, the three burgundy-colored Pullman cars, the Pennsylvania GG-1 electric locomotive, and I could use two more switch tracks." Harrison was ordering big time.

All the guys had money, Gross, Harrison, probably everyone else, he thought. Everything concluded, wrapped up, paid for to the tune of $80.50, and Conrad heading for the door. "See ya around, Fair,' he said on the way out. "Hey, come up to my place and catch my expanded layout."

"There's a kid knows what he wants," Solly said in false wonderment. "Okay, back to you now. What'll it be?"

He wanted to buy the magnetic crane, which was a $19.95 item, but had no place for it on his setup; instead, he selected the electric coal elevator and a hopper car. "That comes to twenty dollars," Solly told him. "Uh, I have eighteen, could I owe you the difference?" Allie asked.

"Sure, kid, sure, come up when you have the money. Hey, I know it's none of my business, but I guess you don't much like that kid who just was in here."

"We're in the same class; I don't mind him, really, he always seems to have more than I do, even when I think I'm doing all right," Allie said.

Solly told him, "Don't let it get ya, because no matter what you have there's always someone out there has more, but these things even out over time. Believe me, I know. In the meantime, enjoy the trains. You got a lot of good stuff there."

Allie's mood brightened with every block traversed on his way home. All in all it was a good trade, the old ring for additional Lionel equipment, and as for Conrad, maybe Solly was right and he'd catch him and pass him one of these days. Besides, he thought, Conrad was pretty ugly with his greasy dirty-blond curly hair and a noticeable overbite that was going to require braces, for sure. Of course, Conrad's parents would take care of that as well as anything else the boy might require. He reminded himself to check his teeth in the bathroom mirror as soon as he got home.

"Just what are you up to now, young man?" Florence Fair inquired of her son as she watched him belly up to their bathroom mirror, spread his lips wide open, and stare at the looking glass closely enough to produce a fine mist on the surface.

"Mom, I'm practicing dental hygiene, only making sure everything is all right, you know, lined up properly, cleaned after meals—"

"Okay, I believe you. Just stay away from the problem your friend, what's his name …?"

"You mean Conrad."

Florence said, "Yes, that one, he'll need major ortho work, he will. God, I hope you won't stick your father with that kind of expense. He'd take a stroke, and then where would we be? Here, let me take a look."

She approached the mirror and observed along with her son. “The teeth look straight to me, Allie. You’re going to be fine, just fine.”

Five

Allie Fair continued to add to his Lionel train layout. In the summer he, Steve Gross, and another friend, Alan Imendi, went up to the "Square" to buy an eight-by-four plywood board on which he would place and secure his track design. It was one of those hot and humid late June days in New York, and the threesome toted the board twenty-three blocks down Westchester Avenue and then carted it up to the Fairs' ninth-floor apartment because it would not fit in the elevator. It took them almost as long to worm the board around the nine flights of narrow staircase as it did to get it all the way from the lumberyard. Steve's advice was to move to the ground floor. Mrs. Fair, exasperated at having to accept the cream-toned piece of wood with its random swirls and lingering chemical scent of the bonding agent between layers, nonetheless took pity on the boys and offered them Hires root beer. Two days later the North Korean army crossed the Thirty-eighth Parallel and invaded the Republic of South Korea.

During the summer, Allie was counseled by his parents to leave the trains be and concentrate on seasonal activities, which is to say he was told in plain terms to be out of the house and in the fresh air, or whatever air the city had to offer on any given day. On weekends, he was detailed to walk a round trip of a mile to Lambaise's candy store and bring home a quart of Breyer's peach ice cream for his father, and to accomplish this mission before it melted. As compensation, he would share in the treat. "Bewitched, Bothered and Bewildered," in a solo piano version by Bill Snyder, was the number one hit at the time. Allie eagerly awaited a new release from Frankie Laine; it was his hope that Laine could surpass "Mule Train" and "The Cry Of The Wild Goose." He also read the strident news headlines about the war and watched the Allied position on the map of the southern peninsula of Korea constricting day by day. It preyed on his sense of confidence; Americans do not get pushed around and do not lose. *When would the tide turn?*

There were the weekend car trips to Jones Beach, and by the time the new school term opened, Frankie Laine had a new single of "Dream A Little Dream Of Me"—a departure from his adventure story ballads—that disappointed him. General MacArthur engineered a brilliant landing at Inchon, on the west coast of the Korean peninsula; within days the Allies encircled the North Korean army and proceeded to chase them far above the Thirty-eighth Parallel. *See, I knew we'd come through. This will all be over soon, just as certain as the Yankees winning the World Series.*

In the Fairs bedroom, the train layout, now more or less permanently nailed down on the plywood, rested behind the headboard, which was not large enough to hide it completely from view. Allie was told that it was only to appear in the living room at Christmastime and perhaps on a few other special occasions. In his free moments, he built railroad-related structures based on plans and designs in *Model Builder* and other magazines, using construction board and balsa wood. For Christmas he asked for and received a passenger car set, silver New York Central cars, the trailing one having an observation deck, in commemoration of which he built a passenger rail station. At the time of the holidays, the Communist Chinese army entered Korea; a large contingent of Marines were trapped at a reservoir deep in the North, from which many managed a daring escape. The war drifted back toward its original demarcation, from which it would seesaw for the following two and a half years, a sorrowful equilibrium.

As Allie trod the paths of his teenage years, it was evident that his interest in electric trains and their accessories had peaked some time beforehand. And in a way, Lionel and its 0 and 027 products had peaked as well. The market was growing for the more compact HO gauge trains, which appealed to the most dedicated of model railroad hobbyists and carried the obvious advantage of allowing for more railroad in less space. HO trains ran smoothly and quietly, the beneficiaries of advancing technology. When it came time for Allie's younger brother, Rob, to take up an interest in trains, the family went for HO, and selected a prefab layout that did not have to rest behind anyone's headboard.

In the latter part of the decade the Fairs finally made the move out of the City into a split-level house in New Jersey. The house had a full-sized basement that would have been an ideal location for an extensive model train setup, but for Allie it was a case of too late. Somehow, somewhere, his old Lionel trains had gone missing, and as time ran on and memories became hazy, all that could be said of their fate was that they were missing in action. Whether the trains had been parceled out piecemeal to this cousin or that nephew, or if they still resided in some carton from the move that was left unopened and sat amidst other dust-laden boxes in the basement or the attic, who could say. The fact was that electric trains were in the young man's past and not relevant for his future. There were analogies to the real world as well; railroads in the macro sense were, if not declining, merely running in place, their position being eclipsed by expanding reliance on air and automotive transport, the latter spurred by a developing nationwide highway system.

It was long after, at a time when Allie had been on vacation with his first wife, that he ran into Steve Gross in a resort hotel in Puerto Rico. They were on their way to dinner, walking through the hotel lobby, when he heard a voice call out, "Hey, Fair, over here!"

Allie turned in the direction of the voice and discerned some familiarity in a face surrounded by masses of facial hair and partially disguised by rose-colored granny glasses joined to an angular body clad in denim. The man was seated cross-legged on a high-backed wicker chair, bookended by two women, either one of which could have qualified for a tryout in a trade group beauty pageant. The taller of the two was a willowy blonde, a pale blue maxiskirt with a side-slit reaching midthigh; her counterpart had coal-black hair parted in the middle held in place with an Indian band, and she wore a scoop neck blouse, a suitable teaser for a promising bosom. Variety, variety. "Gross? Steve? That you?" Allie asked.

"Yeah, it's me, okay. Come here, my man. It's been a while," Steve said, beckoning Allie and Marge Fair over to his ersatz compound across the lobby. He introduced them to his two companions, Astrid (blonde) and Ulla (coal-black), who were described as Swedish and backup singers in Steve's band, The Third Rail. Somewhere in the recesses of his mind, Allie recalled hearing about Steve Gross and his music. He had cut a rock album that had middling success, and now, Gross hastened to say in talking to Allie, he was about to open for Country Joe McDonald on his next gig. "And, you know, Allie, I named the band after your trains, yes I did, man, the third rail, that's the live one."

It turned out that Steve had moved to Beverly Hills but kept a little contact with some of the old neighborhood gang. Allie asked about guys like Conrad Harrison, and Steve said, "That's an interesting story. I heard he was in Nam as a helicopter pilot. He went to the Air Force Academy, you know, but I haven't heard anything lately. Funny thing, No-Fair. He's a warrior, and I'm on the same bill with Country Joe. Go figure."

Funny, indeed. *At least the military might have straightened Conrad's teeth*, Allie thought. As their conversation was concluding and the Fairs were drifting off, Steve rose and whispered in Allie's ear, "Look, I can't shit ya, those girls aren't Swedish; they're from the Bronx—but a better section than the old neighborhood, like near Throgs Neck. And Allie, you were wrong about guitars only being for Les Paul." Marge Fair didn't think much of Steve Gross or his entourage. It was a factor, albeit a minor one, in the breakup of their marriage. Gross remembered the trains, though.

Six

The old man with the young man's name slowly navigated his way around the rain-soaked streets of Chicago's financial district. It was early spring, no time to be in that city or any other one north of the Sunbelt, for that matter. Allie Fair walked with an attitude of struggle, as though there was always a head-wind in his face with which he had to contend, the physical fact being that he relied on a cane, the result of an accident suffered some ten years past. Running late for work one morning, he raced up his commuter station platform only to trip on its uppermost step, sending him to the ground in a heap with his right ankle fractured in four places. Despite three procedures, the healing never turned out right, and he remained with a decided limp from that point onward. The train on that clear morning shut its sliding doors in the usual manner and moved on, an inanimate object paying no mind to a faithful patron writhing in pain at its side. Ironic, he often thought, that such a train buff as he would meet a cruel fate at the hands of something he cherished, for he had never tired of the clickety-clack of rail travel and the moveable views from the car window where even if the route were identical from day to day, if you observed hard enough there was always something new to see.

It was late morning and he was en route to see a client ensconced in an office high atop one of the older buildings on LaSalle Street. He caught the ad displayed on the side of the CTA bus as it planed down the slick roadway, its splash missing Allie's oxford grey cuffs by inches.

Titanic Artifacts and History
The Museum of Science and Industry
March 12 through June 29

Stopping for a moment and then ducking in to the nearest dry lobby, he reached for his cell phone and called his pending appointment. "Hey, Matt," he said when put through to Matthew Garbour, "listen, I know we've got a meeting coming up this afternoon, but can you change it to first thing tomorrow morning? I've got … something I need to do." It turned out that Garbour was agreeable, and they decided to meet over breakfast, and then Allie could catch the 11 a.m. from O'Hare back to LaGuardia. Allie Fair continued to ply his trade, that of investment portfolio management, well into his latter years, although he was winding down on his client base. He was known for advocating a longer-term view toward his recommendations, potentially unrewarding in the fast-paced world of finance, but it was tailored to the goals of his accounts, and the results were, for the most part, better than the competition. So, in terms of a portfolio such as Matt Garbour's, another fraction of a day was not to be of great significance.

Thus the afternoon suddenly opened up, giving him the time to take in the museum's exhibit and then get back to the north end of town, where he was going to have dinner with his daughter, May, the first child of his second wife and one of the principal reasons he never passed up an opportunity to travel to Chicago.

The exhibit was one of the traveling kind, resting for a while in museums in various cities and then moving on to the next destination, the kind of event one would see advertised and say "wow, I want to get to that," and somehow never do because time runs out and the exhibit folds its tent. Interest in the Titanic was at a robust level, having been juiced by the incredible Ballard discovery of its remains in the 1980s and then the successful Cameron film in 1997. The museum promised artifacts raised from the ocean floor as well as a full display of the methodology and equipment that Dr. Ballard used to identify the vessel. Allie checked his raincoat at the front of the museum and hastened as fast as his damaged limbs could take him to the entry point, where he managed to slip in ahead of a school group wherein all of the students wore baseball caps, even the girls. *None of my girlfriends ever wore baseball caps,* he thought. *What is it with this generation? Baseball caps were a thing to be revered, not a part of the commonplace.*

There was an intriguing gimmick he found upon entry, where everyone was furnished with an index card bearing the name of a passenger on the ship, a blatant but effective means to personalize the experience and the eventual tragedy of that voyage. His read, "Thomas Threlfall."

If anything, the Titanic collection exceeded his expectations; there were items brought up from its remains ranging from crockery and luggage to men's formal shirts (undoubtedly cleaned and pressed for the viewing public), reproductions of the bowels of the great ship where the coal stokers worked around the clock, to staterooms of the classes, and even an enormous section of the hull showing its cracked portholes and the steel rivets which, in the end, failed to hold its sections together as the iceberg's hard edges sliced along the bowline, causing the hardware to pop and producing channels for the sea to rush in and send the grand liner to its final berth. At the end, there was an extensive portrayal of the submersibles and the rigs that the Ballard expedition used to find and then bring up a wide range of Titanic items strewn along the ocean's base. The romantic past of the ship came full circle alongside the contemporary technology that located its murky home on the seabed after so many years. At the very end of the exhibit, a wall listed the names of all of Titanic's passengers, and Allie paused to find Mr. Threlfall on the board. Throughout his wended way along the dimly lit maze of the museum's production, his mind reverted to the school paper he had written about the event and a ring given by a librarian, Titanic-related, as it were, handed to him in the hopes that it would lead to a superior grade on the report. TT to MC. Funny, the tricks that memory plays on one's soul; he smiled to himself at the idea that short-term memory loss was either a universal affliction or early indications of Alzheimer's, and yet he could recall the times of his youth as vividly as a cerulean October sky. Was the TT Mr. Threlfall? There could be no certainty inasmuch as the Titanic's manifest displayed three other passengers with like initials.

At the exit area, there was a tony gift shop—after all, the museum had to recoup its costs just like any other enterprise—and he bought a novelty T-shirt for May and a reproduction of Titanic's third-class coffee cup, with the White Star Line logo proudly displayed. A full first-class dinner service was also available, at a price, but he was infinitely more comfortable with the third. Besides, the last thing he needed was another set of crockery, however elegant it appeared in its display case.

He was done there, lugging his purchase in a glossy museum bag and soon on his way to the dinner engagement with his daughter. As he walked toward the exit, he was aware of the school group dispersing and talking amongst themselves. He overheard one of their number say something to the effect of "hey, look at that old guy on the cane. Ya think he might have been one of the survivors?" A staccato response of laughter from his friends reverberated around the surrounding walls. *Allie, he must have been referring to you. Irreverent bastard, no sense of history and not terribly swift with numbers, either.* He didn't look back but moved ahead, thinking that somehow he had satisfied a long-standing subliminal mission and that now he had nothing more pressing to do than to see May and enjoy their dinner date. He had told her to choose the venue, and it did not matter much; there were a lot of selections—in Chicago you had to go far out of your way to have a bad meal.

On the way to May's apartment on Lake Shore, the cold rain splashing against the taxi windows, Allie sat back, really alone, thinking about old memories and mysteries, and how it was important to be an honest guardian of things that were important. The trick was to figure out what was important. His whole life, he had been a consumer, not a producer. Even his work, which was regularly rewarding, wasn't innovative; it was tacked on to the work of others, placing him in the position of being hardly more than a critic, a form of judge. And it was always on to the next big thing, gracing little of his efforts with staying power. Someone like Steve Gross—he created music, for better or worse, depending on your sense of taste, and even if his brief run had flamed out in the seventies (which it did), there was something left behind, perhaps to be rediscovered in more benign times.

That ring, the ancient Lionel trains, they possessed meaning, and along the way he had let them all go. Though mere material objects having fulfilled their share of useful life and childhood pleasures, to be ultimately discarded without so much as a soft goodbye seemed a cold ending. The mysteries surrounding such things would hang on a slender thread and—although long vanished—wait patiently in the wings until some event brought them to recall, as inevitably would happen. *Mysteries were good. They kept the brain active, didn't they?* Did that ring commence its uncertain journey from Thomas Threlfall on that biting and evil night so long ago only to pass from hand to hand and come to an eventual rest in an unmarked repository? It was a question that had no answer, given only to speculation. In an impulse of free association, it evoked for Allie the lyrics of "Whiter Shade of Pale." The song's words, inexplicable in his mind, were, in the end, just what you wanted them to mean, nothing more and nothing less. And so with the ring. Yes, it was Threlfall's gift to Marion; it had to be. As long as he believed in it, that would constitute a true thing.

He was distracted. The taxi had zeroed in on the completion of its journey. "Okay, my man, here's the address. You all right? You seem a little spacey, if you don't mind my saying so," the cabbie said to him. He did mind, actually, caring not at all for gratuitous remarks from hires, strangers at that, but he shrugged it off and proceeded up to May's handsome apartment overlooking Lake Michigan. "Daddy, you look positively soaking," his daughter said. "Come, dry out with a drink, and then we'll be off to dinner."

Green-eyed May Fair, tall with ash-blonde hair, wore a black pantsuit, accented with a pearl choker and looking, her father thought, much like the marketing exec that she was. Still, he was perplexed by the predominance of black as the in choice *(last time I looked there were other colors)* and considered offering an opinion—which better judgment forestalled.

Cocktails consumed, and as they exited the apartment, she told him that he should have called on the cell if he'd been running late, which he had been. "I was a little worried about you. You do have a cell phone, don't you?"

"Sure, but I hate to use it. Too much technology for an old man, and besides, the buttons are too small for my big klutzy fingers. Oh, I know it's stylish, daughter dear, what with everyone on the street talking out loud. I used to think only crazies did that. Sometimes I pretend I'm calling someone, but I'm only talking to my hand. I got the idea from a Steve Martin movie. I guess I've joined them—the crazies, that is."

May merely shook her head following his soliloquy, which took up the elapsed time on the elevator's downward move.

She had reserved a table at a small Italian place on Clark Street. Allie told her about his afternoon at the museum and the reopening—and closure—of a cold case, as it were. "Then, it seems like you solved that problem, Daddy," she smiled, "so allow me a question of you while we are at it."

"Sure, ask away."

"You guys—you and Mom—never told me about my name."

Allie was puzzled for a moment. "Whatever brought that to your mind? Your name? You mean May?"

She continued, her smile widening. "I said there was one question, and you come back with three. But, yes, you know, everyone would call me Mayfair in one syllable, like it was some kind of joke that they all got except for me."

"Well, it's a posh section of London, so that's not so bad," he responded breezily, groping for a credible answer. She turned silent and burrowed in on her father's eyes, expecting to hear more. "Okay," he continued, "when Mom was about to bring you home from the hospital, she hadn't decided on a name, and they needed one right away or else you would forever be known as 'baby Fair,' which would not have been a classy outcome. So Mom put up a choice between Melody or Fan, because she thought it went well with our last name."

"Melody Fair? You mean like in the Bee Gees song?"

"I guess," he said.

She went on. "So how did I become May?"

"Oh, that's an easy one," her father answered. "When I got to the hospital, she told me she had decided on May. And it wasn't so much the connection to our last name as it was after a leading soap opera star of the time. Actually, I think you emerged with the best of the three options. Now you know."

"That's your explanation?"

"It's my story and I'm sticking to it," he said.

May went ahead with her study of the menu. "Let's order, Daddy, I'm starving." He asked after her social life; May was presently unattached, having come through a messy divorce two years previous.

"Still looking, Daddy."

They enjoyed their dinner; she selected a bottle of Montepulciano from Tuscany that complemented their veal chops. As they were awaiting a dessert of fresh berry compote, May Fair said, "All right, Daddy, how's about your name? Tell me about its origin."

"Oh, I once asked my mother where Allie came from. It was about the time I was in junior high. See, I had these friends who, like you, would call me unfair, world's-fair, stuff like that. No one else I've ever known was an Allie. She told me to ask my father." He paused for effect.

May was all smiles now. "Don't string me along. So, what did he tell you?"

"He told me I was named after the great Yankee pitcher, Allie Reynolds, the big chief. But he was full of it, May."

She asked, "How is that?"

"Well, Reynolds didn't get to the big leagues until 1942, and I was—okay—a kid by then."

May processed the answer for a moment and then said to her father that it still could have been true because Reynolds was obviously around at the time of his birth, perhaps just not that well known.

"Nah. That's a stretch. How would an accountant from the Bronx know a minor league guy from Oklahoma. I gave pop the clear impression I did not believe his story. He did compliment me on one thing, though."

"What about?"

"He said that I had done the math—the research on the various dates—and that maybe there was hope for me after all. Beyond that, the subject never came up again."

The evening was ending, and they were in front of the restaurant awaiting a cab. The cold Chicago rain had given way to clearing night skies punctuated by a handful of swiftly moving clouds. May rode with her father to the Drake Hotel. She kissed him good night and then said, "Thanks for tonight, Daddy. I guess we have some mysteries explained, while others still await a solution. Until next time."

Allie Fair pondered all that as he turned the key in the door of the hotel room. He would go on to his morning meeting, then fly home to New York from O'Hare like everyone else. Sadly, there would be no passenger trains for him, being as reluctant as most people would be to invest an overnight riding the rails. The glamour of *North By Northwest,* Cary Grant and Eva Marie Saint in the dining car, hiding in the upper berth, well, that was only in the movies. Nowadays if you tried to re-create the trip, they'd probably run out of food or the train would bog down in Pennsylvania. Better to endure the aggravation of the airport if you wanted to have at least a shot to be home at a reasonable hour.

It is an ongoing effort to make peace with the fundamentals, he thought, *but that's what I've been schooled to do in my world. I've come to view life as a long season of games, and if you win some, you lose others, and some even get rained out. Still, you do not always understand why the results come out the way that they do.*

Experience reaching for resolution, he thought. *I want to be outdoors in early spring to see the pale green of budding leaves on the trees. It is like a splash of peridot against burnt umber, and will make a lovely painting. Yet it is a short window of time when that occurs—the interval between the end of winter and the full bloom of the summer—and although the seasons return and revolve, their passage represents a finite recurrence for all of us, and we cannot know how many such cycles remain.*

There's no such thing as a pause mode. Keep it moving. Like a Lionel train speeding around a curve and derailing, you put it back on its track. Or a disputed call in a stickball game in Crotona Park in 1950. Settle the difference of opinion. Try again. Do-overs.

All that was fine with Allie Fair, just fine.

www.ingramcontent.com/pod-product-compliance
Lightning Source LLC
Chambersburg PA
CBHW020613310726
48979CB00008B/1466/J

* 9 7 8 0 5 9 5 5 1 8 3 1 9 *